Dear Reader,

I don't write a great many short stories, although in assembling this collection, I have to wonder why that is. A shorter work is an opportunity—if not an invitation—to try something different in terms of style or to play with an unusual idea. Short stories are fun to write for that reason, and in addition, offer different structural challenges than books. I love to read short stories: they can be tantalizing in themselves, and also can provide a telling introduction to an author's work.

The works included here were all written as the result of an invitation for me to participate in an anthology with other authors. In the past, invitations have been the only reason I wrote short—though that might change! I was glad to be invited to participate in all of those volumes, but is often the nature of short stories to remain available to readers for only a limited time. So, I'm very pleased now to have the opportunity to pull these works into a collection of my own and make them available to you again.

In addition, putting the stories together makes their similarities to each other more clear. Most of these works have a medieval setting, and all of them include both romance and fantasy elements. Each of them features a strong heroine who makes a choice, a choice that might end up costing everything she holds dear. Historians called the ability to influence one's own situation "agency" and it's an idea that I like to explore in all of my work. In the medieval era, women had more agency than many people believe, and we, too, have agency in our era, although maybe it's less than many people believe. What we choose and why fascinates me. For the women in these stories, the opportunity to choose is more important than the result: I don't know that even Melusine would regret her decision, though the end result is not what she had hoped to gain.

I've included an introductory note before each story, telling you a bit of how it came to be and its history. I've also included an excerpt from my medieval romance, *The Rogue*, because in reviewing these shorter stories, it's clear that Alix and Melusine led me directly to Ysabella.

Until next time, I hope you are well and have plenty of good books to read.

All my best—

Deborah
also writing as Claire

Books by Claire Delacroix

Praise for the Author

"Claire Delacroix is a shining star of the romance genre. Cleverly original, emotional and fast-paced, full of twists and turns, her books will sweep you off your feet!"
—Julianne Maclean, USA Today bestselling author

"A beguiling medieval romance...readers will devour this rich and compulsively readable tale."
—Publishers' Weekly on *The Rogue*

"When you open a book by Claire Delacroix, you open a treasure chest of words, rare and exquisite!"
—Rendezvous

"An engaging tale of lost love found."
—Booklist on *The Rogue*

"Claire Delacroix brings [romance and chivalry] alive with her stunning talent for storytelling!"
—The Literary Times

"[Claire] Delacroix's satisfying tale leaves the reader hungry for the next offering."
—Booklist on *The Warrior*

"An enchanting historical [romance] that mixed a great tale of the fairy realm with a beautiful, sensual love story...an historical as refreshing as it is gripping!"
—Romance Junkies on *The Rose Red Bride*

"Terrific!"
—The Best Reviews on *The Snow White Bride*

"Deborah Cooke is a dragon-master of a storyteller!"
—The Reading Frenzy

"Deborah Cooke's Dragonfire novels are impossible to put down!"
—Romance Reviews Today on *Darkfire Kiss*

"[Deborah] Cooke keeps the pace intense and the emotions raging in this powerful new read. She's top-notch, as always!"
—Romantic Times on *Kiss of Fate*

"An intense ride. Ms. Cooke has an immense talent."
—Night Owl Reviews on *Kiss of Fate*

"Excellent writing, a smart story, and exceptional characters earn this novel the RRT Perfect 10 Rating. Don't miss the very highly recommended *Kiss of Fury*!"
—Romance Reviews Today on *Kiss of Fury*

"Deborah Cooke has definitely made me a fan."
—Romance Junkies on *Kiss of Fire*

Writing as Deborah Cooke

Addicted to Love
In the Midnight Hour
Some Guys Have All the Luck
Going to the Chapel
Bad Case of Loving You (2019)

Secret Heart Ink:
Snowbound
Spring Fever
One Hot Summer Night
Under the Mistletoe (2019)

Short Works:
A Berry Merry Christmas
Coven of Mercy

Beguiled

Tales of fantasy, romance, and forbidden love.

Claire Delacroix
&
Deborah Cooke

Beguiled
by Claire Delacroix and Deborah Cooke

Cover by Frauke Spanuth at CrocoDesigns.

Printing History:
Deborah A. Cooke trade paperback edition
July 2014
ISBN#978-1-927477-41-0

This work has been published in a simultaneous digital edition.

Beguiled

Tales of fantasy, romance, and forbidden love.

Beguiled

An Elegy for Melusine

The story of Melusine is a medieval fairy tale, in that it's a story about fairies that was told in the Middle Ages. It's more commonly known in French than in English, partly because Melusine and her story are associated with the Lusignan family in France—Melusine is said to be one of their forebears. The story has similarities to the fairy tales we know but also some key differences. It doesn't have a happily-ever-after, for example, because it is a kind of a warning about the dangers of fairies and mortals falling in love.

The story was first written down in French by Coudrette in the late fourteenth century, although the more famous version is the slightly later one recorded by Jean d'Arras. Scholars believe that the story was recounted orally much earlier than this, partly because both of these versions are in verse. It could have been a story told merely for entertainment. It could have been indicative of a change in belief, because in the middle ages, fairies became associated with the devil. Or, in a medieval Europe that was more mobile and mingled than it had been previously, the story simply could have been a warning against marrying outside of one's own kind.

An Elegy for Melusine was originally published in the anthology **To Weave a Web of Magic,** along with stories by Lynn Kurland, Patricia McKillip and Sharon Shinn.

I

hey are not the audience I would have chosen, but I have few choices left in these days. If naught else, I have learned to make do with what I am granted—that lesson, apparently, will serve me to the end.

So be it.

I watch them from a narrow window, awaiting my moment. They are more like birds than women, these two, their elaborate garb reminiscent of the fine plumage of birds in courtship. They twitter like starlings, they cackle like hens, they rustle their skirts and huddle together. I suspect from their foolish chatter that they are no more clever than the doves in the rafters.

In my time, they would have never survived childhood.

In this time, they are the ornaments of wealthy men, truly no better than peacocks upon gilded chains. For their own sakes, I hope their husbands get children upon them shortly. Such women do not fare well once they have been savored but failed to satisfy.

But then, my children caused all my woes.

The pair halt upon the threshold and peer into the shadows of the old stone castle. I try to see the place with their eyes, not gilded with memories of mine. There is moss on these floors of fitted stone, and undoubtedly there are mice in the dry brown vestiges of the strewing herbs that had once been thick and fragrant. The merry trickle of water echoes from somewhere within the walls, water that had almost certainly invited itself through a nook. A rogue beam of sunlight shines through the broken roof and sets the dust motes to dancing within it. Those doves twitter in the half-rotted rafters, hidden by the shadows of what remains of the roof.

But still there is grace in the keep's proportions and majesty in its very size. There is elegance in the arches embellished with a mason's carving. The beauty of this abode can still be found here by those with eyes to see.

This pair have no such ability.

"Is this not terrifying, Marie?" whispers one, her eyes wide.

"Blanche, we have entered the castle of Melusine!" says the other. They cling to each other, shiver elaborately, then step into the keep's darkness together.

I barely restrain my sneer. What fools they are! I tread behind them, clinging to the shadows, loathing every word they utter. I debate my prospects but they are few. I have faded too far and weakened too much.

This pair will have to suffice.

"It is hundreds of years old," whispers Blanche, the timid one.

"And said to have been built in a week, for all of that." The one called Marie looks about herself with what might be awe.

"By Melusine," they intone together. The sound of that familiar name upon mortal lips makes me smile.

"How could your Bernard even think of destroying it?" asks Blanche, rapping her companion on her sleeve with a fan made of peacock feathers.

"He says he will build me a larger and finer keep," says Marie, lifting her young chin with a pride that will undoubtedly betray her one day. "He says it will be more luxurious even than Toussèvres."

Blanche's eyes narrow tellingly and I guess that she is Lady of this Toussèvres. Blanche walks further ahead, the amity between the pair somewhat destroyed by these competitive comments. They make their way through what had once been the great hall, their trailing skirts stirring the dust.

"Melusine could see the future because she was a demon," says Blanche as they carefully lift their skirts and climb the mossy steps.

Marie clears her throat, unwilling to be outdone. "Indeed, she knew how to save Raymond's reputation after he had accidentally killed his liege lord. She only did so to ensure the success of her dark scheme."

Now they compete over the details of the history of this castle, each vying to recall more than the other. The result sounds like argumentative starlings or willful jays.

"She built his name, and the repute of his home, and gave him ten sons to further spread his fame," says Blanche. "The great crusading family Lusignan issued from Mère Lusine, or Melusine."

"Her grandson was King of Jerusalem."

"Her son was King of Sicily."

They pause at the crest of the stairs, and I will them to choose the arch upon their right. They do so, granting me no small satisfaction that my powers yet linger, though in truth, there was half a chance they would have chosen it at any rate.

They barely spare a glance to the carving upon the lintel, so laden is it with grime and dust. I know it well enough to see the long current of a woman's hair, the sweet ripeness of her young breasts, the powerful coil of her serpent tail. I reach up and brush it with my aged fingertips as I pass beneath it.

For Fortune's smile.

Their steps falter on the threshold of the room into which I passionately wish them to go. Perhaps some old potency lingers here—it certainly does for me.

I cannot enter this chamber without hesitation, even now, and it is not one that I enter of my own volition. I know, though, that it is the proper place to share this tale for the last time.

Indeed, it is the only place that will suffice.

"Do you think it was here?" asks Blanche in a whisper.

Marie nods. She takes a deep breath and crosses the threshold. Curiosity about the mark reputed to be upon the sill draws them. They halt before the window, look down, and shiver in truth.

There is no sunlight in this chamber, as the sole window faces north. I can see the deadened branches of the forest through its arch, the last vestiges of snow beneath the dark boughs, the roiling blue-grey clouds of a storm gathering in the distance. I had oft thought that one could see to eternity through this window, that detail forgotten until this moment.

My throat tightens with a hundred bittersweet memories, too painful to ponder, too precious to forget.

Blanche reaches out a tentative fingertip to the shape of a woman's foot, apparently carved in the grey stone of the sill. "But Melusine was a demon, a devil disguised as a beauteous woman."

"La Belle Dame sans Merci."

"She had a heart of stone. She beguiled Raymond, to better work her witchery upon the world." Blanche glances about herself, perhaps sensing that they are not alone.

"She made him vow to never look upon her on a Saturday, when she took her bath, because it was then that her true nature was revealed." Marie seems to take a grim delight in the details. "It was then that she reverted to a serpent from the waist down and a woman from the waist upward."

"Every son she bore him had an unholy flaw."

Marie nods. "Geoffroi Great Tooth, born with an enormous tooth."

"Horrible, born with his third eye between the other two."

Marie lifts a finger. "Save Fromont, the sole normal son and his father's pride."

"Until Fromont took his monastic vows, and Geoffroi slaughtered him, burning the monastery to the ground and killing all the monks, not only his brother. And Melusine defended his wickedness."

"So Raymond, who had spied once upon his lady, denounced her before his entire court. He called her what she was and blamed her for bearing him such a monster of a son."

"'Most false serpent!'" the two women cry together, the condemnation sending a shiver to my very marrow.

"He denounced her as the demon that she was and cast her out, as she so rightly deserved," says Blanche with such satisfaction that I long to do her injury.

"She stepped on the sill and took flight as a winged serpent, woman no more because her evil scheme had been discovered."

Each leans on the sill and looks out over the deadened forest. "And she was doomed to remain in that form until Judgment Day." Blanche clutches her heart while Marie crosses herself.

"Mercifully, no such demons walk among us any longer," says Blanche. They eye each other, neither wanting to be the first to suggest that they leave.

I conjure the form of an old woman as my vehicle, not caring what it costs me, and step from the protective cloak of the shadows. I feel the very moment their gazes land upon me, as surely as a touch.

"That is not precisely how I recall the tale," I say, and truly, I enjoy how they jump backward in their alarm.

"Old woman! Who are you and how did you find yourself here?" Marie demands. She snaps open a fan of ostrich feathers and fans herself furiously, as if she was merely surprised to find a trespasser upon her husband's lands, not afraid.

"Have pity," I say. "I am but a good woman who seeks shelter from the forest within these old walls."

"But you would challenge our story?" asks Marie. I see now that her face is sharp and avarice gleams in her eyes. She is shrewd perhaps, rather than clever. She will be unattractive soon, for greed has a way of stretching a woman too taut to be pleasing.

"I said only that it was not the tale that I recall." I feign need, as it will soften them. I cringe as if fearing they might strike me and stretch out a gnarled hand to entreat. "I would but share my version of the tale of Melusine, share it for a crust of bread."

The women exchange the arch glance that the wealthy so oft share in the presence of poverty. Yet more intriguingly, they are convinced that they will never be less than affluent, that the gods will play no tricks upon them.

I decide it is not worth the trouble to peer into their futures to discern the truth. The sharpness of Marie's features and the flatness of both their bellies tells me enough.

"Of course," says Blanche, settling on to the bench beneath the window and arranging her skirts.

"I see no harm in such indulgence," says Marie. She arches a brow. "Though I cannot imagine what difference you can make to the tale. It is so well-known, after all."

"Your version of it is well-known, that I will not dispute," I say. "But it was not always told thus. It was not always believed that Raymond unveiled and foiled Melusine's dark scheme." I hold up my hands, knowing that with this single detail I held their attention in thrall. "Once it was recounted that it was her love for him that proved her undoing."

"Oooo! Tell us!" cries Blanche, her eyes shining.

Marie arranges her skirts with care, preparing herself to be entertained by her inferior. Her smile is condescending. "Tell us the tale you know, old woman."

I begin the tale with ease, for I know it and its beginning as well as I know my own name.

So much had been foretold, but of Raymond's beauty, Melusine had had no warning.

She had known that his steed would be a dappled stallion. She had known that he would be garbed in fine mail, and that his tabard would be the blue of sapphires. She had known that his insignia would be a dolphin, that it would be embroidered in white upon that tabard, that it would similarly embellish his red shield beneath an annulet, that open circle signifying that Raymond was the fifth son of the Count of Forez.

Melusine had expected that her quarry would be riding from the hunt, that his blade would be stained with the blood of his patron, that he would arrive at the very hour that Venus cleared the horizon on the night that the moon waxed full. She had seen all of this in her dreams.

Every detail conformed to what she had been told to anticipate, yet still the sight of Raymond de Poitou nigh stopped her heart.

She had not known that a mortal man could be wrought so well.

Melusine was not accustomed to being startled by mortals. Mortals, particularly mortal men, were slow of wit and heavily built. They were earthbound, concerned only with what of the world they could see and hold, distrustful of glimmers of the world Melusine called her own. They smelled of blood and flesh and earth, as revolting a combination as might be imagined. As a rule, they were as alluring as a creature one might find in the damp shadows beneath a stone.

This knight was handsome, as if he were indeed fey, and he was distraught, as if all the merit of the world was lost. Even more curious, the revulsion she always felt when she came in contact with mortals was curiously absent. Against her every instinct, Melusine was intrigued.

Raymond had discarded his helm, and the trails of his tears were evident. His hair was dark, as dark as obsidian, thick and wavy. He was tanned, his flesh a vigorous golden hue uncommon to the fey yet attractive. He was much taller than she and wrought as well as a mortal man could be wrought.

He rode directly past Melusine and her sisters, no more than an arm's length away. The fey trio drew back instinctively, though they had not yet chosen to step through the veil to the realm of mortals.

Raymond halted at the fountain just beyond them, but only because his exhausted horse refused to continue. The stallion halted, sides heaving, and planted his heavy feet stubbornly against the soil.

"Onward!" cried Raymond. In apparent oblivion of his master's command, the steed bent his head and drank. "Hoy! Jupiter, run!" He tugged the reins, dug his spurs into the stallion's sides, all to no avail.

The horse drank, unhurriedly and with great satisfaction.

"And why should my fortune change now?" Raymond shouted. He shook his fist at the sky, then buried his face in his hands and surrendered fully to his despair.

He wept as only a man unaccustomed to shedding tears can weep, as only a man who believed himself alone could surrender to his unhappiness.

Melusine had never seen a man—mortal or fey—weep, no less weep as if his heart was rent beyond repair. Warrior's tears were potent for their rarity.

His grief puzzled her. She had never anticipated that Raymond would regret the deed he had been fated to do. He was fated to kill his uncle and benefactor and she had assumed that was because Count Aimery's death was his unspoken desire. Thus, she had felt no qualms at proposing a bargain with him, one that would serve to the advantage of both of them.

Her determination faltered that Raymond should be so vulnerable as this, that he should be so troubled by what he could not have changed. Was it just to make a wager with a man so distraught?

Her sisters drew closer, doubtless intrigued that she hesitated. They were as vipers, these two, and quick to mark a shortcoming.

"Why do you linger? This is your chance, bold sister," whispered Melior.

"He is comely enough for a mortal, after all," said Palestine, the malice in her tone revealing that she would have willed it otherwise.

"Show us how readily the curse can be broken, you who are responsible for its infliction."

"You both joined me in our deed," Melusine reminded them.

"It was your idea to avenge our mother thus," said Melior.

"Our father broke his pledge," Melusine said. "The Fates decreed that retribution must be made."

"And yet Melusine, bold enough to enforce the will of the Fates, is afraid of this mere mortal?" Palestine's words were mocking.

Melior gave Melusine a nudge in the direction of the mortal realm. "Has your valor failed you, Melusine?"

"Show us how the release from our mother's curse is won, Sister," said Palestine. "If you dare."

Melusine had never been able to suffer a challenge. She slipped through the barrier of the fey realm and approached her salvation.

They would make a wager, she and Raymond, just as had been foretold, and she knew already who would gain the most. No matter what he chose, Raymond's terms would last solely his lifetime, a mere blink of the eye for Melusine.

While she would possess her heart's desire for all eternity.

The price, to her thinking, was fair.

There was blood upon Raymond's tabard in greater quantity than Melusine had noted earlier. It was Count Aimery's blood that dripped from his scabbard, dripped as if Raymond had sheathed his blade without cleaning it. His sword was obviously fine, graced with an elaborate hilt and a gem as a pommel. His oversight more clearly showed his anguish, for Melusine knew the reverence in which mortal men held their weapons.

Compassion touched her own heart, though she could not indulge in such weakness. She had her own freedom to win and Raymond was no more than the means to her goal.

"And what manner of man does not grant a courteous greeting to ladies?" Melusine asked with a levity she did not feel.

Raymond started, then stared at her as if she were a figment suddenly manifest before his eyes.

And Melusine was startled in her turn. His eyes were an uncommonly vivid blue, the hue of the sky where dusk touches the darkness, where the stars first become visible.

They could have been fey eyes, wrought of a patch of that starlit sky. His tan made his eyes seem even more vibrant a blue. His lashes were long and dark, his features striking.

Her heart skipped in a most unusual manner.

Melusine smiled and glanced back to her sisters, who had also slipped through the veil. They were adorned as fine ladies at a king's court now, jewels sparkling on their brows and at their throats.

Melusine raised a hand as if sharing a jest, letting laughter fill her words. "Truly, the manners of men have become sorry, indeed, if a fine knight cannot grace three noblewomen with a fair greeting."

Her sisters laughed. "What dire course the world does pursue," Melior said.

"How sad—" Palestine pouted "—when men cannot hail ladies with good grace."

Raymond looked between the three of them, clearly astounded. "But I was alone," he murmured. He shook his head, like a man awakening from a dream, then fixed his gaze upon Melusine. "It is the midst of the night, in the midst of the forest. How do you come to be here—and why?"

"I could ask the same of you, sir."

Raymond frowned, wiped his eyes, then doffed his gloves. His manner was polite but cool. "My apologies, lady, for my oversight. I assumed myself to be alone in the wilderness." He made to turn away, making it clear that solitude was his choice.

Melusine caught his sleeve in her fingertips. "And yet you are not alone."

That sapphire gaze lingered upon her, and Melusine guessed that he was shrewd. Indeed, his expression changed slightly, perhaps with the realization that the otherworld touched his own. He was not a common mortal, this one. "Where am I?"

Melusine spread her hands to indicate the glade around them. "At a spring in the forest, one which my sisters and I choose to frequent."

"Upon whose lands do we stand?"

"These lands are soon to be claimed by one Raymond, presently a knight sworn to the service of Poitou and fifth son of the Count of Forez." She watched as he started visibly. "He is destined to be Lord of Lusignan."

His eyes narrowed. "You know my name."

Melusine inclined her head in acknowledgement. "It was foretold that you would arrive here at this time, Raymond of Poitou." She met his gaze steadily, covertly grasping his steed's reins. "The Fates decreed that you would arrive here without your patron and liege lord, Count Aimery, Lord of Poitou, as well as why that would be." She dropped her gaze pointedly to his stained scabbard.

"You cannot know the truth!"

"Your own blade confirms it."

Raymond took note of the blood upon his scabbard and garb, perhaps for the first time, then recoiled. He inhaled sharply and might have ridden away, but Melusine held fast to the reins.

"How can you know of this deed?" he demanded, even as he tried to work the leather from her grip. Melusine gripped it tightly. His voice caught, thick with that grief again. "How could any soul have foretold it? I meant him no harm! Aimery was my patron, my friend. I would have harmed myself afore him!"

Melusine saw the scene then in her mind's eye, saw it with startling clarity. "Anger betrayed you, as it has before," she said. "You meant to strike the boar, you meant to save your lord from certain death. But in your vigor, you struck Count Aimery instead of the wild beast."

His eyes widened, their color pronounced in his fear of her. His whisper was hoarse. "How can you know this?"

"I know much of you, Raymond of Poitou, including how you can see this matter resolved to your own advantage."

"It will be resolved by my death, which is hardly to my advantage," he said bitterly. "No one will believe my tale, though it is true. Am I not the Count's nephew? There are no witnesses of my innocence save the Count and the boar."

"Did Aimery not tell you what he saw in this stars this

evening?"

"You cannot know what he said to me." There was less conviction in his tone than previously.

"He told you that he could not understand the evidence before his own eyes," Melusine continued. "He told you that a man who killed his benefactor this night would gain wealth beyond belief, though that made little sense to him."

The knight paled.

"Do you think your lord Aimery was the only one gifted to read the stars? Their message is clear indeed."

Raymond regained a measure of his composure, though still he was uncertain. "Who are you in truth?"

"I am the one come to grant you your heart's desire."

He looked at her, truly looked at her, and his gaze was hard. "You are fey," he said, snapping the reins from her grip and gathering them as if that was sufficient cause to end their discussion. "Your wager has a dark price, of this I have no doubt." He cast a suspicious glance over the glade, then crossed himself. "God only knows where I have found myself this night."

"You have found the aid you desperately need this night, no more than that." At his arch glance, any lie regarding her nature died upon Melusine's lips. "I would make a bargain with you, for there is something I desire of you and something you can grant to me. The price will not be so foul as you dread."

He hesitated.

Melusine saw more than she would have wished to see in his magnificent eyes. She saw that grief was not new to Raymond, nor was misfortune, and that distrust was a mantle he had learned to assume. She felt a sudden kinship with him, a dawning sense that it had been no accident that he had been chosen for her.

"Are you so anxious to be convicted and killed as that?" she whispered. She peered within his heart and was disappointed to find a typical desire lurking there. "I can see you wealthy, as you yearn to be, with a fine estate and no taint upon your name."

"In exchange for what?"

"Marriage and fidelity."

"Who is your father?"

"The King of Albion," she said, for it was true, and saw a

respect dawn in his eyes.

Still he was curt, tempted but suspicious. "This, then, is your wager? My aid to you in exchange for your aid to me?"

Melusine nodded, noting how he considered the prospect. "In return for my aid, you must wed me. We must live as man and wife."

A smile touched his lips then, his gaze turning appreciative as it slipped over her. "This then is the sum of it? Marriage?" He chuckled, much amused. "Truly I have lost my wits to have assumed I met a fey woman!"

The twinkle in his eyes was beguiling, indeed. Laughter suited him far better than wariness and Melusine had an uncharacteristic urge to touch this mortal.

"Perhaps you are but a clever demoiselle—" he teased "—one who listens where she should not and uses what she hears to her own advantage."

Melusine granted him a scathing glance. She was insulted that he could so readily think her mortal—no less that her objectives were common and unimportant. The truth of her nature—to her thinking—was abundantly clear to any soul of sense.

She had a measure of temper herself and in this moment, it was riled.

"And yet it was foretold that you were a man with your wits about you." Melusine pivoted and walked toward her sisters. "Go then, go and meet your death."

Silence told her that she had surprised Raymond. Doubtless he was unaccustomed to women rejecting his charms! She had thought that only the fey were possessed of such pride.

"What of your heart's desire?" Raymond called.

"My heart will craft another." Melusine lied. "I have all eternity to wait, after all." She granted him another cool smile. "You would appear to have much less time to concern yourself with such matters. How rapidly do you think the Count's heir will declare your guilt?"

Raymond swore with astonishing vigor and she glimpsed the fury of his temper. Melusine turned her back upon the sight, unafraid, and strode back to her watchful sisters.

She was not surprised when she heard Raymond dismount,

not surprised to hear his steps fast behind her, not surprised when he seized her elbow and spun her to face him.

His touch sent such sparks through her that she gasped. He was indeed taller than she, and his smile was more troubling than she had hoped.

The man meant to charm her, 'twas clear, and Melusine would have preferred if she could have recoiled from his touch. She was confused, for this should have been simple, yet his effect upon her made it complicated indeed.

She glared at him, too angered—by her own response and his surety of it—to feign a demure nature she did not possess.

"Tell me more of your wager," he cajoled.

"I see no point in such discussion."

"Perhaps I do."

"Perhaps I do not care."

Raymond chuckled. Melusine caught her breath when he touched her chin, tilting her face so that he could look into her eyes. His charming smile and twinkling eyes undermined her annoyance with him. This mortal had more than a measure of allure, to be sure.

"Tell me," he murmured. "Please."

Melusine took a deep breath, knowing that she had to cede this to him, and looked deliberately across the glade. His touch upon her arm was not as unpleasant as it should have been. Indeed, a tingle emanated from his touch, spreading over her flesh like a wind through the grasses.

"The wager is as I have told you," she said. "The sole constraint I would ask of you—should we agree to make this wager—is that you never look upon me or ask after me on a Saturday."

A frown touched his brow. "Why? What will you do?"

Melusine granted him an exasperated glance. He chuckled at his own folly and shook his head.

So the man could laugh at himself. That was no small thing. Melusine found herself smiling in return.

As they eyed each other, another heat was kindled between them. Melusine could smell his flesh and hear the pulse of his blood, but she did not wish to pull away. He traced the curve of her bottom lip with his thumb, an unexpectedly pleasurable caress.

She spoke quickly, breathlessly, to ensure that her terms were clear to him. "If you make this pledge to me and break it, you will lose everything I have aided you to gain, including your wealth, your land, your fame."

"What of my sons?" Raymond mused, his expression turning mischievous. "There is no merit in wealth and lands without sons to inherit it."

"Sons?" Melusine echoed, horror welling within her.

"Do you not offer my heart's desire? Mine is all you have offered, and sons."

"But...but that means that we will have to lie together..."

He smiled with that roguish confidence. "Indeed. Is that not a part of marriage?"

Melusine could barely speak. The prospect of being despoiled by a man's seed, of lying beneath him, of blood and semen and sweat, made her feel faint. She could not imagine any fate more vile. But Raymond looked determined. "One son," she suggested.

"Ten. The world is unpredictable, lady."

Ten sons! Ten couplings at least. Melusine could not summon a word to her lips so great was her dismay. She fought her urge to deny him, knowing the price that denial would bear.

Yet she was tempted, dangerously tempted, to grant him his will.

Raymond bent and brushed his lips across her temple. Melusine shivered and glanced up, puzzled anew by his effect upon her.

"I shall endeavor to see you pleasured," he whispered, his breath hot against her cheek. "Upon that you can rely."

Lost in his gaze, Melusine found herself curious. Raymond traced a line along his jaw with his warm fingertip, that seductive mischief in his eyes. For the price of her own salvation, perhaps she could fulfill his yearning for sons.

She nodded, her mouth to dry for speech.

"Are we agreed, then?" he asked, his acceptance so ready that she was surprised. "A holding, ten sons, wealth and no stain upon my name, in exchange for marriage and your privacy each and every Saturday. I would accept your wager, lady, and hold you to your terms, if I might know your name in exchange."

"Melusine," she said, her voice soft and unsteady.

"Melusine," he repeated with satisfaction. Later, she would know that she had been lost in that moment, that his utterance of her name was more potent than the strongest spell. "Lady Melusine, consider your wager made."

Before Melusine could reply, Raymond kissed her to seal their agreement. It was the first kiss Melusine had ever tasted, the first time a mortal had laid his lips upon hers.

The unbearable sweetness of it reassured her that the burden she had accepted would not be too much to bear.

II

elusine washed Raymond's blade, his garments and his scabbard in the fountain. The waters eased away the dried stain of the Count's blood, as if it had never been there. Her sisters, meanwhile, cast a fine dust over the trail of blood that marked Raymond's course to the glade. They enjoyed the detail of those ten sons overmuch, to her thinking, and she ignored them.

Indeed, Melusine could think of little beyond her awareness that Raymond stood half-nude near her. The hair upon his chest looked rough and animal to her gaze, his flesh smelled of sweat and blood and carrion, she could taste earth upon her lips. Yet she was drawn to him, as surely as a fish upon a lure, and she could not explain her attraction.

Nor could she explain her agreement to his terms. Ten times his seed would spill within her. Ten times a mortal child would fill her womb. He could not have chosen a detail that would make her more firmly earthbound, more securely fixed in the realm she would spurn.

Could she keep this pledge and not forget all it was to be fey?

Raymond watched her, wary again, perhaps sensing the turmoil of her thoughts. Melusine returned the scabbard and tabard to him, ensuring that their hands did not brush in the transaction. She saw that this displeased him. He dressed with haste, his disgruntled gaze fixed upon her.

He held out his hand for his blade.

Melusine did not relinquish it. "You must trust me fully."

Anger flashed in Raymond's eyes. "Even though you mean to keep my blade, granted to me by my grandfather's own hand? You ask much of me."

"As you expect much from me. You shall have it returned to you in time." Melusine spoke firmly, knowing a warrior would respond to her commanding tone. "Ride now, ride east upon this very path until you reach a wide road. Take it to your right and ride with all speed. You will reach the gates of Poitou with the dawn."

"And then?" Raymond was vexed yet.

"Tell them that Count Aimery has been struck down by a boar."

He shook his head. "They will not believe the tale without his corpse."

"So, you shall take them to it. Return upon that very road with a party to retrieve your liege lord, ride upon it until the sun is at zenith, then look into the forest to your left. Not twenty paces within the forest, you will find your fallen lord."

"There was no road," Raymond said irritably. "We were lost in the thickness of the forest when the boar assaulted us, and lost precisely because there was no road. Your directions are folly!"

"And your pledge to follow my dictate is a thin one."

"You ask me to believe much that is uncommon."

"I am saving you from death," Melusine reminded him. "Much uncommon must occur to achieve such an end."

Raymond glared at her for a long moment, then heaved a sigh. He folded his arms across his chest and smiled ruefully. His anger fled, his mood changing as abruptly as the sun will dart out from behind thunderclouds, and Melusine found herself charmed. "I am not accustomed to finding Fortune matching her steps to mine, Melusine."

"I am not Fortune."

His eyes twinkled. "I suspect you are more fair."

Melusine felt herself flush. "You will find Count Aimery's corpse, just as I have bidden."

Raymond nodded slowly, then shoved a hand through his hair. "But there is yet another detail," he said, his tone more reasonable than it had been before. "They will know that I tell a falsehood by the shape of the Count's wound. It was cleanly made by a blade and any fool will discern as much."

"Your trust is meager," Melusine accused quietly. "We shall gain nothing without it."

"No one can change the shape of a wound."

"Have faith. Faith can accomplish much indeed."

Raymond donned his gloves, dissatisfied again. "Be warned that I will see you hung beside me if this strategy fails."

"It will not fail." Melusine saw no reason to tell him the truth, that he would never again find her unless she desired as much. "Go, for the road already begins to fade."

Raymond swung into his saddle, pausing to look down at her. He was concerned now, his mood shifting yet again. Truly, these emotions held mortals in thrall! "When will I see you again?"

"When you have done as you have pledged, and I have done as I have pledged." She inclined her head to him. "Until then, godspeed to you."

"That salute will not suffice," he muttered, then bent to catch her nape in his gloved hand. He kissed her deeply then, his tongue slipping between her teeth, his rough caress feeding that newfound desire within Melusine. Indeed, she found herself participating in his embrace with a fervor that should have startled her.

She was breathless when he lifted his head, breathless and flushed. He grinned then, a reckless grin that made her heart skip in a most uncommon fashion.

"*Au revoir*, Lady Melusine." Raymond touched his spurs to his steed and rode into the deep shadows of the forest.

Melusine stood, deaf to her sisters' mockery, staring after Raymond until long after the thunder of the stallion's hoof beats had faded. She tasted his mortality upon her own lips and marveled at what she had done.

What had this knight awakened within her?

What fool's wager had he made?

Raymond rode along the road as Melusine had bidden him, guiding a company of the Count's men to some point, he knew not where. Already he had heard the whispers of discontent with his tale of Aimery's demise, and he was well aware that not all believed his innocence.

That the road glimmered slightly just beyond the periphery of his vision did little to reassure him.

He had thought it all a jest. He had thought some pretty

demoiselle played a trick upon him—the daughter of the King of Albion, no less—for no living soul could pledge what she had and keep the wager. He had agreed to her terms, not truly expecting that much would come of it.

But the road had been there, just as Melusine had foretold, and it was curious, so curious that Raymond was uneasy. He had followed her dictate for lack of a better tale, though now he wondered at the wisdom of it.

Even now, he could effortlessly summon the recollection of her. Her hair was long and fair and had glinted in the moonlight as if wrought by a silversmith. Her eyes were a green more verdant than the deepest forest pool. He liked her wit. He liked that she did not believe him to be a fool. He liked how she tasted, so sweet and fragrant that he had half believed she had not been truly before him.

Had he ever seen a demoiselle so fair? He should have credited his initial thought that she was fey. He should not have been so readily persuaded to grant his pledge. In her absence, he fretted as he had been incapable of doing in her presence. The rippling ribbon of fairy road beneath his steed's hooves taunted him.

What if she had lied to him? The fey were known to do as much, especially to win their way in some wager.

What if Aimery's corpse was not as Melusine had declared it would be? What would he tell his fellows then? They would think him deceitful or cunning. Aimery's son Guillaume rode in the company, and Raymond knew that his own future rested in the hands of the Count's heir.

What would he do, where would he go, if Guillaume cast him out? There was no doubt that Guillaume would not suffer a traitor in his hall, or even the man who had forgotten the location of Aimery's corpse.

Raymond could not decide whether it would be worse to find all as Melusine had foretold. What dark powers did she hold within her grip, if she could so change the world at will?

What manner of bride would he find in his bed if he kept his vow? Sweat beaded upon his brow and cold trickle of dread meandered down his spine, though the day was temperate.

He knew when it was midday, though not by the angle of the sun. Nay, there was a prickling at his nape, a conviction that he was watched, and indeed, the fey road seemed to fade ahead of their party. Raymond looked to the left of the path and—to his relief and trepidation—did see something within the woods.

"Here," he said, his voice husky as it seldom was. His finger shook with rare trepidation as he pointed. The men led their steeds into the undergrowth, some dismounting to stride through the thicket. Raymond did not lead the way, though he found Guillaume fast beside him.

"This must be difficult for you, old friend," the Count's son said quietly. "To return to the site of an ordeal is a challenge for the most stalwart warrior. I know the regard that you had for my father."

Raymond said nothing, letting Guillaume think what he would. It was worse, in many ways, that Guillaume was determined to think well of him. They had grown up together and for the first time, Raymond found the younger man's admiration of him was an undeserved and unwelcome burden.

The men shouted. "It is our lord, the Count!"

Raymond hastened forward, anxious to see the truth. It was Aimery, just as he had fallen, in the same garb and the same pose and an entirely different place. Aimery was just as dead as he had been when Raymond left him, and the knight felt his grief wash over him again. There was no hint that Aimery had been moved, and indeed, when they rolled his corpse over, the ground was stained beneath his body with his blood.

As the ground had been where he truly fell. Impossible, yet before his own eyes. Raymond crossed himself, gooseflesh dancing over him as he watched. He did not wish to see, yet he could not look away.

The men peered beneath Aimery's body, grimacing at the wound, and Raymond feared that he would be unveiled as the liar he was.

"What a monster that boar must have been," declared one man. "Look at the damage wrought by its tusks. The wounds are so wide and so far apart."

"So deep," whispered another and shuddered.

"You should not look upon it, my lord," the first counseled Guillaume, who had paled. "Your father had no chance of survival."

Stunned, Raymond stepped forward to see. There were indeed two wounds where once there had been one, and both were ragged as if wrought by tusks and not a sword. He crossed himself again, his gaze rising to the woods.

"Praise be to Aimery," murmured the first man, echoing Raymond's gesture. "May his soul rest in peace." The men all crossed themselves and spontaneously recited the Paternoster.

Raymond's flesh prickled all the while. Melusine was here. He knew it well. She had lingered to see the result of what she had wrought and he could not hide his fear of her and what she had done.

What price for this feat would she demand of him in truth?

"The boar!" One of the squires shouted from a distance.

All of the men pivoted, fearing in that moment that they were under assault.

"The dead boar is here!" cried the boy again. A ripple of relief passed through the company. The men trudged toward the boy, Raymond among them, and one whistled at the size of the boar.

It was the same beast, he would have wagered his life upon it. It had been larger than most, uglier than most, and blessed with a rare abundance of fur. But instead of raging and snorting as it had been when he had seen it last, the boar was dead. Its eyes were yet open, those distinctive eyes. Even in death, one remained angry red and one silver grey.

Raymond bent and touched its flesh, needing to be certain. "It is truly dead," he marveled.

"Aye, and it is a veritable monster," said one man. "This one may haunt your dreams for a long while, Raymond. I have never seen the like of him."

"It must have been overwhelmed by its battle with Aimery." The other men nodded agreement, several commenting on the length and thickness of the beast's tusks.

"We had best make a meal of it," said Guillaume. "There will be hundreds come for Father's funeral and we will have need of all the meat we can muster. Perhaps this flesh will be sweet in exchange for the high price it commanded." He snapped his fingers, tending his duty despite his obvious dismay. Boys hastened to do his bidding.

As the boar was lifted, a gasp echoed through the company. Raymond took a step back and blanched.

Melusine had told no lie, though she returned his blade in a most uncommon manner. It was plunged to the hilt into the boar, the jeweled hilt gleaming in the dappled sunlight.

Raymond swallowed, astonished. The other men clearly recognized the blade, for they hooted.

"Praise be that Raymond was with our lord!"

"You are modest indeed, my old friend," Guillaume said, his voice hoarse. "You said nothing of this brave deed."

Another man gripped Raymond's shoulder. "It takes a rare spirit to face such a fiend, especially in the defense of another."

It was upon Raymond's lips to deny that he had ever done as much, but the entire company murmured assent. They clapped him upon the shoulder, gruffly congratulating him for his valor, and the moment for honesty was passed.

Indeed, with his blade as it was, a denial would have been beyond credibility.

"I did not know for certain that the beast had died," he said as he bowed his head.

"I thank you, for dispensing justice in my stead." Guillaume glanced between Aimery and the boar. "My father was well served to have a man like you pledged to his hand." He embraced Raymond, tears glistening in his eyes, and Raymond felt a fraud.

The others assumed, of course, that he was modest. He was surrounded and congratulated yet again. The others carried away the dead, still chattering about his valor.

Raymond lingered where the boar had fallen, his grip tightening and loosing on his stained but recovered blade. He had not merely been absolved of the killing of his uncle but hailed as a hero.

It was beyond expectation.

It was precisely as Melusine had foretold.

It was a lie. His own memory of events caught in his throat. He had tried to defend Aimery, but he had not succeeded. The praise of his fellows felt tainted for he knew himself to be unworthy.

His gaze fell upon Aimery's corpse, now being lifted to a bier to be carried back to court. Raymond looked at the blood stains upon the ground. He had lost a comrade and a patron, a friend whose loss would not easily be filled. He turned and retched into the undergrowth of the forest, spitting with vigor when he straightened. He wiped his blade upon the leaves and returned it to his scabbard, then wiped his face with both hands.

He would never have willingly injured his patron, not for all the gold in Christendom. Though Melusine might grant him his heart's desire, the price was too high.

He cast a glance over his shoulder, still aware of Melusine's presence. "This is a foul way to make any earthly gain," he whispered unsteadily. "I rescind my agreement. I will not benefit from my lord's loss. I break with our wager, let your vengeance be what it may."

He might have departed then, but Melusine appeared so suddenly that he was taken aback. She might have stepped through a curtain, but there was no curtain in these woods.

Raymond knew then with whom he bargained.

"Demon!" he whispered, uncertain the others could see her though they might hear him. He crossed himself with vigor, then walked away, not sparing her another glance.

The men mounted and urged their steeds back to the road. Raymond noted that the road shimmered even more than previously and that it had faded completely beyond this point. He guessed that none would ever be able to find the site of Count Aimery's demise again. They would make legends of it, they would tell tales of Raymond's valor, and Raymond alone would know the truth of it among men. Fame would be his, but it would be based upon a lie.

When he died, he might well gain a kind of immortality, snared as he would be within the tales of his fellows.

The prospect sickened him.

Perhaps, if he prayed fervently enough, if he avoided the forest, Melusine herself might not be able to insist upon collecting what he had promised. In her absence, he knew he could be resolute.

Perhaps he had best leave Poitiers.

Soon.

Melusine nigh roared with frustration. She could not pursue Raymond, not now, though she knew he meant to spurn her and their wager. The taste of the earth was upon her tongue and she felt the familiar shiver beginning in her very bones.

The sun was already lowering to the horizon and the morrow was Saturday. Melusine had an obligation she could not evade, one that could not be forgotten, one that would not be denied.

She hastened to a forgotten corner of the forest where her shame would not be witnessed. One day per week, the portal to the world she preferred was barred against her. Her curse trapped her in the wretched mortal world while it wrought its price. It was a painful reminder of her fate if she could not break the curse.

Melusine was so tired from her labors of this day that she barely made her refuge in time.

The change came with the shuddering vigor that always took her by surprise. She fought it, struggling against its wickedness as she always did. Her effort made no difference—it never did. The silvery touch of moonlight only made the change more horrific, though she had never had the fortune to metamorphose in the dark.

It was a detail of the curse, wrought by her own mother, that Melusine must witness the price of her deed.

And witness it, she did. No living soul could have torn her gaze away from the unnatural change, no less its relentless speed.

The scales first appeared upon her hips. They grew upon her flesh with startling vigor, like a gleaming pestilence spreading before her very eyes. Even as they claimed her flesh and replaced her skin, her legs were drawn together by a force she could not deny. Her thighs and shins were sealed each to the other, then changed shape, becoming one thick tail. That tail grew as quickly as lightning could strike, coiling in the water where her feet had been just heartbeats before, thick and serpentine.

It was agony to endure and Melusine grit her teeth. Her legs might have been sliced to ribbons from hip to toe, for the vigor of the pain. Her flesh might have been flailed to a pulp, for the fire that burned the length of it. She was singed, she was changed, she was wrought anew in an alien guise. The scales gleamed once her tail was formed, shone in the moonlight, arranged in stripes of argent and azure.

And through it all, she tasted earth. The dark secrets of the soil were upon her tongue, the mysteries of the chthonic mortal world itself. She knew the terminus of every tunnel, the locale of every snake and newt and mole, the destination of every root. She knew the secrets of death and regeneration, she held the keys to Hades and to Hell, she could have swum the river Styx. She could have summoned a mortal soul back from the dead.

Melusine rejected all of it. The earth was not part of the fey world she knew and loved. The fey lived in air and water, and left earth and flame to mortals. She was half-mortal, 'twas true, and this curse had been wrought to remind her of her crime against her mortal father, but she would not accept that legacy willingly.

The mortal world was inflicted and foreign, and though she must endure it, she would never welcome it or allow that there was any merit in its presence. She would step into that world, for as long as she was compelled to do so, but only to win eternity in the domain she loved.

And in the end, she would be rid of this tail. Raymond would have his castle and wealth and his ten sons, and she would have a freedom that would endure long after he had rejoined the earth.

She must persuade Raymond to her cause. She could not be trapped within the mortal world for all of eternity, she could not accept such an exile.

Melusine touched her lips, which still burned from his kiss, and simmered with desire to see him again.

Before the dawn touched the horizon, Melusine realized that she was no longer alone. She jumped in alarm, her tail swishing in the pool, then her mother's chuckle sounded.

"Fear not, daughter mine. It is only me."

Melusine had learned well enough to fear her mother, or at

least her mother's wrath. She settled cautiously into the water as her mother appeared on the bank before her, studying that woman for some hint of her mood.

Presine seemed merry enough, which was perhaps a warning in itself.

"Have you come to gloat?" Melusine asked. "Or to ensure that your curse is effective?"

"I know my curses to be effective." Presine waved a hand, conjuring a stone bench behind herself. She sat down and met her daughter's gaze. "It is my lessons that oft prove evasive. Have you learned anything?"

"Solely that my mother is as a viper when defied, and beyond reason with regard to my father."

"You three should not have imprisoned him in a mountain."

"He should not have broken his pledge to you! Did he not vow to never look upon you in childbirth?" Melusine folded her arms across her chest and glared at her mother. "Though you were too weak to demand compense for his crime, I am not."

Her mother tilted her head to regard her and spoke softly. "What of forgiveness?"

"What of the honor of keeping one's word?"

Presine shook her head. "You have learned little as yet, I see, but perhaps that will change in time."

"What is that to mean?"

"That forgiveness has its place, as does love. We fey have little use for such emotions, and indeed, we believe that mortals can teach us little that we do not know. Their very mortality, though, makes them value life as we do not."

The day had been long and chilly, and her thoughts had been plagued by the recollection of Raymond's burning touch. Melusine feared she was softening to mortals, just as her mother had, but she feared the import of that even more. Thus, she spoke with greater impatience than she should have done. "I value my life, and value it more when I am not plagued by this tail."

"You are not fully fey, daughter mine, and that tail should remind you as much once a week."

"Half fey is sufficient by the old laws to live as fully fey."

Presine nodded acknowledgment. "But the half you have

from your father cannot be so readily forgotten as that. Had you not retaliated against him, you would have become fully mortal. Mortal blood is stronger than fey blood and takes dominance over time."

"No! You never told us as much!"

Presine's smile was wry. "I doubted you would appreciate the revelation."

"Then I am glad indeed that I took the vengeance you refused to take, for I would be fully fey, for all time."

"Would you?" Presine shook her head, then looked up at the last of the stars. "Our time passes, Melusine, and soon there will be no place for us. The realms of fey and mortal draw apart, and the thread that holds them in tether together frays a little further with every passing day. It will snap, not long from now, though the exact day cannot be named. Once it does break, I suspect that the fey realm will be all the paler for its isolation."

"I have heard naught of this."

Presine shrugged. "Nonetheless it is true. You can see the evidence of it in the scorn of men for us and our realm, in their disregard for our powers. Ensure that you choose your realm before the fateful day, for there will be no passing between the worlds from that day hence."

With that, her mother disappeared. Melusine wished she could follow her through the veil and demand more details, but her tail kept her prisoner in this world.

Her mother's warning made Melusine anxious. She knew full well where she would choose to spend eternity, though now she could not be certain that she would have sufficient time to break her curse. She watched the sun rise with impatience, for she had much to accomplish. She had a wedding to arrange, and ten sons to bear, as quickly in succession as possible.

But first, she had a man's heart to win.

Raymond knelt in the chapel, clutching the vial of holy water he had requested from the priest. It was no credit to him that he had crafted a lie to win the priest's agreement to this, but a man had to do what was necessary to protect himself.

The bells had ceased their ringing, the faithful had been summoned and the priest had begun the procession when Raymond had the sense that something was awry.

He felt a ripple in the air, a parting of the clouds of incense, a slight chill touch the back of his neck. He glanced back covertly, narrowing his eyes against the darkness, against the shine of thousands of candles in the shadows.

A woman stood in the portal, wrapped in a dark cloak of heavy wool. He could nearly feel her gaze slipping over the congregation and he had the sense that he was hunted.

Melusine. His heart began to pound. Before his marveling eyes, she dipped her fingertips into the font by the portal and wrought a cross upon her forehead with the holy water.

This would show the truth of it!

Nothing happened. Raymond blinked. He had been so certain that she was the spawn of a demon, so certain that her wicked soul meant him ill. How could this be? She hastened down the side aisle and knelt beside Raymond just before the priest began to sing.

"How..?" he began in indignation.

Melusine shushed him, raising a single fingertip in admonition. "Heed the Mass," she chided, as if chastising a noisy gossip. She folded her hands before herself, bowed her head and joined the prayer with conviction.

Raymond was confused. Demons were always denounced by the sacraments and it was well known that holy water repelled them. But he could see the glisten of holy water upon Melusine's brow. He watched her lips move as she participated in the prayers.

Had he been wrong? Desire unfurled within him at this most unwelcome time, tempting him. He recalled the brief glimpse of her face and found himself too aware of her heat beside him. He gripped his vial of holy water.

Melusine took the bread of Christ's body upon her tongue with nary a flinch. She crossed herself and murmured the prayers as one long accustomed to the ceremony. She recited the Ave and the Paternoster perfectly, her manner as sweet and chaste as a madonna.

His resistance to her abandoned him along with his certainty of her diabolical nature. Her flesh was soft, her lips ripe, her complexion touched with the flush of a new rose. Her cloak did not hide the fullness of her curves and he burned with recollection of her kiss. He watched the delicacy of her fingers as she gestured, he was beguiled by the soft murmur of her voice.

"May God be with you, neighbor," she said to him when the service ended and she rose to her feet. Raymond knew he did not imagine the enchanting smile that touched her lips.

And then she was gone, leaving the chapel in a swirl of wool, her scent lingering behind to torment him.

He had too many questions to let her depart so readily as this. That was why he was compelled to pursue her.

At least he told himself as much.

As if she guessed his intent, Melusine moved quickly through the church. Raymond had to run to catch her. His progress was impeded by many who wished to congratulate him on his kill and his loyalty. Melusine easily outpaced him and he feared to lose her.

He lunged out of the sanctuary and into the thin sunlight in time to catch a last glimpse of her as she rounded a corner in the market.

Raymond ran. He leapt across the square and seized her elbow. She met his gaze, laughter in her own, not surprise.

"I thought the Host would declaim an unbeliever," he said in a hoarse whisper. "I thought the fey could not take communion."

"And I thought mortal men put value in their pledges," she said, then arched a fair brow. "It seems we both have erred." She might have stepped away, but he tightened his grip upon her.

"Pledge to me that you will not flee. Not yet."

She met his gaze, as uncompromising as Aimery had been with a transgression. "Because my pledge is worth more than yours?"

Raymond shoved his hand through his hair. "It is no sin to break a pledge made with a demon, especially when one has been deceived."

"I am not Satan's spawn." Her scorn was unmistakable.

"Indeed, you can be no demon, for you have attended the Mass."

She smiled and leaned closer to him, placing her hand upon

his chest. "You need not fear me, Raymond. I believe all the creed that you believe, and more besides, more that you have never heard."

"Will you drink this?" He offered the vial of holy water.

She smiled, removed the stopper and drank it dry, with no ill effects. Her eyes sparkled at his astonishment. "You place little value in faith, Raymond. Your God gives you succor because you believe in him."

"And this holy water does not injure you because..."

"Because it is water, no more and no less." She raised a fingertip. "All water is blessed. All of this world is blessed. I acknowledge that blessed state and thus it cannot injure me." She pressed the empty vial back into his hand and made to turn away.

"What do you believe, Melusine?"

She paused and he saw a frown touch her brow. "A more honest creed, perhaps. That each will act according to his own advantage, that each will pursue his own ends."

"Regardless of the cost to others?"

"All ways intersect and all actions provoke reactions. No one can predict all of the repercussions of any given deed."

Her words were not reassuring, not to a man who feared what he had done and what his pledge would bring.

Her expression changed suddenly then, as if she guessed that she only fed his doubts. She regarded him coyly, the glorious green of her eyes veiled by her fair lashes. It was an utterly feminine expression, one that awakened his desire once again.

She eased closer and placed her fingertips upon his jaw, her lips curving into a knowing smile. "Tell me the truth of it, Raymond of Poitiers. You said that you were unfamiliar with Fortune. But is it true that Fortune always neglected you, or is it you who have always spurned her kiss?"

Before he could reply, Melusine reached up and brushed her lips across his own, coaxing the heat within him to an inferno.

She spoke a truth, to be sure. Here was the opportunity he had always longed to have, the chance he had known he would never receive. Truly, he had seen time and again that men make their own luck. A beauteous wife, a holding, wealth and ten sons seemed a fat gain for granting a woman her privacy each Saturday.

Perhaps his folly was in refusing the gift Melusine could grant to him.

"I cannot wed without a holding to my name," Raymond said, his voice sounding thick to his own ears. He raised a hand and dared to touch the silk of her hair, dared to utter her name. "I have no estate, no title and thus no right to wed, Melusine. That must come afore the nuptials."

She regarded him steadily. "Have you the will to wed me, then?"

He nodded slowly, his resolve growing with every passing moment. "I render my debts and I keep my vows, upon that you can rely."

"How fortunate that I know how you can obtain a holding." When he began to smile that she would not reject him, Melusine raised a cautionary finger. "If you trust me."

Raymond nodded. "You will not surprise me so readily again."

"Then what you must do is this. The Count's son and heir will offer you a reward for killing the boar that killed his father."

"Guillaume has already done so."

"I shall hope that you did not modestly decline."

"I said that I would have to think upon the matter."

"Good. You must tell him this very day that you desire a holding. You must ask him for all of the land that can be encompassed by a hart's hide, no more and no less."

"But that is not enough to keep a mouse!"

Melusine granted him a stern look.

Understanding dawned upon Raymond. "Doubtless this is your strategy, to test my trust of you."

"The man has found his wits, after all," Melusine said, smiling when he chuckled.

Raymond let his thumb move against her upper arm, tracing a circle. He felt her shiver, but she did not pull away, and he dared to be encouraged that this match could serve them both well. The prospect emboldened him mightily. "And after I have done as you have bidden?"

"Ride back into the forest, by that very road you took yesterday. You will come upon an old man, who will offer to sell you a hart's hide bigger than any in Christendom."

"And I shall buy it."

"No. You will declare it to be inferior and ask if he has another. You must insist upon buying the second hart hide shown to you and no other, regardless of how poorly it looks."

Raymond nodded. "For there is more to it than meets the eye."

"Indeed. And when you have it, take the sharpest knife you possess. Slice the hide into the thinnest ribbon that you can, beginning from the outside edge and cutting in a spiral."

"And that fine ribbon will encompass a larger parcel of land. How clever you are!"

Melusine smiled but did not pause her instruction. "Take the ribbon to the woods and unfurl it as you will. Begin with the fountain where we met, and ensure that it is encompassed within the circle you make. Take witnesses with you, then ask the Count's son to grant you all the land that you encircle."

"It still would seem that precious little land would be so surrounded, no matter how thin I cut the hide," Raymond said. "There will be something uncommon about this hart hide, I wager."

Melusine only smiled.

And Raymond believed. He bent and caressed her cheek with the tips of his fingers. "I will not fail in this, my lady. I shall tell the Count's son that I must have a holding now for I am most anxious to wed." He smiled at her, anticipating a merry nuptial night between her thighs. "It is, after all, no less than the truth."

And this time, when he kissed her with possessive ease, the lady hesitated but a heartbeat before she rose to her toes to return his embrace. Her tongue dueled with his own, her fingers twined in his hair, drawing him ever closer. Raymond knew then an utter conviction that he had chosen aright.

Accepting Fortune's due promised to be an easy burden to bear.

III

he midday meal was in progress when Raymond reached the Count's hall. He spied his brother, Fromont, seated at Guillaume's left, and grimaced. Doubtless Fromont had come to see what could be gleaned from the Count's holdings, under the guise of paying his respects. Raymond had no desire to speak with his brother and tried to slip unnoticed into the company. He sat upon a bench at the back of the hall and had time only to nod to his fellows before Guillaume's voice rang out.

"Raymond! Come! You must sit with me at the board!"

"I am content here, my lord," Raymond replied with a smile.

"And I am not," Guillaume said, with more than a measure of his father's charm. "Come, do not spurn the honor I would show you."

Raymond excused himself and made his way to the high table, trying to smile as those present offered their congratulations on his valor. He felt a fraud, more so when he reached the high table and spied the boar itself, roasted and holding an apple within its mouth, being carved.

"The finest cut for the Count's defender," said Guillaume. The company applauded while Raymond took his seat, awkward with praise he knew he did not deserve.

"My brother is unaccustomed to such favor," Fromont said. "It is only reasonable, as he has never done any deed with success in all his days."

"You know little of your brother since he came to my father's hall," Guillaume said coolly. He smiled at Raymond. "I am not surprised by his valor, for I have seen it often, nor am I surprised that he is as modest as a good knight should be."

Fromont snorted, but contented himself without making further comment. Raymond managed to eat enough to ensure that others did not note his distaste for the meat. He could not look at the carcass without recalling Aimery's insistence upon killing it, and the misfortune that had ensued.

"You are quiet this day," Guillaume said.

Raymond grit his teeth. "As much as I welcome your stewardship, the hall feels empty to me in your father's lack."

Guillaume smiled sadly and looked down at his trencher. "You speak the truth, as always, my most trusted friend." He turned a bright glance upon Raymond. "In my father's memory, as it would surely please him, I would offer you anything as reward for your defense of him."

The meat stuck in Raymond's throat. He knew what he should ask, knew what Melusine expected of him, but he felt he had no right to do so. "The meat will suffice," he said hoarsely.

Fromont made an exasperated laugh. "As witless as ever he was," he muttered, but Guillaume ignored him.

"I must insist, Raymond," that man said, his voice low with intent. "My father will surely haunt me if I do not see this due rendered. Choose, or I shall choose for you."

Raymond's head snapped up in his alarm at this prospect. "As much land as can be encompassed by a hart's hide," he said, his words tumbling over themselves in their haste to be heard.

"What nonsense is this?" Fromont demanded.

Guillaume watched Raymond. "Are you certain, my friend? Your price seems small."

"It is all I desire, my lord."

"Why?" Guillaume lowered his voice. "You may remain at Poitiers for so long as you desire. I will always have need of a loyal man in my household. Think upon the favor you would ask, my friend, and do not waste it on a frippery."

"But I would wed, my lord. I would have a small holding that I might honorably ask for the lady's hand."

Guillaume laughed with delight. "There is the finest news I have heard this day! No wonder you are not yourself. Has she seized your heart truly?"

Raymond could only nod and stare at his uneaten portion of meat.

"Well, who is she?" Guillaume nudged him. "I must know her!"

"I fear you do not, my lord, though with your aid and God's grace that omission shall be repaired shortly."

"Splendid!" Guillaume called for more wine. "A toast to Raymond and his lady fair!"

❧

"You are even more witless than I recalled," Fromont began as soon as he and Raymond had ridden out of the stables. "All of Poitiers yours to take, and you ask for this folly!"

Raymond tried to ignore his brother's bitterness. Indeed, he wished he could have evaded his brother's determination to accompany him. "It is all I desire."

"Then you are more addle-pated than even Father believed. You could have been Count of Poitiers!" Fromont flung out his hands. "You could have ruled all of this! There are those saying that you deserve no less, and Guillaume could not have denied it to you."

"It is Guillaume's inheritance." Raymond looked carefully for the road that seemed to appear and vanish, the road that Melusine apparently could summon. He spied it just where it had been the day before, but only when they were almost past it. Raymond turned his horse quickly and took the path, earning a curse from Fromont but no relief from his tirade.

"Poitiers could have been yours. If you did not want it, you could at least have thought of your own kin." Fromont spat onto the road. "Three brothers yet there are yet at Forez, each and every one of them chafing for a scrap of land. I have to look over my shoulder all the time, so fearful am I that I will be struck down in darkness by the most ambitious of them."

"Who is the most ambitious of them?"

"Whosoever is in a foul mood. Whosoever has been denied some small thing by me. They are all ambitious and they all loathe me." Fromont arched his brows. "You might have spared a consideration for your own brother, for me and my welfare."

"I have ensured that you do not have to care for me."

Fromont snorted. "Hardly that! How much land do you intend to surround with this hart hide? Enough for a privy, perhaps?" He laughed, much entertained by his own jest.

Raymond ignored his brother, for there was an old peasant beside the road ahead. He was removing the hide from large dead hart. He had killed the deer, in direct violation of the forest laws, though he did not appear to be frightened by their approach.

"You should be flayed alive for your impertinence!" Fromont said to the old man, who eyed him with disdain. "You have no right to hunt such a beast on the Count's own land and you know it well."

"The Count has no reckoning of this territory," the old man said. A shiver slipped down Raymond's spine. He noted a glimmer around the old man, a shimmer that might have been wrought of frost and starlight.

The old man returned to his labor. The meat glistened as he worked, the hide appearing uncommonly supple in his hands.

"I would buy a hart hide from you," Raymond said.

"At least you have the sense to buy a large one," Fromont said.

"This one will be large indeed," the old man said with satisfaction, more than half finished with his task.

"Have you another?" Raymond asked.

The old man granted him a sharp look. "You do not want that one. This one is much larger."

"Let me see the other one."

"I am too busy to fetch it in this moment."

"I will wait." Raymond dismounted, cast the reins over his steed's head and let the horse wander. The old man regarded him, not troubling to hide his irritation, and Raymond smiled. "There is no need to hasten."

The old man fussed. His knife moved without its former precision and he nicked his thumb. He swore vehemently, then cast his knife aside. He dug in his pack with haste, then flung a darkened hide at Raymond so quickly that the knight barely managed to catch it. "There! Is that worth your waiting?"

Raymond spread the hide before himself and knew a moment's doubt. It was moth-eaten, this one, and old, with a faintly unpleasant smell. It was no more than half the size of the other.

He recalled Melusine's conviction, though, and the deed she

had accomplished with his own blade. He must show his faith in her.

"How much do you wish for it?" he asked.

Fromont snatched his shoulder and shook him. "Are you mad?"

Raymond stepped away from his brother's grip. "I desire this one."

"Why? You will not even have a privy to call your own! What manner of woman will wed a man who cannot offer her a privy?"

The old man watched this exchange with interest, but named a price promptly when Raymond met his eye.

"Thievery!" Fromont said.

"Aye, it is twice as much as I would take for the larger one." The old man clearly hoped Raymond would take the other hide.

"This will serve me well." Raymond paid the disgruntled peasant, over Fromont's strident objections, then mounted his horse and rode back to the hall.

"Madness!" Fromont shouted behind him. "You deserve every misfortune heaped upon you, upon that there is no doubt. I shall disavow you as my brother, for you are too stupid that we could share any blood between us."

Raymond said nothing, for the prospect suited him well enough.

Fromont had very little to say the next morning, however, when Raymond unfurled the ribbon he had cut from the hide. The narrow band of hart's hide seemed to be endless, and when it was all laid out, Raymond had encompassed not only the fey fountain but a territory miles and miles across.

The company who had come with Guillaume as witnesses gaped in astonishment.

"It is a marvel," said one.

"It is sorcery," whispered another, who crossed himself.

"I do not care. Let it be so!" cried Guillaume. "Well done, old friend! I feared deeply for your lady and yourself when first you revealed this scheme. And this fair land, I confess, is one I have never noted before. You have chosen wisely and have won no less than you deserve."

"But what of this bride?" Fromont asked. "Her countenance must be as bewitched as her counsel."

Raymond, jubilant that Melusine had fulfilled her pledge so well, had no care for his brother's insinuations. "You shall meet her in a fortnight, in this very place. We shall be wedded here, and shall abide here." He remembered her prophecy. "These lands shall be known as Lusignan. You are all invited to join my bride and me and make merry at our nuptial feast."

The company applauded, but Fromont shook his head. "Who is your bride? From whence does she come?"

Raymond had no intention of answering those questions. "What need have you of such details?"

"Can you not celebrate your brother's success?" Guillaume asked.

Fromont scowled. "A man cannot believe all he is told, especially by a woman who provides trickery like this hide."

"I bought the hide. You witnessed as much."

"From her man, upon her counsel, I would wager. You did not happen upon that old man by chance! You led me there, knowing full well what you would find." Fromont leaned closer to whisper. "What manner of woman will you wed, brother mine?"

"A beauteous one, as all shall see in a fortnight."

Fromont snorted. "Not I! Cast aside your life and your salvation, if you must, but do not ask others to share in it. We part this day for all time if you insist upon such folly."

Raymond met Fromont's gaze. "So be it. My pledge to my lady stands true."

Fromont spat on the ground. He left the company and took to the road alone. Guillaume put a hand upon Raymond's shoulder in sympathy. Raymond was embarrassed that he had seen Fromont's poor manners.

"Raymond, about this lady of yours," Guillaume said, his words brimming with laughter. "Has she a sister?"

The company chuckled at this and made to return to Poitiers.

"Fromont is only jealous that your new holding is so fine," Guillaume said. "Any man with blood in his veins would covet such a prize."

"I thank you for the granting of it."

"My father would seem to be smiling upon you, old friend, for the Fates have turned in your favor with his demise."

It was a reminder of Aimery's own prediction that Raymond did not need, but he forced a smile nonetheless.

The first day of the wedding feast dawned sunny and fair, for Melusine had arranged as much. She had labored long and hard to conjure all that was needed for these days of merriment, all that was needed to persuade Raymond that the wager would be as he had hoped and his fellows that success was his indeed.

For three days and three nights, she would host his guests and family. It would be a wedding that all would recall, a wedding with finery fit for recounting over and over again. Peacocks and swans had been prepared for the meal, both cooked and redressed in their feathers for presentation at the board. There were roast chickens aplenty, and stags and pigs, and eggs prepared every which way. The board would groan with the meat.

Pastry had been shaped into dozens of follies, like partridge pies with a pastry partridges sitting atop the filling. Sweet almond marzipan had been colored and shaped like fruit, the confections sure to delight the guests. There was wine from every province and ale for those who preferred it and hippocras to end every meal.

Melusine had ensured that every detail was so rich as to befit a king, all the better to show that her new husband had finally been granted his due. She hoped that all would meet with Raymond's favor.

She would like to see the wariness leave his eyes.

She would like to see him smile.

Melusine smoothed her silken skirts at the sound of hoof beats and gathered her maidens about herself just as the first of Raymond's party left the woods. Raymond rode alongside the newly invested Count Guillaume, the trap on their steeds gleaming in the sunlight as brightly as their mail. Pennants flew above the party, all the guests dressed in their finest garb and jewels.

It was as naught compared to the finery of the fey.

Melusine smiled at the mortals' collective gasp of astonishment. This had been but a field when last they visited the fountain—now a hundred silken tents were pitched in a meadow jostling with flowers. Ostlers strode forth to take the horses, and fair maidens brought cups of sweet wine to welcome the guests. A thousand birds sang in the trees, and the fountain sparkled with music of its own. There were servants aplenty in the meadow, each garbed in lustrous silk, each beautifully wrought. Many sang, their voices sweeter than lutes, and the women had flowers braided into their hair.

The largest tent in the center was tall, wrought of azure silk that shimmered in the breeze. The walls were rolled up and tied with silver ribbons, the tables set within gleaming with silver cups and plates for the wedding feast. To the left was a smaller tent, striped azure and silver, within which Melusine had anticipated Raymond's every desire upon his nuptial night. To the right was a red silken tent, hung with gold, the Count's banner flying from its peak.

The mortals were astonished, and so they should be, to find themselves in an earthly paradise.

Melusine took an embroidered tabard over arm and strode to meet her guests. She had left her hair hanging loose down her back, though a measure of it had been entwined with golden ribbons and worked into a corona upon her brow. She wore a kirtle wrought of silk as blue as a summer sky, which shimmered in the sunlight like fine metal. It was embroidered with silver lions upon the hems, and the tabard she carried was wrought of the same silk and embroidered to match. A silver circlet rested upon her brow and the sleeves of her chemise were visible—that garment was wrought of so fine a linen that it might have been the gossamer of cobwebs.

The stars glimmered in her betrothed's eyes and she caught her breath at his delight.

Raymond dismounted and bent low over her hand, his lips brushing her knuckles even as he held fast to her fingertips. "Lady Melusine! You are more beauteous each time I see you."

Melusine inclined her head, well aware that the others surveyed her openly. She was uncommonly glad to see him again as well.

"Welcome, my lord," she said to him. "I hope that all I have prepared pleases you this day."

"My lady most certainly does," he whispered, for her ears alone, his eyes twinkling. He did not release her hand when he straightened. Melusine felt the warm pulse of his blood when his palm pressed against her flesh, the beat of it making her flush in anticipation of their first night together.

Ten sons.

Raymond introduced her to Count Guillaume. Melusine did not recall the names of the others she met that day, the insistent pulse of Raymond's touch driving all from her thoughts.

"And what do you carry?" he asked.

Melusine felt her cheeks heat that she had forgotten her own intent. She offered the tabard to Raymond. "I made this for you, Raymond, for our nuptials." Her words faltered as they customarily did not. "That you might wear the colors of Lusignan on this day of days."

"Lusignan!" Guillaume repeated. "It is a fair name for a fair holding."

Raymond smiled then, smiled with pleasure, and Melusine's heart fairly stopped. "For me? Truly, you wrought this marvel for me?"

She wondered how often anyone had granted him a gift and guessed the answer afore she completed the thought.

"May it be the first of many marvels the two of you create together," Guillaume said heartily.

If only he knew the truth of it. She and Raymond exchanged a secretive smile, a lover's smile, filled with an awareness that warmed her heart. He had guessed her nature, she saw, and accepted it beyond all expectation.

Melusine's heart warmed.

"Come!" she said. "We have prepared a tent for you, Count Guillaume. Raymond and I will take our vows this day, and a feast has been prepared for afterward. If you would like to retire first, all is prepared for you."

Guillaume bowed. "I thank you for your thoughtfulness, Lady Melusine."

As the Count strode away with his servants, Raymond caught Melusine fast against his side. He whispered in her ear, his voice filled with an excitement he could not hide. "Who are all of these people? From whence did they come?"

Melusine smiled. "They are your vassals, of course."

"I have no vassals!"

"You have claimed Lusignan. These are the vassals of Lusignan, and they will pledge to both you and I during these nuptials."

Raymond glanced about himself, marveling. "This place is from the realm of fey, is it not? You have conjured it, as surely as you conjured the road, as surely as you have conjured these vassals."

Melusine shook her head, glad that she could be honest with him. "Little of merit can be conjured of naught. I would have to be far stronger than I am to conjure all of this and maintain the vision of it for three days and nights."

"Then what? How?" He was intrigued, fascinated but not repelled.

"The realm of fey and the realm of mortals lie entangled, Raymond, some places within one domain and some within the other. A few, like the forest Broceliande, exist in both. Others, like the isle of Avalon, have been in both at times, but in just one in others. Lusignan is not conjured, but summoned. I have summoned these territories from the realm of the fey, to keep my pledge to you. Lusignan has crossed the divide and will remain in the mortal realm for so long as our wager is kept."

He nodded, his gaze trailing over his new holding even as his fingertips traced the embroidery upon the tabard he held. "And if I break my word to you, it all shall slip across the divide once again, disappearing as if it never had been."

Melusine nodded. There was no need to tell him of her mother's news, for there was naught any soul could do to halt the course. And who knew? Raymond might be as dust afore it occurred.

The prospect made her breath catch in her throat.

The nuptial vows had been exchanged, the marital feast had been savored, the toasts to their health had been drained and the new couple were finally alone in the tent that held their nuptial bed,

Melusine saw Raymond's trepidation. He watched her, his uncertainty mingled with his desire, and she knew that he feared to find some horror beneath her skirts.

How ironic that he sensed her Saturday nature, though he had never glimpsed it, heard tell of it, or seen it.

And he never would, unless he broke their pledge. The prospect chilled Melusine and made her doubly determined to win his love.

Sadly, she did not know much of this mortal mating. She had long preferred to match wits with men, not suffer their touch, and refused to think of what she had known would have to happen this night. She unlaced her kirtle and cast it aside, unaware that the candlelight shone through her chemise.

She was aware that he watched her avidly.

"There is naught to fear, Raymond. I am wrought as you would desire," she said quietly. She unbound her hair and laid upon the bed on her back, prepared for however this deed proceeded.

Raymond did not move.

Melusine cast him a smile, then closed her eyes again. "I am prepared. Do what you must to create sons."

Raymond, to her astonishment, laughed. He sat on the edge of the mattress, his weight making it dip. Melusine looked up then caught her breath, for he had discarded his chemise. He was close, very close, his flesh bare and tanned, the hair thick upon his chest.

His eyes danced and a smile pulled at the corner of his mouth. It seemed that he fought the urge to laugh at her. He braced his hands on either side of her and smiled down at her.

"You have not done this afore," he said, with no accusation in his tone. "But surely you have heard whispers."

She shook her head, uncertain what he meant.

"How do the fey mate?"

"With laughter, with words."

"Not with flesh upon flesh?"

Melusine could not fully suppress her shudder of distaste. She looked away from him, not wanting to insult him. "You may proceed," she said, closing her eyes and hoping the deed would be finished soon.

Raymond chuckled. "Your participation would be welcome."

"But it cannot be necessary."

"Is it not?"

Melusine could not resist the sound of his voice, not when he sounded so merry. She opened her eyes and was snared anew by the sparkle of his eyes.

Her own pulse quickened.

Melusine swallowed and dropped her gaze, noting then what he found so amusing. His enthusiasm for the deed seemed to have waned. "I thought you found me alluring."

"Not when you lie like a corpse." Raymond stretched out beside her and caught a tendril of her hair between his finger and thumb. He twined it about his fingers as he spoke, his voice not unlike the low murmur of a brook. "I would meet abed merrily, Melusine. I would see you pleased, as your touch sees me pleased. I would have us grant pleasure, each to the other, and be able to tell our sons that they were wrought in joy."

"I do not know how to do this."

Raymond smiled, an expression as potent as any spell. "You have only to tell me what you like."

"I do not know."

"Aye, you do. You like laughter and camaraderie. What else?" He bent and touched his lips gently to her shoulder, then met her gaze.

"A lighter touch would be more pleasing," she admitted, her heart in her throat.

He kissed her shoulder again, his touch as gentle as a butterfly landing upon a flower, and Melusine gasped.

"Did you see the folly set before the duke?" he murmured, his breath teasing her skin.

Melusine shivered and smiled despite herself. "He thought it was a bird in truth."

"It was so wondrously crafted."

"You must not forget that he had drunk heartily of the

hippocras."

Raymond chuckled. "He insisted that it chirped."

Melusine laughed in recollection of the plump duke's foolishness. "And forced his fellows to listen to the confection."

"Did you note how Guillaume pretended to hear it? He had the others half-persuaded."

"But each time he swore it chirped, the duke insisted it did not." Melusine found herself laughing. She leaned her head against Raymond's shoulder, savoring the recollection as much as the sound of their laughter entwined together.

"It was a fine feast, finer than any I have ever had." Raymond propped himself up on his elbow, his eyes gleaming, and closed his hand around her breast. "I thank you for your labors."

Melusine could not breathe, particularly not when his thumb slid beguilingly across her nipple. Raymond kissed the hollow of her collarbone and she sighed. A tide of desire grew within her, silencing her objections. She knew that it would shortly carry her away, that it would overwhelm her fey reservations.

And she did not care. She wanted to share all Raymond had to offer. She locked her fingers into the thickness of his hair and drew him closer.

"There," she urged when his kiss found a spot that made her tremble.

"Aye, there," he agreed, closing her fingers around his strength.

Melusine's eyes flew open at his apparent enthusiasm. He chuckled, his fingers sliding into the soft heat of her. She moaned, quivering at both the surety of his caress and his happiness.

"We can make magic together, my Melusine," he whispered.

He was mortal. Her response should not have been thus, but Melusine knew it could not be denied. When Raymond kissed her again, she surrendered fully to the sorcery of his embrace, without a single regret.

After three days of feasting and three nights in Raymond's embrace, Saturday dawns upon Lusignan. The bride is absent. Melusine hears Raymond's words, as at a distance, and is relieved, even as the old evil claims

her body.

No sooner does she wish that she understood him fully than there, in the refuge of her forest glade, Melusine dreams a mortal dream. It is someone else's dream, someone else's memory.

It is Raymond's memory.

She sees a small boy, dark of hair and blue of eye, a boy too small to be so wary. It is more clear that he is fey, for he is wrought small and fine and there is more starlight in his eyes.

She peers into the boy's past and recoils from a mere glimpse of his mother, a beauteous fey, but one captured and abused by Raymond's father. The mother escaped her abuser and abandoned her sole child, wanting naught of mortals or half-mortals again.

The father does not welcome the burden.

Melusine winces and looks back to the child Raymond. She sees his four older brothers, his indifferent father, their flesh hanging heavily upon their bones. She sees the hovel in the woods in which they lived, she sees the gruel Raymond was offered to eat, she sees the lice within the pallet where he slept and the rags in which he was garbed. She sees that he is loathed, because he is different.

Her heart twists.

She sees the Earl of Forez—so the father calls himself—summoned to the court of the Count of Poitou. Count Aimery, the man killed by the boar, is younger in this memory, virile and handsome. It defies belief that he and Raymond's father are brothers, but indeed they are.

She sees the Earl of Forez's jealousy when he enters the Count's fine hall and knows his poison will find a target.

"How unfortunate that all your wealth is destined to waste, Aimery," he says to the Count. "As you have not a single son to carry your name."

She sees the Countess blanch at this rude reference to her barren womb; she sees Aimery close his hand protectively over his wife's trembling fingers. "I shall make you a wager, Brother," Aimery says with uncommon grace. "I could take one of your sons beneath my hand and lighten the burden upon you."

The Countess catches her breath and color touches her cheeks.

The Earl of Forez laughs harshly. "I will grant you one of them willingly. Be warned, Aimery, they eat a cursed amount, each and every one of them, and there is not a one among the wretched lot who will come to any account."

Melusine sees the Countess grip her husband's hand, hope making her radiant again.

"Choose," Aimery bids her softly.

She leaves him, descending to the floor of the hall like a jewel come to life. She is a beautiful woman, if burdened by disappointment in her own failure, her skin creamy and her lips red. She is dressed richly, so richly that she glistens as she walks, like a fey queen, though Melusine knows that wealth is as nothing to her.

All the Countess desires is a son, for a son will please her beloved spouse. She would give any trinket, do any deed, if only she could grant Aimery his heart's desire.

She may have such a chance.

The older boys kick Raymond behind them, for he is the smallest and they have drunk heavily of their father's hatred.

But the Countess is not deceived. She has an eye for merit, this mortal. She bends and beckons to Raymond. He hesitates, clearly fearing a trick. Melusine sees evidence that he has told her the truth, that Fortune has not oft been his companion.

The eldest, Fromont, kicks him soundly, ignoring the Countess's sound of dismay. "Forgotten your manners, runt?"

"Not I!" Raymond spares a telling glance to his brother's boot, then steps forward. His face burns crimson, probably with the awareness that every eye in that hall is upon him, but he does not falter. He bows low before the Countess.

Melusine can fairly hear the thunder of his heart.

"At your service, my lady," he says with a solemnity beyond his years. His brothers chuckle and mimic him, his father guffaws.

But the Countess is charmed. She offers her hand to him, as filthy as he is. "Come to me."

Raymond swallows and does as he is bidden. His hand shakes as he reaches to her. He does not touch her but leaves his fingers just before hers, aware of the grime upon his flesh.

The Countess smiles and closes her hand around his with resolve. "And what is your name, child?"

"Raymond."

"Raymond," she repeats with satisfaction, then turns to smile at her husband. "Raymond will be tall and handsome, I wager."

"Do you offer a child in truth, Cousin?" Aimery asks. "Will you spare Raymond, to gladden my lady's heart? I will see him fed and clothed and

trained as a knight.”

Raymond’s father spits into the rushes. “I would be well rid of one less mouth to feed. Take him! He is the most worthless of the lot.”

“You will never make a knight of him,” whispers Fromont viciously. “I am the only one who will be a knight!”

“The world has need of more than one knight,” Count Aimery says, then he smiles at the frightened boy his wife has brought before him. “Welcome, Raymond. Welcome to Poitiers. Join us at the board, for from this day forth, I pledge that I shall treat you as my own son.”

The boy is led to the head table by the Countess, his astonishment as clear to the company as the resentment of his kin.

Melusine hears the faint echo of hope in that boy’s heart, the hope that his luck had finally changed for the good. She wonders how a child so chosen, plucked from the mire against all odds, could still consider himself to be a stranger to Fortune’s kiss.

The glimpse of another memory grants her the answer.

Within the year, the Countess ripens. She is gay, sparkling with her joy. She tells Raymond that he has brought her greatest desire to pass. Melusine cannot tell whether the young boy understands what is happening, why the Countess’s belly is so round, why the Count insists that he will keep his word to Raymond.

Raymond is awed yet by his surroundings, but he grows taller in this household.

A third memory, a vivid one, visits Melusine as the moon rides high over her secluded pool. It is clearly an event that scarred Raymond, for Melusine feels the recollection as polished as a stone that the fingers cannot leave be. She heeds it with care, hoping to learn something of his secret thoughts.

It is dark, night in the hall of Poitiers, but no soul sleeps. A fire burns on the hearth, though none gather near it. Fat candles burn low, the flames sputtering in the melted beeswax. It is warm in the hall, the air filled with the smell of blood and beeswax and the pulse of mortal hearts.

And a sound that cannot be evaded, the screams of a woman in labor. This is beyond Melusine’s experience, this task of bringing a child to light, though she has heard tell of it. Her mouth goes dry, for she too will endure this ordeal.

Aimery is pacing, his anxiety echoed in a watchful young Raymond’s eyes. “All women scream thus when bearing a babe.” Aimery tousles Raymond’s hair, but his words lack conviction.

Aimery is afraid. Melusine smells his fear and marvels at it. The fey have no fear. They are shackled with few of the emotions that so entangle mortals. She is both fascinated and puzzled.

But not for long.

The screams stop so abruptly that every soul in the hall—and there are many in the shadows—catches his or her breath. Aimery and Raymond turn as one to look to the stairs, just as every servant in the hall glances up.

The midwife appears, cradling a bundle. She is as brown and wrinkled as a midwinter apple and her smile is toothless. "A son!" she cries in triumph. "A hale and healthy son."

The company cheers, more than one commenting that the lady will be pleased. Melusine smiles in her turn that the Countess will have her yearning fulfilled. The servants prepare to congratulate the lord, but he pushes them aside in his anxiety.

"And my lady wife?" Aimery demands.

The midwife closes her eyes and turns away. The hall falls silent on a gasp of disbelief.

What is this?

The midwife's voice is thick. "Her last wish was that the boy be named Guillaume."

"Nay!" The Count runs up the stairs, shoving the midwife aside to enter his wife's chamber.

"She bade me remind you of your pledge to Raymond," the midwife says softly. A trio of women in the hall, elderly servants all, begin to weep.

"Margot!" Aimery's shout echoes throughout his hall. "Not Margot! Say she yet lives."

But she does not, and every person in the hall knows what he refuses to believe. More than one weeps quietly. The midwife rocks the child who has begun to cry in his turn. Small Raymond turns back to the fire, a frightened boy uncertain of his future yet again, his eyes filled with tears.

Fickle Fortune! Only now does Melusine begin to understand the price of the mortality borne by those in this realm. Though she has known affection, it has never been so potent as this. These people mourn the loss of a beloved, mourn in a manner unknown to the immortal fey.

They mourn because Death has stolen one of their number away, stolen the Countess for all time. Is love more potent for mortals? Is their love more poignant for the fact that it can be lost at any time? Is this the compensating gift granted to them, in exchange for their inevitable demise?

In the silence of the forest, Melusine wonders. What is it like, to be as beloved as Aimery's Margot? What is it like for mortals to twine their hearts together, to make one from two, to pledge fealty each to the other for so long as they both shall live? A desire lights within Melusine then, a yearning to know the truth of it.

The sun gilds the horizon and Melusine changes form, with the usual relentless pain. This time, though, her tears are not shed solely for her own agony. She weeps for the Countess Margot, cheated of seeing her greatest dream come to fruition. She weeps for Aimery, who surely desired a son but not in exchange for his lady wife.

And she weeps for Raymond, a boy taught too often that Fortune could not be trusted to favor him for long.

IV

ithin eight days of their nuptials, the forest around the greatest hill in Raymond's new domain of Lusignan had been cleared away. The laborers had emerged from the forest, arriving silently one morning without warning. No one knew them or from whence they had come. They spoke little, though they worked with unholy vigor.

Raymond chose not to ask for details.

These laborers dug enormous ditches, beneath Melusine's command. They laid foundations and crafted a dungeon deep and wide. They began to build a stone wall, a wall that grew higher and higher with such remarkable speed that people came merely to marvel at it. Two commanding square towers rose above those walls.

The walls were rife with arrow slits, and the top of the wall was a crenellated battlement. Three men could walk side by each along the crest of the walls, arms outstretched and fingertips barely touching. There were three gates, each protected by a heavy portcullis and numerous cunning vantage points for archers.

Raymond had not guessed that his wife had known so much of military matters and defense.

There was a chamber within the keep, close to where the lord's chamber would be, and curiously, it was completed first. It had only very high windows, so narrow that a bird could barely peek within them, and it was to this chamber that Melusine retreated each Saturday. Raymond did not know what she did there, and he told himself not to care—it was sufficient for him to know that she was close at hand, not disappearing into the forest alone.

Having grown accustomed to Fortune's lack, Raymond knew to embrace her gifts when they appeared. He found himself laughing at small things, and his lips seemed to be curved always in a smile. Raymond found himself, standing in the fields, merely watching the laborers at their craft, marveling that it should be his. He greeted each morning, not with wariness, but welcoming its possibilities. One day he found himself whistling and realized that this new effervescence within him was happiness.

Melusine could not help but know that he credited her with the change in his life and circumstance. Raymond was besotted with her, fascinated with the rounding of her womb. He seduced her each night, learning what she favored and what she did not, taking delight in her pleasure.

It was more than the mating itself—they became fast friends. They nestled together in their tent at night and spoke of nonsense, of names for the child, of what he would look like, of whether the babe would indeed be born a boy.

Raymond was determined to show himself worthy of his lady's gifts. He strove to be a fair lord to his vassals. He oversaw the courts himself and was visible among his people. He listened to them, considered their desires, ensured their defense. He planned a mill and a pond for breeding fish, to clear acreage for farms and pastures.

Raymond believed his marriage was a good one—he courted his wife both day and night that she might be persuaded of the same.

❧

It had been some nine months since their nuptials, when Melusine came to Raymond in the fields. She carried a gift for him in her hands and hoped desperately that he would favor it.

"What is this?" he asked, kissing her cheek in affectionate greeting as was his custom. "This child has made you as soft as a rose petal," he whispered and she felt herself flush.

"I have wrought you a gift," she said, then she fought a smile. "With my own hands, even." He feigned such amazement that she laughed, and she proudly showed him the needle pricks upon her fingers. He kissed each one dutifully, prompting her laughter at his playfulness.

"It must be precious indeed." Raymond shook out the burden of cloth and gasped in wonder. It was a pennant, long and slender and wrought of silk.

"It is a pennant for Lusignan. I designed the insignia," Melusine said hastily when he said naught. "I hope you find it fitting."

"Fitting!" Raymond laughed aloud and shook it out into the wind. "Melusine, it is magnificent! Look how long it is, how bold the colors!" The vassals near him commented with enthusiasm, but Melusine had eyes only for Raymond's smile.

She had chosen a background of ten horizontal stripes, alternating azure and silver, though she hoped he did not ask the reason for their color. Atop the stripes, she had embroidered a red lion, thinking it appropriate.

"It is glorious, Melusine. I will be delighted to bear this mark upon my shield." He examined it in wonder, exclaiming over the quality of the embroidery, then stared at her in understanding. "A pennant? Does this mean that the castle is complete?"

Melusine nodded and smiled. She offered her hand to him and he seized it, pressed a kiss upon the back of her hand, then placed it upon his elbow.

"Let us unfurl this banner where it belongs." He led her to the keep, ensuring that her way was unobstructed and letting her lean upon him when she grew tired. The babe was heavy these days, and she appreciated his gallantry when she felt so graceless and large. They strode beneath the portcullis to the cheers of their vassals.

"Truly, this is all to be our own?" he asked.

"Truly, Raymond, it is no less than you deserve." Melusine rose to her toes to kiss his cheek. He turned so that her embrace met him full upon the lips, much to the pleasure of the company.

Melusine gasped and it was not from his kiss. She had had small convulsions these past days, enough to make her catch her breath, though this one had nearly taken her to her knees.

"What is it?" Raymond was immediately concerned.

"The babe." She was flustered. "Your son intends to arrive shortly." Melusine closed her eyes and caught at his arm as another convulsion clutched her womb.

Her waters broke then, the dark puddle spreading across the stone floor. Melusine leaned against Raymond, needing his strength. She could hear the reassuring thunder of his pulse, and found comfort in his warmth. She wished she could bear the child there, in the circle of his arms, but knew it was not to be.

"This was not the way I would have first entered our chambers," Raymond teased. "You need not fear—I shall see the banner hung this very morn. You and the babe can look upon it when you are able." He caught her in his arms and climbed the stairs, trying to tempt her smile all the while.

She saw that he was frightened as well, but could say nothing to reassure him. They were no sooner in the lord's chamber than the ladies were pushing him out the door.

Then the pain began in earnest. It was worse than that of her weekly transformation because it endured so long. Melusine found herself screaming as the Countess had screamed in Raymond's memory. It was barbaric, to bear children as beasts of the forest bear their young, but she would fulfill Raymond's terms.

Or die trying. The prospect terrified Melusine as little else could. It was purely mortal to procreate this way and she supposed she could only have done it because she was half-mortal.

But could she die in the deed, as the Countess had?

If she did die partaking of this mortal folly, would any mourn her loss?

⟡

Melusine's first son bawled mightily upon his emergence into the world. It was past midnight and Melusine was exhausted from her efforts. She lay back upon the pillows, hearing herself pant like an animal even as the blood ran from her.

"What a large babe!" the midwife said. "It is no wonder you labored so long and hard, my lady." The women gathered closer as Melusine felt only relief that the ordeal was finally over.

And she was yet alive.

She had only nine more times to do this deed. She closed her eyes, feeling the extent of the ache within her, and listened as the women commented upon the babe's size and vigor.

Then there was silence, and Melusine knew that something was amiss. She sat up as best as she was able, fully aware of the sweat upon her brow and the blood upon her flesh.

"Let me see my son," she commanded. She had to demand him again before the boy was laid in her arms.

She immediately saw why they had hesitated. This child she had created within her womb was not wrought poorly, but his eyes, his eyes were troubling. They were not the eyes of a mortal babe, nor those of a fey child, and the very sight of them sent a shiver down her spine.

One eye was angry red, the other silver grey.

They were just as the boar's had been, Melusine realized with a start, like those of the boar that had killed Aimery. She knew a foreboding then that the truth that she and Raymond had buried would force its way to light, one way or the other.

Why else would her child remind her of that boar? Why else would she suddenly feel guilt that the truth had been disguised, that proper compense had not been made?

Melusine shook her head, willing such nonsense to disperse. She was tired, no more than that.

"His name is Urien," she said, the words as dust in her mouth.

Raymond came into the chamber then, impatient with the women who would have kept him from his wife's side. Melusine saw the anticipation upon his face, saw the happiness within him, but there was no point in hiding the truth.

They had wrought this together, after all.

Melusine offered him the bundle that was his son. She watched, heartsick, as revulsion filled his eyes. He took the child, but with reluctance. Melusine knew with immediate certainty that he blamed her for the child's flaw. She turned away, stung, and kept her darkest fear from him.

Let him believe the taint was hers.

She would do better with the next son.

Melusine's wish was not to be.

Oblivious while her second son filled her womb, Melusine built the city of Lusignan outside the castle walls, her workers casting it up with a speed that left all speechless. She added a tall, ornate tower to the keep itself, desperate to show her husband how she cared for his favor, how she would prove herself worthy of their wager.

When it was completed, Raymond's smile did not reach his eyes.

Her gifts were worthless. Melusine felt a despair such as she had never known. She felt an affinity with the Countess and could only hope that this child was wrought more fair.

Raymond carried her again to the bedchamber when the pains began anew, kissed her brow and wished her well. A thousand things remained unsaid between them as the pain claimed Melusine.

To no avail.

Hugues's flesh was so fiery a red that it might have been cut from the heart of the sun, and indeed, touching him left burns upon his nursemaids. Though he did not resemble the boar, there was something of a beast about him.

Melusine conceived promptly again, though that did not slow the frenzy of her pace. She established the towns of Mel and Partenay while her belly rounded, determined to show her spouse that wedding her was not without merit.

But Raymond became grim and distant, despite his polite acceptance of her earthly gifts. They did not whisper abed any longer, and indeed, he did not always share her bed. Once he knew she had conceived, he slumbered elsewhere. Melusine ached with loneliness for his company, for the sparkle of his smile.

There was but one way she could win either again.

Guy had one eye lower than the other, but otherwise was finely wrought. A ghost of a smile curved Raymond's lips when he examined his son and Melusine dared to be encouraged.

Raymond returned to her bed, professing his certainty that the "ill-fortune" affecting their children was diminishing. Melusine resolved that she had not accepted the fullness of her wager with sufficient joy. She greeted him abed with enthusiasm and surrendered utterly to the pleasures of mortal loving.

Of course, Raymond's seed took root again and did so with astonishing speed. Haunted by the prospect that she might die in labor—for it grew more difficult each time—Melusine worked tirelessly. She established the town of Rochelle, upon the coast. As always, Raymond knew how to make the best of her offerings: he licensed a shipping trade in wine from that port, which added many tithes to the Lusignan coffers.

Anthony was born with a bleeding gash in his cheek. The midwife said it was like a wound wrought by the claw of a lion and set to tending it. Melusine thought it more like the gash of a boar's tusk. She knew, deep in her heart, that the wound would never heal in all his days and nights.

It never did.

Nor were the shadows dispersed in Raymond's eyes. He did not laugh as much as he had in the early days of their marriage. His brief certainty that all misfortune was behind them had died, leaving him somber as he had been when first they met.

Melusine bent her attention upon her sons, scarred as they were, ensuring that they were a credit to their father. She raised them to be courteous, to be valiant and true, to keep their word and speak their thoughts. If one could overlook their physical flaws, their natures were worthy indeed. Melusine persuaded Raymond to take Urien as a squire, to begin the boy's knightly training. The boy fairly blossomed beneath his father's attention and was so quick a study that Raymond was impressed.

Then Raynold was born with only one eye. Time proved that he saw more clearly with that single eye than most people do with two. That was not sufficient to sate his worried parents.

Their couplings became silent now, quick, dutiful and devoid of joy. The matings that had once created such joy became a misery and an obligation. Melusine felt the full weight of her earthliness without the compense of Raymond's love. Indeed, her weekly metamorphoses became more painful than they had been, more redolent of the earth.

Geoffroi was born with a great square tooth already protruding from his mouth. Melusine took one look at him and buried her face in her pillow, unable to evade its similarity with the tusks of boars. Were boars not said to be born with their tusks intact?

Raymond returned to the marital bed grimly. The pair did not look into each other's eyes, they did not tease each other, they did not waste time with the pursuit of pleasure. Melusine suspected that she was not the only one counting that they had four more children to bring to light. She half-feared she would give birth to a boar itself, should this continue.

Raymond no longer defended Melusine against the whispers of her nature that they oft heard. She dared not voice her suspicion that it was his deed turned against them. It would have been too much for the man to bear. Already he saw his wish for ten sons tainted. Despair sat between them at the board like an uninvited and unwelcome guest that could not be ousted.

Melusine was despondent when she rounded again, and Raymond barely acknowledged the news when she told him.

Their seventh son, however, was the son who changed all.

The babe was beautiful.

Melusine could not believe it. His hair was dark, like Raymond's, his eyes a merry blue, his lashes dark and thick. Though she had examined the babe a dozen times, she could not find a flaw upon his flesh. He had not so much as a mole.

But there was something about this babe, something that cast a shadow over Melusine's joy. She smelled a poison in him, though she could not name it or its source.

Perhaps she would have preferred that any flaw he bore was visible, not hidden in his heart. Perhaps she was too suspicious to accept Fortune's kiss, as Raymond once had been.

She was still struggling with her response, still holding the babe, when Raymond came to her side.

"What is amiss with this one?" he asked, indifferent as he had not been when first they wed.

"Naught," Melusine said. She offered him the child, withholding her doubts, until she saw his response.

"He is perfect!" Joy suffused Raymond's features. He held the boy high and laughed, turning in place while the midwife chided him. He bent and captured Melusine's chin, then kissed her deeply. "Praise be, Melusine! The curse is behind us, finally."

Her heart thumped to see him so pleased. "So it would appear."

"We shall invite every soul to his christening!" Raymond was exuberant. "We shall have a feast to rival that of our wedding. We shall have everyone gaze upon his beauty, share our joy.”

“As you wish.”

Raymond hesitated at her bedside, bouncing the child in his arms. “Might I ask a boon of you, Melusine?”

She shrugged, unable to shake her foreboding.

“I would name him Fromont, for it is a traditional name in my family.” Raymond took a deep breath. “And I would invite my brother to the christening. Perhaps he should be godfather. It is time that we put old wounds behind us.”

“As you wish,” Melusine agreed, closing her eyes when he bent to kiss her cheek. She was tired, tired to her very bones.

And she feared she knew now what taint the babe Fromont bore. It was the toxin of Raymond’s half-brothers and father that she smelled upon the child.

It was jealousy and she feared its import.

The third day of feasting happened to be a Saturday.

It had been a folly of planning on Raymond’s part. He had not forgotten about Melusine’s weekly departure, but had been so delighted that he had overlooked it. Truly, if she had been of more aid in the arrangement of events, as was her wont, it would not have happened.

But Melusine seemed very weary after this birthing and was slow to rise from her bed. In his determination to resolve all and leave her the time to recover, Raymond neglected that one detail. He supposed, in hindsight, that they had gone their own ways for so many years, that he had become less aware of her daily doings.

Raymond awakened on that day, not surprised to find her gone and the door to her private chamber locked against him. He took the babe Fromont from the nursemaid and carried him down to the hall, smiling upon his other sons as he went. His brother and the babe’s namesake was already at the board, his manner such that Raymond knew he would make trouble this day.

“Is your wife too lazy to be the good hostess this day?” Fromont demanded by way of greeting.

“It is no sin for a new mother to rest.”

“Slovenly is what our father would have called it. A woman

should be about her tasks within days of bearing a child."

Raymond felt a flicker of temper, but he damped it deliberately. He bounced his son and savored the ale and bread brought to him. Fortune smiled upon him again, and he would not fail to appreciate her charms.

Fromont grew ever more agitated as time passed. "Does your lazy wife insult her guests?"

"Of course not." Raymond smiled. "You shall see her at chapel on the morrow, no doubt."

"On the morrow!" Fromont snorted. "Does she mean to neglect us all of this day? What manner of hostess is she?"

Several of the other guests eyed each other, their doubts awakened by Fromont's nonsense.

"Melusine is tired from the delivery of our child," Raymond said firmly. "You will sate yourself with my company on this day."

"All the day, she will rest," Fromont said. He rolled his eyes. "Truly I should like to be the Lady of Lusignan, the better to lead a sluggard's life."

His squire snickered. The hall became silent.

Fromont leaned close to Raymond. "Is she oft absent like this?"

"What matter to you?"

Fromont tapped a fingertip upon the board. "I shall tell you what matter to me, brother mine. I have heard that the Lady of Lusignan is never seen on a Saturday. I have heard that the Lord of Lusignan is bewitched by his wife, too enchanted to demand of her an explanation."

"You have heard nonsense."

Fromont sat back, his expression sly. "I have heard that the Lady of Lusignan has a lover, that she spends a day abed with another man once a week and her husband has not the wits to ask after her absence."

Anger flickered within Raymond. "You cast aspersions upon the character of your hostess, foul manners in any court."

"I repeat only what others are saying." Fromont smiled. "And I do so because I care for your welfare, brother."

"You have never liked Melusine," Raymond said, his voice rising hot. "I will not listen to whatsoever you say against her."

"I have always been skeptical of your lady, I must admit." Fromont sat back. "I have always suspected that she is fey. There is something ethereal about her."

Raymond could not guess whether his brother guessed that he had named his own secret certainty.

"Certainly, your holding seems to have been conjured from naught, and all has been built with unholy speed..." Fromont snapped his fingers. "As if by magic."

"Melusine has found diligent laborers."

"Yet the lady does not seem to have aged in all the years you have been wed. How long is it now? Twelve years? And not a silver hair is there upon her brow." Fromont chuckled. "While you, brother mine, have more than a few."

"Who knows what women do in their vanity?" Raymond said, summoning a smile with an effort. "Perhaps she spends her Saturdays removing those errant silver hairs."

Too late he realized that he had confirmed Melusine's weekly absence. Fromont's eyes gleamed with malice.

"Perhaps." Fromont surveyed the hall. "If she were fey, she might well be on her knees in the chapel all this day, doing penitence for her nature to earn the Lord's forgiveness."

"You repeat the nonsense of old women."

"Perhaps." Fromont's gaze dropped to the babe in Raymond's arms. "But what if these sons of whom you are so proud are not of your own seed?"

The very thought sent a shiver through Raymond and sharpened his anger.

"They cannot be of your own seed, Raymond, not with such monstrous scars."

The possibility grew more plausible to Raymond.

"What if the flaws upon them are a mark of God's disfavor? What if they are an indictment of adultery?"

The very prospect infuriated Raymond, firing his temper as it had not been roused in years. The notion made dangerous sense. He knew that Melusine had not been anxious to meet him abed. Did she prefer to mate with one of her own kind?

Whose sons did he raise as his own?

Fury that his wife cuckolded him blinded Raymond to the

trouble his brother stirred.

Fromont lowered his voice and tapped Raymond's arm. "What if Melusine couples with demons each and every Saturday? Should you not know what occurs within your own hall? What manner of a man would not put a stop to such doings?"

How dare Melusine so deceive him?

How dare she steal from him the sons she had pledged to bear?

Raymond pushed the babe into a nursemaid's arms and rose abruptly from the board. He strode from the hall, anger hot within him, and made his way to the chamber of her treachery.

Fromont was right—it was time Raymond knew what occurred within his own hall. No door should be locked against the Lord of Lusignan.

No sound came from behind the door. No light glimmered beneath it. Raymond dropped to the floor but found he could not peer beneath the door. It was crafted by some fey means to ensure that none could glimpse whatsoever occurred within the chamber behind it.

That made it perfect for an assignation. Why would Melusine have bothered to craft it so, if her secret had not been foul?

Raymond would not be swayed, not now that he was determined to know the truth. He took his dagger from his belt and embedded the point in the wood of the door. He silently spun the sharp weapon, gradually cutting away the wood. A dent appeared, then the dent grew deeper. Finally, his blade broke through the thickness of the wood, and he worked at the hole until it was the full diameter of the blade.

He hesitated for a heartbeat.

Melusine would never know that he looked. Raymond told himself as much, shook off his foreboding, then put his eye to the hole.

At first, Raymond saw nothing amiss. Melusine was bathing. Indeed, she was alone in the chamber and that relieved him mightily. She sang softly to herself.

Raymond's anger faded to naught and he found himself

admiring the beauty of his wife. He had not looked upon her leisurely in years, and now he indulged himself. He liked the ripe curve of her breasts, the rosiness of pregnancy that yet clung to her flesh. Her skin would be softer than silk, her hair smooth beneath his hand. He was tempted to join her there, to make merry in the bath together, and he raised his fist to knock.

Then Melusine reached for a cloth that was just beyond her grasp. She raised herself out of the water and Raymond's knees fairly gave out beneath him.

His wife had a tail.

He blinked but the sight remained. From the navel down, Melusine was wrought as a serpent. Scales of azure and silver covered a long twining tail that replaced her long lean legs, its stripes the same colors Melusine had chosen for the banner of Lusignan. Raymond shuddered in revulsion, and leaned his brow against the door, unable to look upon the horror of her any longer.

This was what Melusine did not want him to see. He was momentarily tempted to spurn her, to cast her out for the monstrosity that she was.

Then he found himself thinking of the kindness Melusine showed to their scarred sons, how she had taught him to look beyond the physical marks they bore to their noble natures. Raymond had to admit that she was right. Their sons were gracious and well-mannered, their prowess at arms exceeded only by their skill at poetry. Though the shock of his first glimpse of each of them had been profound, he loved them all now.

Though none as much as he loved little Fromont.

Raymond's heart wrenched. Melusine was his wife, his lady and his love. She had saved him from death, she had kept her pledge to him. She was loyal and just, kind and honorable. With her aid, he had made far more of himself than ever he might have otherwise. Her counsel was good, her patience was uncommon. Melusine had brought him joy and hope, such as he had never known before.

Raymond loved her. The realization astonished him, all the more because he was utterly convinced of its truth. Still the balance between them was a poor one: Melusine had granted

Raymond his heart's desire.

And he had rewarded her with treachery.

Raymond stepped away from the portal, ashamed of his weakness. He sealed the hole with wax and returned to the hall, newly determined to prove himself worthy of his lady's affections.

Once there, he turned to his older brother. "You worry for naught, brother of mine!" he said. "My lady wife slumbers alone, as I told you, as a women tired from bearing a child will do. You make a tale where there is none."

"She should join us in the hall, then, if nothing is amiss."

Raymond's temper flickered again, though it was directed more truly this time. "Hasten yourself, Fromont. Any man who speaks ill of my lady wife is not welcome in my hall." He lifted a cup of wine to his lips. "Begone afore I drain this wine."

Raymond saw then the jealousy that had prompted Fromont's denouncement. It was Lusignan's wealth that attracted his brother's venom, no more than that.

Guillaume had warned him once, but Raymond had let his temper lead him to an error.

Never again.

But Melusine knew what he had done.

Raymond realized as much when his lady came to their chamber on Sunday, just after first light. She was hesitant, uncertain as never she was, and he immediately guessed the reason for it. She came to the side of the bed and looked down upon him, her expression sad, her fingertips trailing across the linens.

'Twas as if she took leave of him.

His heart in his mouth, Raymond smiled at her, feigning ignorance. "Good morning, lady mine."

Melusine jumped. "I did not know you were awake."

"I have waited for you, for your heat beside me in our bed."

She studied him carefully, reluctant as he had never seen her. "I dreamed that you were angry with me."

"Dreams are folly," he said, pulling back the linens for her. "You should know better than to heed their nonsense. How could I be angry with you, with seven fine sons to my name?"

Wariness lit her eyes. "They are not all fine."

"They *are* all fine," he insisted. "They are an honor to us both in their chivalry, their bravery and their skill. I do not doubt that they will win great fame and beauteous wives in their time."

Still Melusine did not touch the bed. "Forgive me. My dream was most unsettling." She crossed the chamber, her fingers knotting together. "What of your brother?"

"Fromont has left and has been bidden not to return."

She glanced over her shoulder, surprised.

"His wicked words are not welcome at Lusignan."

Melusine turned back to the window, clearly uncertain. "We should grant a stirrup cup to our departing guests."

"They have feasted beyond expectation for three days and nights. I would let the castellan bid them farewell. Come to bed, Melusine."

"It is too soon, Raymond, too soon after the babe."

"I would hold you close, no more than that."

Still she did not come to him.

Raymond rose and, when she did not turn, caught her shoulders in his hands. He kissed her nape, loving how she still shivered slightly at his touch.

"Your dream is backways 'round, my beloved Melusine," he whispered, pulling her back against his chest. "I have a gift for you, one I have been saving too long."

He retrieved the silk bundle from its hiding place in his trunk. He did not tell her that he had purchased the gift in anticipation of the birth of their first son, but had been too devastated by the sight of Urien's eyes to give it to her then.

He half-suspected Melusine would guess as much.

She unfurled the silk, so carefully that she might have expected to find an asp within it. She caught her breath when the jewel lay in her palm, then looked up at him. There was a shimmer of tears in her wondrous eyes. "You bought this for me?"

"I met a jeweler in Paris, on one of my journeys there. He had the most uncommon skill. Do you like it?"

She shook her head and said naught.

Raymond reached out and touched the gilded gem, unable to resist it even now. The gem was a great freshwater pearl, as large as his thumb, yet wrought in a curious curved shape. The jeweler had used the lustrous pearl as the tail of a figure of Neptune, creating a fine filigree of scales that held the pearl captive, making the rest of the figure out of gold. Neptune had tiny emeralds for his eyes and the tines of his trident were topped with garnets.

Raymond wondered suddenly if he had found the piece so alluring because he had guessed something of his wife's nature. Melusine watched him, clearly wondering much the same.

"I could not resist it," he said, shaking his head at his own impulsiveness. "It cost a small fortune, I must admit." He met her gaze guiltily and pushed his hand through his hair. "We did not, in fact, lose so much coin in the trade of wine as I had told you. I lied, Melusine, that you might not guess that I had bought you such a gift. I had to bring it to you." He smiled, hoping she would forgive him, and forgive him for more than that lie.

Melusine touched the stone with her fingertip. "It is most unusual," she said, her voice soft.

"It is beautiful. It is magical. I could not leave Paris without possessing it for my own." Raymond met her gaze deliberately, hoping she would glimpse what was within his heart. "Is it any wonder that it reminded me of you?"

Melusine smiled then, a smile that lit her eyes. It was the greatest gift he had ever been granted, for that smile told him that she would not leave.

"You speak wisely, Raymond, for the castellan can see to our guests. I would savor a few hours abed in your embrace," she said, reaching to caress his jaw. "I thank you for the gem."

Raymond was buoyant. He had been forgiven, beyond all expectation, and it was more, far more, than he deserved.

V

here was winter upon Raymond's brow when Melusine saw her mother again.

To be sure, her mother was the furthest matter from her thoughts. She had heard that foul rumor again, the one that troubled her so much, and she knew not what to do. Melusine climbed the stairs to the lord's chamber as snow swirled outside the narrow windows.

She had to do something, though she hesitated to ask Raymond's counsel. This matter would be strike to his heart. Fromont, who had always been studious and serious, had joined the monastery at Maillezais—and this over Raymond's objections. Still the gleam in his father's eye, Fromont had taken a plump endowment to that monastery. He learned quickly, he always had, and Melusine had not doubted that his vocation was genuine.

Which was why the rumor about Maillezais troubled her so.

Three more boys had been born to her after Fromont, bringing the tally to Raymond's desired ten sons. The eighth had been another monstrosity, as if all the goodness of her womb had been devoured by Fromont. Born with three eyes and of so violent a temperament that he tore her womb even on his departure, Melusine had named him Horrible. The ninth, Raymond, and the tenth, Thierry, had been blessedly normal mortal children, though neither could dislodge Fromont from their father's affections.

Presine startled Melusine, no less by her presence than her welcoming smile.

"What is this?" Melusine asked. "You have not been glad to see me for years."

Presine laughed. "How long have you been wed, daughter mine?"

"Thirty mortal years." Melusine shook her head, marveling at how quickly the time had passed. "I have learned something of forgiveness in that time."

"Have you? You were always a clever child." Presine hugged her unexpectedly. "You were not just the eldest, but my greatest joy. That is why I came to warn you."

"Of what?"

"I told you of the worlds drawing apart. In these days, the thread frays with ever increasing speed. The moment of parting is upon us, and I would not have you trapped in the mortal realm."

"Would you not remain with Father?"

Presine laughed at the very thought. "In a mountain? Nay! He has been dead these twenty years."

"I did not know."

"It is of import no longer. I cannot mourn him for all of my days as mortals mourn for all of theirs. I am young yet, for a fey, and there is much yet to savor." Presine smiled and offered her hand. "Come with me to the domain of the fey, Melusine. You have always preferred that realm. I would not have you lost beyond the divide."

Melusine hesitated, thinking of this matter of Maillezais yet unresolved. It was easier to consider that than the notion of leaving Raymond.

"Is your wager not rendered in full?" her mother asked. "Have you not delivered ten sons and all the wealth your spouse might imagine?"

"Of course." Melusine eyed her mother. "What of my own curse?"

"You had only to compel a man to love you for all of his life, without breaking his pledge to you. Has Raymond broken his pledge?"

Melusine looked away, unable to lie. Her mother chose to interpret that rather differently than it was meant.

"Ah, and he has stolen your heart in keeping his word so well! This is how you have learned of forgiveness." Presine laughed merrily. "You were always one much concerned with the merit of a promise. I am certain that the curse can be lifted, especially if you are in the realm of the fey and the divide has occurred."

Melusine was not so certain.

Worse, she did not want to leave.

Not yet.

"Come now, before it is too late!" Presine urged impatiently.

Raymond's tread sounded on the stairs, slower than it once had been but still beloved for its familiarity. Melusine turned, anxious as always to see him again. They had been apart all this day and she yearned for his embrace, as she did most every night. Tenderness assailed her and she half-smiled, imagining the light that would claim his eyes when he saw her.

She had done well to forgive him.

Presine whispered in her ear. "There is no time for farewells, and they will serve naught at any rate. Disappear, you know that you can."

"It would break his heart if I abandoned him without explanation," Melusine argued, knowing that it was her own heart's breaking that she dreaded.

She loved Raymond. The truth stunned her with its simplicity, and she knew then what she had to do.

"He is mortal," her mother said. "Like your father, he will not have long to endure any pain."

Melusine turned at that and confronted her mother. "Nor will he have long left to savor this world. You defended my father once, against me, and bade me forgive him."

"I was angry that you defied me." Presine shrugged. "There is nothing eternal between men and fey—so we are taught and so it is true. Come with me, and be among your own kind."

Melusine did not move. "I will be among those I love, for so long as I can endeavor to do so."

Presine was aghast. "But you could be trapped in their realm!"

A tranquility filled Melusine, a satisfaction that her beloved drew nearer, a certainty that there was nowhere she would rather be than here, awaiting him. "So be it. Farewell, Mother."

They stared at each other, shocked that they might never have the power to see each other again. A sound filled the walls, erupting from everywhere and nowhere, a great tearing.

The divide was upon them.

Presine offered her hand one last time, but Melusine stepped away. Her mother shook her head and then she was gone. The rending grew to a deafening roar, then fell silent.

It was as silent as the grave, silent save the measured tread of Raymond's steps. Nothing looked different, but Melusine could feel an absence that had not been there before.

The realm of fey was gone.

Forever. The door opened behind Melusine even as she struggled with the truth of it.

"You look troubled," Raymond said.

"I am only concerned about a rumor I heard this day."

He drew his chemise over his head, older and thicker than once he had been, though still hale and strong. "Tell me of it."

The words caught in Melusine's throat, for she was certain they would cut Raymond deeply. He could not be objective about their son Fromont, so much did he love the boy.

And she did not want to trouble him this night. She did not want to argue, or even debate.

She wanted to sleep, secure in his embrace, for the world she savored was lost to her for all time. She shrugged and spoke lightly. "I should not heed rumor, much less repeat it. Come to bed, Raymond, and force such frippery from my thoughts."

He smiled, as roguishly as ever he had. "My lady's wish is as my command." He caught her up in his arms and tickled her until she laughed helplessly, then they tumbled into bed together.

And Melusine had no regrets for the choice she had made.

Morning brought the return of their crusading sons—for Christmas was nigh upon them—and a hall bursting with noise and merriment. The wine flowed as abundantly as the tales.

Urien told of how he and Guy had aided the King of Cyprus, and how their deeds had inspired awe in the men there. Despite their valor, the King had been wounded in the assault. Upon his deathbed, the king had granted not only his realm but his most beauteous daughter to Urien's hand. Ermynee already had borne a son, Greffon, and Melusine delighted in meeting her first grandson.

Not to be outdone, the brother of the King of Cyprus had endowed Guy with the kingdom of Armenia, and his lovely daughter Flourie in marriage. Flourie too was ripening with child, though she flushed mightily when Melusine commented upon it.

It was clear to all that both sons were as smitten with their brides as their brides were with them, and Melusine and Raymond exchanged a smile of pride.

"You raised them well," Raymond said, pressing a kiss to Melusine's knuckles.

Anthony and Raynold had traveled together to relieve a besieged holding in Luxembourg, discovering only later that the daughter of the duke of that place was its reigning authority. So grateful was this damsel named Christian that she wedded Anthony. Raynold had then accepted an invitation to defend Bohemia against the Saracens, winning both the hand of that king's daughter, Eglantine, and the crown of Bohemia for his triumph.

Geoffroi recounted how he had defeated the giant Guedon in Rochelle. Ever aware that his father found fault with him, Geoffroi took great pleasure in reminding Raymond that he had tried to dissuade him from this task.

"It is true," Raymond agreed easily. "I thought the fiend too doughty an opponent for you and I feared for your survival. You are too young to be lost to us."

"But I was not lost," Geoffroi said with satisfaction. "You underestimate me, Father, as always you did."

"I am not displeased to have been mistaken." Raymond chuckled and called for another cask of wine was opened. A great fire burned merrily upon the hearth and there was much laughter in the hall. A roast stag was carried to the board at midday, followed by dozens of other delicacies.

Melusine seized a quiet moment after the meal to speak with Geoffroi, with whom she had always had a kinship. "I would ask a favor of you."

"Any deed you can ask of me, I will do, Mother."

"I have heard a rumor, one that upsets me greatly. I would know if there is truth within it before I cause your father concern."

"You know that I shall do your service first and foremost."

"It is whispered that the monks of Maillezais have lost their way." Melusine licked her lips and spoke with care, aware of

Geoffroi's bright gaze upon her. "It is told that they are lecherous, one and all, that they have encounters with the local women and that they are sinners beyond compare."

"But Fromont is there!"

"Perhaps he is beguiled. Perhaps he does not participate in such folly. Perhaps he errs and does not know it." Melusine gripped her son's hand. "Perhaps the rumor is a lie. Unearth the truth for me, before your father hears tell of it."

"I shall see justice served," Geoffroi said, a flicker of his father's anger in his eyes.

"No! I ask you only to learn the truth!"

But Geoffroi strode through the hall, deaf to her calls for his return. She could not catch him, this son of hers so much taller than she. Too late, Melusine recalled how Geoffroi and Fromont had long competed for their father's favor, though Raymond's eye had never left Fromont.

Too late, she feared what Geoffroi might do.

She had not long to fear.

Geoffroi returned within a week, the smell of woodsmoke upon his clothes. There was fury simmering yet in his eyes though he stood triumphant in his father's hall.

"I have dispatched wickedness from your realm again, Father," he declared, his resonant voice drawing the attention of all.

"What is this?" Raymond asked, bemused by this son as so oft he was.

Melusine prayed that the portent pricking her flesh was wrong.

"The abbey Maillezais is burned to the ground," Geoffroi said, not troubling to hide his scorn.

"Maillezais? Surely Fromont is not yet there?"

"He was and he is."

Raymond clutched the board, his face ashen.

Geoffroi met the gaze of every soul in the hall, his conviction that he was right unshaken. "I went to Maillezais, to seek to root of rumor at Mother's request, and I found that rumor had not done the truth credit. I found those monks fornicating in the chapel. I found them gorging themselves, I found them sleeping, fat and sated in every corner."

Geoffroi sneered. "I found the gold stacked within the cellars, and indeed, evidence of every mortal sin practiced at that monastery. They defiled the very place on which the abbey was located and were an abomination to God."

Raymond crossed himself, his hand shaking. Every eye in the hall was fixed upon the jubilant Geoffroi. Melusine made her way to her spouse and touched his arm.

"Do not be angered, Raymond. It will serve naught."

He shook off her touch and stepped away from her, his gaze fixed upon Geoffroi. "What wickedness have you done?"

Geoffroi smiled. "I have done God's work this day. I have purged Maillezais of sinners. It is writ that heretics should be burned, and so they were, all of them. I barred the doors and stacked the wood high so that none could escape. I burned Maillezais to the ground and took the taint of its sin from this world. God will judge them now, and he will not be merciful."

Silence filled the hall.

"What of Fromont?" Raymond's voice was hoarse.

"Dead, like all his sinning fellows."

"Nay!" Raymond roared, the single word fit to raise the roof. He bounded toward his son, seized his tabard and shook it as if Geoffroi was no more than a boy. "You do this out of malice. You have always been jealous of the favor I showed to Fromont. Tell me you lie!"

Geoffroi lifted his sleeve toward his father's nose. "Smell the smoke. Ride to Maillezais and see for yourself. Ask my men."

Those men nodded as one, many of them clearly uncomfortable with what they had done. "It is true, my lord. Maillezais is no longer."

Melusine braced herself for Raymond's response, but she was unprepared all the same.

He spun and shook a finger at her, bitterness contorting his features. "Most vile serpent! This is your fault, and your fault alone. I should never have taken your wager, never have suffered your kind in my bed. I should never have believed you, never have let you beguile me. You are fey and you are monstrous. Naught of any merit ever came from your womb! Look, look what your wickedness has wrought!"

Every gaze fixed upon Melusine. She stood alone in the center of the hall, her back straight, her chin high. She felt the assembly slide away from her, saw the recrimination and rejection in her beloved's eyes. She felt more alone than ever she had in all her days.

"Not even Fromont?" she asked quietly.

Raymond looked down, unable to hold her gaze.

It was done between them, for he had denounced her before all. Melusine could not pretend that he had not broken his word to her, not before so many witnesses.

"My lady?" asked a servant.

Melusine pulled her sleeve away. "I am your lady no longer, not now that your lord has cast me out."

The woman's face worked silently for a moment, then she broke into tears.

Raymond pursued her, his steps increasing in speed. Melusine turned away from him, devastated by his rejection. She crossed the hall and climbed the stairs to the chamber that only she had ever entered. She threw open the door, well aware that they trailed behind her.

It did not matter now. Nothing mattered now.

"Melusine!"

Raymond was behind her but she did not want to look upon him again. He caught her elbow and compelled her to face him. Melusine met his gaze, afraid to see his revulsion at such proximity.

Instead she found despair. His eyes gleamed with fey lights, just as they had when first she met him, but the shadows were a thousand times darker than they had once been.

This was the gift she had rendered to her beloved.

At the painful truth of it, Melusine wept.

Raymond eased a tear from her cheek with his thumb. He framed her face in his hands and she felt his hands shake.

"God in heaven, my Melusine," he whispered. "What have I done?"

He knew what he had done. Melusine stepped away from him, though it was the last thing she wished to do. In truth, she had no choice and they both knew it well. Her vision glazed with tears, she left his side, trembling beneath the weight of her disappointment.

"You will see me no longer," she told them all, her voice hoarse. "So it has been decreed and so it shall be. But one thing I will ask of you and that is that you do destroy one fruit of my womb." She pointed to Horrible, who had killed two nursemaids in his infancy, who she could not supervise if she was not here. "Do not suffer this son to live. I ask this of you and this alone."

With that, there was no reason to linger. Melusine lifted her skirts and strode to the window. The assembly fell back, their eyes wide. They could not disguise their newfound fear of her, though, and that was bitter. Just this morn, they had regarded her with respect and affection.

"Melusine!" Raymond cried, his voice anguished. "Stay!"

"I cannot."

"But you weep!" he insisted, then appealed to the gathered household. "All know that the fey cannot shed tears."

Many of the company nodded, as if their assent alone could change her circumstance.

"And all know that the sworn word of a man of merit is worth more than gold. Even I was fool enough to believe that."

Raymond had the grace to pale.

The pain was growing within Melusine's legs, spreading through her more vigorously than ever it had before. The change was upon her, and its sole merit was that this would be the last time she had to endure it. She was devastated to realize that she would change before so many horrified gazes.

But there was yet a moment to flee. Melusine leapt to the broad stone sill beneath the window, felt it give and shimmer beneath her foot, then strode into the open air. The wind lifted her, rising beneath the leathery wings that had sprouted from her back, caressing the scaled serpentine tail that trailed behind her.

When she parted her lips to cry farewell to all of those she had loved, the harsh scream of a dragon was the sole sound she could emit.

She did not truly expect the realm of the fey to embrace her, but all the same, it was a shock to find that curtain sealed against her. She was indeed an exile.

All because she had dared to love a mortal man, because she had dared to believe that love could make all come aright.

Blanche and Marie twitter but I have no patience for their foolery now. Just the sharing of the tale has emptied me, emptied me for the last time. I have no anger any longer, no remorse, no sorrow. I have no regrets. I am as an empty shell.

Or the discarded skin of a snake.

In my mind's eye, I see the repercussions yet again. I see Raymond wither, his heart broken by his own deed and his last days filled with solitude and regret. I was there, but he could not see me, could not feel me, could not sense my presence any longer. Indeed, I flew around the ramparts, bemoaning his pending demise, though he alone did not heed me.

It was unbearably sweet to hear my beloved call my name with his last breath, unspeakably bitter that he did not know that I was there.

I see my sons losing their every advantage, I see their children born with frightening deformities, their marriages sown with dissent. I see marauding armies claim precious Lusignan, the lands and vassals unable to retreat to the realm of the fey. So much I watch, powerless in memory as I was in fact to avert the course of events.

I see this old castle as it crumbles and fades over the centuries, claimed by mice and vines, filled with rain and wind. I know that I cannot bear to watch it fall on the morrow.

"So, now you know the true tale of Melusine," I tell these foolish girls. "How her mortal blood grew dominant, how her yearning for mortal emotions cheated her of all she held so dear."

Marie laughs, a little too loudly for her merriment to be genuine. "You cannot know the truth of it, old woman. It was said to have happened hundreds of years ago."

"If it even happened at all," adds Blanche. She casts me a coin, but that token will no longer suffice.

I will have my price of them.

I draw myself up tall and cast aside my cloak. For the first time in all my many days, I take joy in changing before mortal eyes. Horrified, fascinated, they cannot look away, yet they cannot stand to watch.

The scales begin the form over my flesh, no longer so young and supple as once it was. These scales march over my skin with the same voracious speed, but they are gnarled and dull, like the toenails of the aged. The silver and azure stripes are faded, no longer gleaming. My bare breasts no longer are pert and firm, my hair is no longer long and flaxen. It is all part of what I am. I show them my wrinkled breasts and my greyed hair, I show them the compense that heartbreak has had from an immortal.

I show them all that I am and all that I was and I laugh as they scream in terror.

I laugh louder as they try to flee. Such women as these do not deserve to live. With the last vestige of power within me, I change their shapes, just because I can. One becomes a partridge, the other a peahen, both female, both plain, both clucking and pecking futilely at the stone floor.

I lift my arms high, savoring this last heady taste of the power that once flooded my veins.

That once I took for granted.

Then I step on the sill, the footprint perfectly fitting my own even after all these centuries. My leathery wings unfold behind me, creaking as they beat against the air. I cry out as I fly around the high ramparts one last time, then I leave Lusignan forever. I cannot hold my form for long, but I take great joy in shocking as many mortals as I can.

As to where my heart will go after my form fades to naught, who can say? The memory of my beloved burns bright within it, and of regrets, I have not one.

Amor Vincit Omnia

"Amor Vincit Omnia" is a Latin saying that translates to "Love Conquers All." There are many pieces of medieval jewelry inscribed with this expression, and not just the rings one might expect. This romantic notion seems to have been a popular one, perhaps because there were obstacles to the course of true love in a society in which many marriages were arranged.

When I was invited to participate in a digital anthology called **Seven Deadly Sins**, it occurred to me that love could heal so many wounds. This collection included twenty-eight stories, all written by different romance authors, four for each of the deadly sins. I chose *Covetousness*, which was changed to the more modern term *Greed* for publication. Of course, I prefer the medieval choice of word, as it implies more dimensionality to me—never mind a complexity that would require love's power in order to be conquered.

This piece was a particular challenge to me as it had to include a romance in less than three thousand words. It also gave me a chance to feature an unusual heroine for the romance genre and give her the happy ending I believe she deserved.

Venice 1205

went to watch the ships arrive.

But then, I always meet the ships. I could tell you that 'tis simply good business to be present where one's revenue is most readily made, for that is part of the truth at least.

The ships were numerous on this day, for victory had not diminished the ranks of what had been a considerable fleet on its departure. Three years ago, some four hundred and eighty ships had sailed from this harbor for points east, led by the vermilion-painted galleon of the doge himself.

They had conquered and now they returned, the ships low in the water with their wealth of plunder.

'Twas not the most promising weather. The skies hung low and the clouds threatened to burst all the morning long. The ships brooded at anchor, awaiting the signal that the ceremonies began.

For there would be festivities. The Republic had been paid and then some—indeed, it could be said that the fall of Constantinople was a victory beyond expectation. Venice was now lord of a quarter of the world, as defined by the Romans, and half a quarter again.

On this day, she would lavish a carefully calculated measure of her winnings upon her residents. If naught else, this was a city of calculation. 'Twould be expected that the arriving men would be more free with their newly acquired wealth and this was what had brought the crowds to the Piazza San Marco.

No less what sparked their jubilant mood

There were moneychangers and jewelers, armorers and tailors, entertainers and pedlars aplenty. Stalls had been set up by those roasting meat, by bakers, by confectioners, by herbalists with a cure for whatever might ail a returning adventurer. The square echoed with their cries as they hawked their wares to the expectant crowd, jostling each other good-naturedly in anticipation of the coin they would have in their purses this night.

And of course, we women were there. Not a respectable matron among us, we were plumed and adorned, powdered and painted and displaying our wares. There were the women of the common bordello, the Casteletto, that house reputed the length and breadth of Europe, but their charms seemed tawdry to me.

I knew the price of living in that house all too well.

My girls were veiled in the Eastern tradition. 'Twas a half veil that they wore, wrought of the sheerest silk and ending just below their noses. Stitched to a circlet, the design was most clever to my thinking—it alluded to mystery. It drew a man's attention to the carmine-reddened fullness of the girl's lips and thence to the ruddy perfection of her nipples, visible through a similarly sheer chemise.

Provocative indeed.

A more practical consideration was that the veil kept the sun from marring the pallor of their complexions. I insisted that they line their eyelids with kohl and dust their faces with rice powder. The effect was both exotic and ethereal.

In a city like Venice—of whose ilk there is no other—where the ostentatious is the norm, display must be bold indeed to attract the eye. My girls were recognized readily in the marketplace and sought out by men of discriminating taste.

And that was not the only element of our presentation. I was in the habit of employing dwarves and had brought them all on this day. They are, in my experience, men of stout hearts and unswerving loyalty though they may be gruff of manner.

And their plight touches my soft heart—oft imported as an oddity for a wealthy man's retinue, 'tis not uncommon that they are cast from the man's house when his taste changes and left to fend for themselves. Mine is a house of orphans, in more ways than one.

Dwarves are also far stronger than men of greater stature oft realize, a fact that has proven to our benefit on more than one occasion. This trade, after all, is not without its risks.

To which end, Asim had also joined our party. An enormously tall and muscled Negro, he had been included in my purchase of the house. I offered him his freedom shortly thereafter, though his efficiency in managing the house is ruthless and his instincts in assessing men uncanny. 'Tis whispered that he has a sixth sense and I know not whether 'tis the truth or whether he simply observes the world with greater care.

He promptly offered his services at a princely sum, which I was glad to pay. He told me then that he had no other place to go and I, understanding this experience all too well, have never spoken again with him of our respective origins.

He wore only a gold and black linen sarong on this day and a necklace wrought of heavy gold coins. He had oiled his skin so his gleaming flesh gave the look of an ebony sculpture, an illusion much aided by his characteristic stillness. He was bald, though whether by nature or design I could not say, and wore a large ruby in one earlobe.

In Venice, unsurprisingly, he was known not for his striking appearance but for his impassivity.

The maids of the household had come, as well, and there were boys who held silken awnings above the girls in case the rains did come. I thought our appearance quite striking. They were beauties, the six demoiselles in my employ, their fair hair spilling down their backs in carefully arranged curls. I fussed and I clucked in a most maternal fashion, even though I was garbed just as they and neither so old nor so wealthy that I did not welcome trade myself.

There is an art to staging spectacle, to keeping a crowd waiting while their anticipation builds then ensuring that expectations are met. Venice excelled at such art. We waited all the morning, with growing impatience, while the skies threatened rain and the great galleons bobbed at anchor. The younger girls began to complain in the very moment that Asim pointed to the lofty tower of the campanile.

He said naught, of course, and there was no outward sign in the moment before he pointed that anything would occur. The girls turned, looking young despite their dress, and hooted when the first bell rang.

A cheer rose as the bells began to chime in a celebratory cacophony. Thousands of white pigeons were released at once from the tower, so many that they darkened the skies further as they passed. Cymbals clashed and handbells were rung, lengths of shimmering silk were unfurled from towers like long flicking tongues. And the shouts of welcome began.

The men poured down the sides of the galleons, nearly capsizing the bevy of smaller vessels that met them. An experienced eye could see the truth of victory in the way those men rowed, so vigorous, so persuaded of their own invincibility.

More than one of the women standing near me smiled in anticipation. We all pressed closer, anxious to be near the lip of the sea to have best pick, but then, there were so many men that none would go lacking on this night.

'Twas not long before the square thronged with new arrivals, shouting men, backslapping men, men whose gazes eventually slipped over us. Aye, there were many disinterested in the festivities planned by the Republic.

I struck hard bargains for the beauties in my retinue, a decade of greeting returned soldiers having given me an eye for a man's resources. I would have none of those Saracenate *bezants* from the Latin Kingdoms—though wrought of gold, their fine diminishes by whim and they are devalued too oft to be reliable. And I had the most beauteous women, so the vagaries of the market were with me.

Guiliana was skittish, for she had recently had a coupling turn violent. I was particularly determined to ensure that she had a suitable partner on this day and knew that Asim watched me with a sharp eye. He is not unprotective of our little lambs and had interrupted in a most timely fashion. All the same, I have no doubt he blamed himself as much as I blamed myself for that sorry incident. To my relief, a local dignitary of my acquaintance returned from his adventures and made directly for me.

We greeted each other warmly and exchanged pleasantries. He was an older man, handsome and vigorous, yet tender abed. He had been one of the first I had known in this city and my first regular client. I knew he could be relied upon and that he liked innocence.

His gaze fell upon Guiliana, so obviously uncertain of herself, and I caught Guiliana's hand in my own. He smiled at her, a reassuring yet not entirely paternal smile, and she blushed in a most becoming fashion. Asim nodded approval over her head and I made a finer deal than I had expected.

From each client, I had my payment in advance, as usual. My

reputation for fair dealing was sufficient to ensure that most met my terms with little argument—or else the men's desires were too overwhelming—even when I sent them to the moneychangers with those cursed *bezants*.

I am not so fool any longer to trust to a man's noble instincts. Such is an error one makes only once. I dispatched each girl to the house, not only with the man who had bought her favors but also with a retinue of my own employ to ensure that she arrived there safely. Asim escorted Guiliana at my nod of approval.

For all the noise and anticipation, the entire matter was concluded very quickly.

I had ceased to be surprised by such efficiencies, for one learns quickly that lust is a demanding master. My doves successfully contracted, I was not above scanning the piazza one last time.

I have what could be called a policy of charity. Usually there is one girl—a shy one, a new one, one whose beauty is only just blossoming—who is left without a companion. And there is always one man with a yearning but no coin to pay for its satisfaction.

And truly, more experience never was a liability for a whore.

I have had the good fortune to choose honest men for such indulgences and oft have seen much benefit returned to me years later, when that man has made his fortune. Favors are never unwelcome, nor are paying clients.

But that is not the root cause for my doing this. I have known all too well what 'tis to have naught in one's purse, to be hungered and without solace. I have known the meanness of this city so concerned with revenue, and this, in a small way, is my attempt to aid another. All the men who visit my house are offered a meal as part of their fee, so in this act, I feed one man's earthly desires of both kinds. If there is a God and there is a judgment, then I would have something said in my favor in that court when I reach it.

But on this day, there was none left from my house but myself. I was pleased enough with what had been wrought and the coin that weighted my purse. Still I could not help that backward glance.

'Twas then that I glimpsed one man rowing alone to the dock.

He moved with sure strength, rowing with the determination of a man filled with his own convictions. His shoulders were broad and he was clearly strong, for the small boat skimmed across the shimmering water as though it had been propelled by the efforts of three men. His hair was of an auburn hue, a shade for which I have a particular affection, and seemed a riot of unruly curls.

There was something so compelling about him that I stopped to watch.

He leapt to the dock with such ease that I was startled by the glint of silver in his trimmed beard when he turned to survey the piazza. He was man familiar with boats then, perhaps a sailor or a captain or a merchant who shipped his own wares.

He was well dressed, though simply garbed, his cloak caught at one shoulder with his only ornament, a round pin that glittered gold in the sunlight. There was no embroidery on his hems, no lavish adornment of any kind. I wondered whether he could not afford it or whether he had no taste for it. His boots were finely wrought which made me conclude the latter.

I was intrigued. He glanced around the emptying square with a brusqueness that hinted at impatience in his nature, surveyed the last of the parade of women, then strode directly toward me. The purpose in his stride made my tired heart skip a beat.

Here was a man who spied his desire and made it his own.

'Twould not be so terrible a fate.

His gaze flicked over me as he approached, no doubt seeing all he truly needed to know. His eyes were that uncommon shade of blue that threatens to turn to green or silver when the light is right. Eyes the hue of the sea. The silver had infested his hair as well, but he had the manner of man much younger. There were lines in his tanned face, but they were interesting lines. Lines from laughter. Lines from endurance.

I found myself quite uncharacteristically breathless when he stopped before me, this man of vigor and experience.

"I seek a woman," he said in crisp Venetian, by way of introduction.

I shook my head, amused by his blunt speech. "All men arriving in this port seek a woman. Sadly, you have tarried too long to have your choice."

"Not any woman. I seek a specific woman." He smiled with sudden humor and his eyes twinkled, exactly as the waves of the sea will twinkle when the sunlight dances upon them. "Although you undoubtedly will tell me that one is much like another, at least abed."

I merely smiled.

His own smile faded, his impatience reappearing as he scanned the square.

Then he eyed me, his expression shrewd. "I have been told that courtesans know all there is to know in any town."

"The claim is not without merit."

"Will you help me find a woman?"

"A specific woman?" I asked, unable to keep the teasing lilt from my voice.

He nodded curtly. "Aye."

"There are many women in Venice."

"I seek only one."

"And many more in the lands beyond." I tilted my head to watch him, intrigued by his insistence.

"But the one I seek is beautiful."

I laughed. "Surely you have heard it said that beauty lies in the eye of the beholder alone? If I had a *grosso* for every time a man told me of the beauty of his love, then I should be a wealthy woman indeed."

His gaze slipped over the silks I wore, the fine leather slippers, the jewels woven into my hair, the veil over my face. Four maids attended me, each garbed more richly than many a lady in those barbaric distant Frankish lands. The display of my assets did not go unnoticed. I held his gaze more boldly than any street urchin and arched one brow high as I smiled.

He surveyed me, then looked away in disgust. "It seems you have had a *grosso* for that, for your attire is far from modest."

His disgust irked me, though my skin should be thickened against such barbs by now. "Not for that, but a *grosso* every time nonetheless." I smiled, my coldest smile. "If not more."

He frowned again and would have stepped away. "I seek an answer from the wrong person. Forgive me for troubling you."

But I was not quite prepared to let him leave, this man who thought he knew all there was to know of me as quickly as that. I called after him. "Why do you seek your woman in Venice?"

"Because 'tis here she must be!" He spun to face me. "'Tis here that I will begin to search for her. With or without your aid." He shoved one hand through his hair, looking suddenly tired and older. "Forgive me for wasting your valuable time."

You know already that my heart is soft. I felt sympathy for this man, that is the simple truth of it. And I was curious. In that moment, I made an impulsive choice, as I so seldom do. "Wait."

He halted, then turned as a man who doubted his ears.

"Come with me." I offered my hand.

He looked me up and down and I knew he understood that I did not invite him to converse about the weather. "I have no coin."

This surprised me. "But I thought all returned wealthy from this endeavor."

"I had wealth but I have it no longer." He smiled wryly. "Does this change your invitation?"

I have an inexplicable affection for men who surprise. He was not hard upon the eyes, after all, and I was becoming more curious by the moment. "I offer the hospitality of my chambers in exchange for your tale."

He closed the distance between us with a trio of quick steps, those eyes bright with hope. "You will help me?"

I shrugged, more affected by his anxiety to find this woman than I wanted him to know. "Perhaps. Perhaps not." I tilted my head to regard him. "Everything, after all, has its price."

He looked around himself. "Especially here."

I smiled again. "Aye. Especially here."

He smiled back at me and this time, his smile lit his eyes. He stepped closer and offered his hand, as a nobleman will offer his hand to his lady. I was touched by this gesture, for there are few noblemen who treat whores with such courtesy in public.

I took his arm and felt a tingle of desire. He smelled of sun and wind and sea, clean and masculine scents that have always appealed to me. He was fit and strong, his hands were well wrought and there was a thrum about him that told me that he would not disappoint abed.

"I am Millard, once of Aigues-Mortes," he said, his voice low as though he confided a secret, and I felt the rumble of his voice against my hand. "You have beautiful eyes," he murmured, his gaze searching. "Their shape reminds me of an old friend."

"Not of your specific lady?" I teased and he snorted with laughter. There was no condemnation in his sweeping glance this time, just a rueful acknowledgment of my trade.

"Nay, never that." But Millard squeezed my fingers, which made it difficult to take offense.

Perhaps I would help him.

Perhaps this charitable donation would not be such a sacrifice, after all.

ॐ

Asim had ensured that all was ready, the meal laid in the best room on the *piano nobile*. This floor of the house was one level up from canal or street, and comprised the most lavishly appointed rooms, which were used for the entertainment of guests. The girls and their companions were absent, though undoubtedly they would send for fripperies from the table to be brought to their individual rooms. Asim ensured only that the food was plentiful and that 'twas artfully displayed here.

My guest looked about himself with some curiosity but no avarice, which surprised me. Indeed, he seemed spared of the assessing nature of so many in this city, a welcome change. I invited him to a seat at one end of the table. A boy from the kitchens poured red wine into fine goblets, left the vessel, then bowed and disappeared.

"I thought you offered other entertainments than a meal."

I took my own seat. "Payment is always collected in advance."

He chuckled and lifted his goblet of wine. "To fair business practices."

And we drank.

He stared at me over the rim of his glass, as though he would pierce the sheer silk with his gaze. "Do you not remove your veil to dine?"

I shook my head.

He regarded me with undisguised curiosity. "Do you take it off abed?"

"Render your payment if you wish to know."

Millard might have said more, but something in my expression may have persuaded him that he would not win any change in my choice. So he surveyed the meal, commenting on the simple fare of ships as he chose from Asim's array.

Millard ate with enthusiasm, exclaiming over this dish and another, never hesitating to try even what he did not know. His curiosity was a delight, his zeal for sampling undiminished as the meal progressed. He was a charming companion, with a full arsenal of anecdotes.

I toyed with my own meal, imagined that this large, purposeful man would show the same zeal abed. I thus forgot my own hunger, at least for the meal, and watched his hands. A man's hands tell much about him, in my opinion, and these told a thousand tales. They were capable and strong, gentle and adept, tanned and calloused.

Watching them made my mouth go dry as I imagined what else they might do well.

Asim hovered discreetly, for I could feel his presence in the shadows by the stairs. I do not know whether he hovered for me or for Guiliana, though I listened intently to the sounds coming from the rooms above. I do not have Asim's sixth sense, and this risky trade demands my keenest observation.

'Twas because I listened so intently that I heard the muffled gasp of Guiliana in her chamber, a gasp of such delight that it made me smile. And 'twas because I listened that I heard the affectionate chuckle of a large man lurking in the shadows.

My guest straightened at the distant sound, his gaze flicking over me. "Pleasure genuine or feigned?"

"Genuine, I am certain."

Millard watched me closely. "And you are relieved."

"Who would not be? She was much troubled earlier this day."

His eyes narrowed. "You sound almost maternal."

I laughed beneath my breath. "'Tis a sad commentary that I am like to be the best mother these girls ever had."

He grimaced. "Even if they have been stolen or bought from

their own mothers?"

There were those who did as much and I knew it well, but not I and I was oddly determined to ensure this man misunderstood me no longer. "These girls come to me when they have no choices left. They are destined to be whores, by dint of some misfortune, and 'tis either my abode or the Casteletto. Have you been there?"

He shook his head. "'Tis much reputed."

"'Tis a hell." I spoke with heat. "I spent five years locked within its walls."

"Then why did you enter it?"

"Because I was not yet ready to starve. But I knew from the first that I would survive that place and I saved every coin that I could, secreting them in my mangy pallet. I stole when I had the boldness for it and I begged extra payment from those who visited me regularly. I was robbed twice, but after five years, I left and never darkened that threshold again."

"But still you labor upon your back."

I snorted and drank of my wine anew. "Not always upon my back. Men here are inventive."

"You could have surrendered your trade."

"To do what? Marry honorably? Unlikely at best for men are apt to be harsh in their judgments of my kind, though 'tis they who have made us what we are."

If I sought reassurance from him that he was not of this ilk, he gave me none.

He waited expectantly, watchfully.

"And the convent is not to my taste," I continued sharply. "Nay, I bought this house and I give young women who are destined to make the same choices as I was forced to make the opportunity for better circumstance. 'Tis true that the trade is the same, but they live in comfort and safety, they eat well, they are visited by competent physicians, and they are only here because there are no other avenues open to them."

I took a long draught of my wine, alarmed to find myself trembling in my anger. 'Tis not my custom to drink in the company of my guests but Millard, with his conviction and quick judgments, troubled me more than any who had ever crossed my threshold.

"You are quite protective of them."

"They are here because no one else was." I dropped my gaze, certain I had said too much.

"Then perhaps you are not so poor a guardian as you might have me believe."

I looked up in surprise at that but Millard had returned his attention to his meal. 'Twas clear he knew little of the truth of our occupation. That reassured me oddly, for 'twas likeable that he did not visit brothels in every port. Restraint is an admirable quality in a man, and one I admire more with each passing year.

He similarly did not overindulge in the feast laid before him. I have seen many a man gorge himself to sickness on the finery of my table. But not this one. He complimented the fare with simple approval, sipped his wine and regarded me with amusement over the lip of the glass. "My payment would seem to be due."

I merely nodded.

He took another swallow, then set the glass upon the table. He leaned forward, tenting his fingers together, as intent upon the recounting of his tale as he seemed to be about every other task that fell to his hand. "I was born in Aigues-Mortes, a port on the south coast of Frankish territories. My father had his own ship, though his trade was not an overly profitable one. My mother died when I was too young to recall her well, in the labor of bearing what would have been my younger sibling. After that, my father took permanently to the sea. I was raised with a ship heaving beneath my feet, in a world of men and adventure and foreign trade.

"My father spoke always of fame and fortune, most frequently of fortune. He always had a tale of the fortune we would soon discover, the journey that would make our names, and I caught his fever for riches. 'Twas a quest we led, from one end of the sea to the other, and when he died without having found that treasure, I was doubly determined to succeed.

"Shortly thereafter I met a woman." Millard shook his head in reminiscence. "A beauty and the daughter of a vintner whose product I shipped. She was young, so young that her father had not yet realized that she stood on the cusp of womanhood. He sent her to my ship with messages and missives, an errand boy in flicking skirts."

"And you took advantage of her?"

"Nay, not that." He frowned and pushed his glass across the board, clearly sorting his memories. "I desired her. She was a beauty and she made no secret of her own admiration for me."

"She was determined," I guessed and he nodded.

"Aye, she was most romantically inclined. I cannot say that I did not anticipate her visits to my ship. I always held a part of myself back, as though there was a wall betwixt us. I loved travel and I loved adventure, I was pledged to a quest that no woman could challenge."

"So you left her there?"

"Not quite so readily as I might have preferred." He shook his head, his firm lips curved in a smile of reminiscence. "She guessed my intent better than I guessed it myself. She returned unexpectedly on the night I meant to lift anchor and we argued, most heatedly. She insisted that she loved me and that we were destined to be together."

"But you left all the same?"

"I was eighteen years of age. I could not bear the thought of shackling myself to a bride in those days." He rose and strode to the tall windows that faced the canal, folding his hands behind his back as he continued. His hands clenched and unclenched. "In those days it seemed to me that my father had surrendered his chance by wedding my mother and thus spending part of the year ashore. I was young, I was confident and I desired my due. I thought a woman could be found at any time."

He bowed his head. "When she left, certain she had persuaded me, I slipped anchor and rode the crest of that night's tide. I never returned to Aigues-Mortes again. Instead, I sought my fortune these fifteen long years."

He recounted the details of his quest with the attention only a man can show for such ordeals. 'Twas not a tale unlike so many others I had heard of fortunes won at great hardship. Perhaps I yawned, though it would have been indelicate to do so.

He glanced up and caught me, then laughed beneath his breath. "You are bored and I have scarce begun."

I lifted a brow. "Then you had best hasten to the interesting part."

He chuckled, evidently amused by my tart tone though unoffended by it. "I suppose 'tis not that remarkable a story."

"'Tis not, thus far."

He folded his arms across his chest and regarded me with mingled triumph and mischief. "Ah, but 'tis not common for a man to win a fortune, then cast it away."

"Not in these parts."

"Nor any other." He leaned forward, tapping one heavy finger on the table, holding my gaze as though he would compel me to not only listen but agree with him. "All those years I had suffered, all those sacrifices I had made, all in the hope of winning a fortune for my own. Yet once I had it, 'twas not satisfying in the least."

"Where did you win it?"

"In Constantinople, as all these others did. Three days of customary looting were allowed after the walls of the city fell. I had never seen the like of it. Fingers cut from the hands of the living to win their rings, women and children slaughtered, churches pillaged. Altars were chopped into pieces that they might be transported more readily. There was violence too, when more than one wanted a choice piece. Men were murdered in churches and left to rot for the want of a golden chalice."

"And you had your due?"

"And then some! I was in the thick of the looting. I was mad with lust for gold and gathered more than I could carry. I stowed it and hid it and piled it in secret corners. I evaded the obligatory official division of the spoils, as so many others did, intent on not sharing what I saw to be mine." He shrugged, dissatisfaction in the set of his lips as he surveyed my abode. "You too are surrounded by wealth and no doubt much accustomed to its charms."

"Such as they are."

"Indeed! Goods and gold and precious stones do not make a man happy, nor give him contentment." Millard sighed. "I had been driven all my life to seek out wealth and make it my own." He shook his head and smiled. "Yet it gave me no solace to have found it. I wanted more and coveted the possessions of others, I pilfered and hoarded and guarded my trove like a vigilant dragon.

This, even though it gave me no comfort in and of itself, and I refused to part with so much as a denier of it to acquire comforts.

"The booty increased my fears, for I fretted that countless others schemed to steal my prize. 'Twas stolen itself, after all, and 'twas only when I lay awake nights merely to ensure my possession of it that I realized the folly of what I had done. I learned the false allure of riches all too well. "

He shook his head. "And the goods themselves tormented me. Each reminded me all too well of its origin. They seemed fraught with incriminations, those trinkets, and taunted me to guess at the fate of the one who had owned them last. Indeed, I oft knew the fate of the possessor and I saw that one's anguish when I looked upon the prize.

"So I realized all too late that I had dreamed of a false reward, that I had charted the course of my life in vain. I lay awake, seeking in my memory the one thing that had sated my desire, a true guiding star. 'Twas only then I realized that I had cast aside the greatest gem in favor of an elusive setting."

"What gem?"

"The woman." He picked up his glass and turned it, watching the sunlight catch in the ruby hues of the wine. He smiled in recollection, a sweet smile that tugged at my heart. "The woman who loved me more than I deserved, yet a woman who I found all too easy to leave behind in my quest."

"And this is the woman whom you seek now."

He nodded and replaced the glass upon the table, its contents untasted. "I told myself once that I sought wealth so that I could give her what fripperies she deserved, but that was a lie. I sought wealth for myself and for my own satisfaction alone. She never desired it." He sighed. "And so, as better befitted her memory, I surrendered my wealth."

"Surely not all of it."

"Aye. All of it." He glared at me, as though daring me to disbelieve him. "I showered coin upon churches and strewed it into the hands of beggars. I gave to the monks and the nuns, to anyone who asked it of me. I aided widows and orphans and men left maimed by war or the wrath of God. I was rid of it all in a surprisingly short time, yet even that did not ease my yearning."

"So now you seek the woman."

"Aye. Will you aid me?"

"What do you want of her? Forgiveness?"

He smiled. "More. I would have her hand in mine. Will you aid me?"

I rose to my feet and paced the length of the room, choosing to avoid his question. I know too much of men to believe that all they claim is true. "Why should she be here? You said yourself that you came from Aigues-Mortes."

"She vowed to follow me if I were so fool to leave her side." He shook his head, bemused. "She was convinced that our love was strong enough that we could not be parted. She told me that she would meet me here, once I recovered from my folly." He shrugged. "My folly is gone and I am here. I can only hope that she is."

I turned to face him, seeking the truth in his features. "Did you love her? Do you still?"

"Aye and aye again." He met my gaze, his own filled with resolve. "I did not imagine how much at the time. Perhaps I did not wish to know the truth of it then."

I was skeptical. "And so, you assume that she waits vigil for you because 'tis now convenient for you to seek her out."

"She swore to do as much."

I made an exasperated sound. "How long have you sought your fortune?"

"Fifteen years."

I laughed then, for there was naught else I could do. He was startled, but I have a distinctive laugh and it startles many a guest. I sobered with an effort, though I could not keep my lips from twitching. "Fifteen years is a lifetime for many women. If she wedded, she could have had eight children by now. Perhaps ten." I paused, enjoying his dismay. "Provided she survived each labor."

He frowned, his agitation revealed by his restless rearranging of the cutlery. He leaned forward and the brooch he wore caught the light, the gems upon it winking at me and feeding my anger with him. "But surely not..."

"Surely so," I corrected harshly. "The risks of childbearing are high, of abortifacients yet higher. I have lost many a young woman in both pursuits, and I can afford the best physicians. How competent are the physicians in Aigues-Mortes?"

He swallowed and did not answer me. "She might not be wed."

"Nay, she might be dead of other causes. She might have been beaten or robbed or raped or have fallen ill with an ague that she did not survive."

To his credit, he looked sorely discomfited.

"Did you sample her?"

He nodded, a man filled with remorse. "I could not resist..."

Oh, 'twas an old excuse and one that earned naught from me. "Perhaps she even died in bearing the fruit of your seed. How much coin would her father have spared for a physician if your lover confessed to carrying your bastard?"

Now he was truly alarmed, but I gave him no quarter.

"Even if she did not conceive your child, if the lack of her maidenhead was discovered by her family, either on her wedding night or before, then she might have been cast from their doors. If she contrived to reach this city and if she is not dead since, then I assure you I know her employ now."

He paled and stood up hastily, pacing the length of the room more quickly than I could have done. "I never thought of it."

"Men seldom do." I sat heavily and drank once more. My hand was shaking but I felt no remorse for tearing the scales from his eyes.

He pivoted at the far end of the room. "You are harsh with me suddenly. What has changed your manner?"

"A lie," I said with heat, not intending to confess any such thing. "A lie has changed all."

"I told you no lie!"

"Aye, you did." I stood and cast my pristine napkin upon the board. "'Tis time you left my home."

"But what of your services?" There was a glint in his eye that I knew all too well, though the sight of it sickened me in this moment.

"Your payment is not deemed fit. Be glad you had a meal at my board. 'Twas more generous than you deserved."

He strode back to me, angry now that I assaulted his

character. "But what lie? What did I tell you that you believe to be untrue? I demand to know."

I reached out and touched the pin on his cloak with one fingertip, letting accusation narrow my gaze. "This is the lie. You did not give away all your wealth."

"I did! I did! All but this!" Millard cupped his hand protectively over the pin.

"If your tale is sincere, then give it to me as your payment. I shall then render the service you desire." I smiled coolly and put out my hand.

He stared at me, then shook his head. "I cannot."

"'Tis not so valuable as that," I scoffed, though my heart pounded madly with my audacity. "Pearls and amethysts are readily replaced, even by a man with little coin."

"'Tis not the value of the brooch that is of import!" Millard closed his fist over it. "*She* gave it to me. And if you guess aright, and she draws breath no longer—" his voice caught and was lower when he continued "—then 'tis all I have left of her. If naught else, 'twill remind me of my folly."

"As she did when you might have denied it."

He bowed his head at the truth in that and turned away, a defeated man. "Aye, as she did."

Oh, it has been said that my heart is too soft for this trade. He walked toward the door and I could not let us part this way.

"When she granted this to you beneath the stars, on the wharf in Aigues-Mortes, where she pledged her love to you."

Millard turned, incredulity in his eyes.

I took a deep breath. "And you were so concerned with the taste of the wind and the timing of the tides that she feared you did not even hear her words. She knew you would leave that very night and feared never to see you again."

"How can you know this thing?" he whispered.

"The same way I know 'twas then that she gave you that pin. The same way I know the inscription upon its back."

His gaze flew over me. He licked his lips and took a step closer. "It cannot be." There was an echo of hope in his voice though and I dared to feel some hope of my own.

"*Amor vincit omnia,*" I whispered unevenly. "Love conquers

all." The moment I had awaited for fifteen years was suddenly upon me—the moment I had anticipated and the one I had dreaded. All my artfully composed explanations had abandoned me, but there was no turning back at this juncture.

I removed my veil and cast the circlet on to the table, lifting my chin with pride. "Does love conquer all, Millard? Or is that merely another old romantic fable?"

He gaped at me. I stood my ground, knowing all too well what Millard saw, what I had become in fifteen years to ensure my own survival.

To keep my pledge to him to be here, waiting for however long it took.

I feared what he would say, feared that he would spurn me now and leave me with naught but this life as my only prospect, feared that he would shred the only dream I had ever had before my own eyes.

"Alix," he whispered, incredulous.

Suddenly a joy lit his features, a jubilation that needed no more words and left no doubt in my heart unanswered. I was in his arms, tasting salt in his kiss, though whether the tears were mine or his, I could not have said. In no time at all, we were in my chambers, entangled with each other and the linens, whispering, confiding, discovering once again.

Amor vincit omnia indeed. I slept beside him that night and every night thereafter, certain of the truth of it. Millard had returned and his heart was mine, as it never could have been mine, all those long and lonely years ago. We had both changed, but I could only believe that we would be happier for it.

And I had, after all, called our future right before.

The Leaves

On September 11, 2001, at nine in the morning, I was making tea in my kitchen and the radio was on. I heard the news report about a plane colliding with one of the World Trade Center towers. I assumed—as many did—that it was a small aircraft accident. I turned off the radio, took my tea and sat down to work. Although I had intended to revise a contracted book that was coming due, this story fell out of my fingertips instead. By ten, it was done. I went to get more tea and listened to the news again, which was when I learned of the terrorist attack in New York.

I'd never written a creepy short story like this one, and I hadn't written a short story in a long time. This piece was darker than the stories I'd been telling up to that time, and it wasn't a romance. Because it was so different from my previous work, I had to think that there had been something wicked in the air that morning. Now I can see this story as the first piece in a stream of darker work. It has similarities to both my vampire short story *Coven of Mercy* and to the urban fantasy romances in my Prometheus Project.

This story was previously available in a self-published digital-only edition.

It began in October. She had seen a lot of Octobers, Mildred had, but this one was different.

Not the month, but the leaves.

Oh, they turned brilliant colors as always they had, and they shone against the clear blue autumn sky as always they had, and they scuttled along the streets as always they had.

But this October, they followed her.

Mildred thought at first that it was her imagination. She heard the crackle behind her of falling leaves one day early in the month when she walked to the corner store. She shopped every day for something. It got her out of the house, she told anyone who asked, got her out in the world, gave her exercise, kept her young. She liked talking to people, even the Asian man who had bought what had once been Mr. McConnaughy's convenience store, the man she could barely understand.

She lived in the house that had been in George's family for generations. Once it had been surrounded by a farm, but George's father had sold off the land as the city came ever closer. It was surrounded now by tract houses. It stood off by itself, at the end of a long gravel driveway, the family having chosen to keep a large lot around the house. That property was filled with trees, some planted by George, others by his father, others even before that. Those trees towered over the house, shading it and sheltering it.

Mildred loved the trees. She loved the sound of the wind in their branches. She loved the cool shade they cast in the summer and the stark look of their bare branches against a clear winter sky. But most of all, she loved all the hues that the leaves turned each fall. She felt each year as though the house was surrounded by a kaleidoscope of color.

The sight of the changing leaves always made her glad to be alive.

She was coming home with a pint of cream on that day, a treat for the ginger cat who slept in a patch of sunlight on her front porch and seemed disinclined to leave, when the leaves rustled on the drive behind her. She smiled and looked up through the canopy of red and gold and orange at the sky of robin's egg blue.

She closed her eyes when the honeyed autumn sunlight touched her face and willfully ignored the ache in her old joints. She imagined the sunlight slipping through her veins like glistening gold, touching, warming, invigorating.

And then the rustle became louder.

It came closer.

She thought it must be the wind.

The leaves scuttled and danced, chasing around her ankles in a flurry that seemed almost aggressive. One clung to her support hose and wouldn't shake free. Mildred tore a hole in her stocking working it loose.

Then it clung to her gloved fingers.

"For goodness' sake!" She shook her hand, then finally rubbed her glove against the rough bark of the closest tree. Still it wasn't easy to dislodge the leaf, but she managed to shake it free.

Mildred felt the first tinge of fear when the rustle continued behind her. For the first time, the driveway seemed too long and the house too far from the bustle of the neighborhood.

She walked more quickly, knowing that she was being foolish, and reached her porch all out of breath. The ginger cat yawned and stretched luxuriously. Mildred was reassured. She was getting nervous, jumping at shadows. They were just leaves.

She believed it until she heard something like a cluster of children racing closer, whispering, giggling, conspiring. She turned to see a tumult of thousands of leaves cart wheeling down the laneway toward her.

The sight struck terror into her heart. Mildred scooped up the cat and hurried into the house, fumbling with her keys in the old lock. She slammed the heavy wooden door just as a barrage of leaves flung themselves against it with a shout.

One slithered beneath the door and lifted toward her, riding no breeze she could discern. In panic, she stamped on it, stamped on it until long after it was crushed on the floor, silent and battered and still.

Mildred turned both deadbolts, took a deep breath and smiled at the mystified cat. She took it to the kitchen and put the kettle on to make herself a cup of tea. She liked how the cat rubbed against her ankles and reasoned it was glad to be inside. It was even more glad when she poured the cream into a bowl and set that on the floor.

She told herself that she was getting old and silly, but her hand trembled as she lifted the teacup to her lips.

Mildred didn't go out again that day.

Or the next.

She didn't even open the door.

This was, of course, because she was busy.

Mildred dug an old litter box out of the basement for the cat, cleaned it and filled it with sawdust. The cat must have lived in another house because it knew exactly what to do.

And its presence comforted her. She was glad to have been adopted by this tawny creature. It slept on the landing in the patch of sunlight that came through the little leaded window above the stairs.

It had been three days since she'd gone out and Mildred was thinking she should get some more cream for the cat. Maybe a can of fish. She sat in the chair in the living room that allowed her to watch the cat in the sun. She drank her tea as the cat slept, reassured by the play of sunlight on its fur, the sweet drowsiness of its face.

Then the wind flung a barrage of leaves against the living room window so abruptly that she jumped. They seemed to wriggle as they slid down the glass. She had the strange idea that they were seeking some illicit way into the house. Mildred even thought she heard them murmuring to each other. She shivered and watched, unable not to watch, until the last leaf had fallen to the ground.

To her surprise, the cat had moved to her feet. Its tail swished. Its ears pricked as it too watched the leaves, its eyes narrowed to a hunter's gleam.

They went together to the window, the cat leaping to the back of the sofa. It had to be her imagination that the leaves seemed to swirl toward the house, as if responding to the sight of her.

The cat folded its ears back.

Mildred scratched its neck, liking its warmth and the softness of its fur. It was a good moment to not be alone.

The wind was up, she told herself firmly. It was no weather for old ladies unsteady on their feet to be venturing down to the corner. Winter was coming, Mildred could smell its bite. It was time she got accustomed to staying home once in a while.

It was an excuse and she knew it, but she didn't go out.

The following day, Mildred awakened angry and defiant, a ginger cat sprawled across the pillow she still thought of as George's. She named the cat George, then and there, and rose with purpose. The day was still, the sunlight pooling golden on the lane. The wind was gone.

So was the cream.

Mildred marched out into the world, for George. She was not going to let that cat go hungry because of leaves.

She liked that he watched her through the front window, from his perch on the back of the sofa. Even when she looked back at the end of the laneway, she could still see his golden shape there.

It was a beautiful day, the kind of October day that made her remember hayrides in the country and first kisses and weddings and babies. She was smiling as she bought a quart of cream for George and a package of ginger snaps for herself. The Asian man spoke to her, and she couldn't tell whether he had commented on the weather or the news.

Mildred smiled all the same and thanked him. She said it was a lovely day. He said something and they smiled at each other.

Then she squared her shoulders and stepped out into the street again.

She was halfway down the laneway, just beginning to convince herself that the incident earlier in the week had been nonsense of her own devising, when she heard the rustle of leaves again.

She glanced over her shoulder to see a flurry of orange and yellow closing fast.

Mildred panicked. Even though she quickened her pace, they quickly surrounded her.

The leaves swirled around her in a column of radiant hues, a cloak of many colors. They obscured the property that she knew like her own hand, pushing her glasses askew, striking terror into her tired heart. She feared they would carry her off forever, that she would be lost forever, that she would disappear as if she had never been.

Terror gave her strength.

Mildred burst from the cloud of leaves and ran to her porch, her chest heaving with fear and exertion. George watched with bright eyes from the window. Her hands were shaking so hard that she missed fitting the key into the lock. She dropped her keys and had to stoop to pick them up again, losing precious time. She heard the leaves mustering again as the lock finally clicked. Mildred fell into the sanctuary of her foyer and slammed the door behind herself.

A trio of leaves slipped through the crack.

She turned both deadbolts, then cried out when she saw the leaves. Like the first one that had invaded her house, they rose toward her in defiance of everything she knew. There was no wind, no draft, nothing that could propel them.

But they still came.

Mildred retreated, but to no avail. The leaves chased her. They pursued her to the kitchen. She was backed into the wall beside the stove, but they fluttered right in front of her face.

She was cornered.

She had the strange sense that they knew it.

That they had planned it.

That they had a scheme for her.

Just when she thought her heart might explode in fear, George arrived in her defense. Mildred saw a ginger streak dart through the swing door to the unused dining room. The cat pounced upon the leaves, then shredded them. His eyes gleamed and his tiny teeth shone as he reduced them to nothing.

Confetti.

Harmless confetti.

Mildred heaved a sigh in relief and straightened her glasses. It made no sense but she couldn't deny what had happened. The cat had even responded to the leaves.

George tipped back his head to meet Mildred's gaze and mewled in complaint.

She smiled, knowing exactly the reward he wanted for his services. She took a deep breath, put the kettle on and poured George a generous serving of cream.

She put those shredded leaves down the toilet, even before she hung up her coat, making sure she didn't miss one tiny piece.

Mildred flushed it two more times, even though it was a waste of water, just to be sure.

Mildred did not go out the following day, even though it was Sunday and she should have gone to church. It was a longer walk to church. She was terrified of what might happen in that extra block.

The leaves threw themselves against the living room window, as if to protest. George sat on the back of the sofa, batting in their direction, his paw colliding with the glass over and over again.

The next morning, Mildred woke up to find two maple leaves on her shoulder. Right there, on her nightgown.

She sat up hurriedly, disturbing George. He took one look at the leaves and destroyed them.

How had they gotten in? She'd left the bathroom window open, just a crack, the way she always did, but there was a new screen on it.

Had she left anything else open? She was sure she had checked the doors two or even three times. Mildred got out of bed more quickly than she usually did.

She froze on the threshold of the bathroom and stared. The window screen was torn, It had a thin slit right in the middle, which was new.

Even worse, dozens of leaves were piled against it on the outside.

They twitched. They writhed. They squirmed. They might have been trying to bend themselves through the opening. It was a still morning, so the wind was not to blame.

Mildred slammed the window and locked it, her breath coming quickly.

☙

That was the day the battle was lost.

That was the day Mildred realized she could not keep them all out. Leaves slipped through the mail slot with bills from the gas company. Leaves came down the chimney and wiggled through the closed flue. Leaves rattled against the fans in the kitchen and the bath, having found their way through the vent. They were trapped against the inner screen, but she was never sure for how long. Leaves weaseled through the slender crack between the windows and their frames. Leaves came through the storm drain in the basement and lifted the catcher from below.

She could hear them rustling everywhere it seemed.

And once they were within the house, they hunted her. They chased her; they harassed her; they shoved themselves against her and plastered themselves against her skin. She found them on her face when she awakened on Tuesday morning. They were between her breasts. They were in her shoes.

The leaves terrified her. Mildred didn't know what they wanted. She didn't know what had changed.

She didn't know what she would have done without her stalwart feline defender.

She did know that if she told anyone about her experience, they would think her old and senile and stupid. She knew that then she would be forced to leave this house she loved, leave George, leave her life from some hideous existence in a care facility.

And that frightened Mildred more than the leaves.

☙

That prospect was what drove Mildred finally to make her peace with the leaves.

It wasn't a lack of food or even a lack of cream for George. Mildred had lived through a depression and a war. She knew how to make meals from what came in cans and she had many, many cans in her root cellar. She was prepared for disaster.

But she resented being trapped in her house. She resented the feeling that she was old and foolish and afraid of autumn leaves.

November had come, the sunlight had taken a colder tinge,

and she told herself that George was in need of a better reward than evaporated milk.

She was determined to go out.

She was determined to have her life back.

Mildred put on her warmest coat—the tweed one with carved horn buttons that had seen forty years of diligent service—and her sturdiest shoes. She chose her favorite (and secretly lucky) hat. She tugged on her gloves and knotted her scarf tightly at the neck of her coat. She took one of the old George's canes, she patted the new George, and she marched out into the world.

And it was fine.

The leaves were touched with frost now. Some were scattered across the brown lawn like fallen soldiers in a war of seasons. There was a great mound of them alongside the laneway, piled high and flattened with rain. The lawn service had piled them up there. Mildred made a mental note to call and remind them to come and shred them for compost before the snow fell.

She was certain there were more fallen leaves than she'd even seen before.

But they all looked wet and limp. They were still and already darkening, their bright colors faded. They were dead. Mildred found that the sight put new vigor in her step. The air was bracingly cold, the light almost painfully bright.

She said hello to everyone she met. She spoke at length with the Asian man in the grocery—although she was not at all sure that they were talking about the same thing at every point in the conversation, it was very pleasant. They both smiled a great deal.

Then Mildred took George's cream and her cookies and headed home. She touched the brim of her lucky hat more than once as she approached the laneway to the house.

She had been foolish.

She was relieved.

Mildred was almost on the porch, triumphant in her conquest. She waved to George, who had not moved from his watchful perch in the living room.

She was just beneath the mighty beech tree when there was an unruly gust of wind. It was so strong and sudden that it nearly flipped her hat off her head. Mildred clutched the brim.

Then she heard the rustle of leaves overhead.

Mildred looked up in alarm. The beech was always late to lose the last of its leaves. She'd often thought it wanted to hold on to summer a bit longer. There were still quite a few of them on its highest branches.

But this wind was freeing every stray leaf. They even looked to her as if they were struggling to break free in the same moment.

To take advantage of opportunity.

It abruptly seemed to have been very foolish to come outside. Mildred felt as if she had underestimated the leaves.

She hurried to her front door.

She heard the leaves rustling.

She saw them falling all around her. She didn't dare look back. Her breath came quickly as she raced for the porch. She had her keys in her hand, the one that unlocked the door at the ready.

The rustling was so loud that there must have been thousands of them. Mildred was sure the sky had turned dark, their sheer numbers blocking the sun.

And they all headed directly for her.

She was the eye of the storm.

She cried out and ran for sanctuary.

She made the first step on the porch and they were around her ankles.

They swirled up to her knees as she stepped up to the next. They seemed to be frantic or frenzied, shaking with excitement. They spun and danced, gleeful and celebratory as they wound around her legs.

Mildred stumbled on the third step as they rose higher, surrounding her, pressing against her.

She lost her balance when they slipped beneath the hem of her coat. She clutched the railing as they slithered up her sleeves, behind her glasses and under her hat. They were in her shoes, they were under her stockings, they were inside her underwear. They giggled and chortled, but their glee terrified her. They jammed themselves against her mouth, her ears, her nose.

Mildred fell on her own porch, blinded by their assault. She tried to cry out, but they slid into her mouth, silencing her.

She heard her ankle crack and knew that she would run no

more.

Then they were upon her, millions of leaves, oak and maple and poplar and elm and beech. They suffocated her, buried her, engulfed her.

Silenced her.

Forever.

The coroner didn't look past Mildred's broken ankle. "You know how old people are," he said. "They think themselves young again. They play in the leaves, remembering their childhood. But they aren't young and their bones are fragile. She tripped on the steps. She fell. She must have panicked."

What else would explain the leaves beneath her fingernails?

In her mouth?

In her nose?

The coroner had far more interesting puzzles to solve that week. His superiors, also overburdened, were content with his version. The papers didn't run the story. The police closed the file.

Mildred's memorial service was sparsely attended: just the Asian man from the corner store, the lady from the church who had adopted George, and the minister. The lady from the church brought the cat, although the minister sniffed at her whimsy.

'Another foolish old woman' was surely what he thought.

None of them—except maybe George the cat, who had witnessed it all—guessed what the coroner would have found if he had looked more closely.

How would he have explained the leaves jammed down Mildred's throat?

The ones balled in her stomach?

What about the leaves burrowed into her every orifice?

Shoved beneath her eyelids?

Worked beneath her skin on her palms?

Mildred would have said she was their prey. She would have said the leaves had stalked her, that they had been intent on destroying her all along. She would have said that they had won the hunt.

Mildred would have said it was malice behind it all.

Hate.

But the leaves, the leaves would have called it love.

The Kiss of the Snow Queen

This novella was the result of an invitation to participate in a follow-up volume to the anthology **To Weave a Web of Magic**. Again, the stories were to include both fantasy and romantic elements, and the participating authors were myself, Lynn Kurland, Sharon Shinn and Sarah Monette. The only guideline was that the anthology title would be **The Queen in Winter**.

The first story that came to mind for me was Hans Christian Anderson's *The Snow Queen*. I always found the description of Kay having a shard of ice in his heart to be very poignant and evocative. That name turned my attention to Cai (Kai, Keu, Cayous), one of the knights of the round table in the Arthurian cycle of stories. Cai is interesting to me because his role changed so radically over the centuries, shifting from the foremost knight and ultimate hero of the Welsh sources to Arthur's seneschal (and a minor character) in the stories told by the French troubadours. In the Welsh poem *Pa Gur yw y Porthawr* (*What man is the porter*), for example, Cai is given credit for killing the Cath Palug, a monstrous 'clawing cat' that terrorized the people. There is a similar tale of Arthur fighting a monstrous cat called the Chapalu (or Capalu) near Lake Lausanne (located in modern Switzerland) in the French poem *Merlin*, although the cat is triumphant in that version.

I chose to set my version of Cai's battle against the Cath Palug in the ancient kingdom of the Burgundians, in the early Middle Ages when many believed the gods walked among men. Of course, much like Anderson's Kay, my valiant Cai can only win the day with the help of Gerta, a woman with the ability to see beyond the immediate present.

I

he stirring of shadows in the bronze mirror would have awakened Gerta, had she slept. She had been awake all the night, so she was immediately aware of the motion within it. She watched it warily, reluctant for once to heed its summons.

She had done wrong, and she knew it well. She had used the mirror against its purpose, against her mentor's counsel, and it had been three days since her transgression.

Gerta feared to see what reckoning the mirror conjured. Such forces could be willful, perhaps as willful as she had been in trying to bend the mirror's power beneath her own inexperienced hand.

But what choice had she had?

The mirror in question was a bronze disk, one face of it polished highly. Most people saw their own reflection within it, but Gerta, as a seer, saw distant events and portents displayed upon it. Her gift was rare and, as soon as it had become evident, she had been apprenticed to another seer. Isold had been her mentor from childhood until that woman's death five years past.

So much had changed with Isold's demise. Gerta still yearned for the days before the arrival of the Cath Palug in her father's realm, for that fiend was the root of all evil that had followed.

The mirror tickled her thoughts, persistent as it seldom was. Still Gerta lingered abed. Her training was not complete, but she had the wits to know trepidation.

Gerta's chamber was at the summit of the sole tower in the abode of Gundobad, the king of Burgundy. She had long thought its location befit a seer, for it would protect her chastity, but now she understood that her chastity had been protected for another reason.

Her chamber was still dark, for it was not yet dawn, and the hall below was blessedly quiet. She could have slept in her exhaustion, had she felt confident that she would not be assaulted in her slumber. The trunk pushed against her door was no guarantee, nor was the dismissal of all maids who might have betrayed her while she slept. Gerta rubbed her eyes, exhausted and hungry from three days secured here alone in her defiance. She looked toward the mirror, hoping fiercely that her summons would bring relief.

There was only one way to be certain. Gerta rose to heed the mirror. She had best know the worst of what she had done.

She was still dressed, wearing her favored plain robe, the one that did not look like the choice of a king's only daughter. The robe was blue, the pale blue that came from woad, woven finely from wool and devoid of embroidery. It covered her from chin to toe, the sleeves hanging modestly over her hands. To leave her hair unbound but cover all of her skin, with the exception of her fingers and her face, was the modesty Gerta had been taught to better protect her gift—though such modesty had served little in this place.

It was when Gerta bent to pull her leather shoe over her heel that she noticed the odd shimmer in the air. There was fog in the valley beyond her window, which was not uncommon in itself, but this fog was strange. It had slipped over her sill like quicksilver and now pooled on the floor of her chamber. It seemed to swirl there, shimmering, as if an unnatural wind stirred in her chamber.

As if it moved by some force of its own.

As if it awaited her.

The mirror tugged at Gerta, but the fog both fascinated her and made her afraid. This was a fog wrought of shadow: there was darkness within it, a foreboding darkness.

Instead of going to the mirror, Gerta glanced to the window. All souls in the valley slept, thanks to Gundobad's generosity with thin ale these three days, but the current of fog was in motion. In contrast to the stillness, it wound like a river, moving sinuously between the quiet huts below.

Gerta frowned, for this fog showed purpose as natural fog never did. It unfurled across the valley like a ribbon, a ribbon with a clear destination. It did not trouble itself to fill the furrows or coil around the mountains that framed the valley: it made directly for its goal. It had cut a path directly to Gerta's window. She leaned out and saw that it ascended the wall with that same purpose.

It hunted her.

Or it replied to her unorthodox summons. Gerta turned to regard the rising mist on her floor warily, her heart skipping with the surety that she was prey.

The fog drew closer as she watched, slipping around her ankles, for all the world like a possessive caress. Her skin chilled immediately, as if she had plunged her foot into ice water.

Gerta leapt out of its clutch and imagined that she heard faint laughter. She crossed her plain chamber hastily, lifted the bronze mirror and turned its polished face upward. Within the circle of bronze, shadows swirled and churned, echoing the motion of the fog. She stilled her breathing, ignored the strange sense that she was being watched, and opened her thoughts to the mirror.

The shadows resolved so abruptly that Gerta jumped. A man's face was suddenly before her, a face so clearly shown that her heart skipped. It was a man's face, radiant with virility, tanned and golden and as confident as the midday sun.

It was more than his face shown in the mirror—the mirror had become his face. Gerta might have had her hand upon his throat instead of upon the handle of the mirror. Indeed, the handle felt warm and had the texture of flesh beneath her fingers. She had never had such a vivid vision and some part of her wished that had never changed.

She was in the presence of a potent sorcerer, to be sure—and he had replied to her summons. Gerta's mouth went dry.

He was sufficiently handsome and sufficiently close to disconcert a maiden like herself. His eyes were blue, a clear vibrant blue, and lit not only with shrewdness but with an appreciation that could make a woman lose whatever inhibitions she held.

"I come, at your summons, to serve your will," he said, his voice a pleasant timber that sent a shiver through her.

Gerta shook her head, for she should not have been able to hear him. "What you have done to the mirror is not possible..."

He smiled, as if amused. "Many things are possible, if we have the will to believe them so."

He seemed to be surveying her, which was also impossible:

the mirror granted views but did not allow for communication.

All the same, this man heard her and she heard him. Gerta caught her breath, wary of his power even as her thumb moved across the handle of the mirror. She could feel his pulse and the heat of him and seemingly could not halt the motion of her thumb. She had never touched a man, and no man had been permitted to touch her—this caress was forbidden, stolen and beguiling all the same.

That must be why her heart raced. It could have naught to do with the warmth of his gaze.

"You are a sorcerer," she guessed, for Isold had told her of such men.

He nodded. "As are you, for this is no small spell you wove."

Gerta felt herself flushing. "I know naught of spells..."

"Yet you cast a fearsome one all the same." His fair brows pulled together briefly. "Such talent is not unknown, but it has need of a mentor, the better that it can be tamed." Then he looked upon her, both assessing and appreciative.

"That is not why I sent the summons." Gerta averted her gaze. "My mentor is dead these five years, and I knew not what I did," she confessed, then could not help but look for his response.

He smiled, a smile that lit his eyes. "Then you have need of another mentor. Perhaps that is why your summons found me. I have need of a pupil and perhaps of a partner."

He put a slight weight upon the last word, sufficient that Gerta understood his meaning. She had guessed that there would be a price to be paid for her audacity, but she had not expected such a high one.

"You should know that I am maiden, once and always," she said with breathless haste. "The loss of my chastity will be the sacrifice of my gift as a seer. So I was taught and so I believe."

"That cannot be true," he said patiently, "for then we should have no wager."

She could not dismiss him, nor could she pledge what he asked of her. Gerta wished ardently for counsel, but knew she would find none in Isold's absence. Worse, she felt herself slowly blush beneath his regard, her face suffusing with heat.

She knew she should tear her gaze from his, but despite

herself she was intrigued. Her pulse quickened that there was another of her kind who breathed, at the prospect of having a tutor again—and she was honest enough to acknowledge that it quickened for another reason, as well.

"Who is to say what gift will come in the place of the one you have?" He regarded her warmly, clearly undeterred, and a treacherous part of Gerta was glad of this. His voice was filled with both confidence and compassion. "A whole is wrought of two halves, Gerta, and is greater than the sum of its parts. You must trust in the way of things, in the fact that your summons came to me, of all men." He winked at her then, silencing whatever she might have said. "But before we speak of this and much more, there is a task I must perform for you. Your request must be fulfilled."

Before Gerta could protest, he became smaller and the mirror became its usual self again, the handle reverting to cold metal. It was as if he stepped back, and she felt the loss of his attention.

Then she cried out. She recognized the place where the sorcerer stood and understood with sudden clarity the fullness of what she had done. He stood before a cave, a cave that was as familiar to Gerta as the lines in her own hand.

The mirror often showed her warriors who met their end at this stone portal: this was the abode of the Cath Palug, the beast that had ravaged her father's land, the fiend that had destroyed her father's kingdom and driven his people into exile.

The mirror had found a trick to resolve her request, for the demise of the Cath Palug would defeat Gundobad's intent that Gerta should wed his son, Sigismund.

But no man could defeat the Cath Palug. Those who fought the great cat paid with their lives. She had cast into peril someone who aided her.

Again.

"Do not do this thing! Do not face the Cath Palug!" she shouted, but the sorcerer strode to the opening of the cave, apparently unable or unwilling to hear her any longer.

Gerta felt sickened by her deed, impotent as never before. She had called for aid; she had used the mirror to make a cry for assistance to selfishly secure her gift.

And now this sorcerer would die, for answering her call.

As she watched, the sorcerer laughed, raising his voice in a whistle of summons. He even called the beast! Gerta caught her breath at his daring. Daughter of a warlord, she liked that this sorcerer was a warrior as well and that he did not flinch from a foul deed. And she admired his boldness, to be sure.

She did not like that he would pay for his valor with his life.

She saw the cat's profile appear against the darkness of its hovel, saw its eyes glint. It was large, larger than a man, and possessed of a hunger that could never be sated. It had grown larger since last she had glimpsed it, grown by feasting upon the meat of the warriors it ruthlessly slaughtered.

It crouched. It snarled.

It leapt.

The sorcerer raised a massive spear against the beast and made to drive it into the beast's breast. The Cath Palug snapped the spear as if the weapon were a mere twig, then roared in fury. The sorcerer drew his sword with startling speed, but the cat caught him around the throat, closing its powerful jaws around the pulse of his life.

Gerta cried out. The Cath Palug was strong and fast, stronger and faster than most warriors anticipated. Those who faced it had little chance to learn from their errors.

To Gerta's astonishment, the sorcerer bellowed and smote the beast with a blow that should have killed it. He was strong! Gerta thrilled at the evidence and dared to hope that he might triumph. The cat retreated snarling, its wound flesh-deep only, its blood staining the snow.

The sorcerer swore under his breath and the pair circled each other warily. Gerta's grasp upon the mirror was so tight that her knuckles were white.

But truly, what difference if this sorcerer claimed her or Sigismund did? Her gift would be sacrificed either way. She had never feared so much for the life of any man who faced the Cath Palug, and there had been many, some even as valiant as this man.

What had changed?

The answer came most unexpectedly, so unexpectedly that Gerta dropped her mirror.

"Well, it's not that complicated," a male voice said immediately behind her. His accent was as unfamiliar as his voice. "Work with me here, Gerta, my girl; you're clever enough."

Gerta pivoted in terror as the mirror clattered to the floor, but her chamber was empty. Her gaze darted to the portal, but the trunk still barred entry. The light was turning pearly with the promise of the dawn and there was no corner in her chamber in which a man could hide.

She was alone, to be sure.

When Gerta could not summon a coherent word, the voice continued. "He's your destiny, of course."

She peered out the window, thinking there must be someone outside, hanging from the sill or the roof with uncommon agility. Nay. She leaned her ear against the portal, thinking some bold soul assailed her from the corridor beyond. Nay. No man crouched in the rafters, either, and the trunk held only the few garments of her own that always it held.

She stood in the middle of the room and turned slowly. She was losing her wits.

A man she could not see whistled low and Gerta jumped. "Some girls have all the luck. He is one handsome piece of work, Gerta, and that smile...mm mmm mmmmmmm."

"Who spoke?" She drew her small eating knife and held it before herself. "Who are you? Show yourself."

"Oh, baby, I'd do it in a minute if I could. Give me a kiss and help me out."

Gerta felt a caress across the back of her neck, in the shadow beneath the weight of her hair. A stroke of strong fingertips that made her tingle in a new way. She gasped and turned, but there was only the shimmer of the fog behind her.

"Who are you? What are you? And what do you desire of me?"

Rich male laughter echoed in her chamber, so resonant that it could not have been her imagination. This was no trick of the sorcerer in the mirror, for the voice differed. This one was deeper, darker. Older.

Undoubtedly more skilled than she. Gerta's breath came

quickly in her fear. There was only the sinuous fog in her chamber, the fog that was like no other fog she had ever seen, a force she did not know how to conquer.

She straightened with bravado. "You must depart immediately. Your voice reveals your gender and it is forbidden for a man to enter my chamber."

There was a smile underlying his response. "Fortunately for you then, I'm not a man. This must be your lucky day."

Gerta did not have the audacity to ask what he was. "Fortunate for me? How so?"

"Isn't the woman the one who pays the price for tempting a man's lust? A strange custom to my thinking, but not an uncommon one in mortal societies. Take Sigismund, for example."

"I will not take Sigismund!" His words struck a bit too close to the bone for Gerta's taste and she raised her knife higher as he laughed. How could this strange intruder know such details of her life? "I command that you show yourself!"

He chuckled, as if the idea was absurd, the sound coming from no distinct source. Perhaps she was going mad. The prospect of being tied to Sigismund for the remainder of her days, of being trapped in this violent household with no hope of release, perhaps could do that to a woman.

"His name is Cai," the voice continued confidentially. "Cai the Tall, one of the nine enchanter kings of England. He's from Wales, actually, but details, details."

"You evade my demand."

"I'm telling you what you really want to know, Gerta—what you need to know. Why else do you think I'm here? This Cai guy has some pretty serious credentials. Companion of kings, slayer of giants." He cleared his throat softly and Gerta hated how avidly she awaited his words. "I'm thinking you two kids have got something in common. Face it: you could do a lot worse, my girl."

"I am no girl but a woman in truth..."

"You won't be a woman until you are claimed by Cai and you know that as well as I do."

"No man may touch me," Gerta began to protest but the intruder's voice dropped to a whisper, a current of low sound that seemed to slither into her ears.

"So, how do you think Cai will be in bed, Gerta? Rough? Wild? Tender?"

The treacherous whisper left a warm course over her lobe and into her ear, leaving a heat of speculation in its wake, one that reached all the way to her heart. Gerta felt as if she had suddenly stepped into a beam of bright sunlight, as if her very flesh was aflame. Gerta could feel the course of her own blood, could not evade the thunder of her pulse.

She was awakened.

She seemed to feel a caress, one that slid down the length of her arm. A man's fingers might have entwined with her own, his palm over the back of her hand, though she could see nothing. She stared at her arm in mingled astonishment and dismay, unable to account for her response to the leisurely caress. It could not be called anything else, and her mouth went dry as she thought of Cai touching her thus. Such a gentle caress could not have been from any other man she knew.

Her hand was then lifted by an unseen force, a tingling kiss planted on her palm. She could fell the press of a man's lips against her flesh. She stared at her hand in marvel as tingles spread through her from that point.

Then she cried out at the flick of the tip of his tongue across her palm. "Do not do that!" She backed away, wiping her palm upon her skirts.

"Listen to your pulse, Gerta. How about that warmth in your belly?" The voice might have been whispering her ear then, the feel of breath against her throat making her shiver. "How about that heat down below there?"

"Leave me be!"

"Cai will certainly be lusty. Men like their earthly pleasures, sorcerers even more so, not that there's anything wrong with that. And he wants you, I can tell." He chuckled. "But then, who wouldn't?"

Gerta felt herself blushing crimson. "Who are you? What are you? What do you want with me?"

"What everyone wants, pretty much, except I can't do much about it." He laughed then, although Gerta did not see the humor in his words. "Consider me a catalyst."

"I do not know this word. Your speech is strange, as if you are a foreigner."

"You could call me that, for sure." He sighed. "How about a matchmaker? Do you have those? Someone who smooths the way, so that everyone gets what they want?"

"I do not desire to be claimed by a man."

"But you called..."

"To keep Sigismund's hands from me! What else could I do?"

The voice interrupted her. "Don't you think it's fair that if Cai defeats the Cath Palug, he gets the bonus prize?"

"I will be no man's prize."

"Will your father see matters your way? I think not. If our friend Cai kills the Cath Palug, I'm thinking Daddy-O will have a little reward for him." He paused. "Like you, for example. Prize, bride, it's all pretty much the same in a barbarian culture, don't you think?"

The voice was right, much to Gerta's dismay. Her current situation revealed that her father would be glad to trade her for his own advantage—he had not fought Gundobad's decree.

"Think about it." The voice surrounded her again, sliding into her own thoughts as if it would mingle with them. "A warrior's hands upon you, a partner both strong and gentle. Two minds as one. Haven't you felt a bit lonely since you lost Isold You've got to believe it could be worse, Gerta."

"He will not win." She folded her arms across her chest. "This discussion is of no import. No man defeats the Cath Palug."

"Someone's got to do it sometime. All good things come to an end and all that."

"Nay, the Cath Palug is invincible."

"No one is invincible, babe."

Gerta caught her breath. She could feel the weight of a man's hands on her shoulders, as if he stood behind her and nuzzled her neck. Despite herself, her body was responding to this strange intruder, a part of her mind considering the pleasure that might come of a man's touch. If he had tried to force her, she could have spurned him; if he had been substantial, she could have struck him. But he seduced her and his touch was dangerously persuasive. As it was, her feet seemed rooted to the floor.

"Not even you," he breathed.

"I will succumb to no man's touch."

"You've done pretty well so far. Doesn't ol' Sigismund call you the ice maiden?"

Gerta glanced over her shoulder and almost caught a glimpse of a man. She blinked and whatever she had seen was gone. "How do you know this?"

He chuckled. "I know a lot of things. Think: you and Cai would be two of a kind," he whispered, seemingly leaving a line of kisses along her throat. Gerta swallowed, trying to fight the allure of his caress and not doing as well as she would have liked. She stood straight, hoping she appeared to be unresponsive.

"Aren't you lonely, sometimes, Gerta?" The words were so softly uttered that they might have been her own thoughts. "Wouldn't it be great to have someone to talk to, someone who understood the burden of your gift, someone who knew how best to use it?"

Gerta's eyes flew open. This was sorcery! She had to flee such a persuasive spell! She darted to the door and shoved the trunk aside, only to have it slide back into place before she could open the portal.

"Oh, no, you don't want to go out there. Do you really think Sigismund isn't watching the door? "

Gerta fought the weight of the trunk without success. It seemed to be fixed to the floor, and had the same dark shimmer about it as the fog. She guessed that she would never move it.

"I won't be able to do much if he gets his hands on you, and no one else will help you here."

There was truth in that, truth that halted her. Gerta looked around herself in panic, knowing she was captive. Never had she felt so trapped by a lack of choices. Her breath came quickly but she could not slow it.

"Your arrival in his bed is three days past due, and I'm thinking the boy is getting a bit restless. It's not going to be fun, Gerta, when Sigismund takes what he thinks is his due."

The fog, Gerta realized, had piled itself in the corner where it shimmered like a dark opal. If she squinted, its shape might be similar to the silhouette of a tall and well-muscled man.

She straightened, liking that there was something to confront. "What do you desire of me?"

"That would be the million dollar question."

"I do not understand all of your speech."

"A kiss would be a good start."

"You will not have one, so long as the choice is mine whether to surrender it."

He sighed, then his tone turned chiding. "Ah well, then, don't miss the good bits on my account. Cai conjured up this show for you, after all, though even he never guessed how it would end. You should at least have the courtesy to watch."

Gerta felt her eyes narrow. "How can you know what the mirror will show before it does?"

"Oh, come on, Gerta. You could guess if you wanted to. It's not rocket science. Go on, give the man the grace of your attention. It cost him big to work this spell."

Would Cai defeat the Cath Palug? Gerta glanced at the mirror, curious but uncertain whether it was wise to turn her back upon this strange intruder. She prickled, though, with the surety that the mirror's turmoil still unfurled.

The intruder chuckled again and Gerta knew he had guessed her thoughts. Odd, she had always thought herself adept at hiding them. She snatched up the mirror and looked within it, willfully ignoring her unexpected and unusual guest.

To her surprise, the mirror had waited for her. This had never happened before, and she felt a grudging respect for Cai's abilities. She could learn much from a sorcerer of such power, and a part of her yearned for such knowledge. Had this occurred already? Or was it yet to occur?

Could her choices affect Cai's survival?

"Now, you're thinking," the voice mused.

She thought no further before the beast spring again. It buried its claws in Cai's hauberk. They were black, those claws, long and sharp and gleaming like obsidian. Gerta had seen them slice men open like knives. Cai bellowed in pain and fury. His blood ran crimson, the Cath Palug's claws buried almost their full length in his shoulder.

There was too much blood. Gerta bit her knuckle and could not so much as blink less she miss something of import. Cai stumbled as he bled, and then he fell.

To Gerta's dismay, no soul came to his aid. Surely he had not embarked upon such a quest alone? But sorcerers oft labored alone, especially when they believed their success inevitable.

A lump rose in Gerta's throat as the cat, the cursed Cath Palug, grasped Cai's hauberk with its teeth. The sorcerer murmured but could not rouse himself to fight off the fiend, so fearsome were his injuries. The growling cat dragged the warrior into the yawning darkness of its lair.

There was naught left but a trail of the sorcerer's blood, brilliant red against the snow, marking the path to the cavern.

Cai was still alive, Gerta knew it, and she guessed that the beast would torment him before killing him. The prospect sickened her. Such nobility of intent deserved better reward than this. Gerta put the mirror down with force, angrier than she ever had been, and turned away.

This was her fault.

She looked to the shimmering shadow, disliking that she would be fulfilling his expectation. "What must I do to aid Cai?"

II

hat's the spirit! See? Two of a kind," the intruder said with such surety that Gerta longed to do him injury. "That's some kind of connection. So tell me, what changed your mind?"

"He is not yet dead," Gerta said, her words thick. "The cat will torment him before killing him."

"Compassion is good. It could come in handy."

"I do not understand."

"You don't need to. Yet." The intruder cleared his throat, and Gerta wondered if he meant to say something unpleasant. "You know, I hate to raise the possibility, but the Cath Palug might not kill him at all."

Gerta's lips tightened. "He will die eventually."

"Maybe not."

"I do not understand your meaning," she said with impatience. "I thought you intended to show me his triumph."

"Ah, well, you can't have everything. Besides, you didn't want him to succeed."

"I did not condemn him!"

"Not like you've done to others," the voice mused.

Gerta strode across the room, trying to put distance between them. "I do not know what you mean."

"Then you're dumber than you look."

"I..." Gerta silenced her angry response with an effort, for she sensed that the intruder simply wanted to rouse her ire. "What must I do to aid Cai?"

"Obviously, you're going to have to go to the cave of the Cath Palug and intervene."

Gerta stepped back in shock. "I cannot do this!"

"Why not?"

"I am a maiden. I am not a warrior. I cannot defeat the Cath Palug when a man such as Cai cannot do so." Gerta's protests sounded like excuses even to her own ears. "My father would forbid it!"

The shadow laughed. "And why would you care about his perspective?"

"And it is three days' walk to Lake Lausanne. Cai will be dead before I can arrive there."

"Gee, and I thought you felt a little responsibility, maybe a bit of guilt."

"I cannot do what you decree. It is beyond my abilities."

"So, you're afraid." The voice made a clucking sound. "What happened to good ol' fashioned nobility?"

"I cannot do this!"

"You mean that you will not do it. There's a world of difference."

He was right. Indecision warred within Gerta and she turned to pace the chamber. She dreaded what Cai would endure in that cave, yet at the same time, she knew what would be demanded of her if he survived.

Did her compassion extend to the sacrifice of her gift? What would Isold have done? Gerta knew, which only fed her guilt.

The shadow spoke with easy confidence. "So, let's walk through this one. The sorcerer from whom you could learn a million things—give or take—could very well die because you didn't do anything to aid him, and it would be your fault because you summoned him in the first place. That would be dirty pool, no matter how you look at it."

"I cannot be responsible for every event!"

He ignored her outburst. "So, Cai dies, the Cath Palug continues to kill, and your father remains in exile, which means that the deal he's already struck with Gundobad will stand. You'd get to stay in this fabulous place for the rest of your life, with Sigismund on top every night. The thing is, you might not live that long, so maybe it's worth it."

"Cease your chatter!"

"How long do you think it's going to take Sigismund to figure out how to get in here? He's not the sharpest tack in the box, but it's not a really tough problem. He should be able to manage a rape pretty soon now, and that would pretty much end the stand-off. You can only lose your chastity once, after all, and once it's gone, it's gone."

"You are impertinent!"

"Oh, come on, Gerta, why else did you bar the door?"

"I must protect my chastity."

"Yeah, from Sigismund. Tell me, did those bruises heal?"

Gerta's hand rose to her upper arm of its own volition. "You cannot know this. It was resolved between my father and Sigismund's father, Gundobad. The wergild was paid for the insult Sigismund made to me."

"And then the deal was cut. He's going to have you, probably tonight, unless the Cath Palug dies."

Gerta turned away. "Cai might triumph over the Cath Palug."

"Okay, I can work with that. Let's imagine that Cai does win, but he's in pretty rough shape, isn't he? He'd probably be so damaged that some other guy could beat him to the punch, could come trotting to your father and pretend that he had killed the Cath Palug, and your father would then give you away to an imposter. Much as I admire a little opportunism, you're selling yourself short here."

Gerta felt the color drain from her face. It was all too plausible.

"But, you're right, Gerta, it's a much better plan to just stay here, to just wait for Sigismund to take down the door."

"You are sardonic."

"You're forgetting that power comes from making your own choices and then doing something about them." His voice lowered. "You're forgetting that redemption has to be earned."

It was unthinkable that she could confront the Cath Palug and win, but then, maybe there was something unnatural about the beast. She had conjured a spell of power, Cai had said so. Did she even know the fullness of her abilities?

Gerta turned to the window, her eyes widening when she saw the frost that had inexplicably filled the valley. She clutched the sill with cold fingers, astonished at the scene before her.

"Well, I'll give you the inside story, Gerta, seeing as I can see the proverbial writing on the wall here. The only man who can kill the Cath Palug is our pal Cai, but he can only do it with your aid. You've got to do it as a team, and I'm here to coach."

Gerta's gaze flicked over the valley, distracted by the sight. The fog was inexplicably gone, the valley garnished with hoarfrost. Every branch glistened, every tree had become a jewel, and the very snow sparkled as if strewn with gems. Icicles hung on the edges of the roof, the first blush of daylight making them tinkle and twinkle. It was both beautiful and unnatural.

Treacherous.

"But it is May," she said, almost to herself. "It is too late for such cold." It should have been a magical sight, the glitter of all that ice, but there were shadows within it that made Gerta dread its intent.

Could ice have intent? Could ice have malice? She would never have given such a thought credence, not before this morning. She would never have thought fog could speak with her, either, or that the mirror could be used by another to address her.

"It's the ice, you see," the intruder said, as if that was a reasonable reply and indeed, it made a certain sense. "Ice is at the root of everything, and the Cath Palug is just one of its instruments."

Menace carried from the ice as surely as the scent of wood smoke assails the nose, as surely as the unseen presence of the Cath Palug made men's hearts beat in fear. Gerta felt the intruder join her and glanced sidelong, barely catching the glimmer of his silhouette.

The hairs on her left side, those closest to him, stood slightly and prickled, as they would when changing garb in midwinter, as if there was something about him that could quicken her very flesh. She had a definite sense that she stood too close to something she should not approach at all.

Yet like a moth lured to the flame, she was tempted to move even closer. What she did was hold her ground, savoring the tingle that danced through her body. "You brought this ice," she accused, recalling the dark shimmer of the fog and seeing a similar shimmer in the hoarfrost.

"Not exactly," he said. "It followed me. Unfortunately."

"From where?"

A smile filled his words. "Well, that would be the point, wouldn't it?"

She could almost see him, leaning his elbows on the sill. He was handsome in a darker way than Cai, but shared that man's confidence. He was sure of himself and sure of his own allure. He smiled at her and there was something wicked in that expression, something so alluring that Gerta recognized it as dangerous.

Then she blinked and could not see him clearly any longer.

Her breath caught in her throat. She could smell him beside her, though, the warmth of another presence, the heat of a man in her own chamber. She could feel the leap of her pulse, the awareness of his presence in every fiber of her being, and she knew that the spell he wrought was one to which all women were susceptible.

Surely she was more clever than that?

"You are more substantial than you were," she said.

"You're yearning. Lust isn't as good as the real thing, but I can make it work."

"I feel no lust for fog!"

"What about Cai?"

Gerta shivered and averted her gaze.

"You've got to realize that a fear unfaced is one unvanquished," he said gently. "And a foul deed for which you have not done compense, is a burden of guilt upon your back. I should know."

Then he moved away, the fog dispersing around the floor of her chamber, as if granting her time to consider her course. He could well afford to grant her that time, for he was right. As much as she would have liked to deny it, Gerta truly had no choice but to aid Cai.

Perhaps she would fail.

Perhaps she would not lose her gift in the end.

It did not matter. She had to aid him, even knowing what the price to herself might be.

Gerta had no idea what she might need to vanquish the Cath Palug, but there was little she had to take. Her father had sold what few trinkets they had had to maintain a vestige of his kingdom for as long as possible after the arrival of the Cath Palug.

It had not been sufficient to keep them from becoming exiles, from seeking Gundobad's hospitality. Gerta opened the trunk and removed the fur-lined cloak she had stored there for the summer, donning it with impatient gestures. She belted it around her waist, then pulled on her thick boots. She had two knives and took them both, placing them in a sack along with a few other belongings, a comb, another shift, a partial loaf of bread she had not eaten yet. She lifted the mirror, intending to take it, and the intruder cleared its throat.

"Not that. Don't take that."

"It is my tool."

"It can be used against you."

Gerta gave the fog a quelling glance, then shoved the mirror into her sack. She did not imagine his sigh of forbearance. "You must tell me of this ice, so that I understand it better. A foe cannot be defeated which is not understood."

"The ice is only a tool, or a weapon at best."

"To understand a weapon is to better understand the one who wields it." She granted him a glance. "And perhaps it can be turned against the one who wields it."

"Fair enough." There was a smile in his voice that made Gerta feel proud of herself.

Despite the lack of a clear plan, she felt a shiver of anticipation at the boldness of her quest. She would depart with no more than a shadow as her companion, albeit a male shadow, to aid another seer. She had undertaken no deed so daring since Isold's demise.

In the absence of Isold, Gerta had not known who might have aided her if she overstepped herself. She wondered if Cai had summoned her because he had suspected he might have need of aid. But she could not reconcile that with his complete confidence.

Nay, she believed that he had summoned her so that she could witness his triumph. Had the battle gone awry because he had expended too much of his power to command her mirror? The prospect of her own apparently infinite culpability gave haste to Gerta's gestures.

She turned to the portal with more determination than she

might have expected, but the voice sounded suddenly close by her ear.

"Not that way. The last thing we need is Sigismund to tag along."

"But there is no other way."

He laughed. "Isn't there?"

Gerta felt herself caught around the waist, as if a man pulled her fast to his side with one strong arm. In a heartbeat, she was aware of the intruder's height, of his heat, of the pulse of his heart so close to her own.

A man held her against his body! His strength was undeniable as was the curious rush of pleasure that slid over her flesh. Her breast was crushed against him, and the sensation was not unpleasant. Indeed, her body responded to the feel of him with enthusiasm.

"Unhand me! It is forbidden for a man to touch a seer. You will be compelled to pay the wergild..." Gerta struggled to no avail. Her captor carried her easily to the lip of the window, caught her knees beneath his other arm, then leapt into the very air.

They plummeted like a pair of stones.

He would see her killed! Gerta parted her lips to scream but made nary a sound.

For her captor's lips closed over her own in a possessive kiss.

For a dangerous moment, Gerta was shocked to immobility, which only granted her assailant the chance to deepen his kiss. His embrace fanned the flame that Cai had awakened. His tongue found its way between her lips and Gerta gasped, then was amazed at the pleasurable sensation he granted with his caress.

Then she pushed him away, realizing her own weakness. She had but a moment to hate his low laugh of triumph before she realized that they did not fall any longer.

They moved parallel to the ground, over the roofs of the huts clustered outside Gundobad's portal. Gerta frowned. She heard the beat of leathery wings and looked up. She could see her captor faintly, mischief gleaming in his eyes, his smile flashing white. She dared not look long upon him, for there was something in his avidity that stung her eyes.

It was when she looked down, to the shadow they cast upon the ice, that her heart fairly stopped. A shimmering dark shadow possessed of leathery wings held her captive. Gerta thought of predators returning from the hunt, of owls and hawks.

What manner of monster had claimed her, and what was his intent in truth? She did not even know his name, much less his nature.

Suddenly, her choice to aid Cai seemed wrought of folly alone.

Gerta fought with renewed vigor in her terror, though to no discernible effect. In fact, her captor held her more tightly, which only reminded her of Sigismund's recent assault. Gerta twisted and writhed, nigh mad in her fear. Her captor swore mightily, and their course over the valley dipped low, but he held fast to her waist.

"Unhand me!" Gerta cried. They had already flown past the cluster of huts and ascended rapidly to the pass at the far end of the valley.

"Remarkable as it may seem, you're more useful alive." He sounded as if he spoke through gritted teeth.

"I demand that you release me!"

"I think you're right," he agreed with sudden amiability. Gerta did not have time to distrust his new tone. "You're too much trouble."

And he let her go.

Gerta screamed as she fell toward the earth. There was no one this far from the village to hear her, no one who might aid her—even if it were possible to do so. She tumbled earthward with fearsome speed, her hair whipping around her face, her skirts blowing above her knees. She had no care for modesty, for she knew that she would be broken in a thousand places upon impact.

She screamed for it was all she could do.

Suddenly she heard a swish of wings and, not the height of two men from the ground, her captor plucked her out of the air. She clung to him, her breathing ragged and her pulse racing, and he carried her ever upward.

"Appreciate me now?"

"You did that apurpose," Gerta accused, once she had recovered her breath. "You meant to put fear within me…"

"You've got to admit, it's got its uses."

"You are a wretch, and a cur. You are scoundrel and…"

"Look, Gerta, babe, not to be rude, but that's all old news."

Gerta closed her mouth, fumed and hung on to him in silence. Her captor eventually landed, stumbling only slightly on the shimmer of ice, and set her on her feet. They were at the end of the valley; the castle and village no more than distant shadows. He exhaled mightily and might have made some unwelcome comment, but Gerta swung her fist in his direction.

"Cur!" she cried, but her hand swept through the cloud that was her captor with no resistance. At most, she felt a chill on her flesh.

He laughed.

"No man shall touch a seer! No man shall embrace a seer, lest her gift be sacrificed. So is it decreed within the laws of every land."

"Gerta, hon, we've been over this. I'm not a man, so you've got nothing to worry about on that score." He sounded tired, and Gerta felt a prickle of concern for him, one that she quickly dismissed. He exhaled mightily and seemed to dim slightly. "Gotta rest a minute, Gerta. I haven't manifested in a long time. It's a lot harder than I remember." He sighed. "Or maybe I'm just getting too old for this intervention crap."

As she was coming to expect, Gerta did not fully understand him and that did little to reassure her.

He seemed to peer at her, though his features faded in and out of view. "You've got to weigh, what, one forty? One fifty? There's a lot of you to love, Gerta. No wonder I'm bagged. Trust me to glom onto the substantial ones."

Though she did not understand his measure, his tone told her that he did not truly flatter her. Gerta straightened. "I am robust, which is a mark of health. The feeble do not survive."

"I guess they wouldn't in these conditions."

Gerta frowned, for she saw naught amiss with her living conditions beyond the presence of Gundobad and Sigismund.

He continued. "Being a robust woman, don't you think you

should see your royal lineage continued by having kids yourself?"

"I do not understand. How would my possession of young goats continue the royal lineage?"

"Sorry. Children. I meant your bearing children."

"To be a seer is a greater calling."

"Yeah, I see that your father believes that. I don't think everyone's on board with this rationale, Gerta, and if you're going to give it up, why not give it up to one of the good guys?"

He did not seem to expect a reply and truly Gerta did not have one. She looked around herself, felt her belly grumble, and had a thought. "It is three days' walk to Lake Lausanne, where the Cath Palug holds Cai captive. If you fly us there, we could arrive more quickly to assist him."

"Assuming I could fly that far. Unless, of course, you wanted to do the horizontal mambo. Maybe a couple of times. That would give me the stamina for a long flight."

"I do not understand."

"I told you, Gerta, I get power from lust. Your lust. Kisses are well and good, but for that kind of effort, I'll need sex. With you. Multiple times."

Gerta took a step backward in shock. "Nay!"

"Then do me a favor and at least fantasize a bit about our boy Cai. You're going to need me when we get there, and the stronger I am, the easier this whole thing will be."

"But Cai..."

"Will have to hang on, all by himself. Give him some credit. I think he can do it. And unless you put out, we don't have a lot of choice."

Gerta turned away, unable the accept the burden demanded of her to right her error.

Meanwhile, her companion straightened. She found it was easiest to perceive him from the periphery of her vision, as if glimpsing him from the corner of her eye. He was taller than she, those large leathery wings arching high over his shoulders. He patted her shoulder companionably. "If it makes you feel better, I didn't expect otherwise. I think we should arrive in time."

"And you?"

"I'll drift along. Don't mind if I fade in and out. I'll be here."

He grinned at her. "And remember, you can always make this easier for both of us."

"Willingly? Never!"

He chuckled. "Too bad you're so cute when you're outraged. It makes it tougher for me to behave myself."

She felt a fingertip flick across the tip of her nose.

Gerta took a step away from him, disconcerted. "What are you? Who are you?"

"Well, that's a long story."

He did not seem inclined to share the tale. He was a sorcerer, Gerta decided, a sorcerer who could depart from his body. Isold had told her of such power. Gerta had always suspected that it was no more than a tall tale, but here was evidence of its truth.

Perhaps she could persuade him to teach her this trick.

"The ice then," she said with resolve. "You must tell me about the ice as we walk, as you insist it is at root of everything."

"I thought you might have more interesting questions now."

Gerta did not misunderstand the undertone of his comment. His voice was low, teasing, as if he deliberately coaxed that new flame within her. Her lips were burning yet from his audacious kiss, and though she had fought his embrace, she felt a heat within her that she had not possessed before.

He had stirred something to life, with his words and his touch, and Gerta doubted it would ever be fully quelled again. It had been easier to reject intimacy with conviction before she had sampled the pleasure it could bring. True to his earlier comment, her companion seemed to have gained vigor from their embrace, for he was more clearly discernible than he had been yet.

He seemed to float beside her, a dark shimmer just beyond the edge of her vision. Gerta strode toward the summit of the pass with confidence, ignoring the weight of his gaze and the resulting heat of her flushing cheeks.

"The ice. How is it at root of everything?" she asked. "And what does it mean for Cai?"

"I don't suppose you might be Christian?"

"Of course, I am Christian. We were immersed in the river at my father's command, after our arrival at Gundobad's court and his insistence that we join his faith before joining his household."

"Baptized," her companion provided. "You were baptized."

"Aye, that was his word."

"Don't suppose you had catechism class?"

She glanced his way. "I do not understand this catechism."

"Lessons about the faith."

Gerta waved a dismissive hand. She had never been very interested in the teachings of Gundobad's bishop, and to be fair, he had never been interested in what she might have taught him.

"Didn't the bishop tell you any stories?"

"Oh, he told one, but I thought little of it." She felt her companion's expectancy but shook her head. "It is your task to recount a tale first. There will be time aplenty for mine."

He laughed lightly. "Fair enough. You sure it's this way?"

"Do you suggest that I do not know the way to my father's abode?"

"No, no, it just looks like a rough road."

"All journeys of merit are arduous."

"Well, ain't that the truth."

Gerta was glad that she was young and strong. She could walk two days with little food, for they would cross mountain streams where she could drink fresh water. And by midday on the morrow, they would reach the hut of the old woodcutter. Gerta could walk far on the promise of old Egan's company, his savory cooking and his warm hut. There was a man who had served her father well, a man with a heart filled with kindness. It would be good to see him again.

Gerta walked more quickly at the prospect.

It took a while for her companion to find the thread of his tale, but Gerta did not prod him further. She concentrated on keeping to the path and keeping her footing, for the ice was spread thickly and the slope inclined.

"You see, your bishop could have told you stories that would have answered a lot of this, but since he didn't—you know, you could report him to the big guy for that—I'll have to start at the beginning. Or close to it."

Gerta walked in silence, fairly hearing her companion think.

The tale the bishop had told had supposedly been of the beginning, and she wondered whether her companion would tell the same tale.

"Once, there were beings, let's call them angels for the sake of argument."

"Angels," Gerta echoed, trying this strange new word upon her tongue. This could be no tale she knew.

"These angels existed at the beginning of all time. For a while there, God considered them to be his first and greatest creation."

"God?"

"The force that or who created everything, the world and everything in it, the stars and the sun. The force that exercises supreme authority. Your bishop called him God, didn't he?"

"I paid little heed to the bishop. Though it is courteous to acknowledge the gods in which other peoples believe, but I do not believe in this God." Gerta studied the frozen ground. "I believe in the sun and the moon, the earth and the sky, the power within us and some power without, the cycle of death and birth that occurs every year."

"Fair enough," the voice agreed. "What about good and evil?"

Gerta shrugged. "There is good and evil in all of us and in all things. The balance or lack of it is part of life."

"Phew! I could really get to like this non-Abrahamic religion thing, you know? The whole polarization of good and evil has always been a bit tough for me to swallow. Dualism is too simplistic, too straightforward to have much to do with the real world. I've never liked it."

Gerta said naught, for he might as well have been speaking the language of foreigner.

"I'll guess that the Burgundians are Arian Christians, isn't that right?"

Gerta frowned. "It sounds familiar. Would some Arius have been their leader?"

"Bingo! Well, consider yourself smart not to have bought into their whole game. They're going to be ousted as heretics soon and it won't be pretty."

"I see," Gerta said, although she did not.

"Okay, so back to our story. Essentially, the bloom faded

from the rose and God decided to go with another creation. People. He made men and women."

"I know this tale of God's creation of men. Adam and Eve were in the tale recounted by the bishop."

"Ah, so he told you about the Garden of Eden."

"'In the beginning, God created the heaven and the earth,'" Gerta recounted, then shook her head. "But God wished for people to be serfs in service to him, as if they had been conquered in battle."

"Why do you say that?"

"Because He refused them knowledge and the understanding of good and evil. He wished to keep them in ignorance of their own nature and their place in the world. It is not natural for people to refuse to learn or to be denied the opportunity. It is what one does with serfs, to keep them from lusting beyond their place." She could not keep herself from sneering. "This bishop blamed women, blamed Eve..."

"Eve and her temptation. You know, I always liked Eve. It was more than her being such a hot babe; she had what the French are gonna call a 'certain *je ne sais quoi*.'" He made a sound, like the smacking of lips, which Gerta ignored.

"...for taking of the fruit that was left in her very sight. By why would it have been left before her, if it was not hers to claim? If you do not wish any soul to covet some possession you own, you do not display it to them. You do not show it to them and forbid them to desire it. This is not reasonable. Treasures should be hidden, their merits shared with a select few."

"Sounds like Gundobad's logic to me. His son should get to have you and you should pay for the sin of tempting Sigismund's lust by the sacrifice of your gift. Blame it on the women. It's an old game, almost as old as me, if it makes you feel any better."

But Gerta did not care about this assertion. She spun to confront her companion. "How do you know so much of the details of my life?"

III

know more than you ever want to, Gerta honey. I really hope that you don't have any affection for Sigismund..."

"Not I!"

"Good, because this guy's bad to the bone, you know. He's going to kill his own son one of these days." He grimaced. "He's not really a primo catch, if you know what I mean."

Gerta was not surprised by these tidings. "His father Gundobad is mad and violent," she whispered, fearing to be overheard even so far from listening ears.

"You've nailed it in one. Not everything passed from father to son is worth keeping." To Gerta's relief, her companion left that notion alone, for it was troubling to find herself in such vehement agreement with him. "So, back to our story. God thought his new work was a triumph and so He wanted the angels to serve people."

"So, they would be the serfs!" Gerta shook her head. "This is some God who desires only such service from his creations."

"Don't all gods desire service?"

"Respect, this they all demand. Flattery and offerings, not slavish obedience." Gerta took a deep breath, seeking the means to explain the difference. "The old gods seek deference, but they do not command mortals. They can do deeds to aid or to plague men, which is why their aid is requested, but they do not dictate our choices."

"What about fate?"

"Who can say? It might be that the nature of a man so shapes his choices that his destiny can be determined from his birth."

"Character and deed perfectly entangled," her companion mused. "But then, who created the character of the individual?"

"Who can say? There are mysteries not ours to examine."

"So, it might have been your destiny to come along with me?

This journey might be the culmination of everything you've learned so far in this life?"

"I do not doubt that you have tricked me," Gerta said sternly. "If naught else, you did not reveal your nature truly to me, not before I had no choice but to continue."

"You could turn back. It's not that far to the village. You could be there by sunset."

Gerta glanced over her shoulder, half-tempted. They had climbed almost to the pass through the mountains and she was breathing heavily from her exertions. In truth, they had come farther than she had realized, for she had been so interested in their conversation. The sky was a clear blue, the sunlight making the ice sparkle like gems.

Her father was far behind her, the father who had betrayed her. So was her betrothed, the man who would rape her daily once it was his right.

Gerta turned her back upon the valley she had come to think of as her home and began to climb onward. It was surprisingly easy to do. She recalled the blue of Cai's eyes and felt an unwelcome thrill of anticipation. The path became steeper from here and she bent herself to the task of climbing, savoring her own strength. She felt alive as she had never before.

"Not going back?" her companion taunted.

"I owe it to another sorcerer to grant my aid in his distress," she said stoically. "I need to repair what I have set awry."

"And that's your sole motivation, is it?" her companion teased. "You know, I think you just want to know how Cai tastes."

Gerta's face burned. She stared at the snow before her and marched onward, ignoring the shadow that drifted behind her. The silence pressed against her ears and she suspected that he knew what she was thinking.

She was thinking of his earlier comments. She was thinking about the surety in Cai's gaze. She was recalling how her mouth had gone dry beneath his perusal; she was recalling how alluring she had felt as he looked upon her. She was wondering about the weight of a man's hands upon her body, the dance of his tongue with hers. That heat in her belly that resulted from this consideration was not unpleasant. She recalled her captor's kiss and was suffused with heat. That had not been so difficult to endure.

Isold had taught her that the passion kindled by men was a fleeting pleasure, one that would cost Gerta the greater power of her gift. Yet here she strode toward a man intent upon claiming her, a man who understood the price she would have to pay and would demand it of her all the same. Instead of fleeing Cai, she went to his aid.

Was that the true danger of her journey? Gerta did not know, but all the same, she did not feel that she could turn back. She knew that she would dream of Cai being dragged into the Cath Palug's cave. She knew that she would imagine the torment he endured there. She guessed she would know the moment that he died.

And she knew that if she remained at the court of Burgundy, she would not be able to live with the fact she had done nothing to aid him. Her gift, it seemed, was forfeit anyway, and she chose to surrender it to Cai instead of letting Sigismund steal it.

She strode toward the pass, undeterred by the deep snow, not sparing Burgundy a backward glance. Her future lay ahead. Gerta was certain of it, though she could not guess what her future might be.

"You spoke of angels," she reminded her companion sternly, wanting an escape from her thoughts as much as his tale. "Continue your tale, if you please."

She half-expected him to deny her, as he seemed inclined to provoke her. Instead he said nothing. She glanced his way and was shocked by how vividly clear he had become. He was even whistling slightly beneath his breath.

He winked at her, a vision of masculine pride. "That's the spirit, Gerta, babe. It's a rotten job thawing you out for Cai, but somebody's got to do it." He seemed to be enjoying himself overmuch, to her thinking. He flicked his tongue at her, both bold and beguiling. "Whatcha going to dream about tonight?" he whispered, eyes shining. "Maybe we can get in a little practice before the main event?"

Cheeks burning, Gerta turned away from him and stumbled

onward in the snow.

☙❧

Only a few moments passed before Gerta's companion resumed his tale. "Well, as I was saying, God wanted the angels to pay homage to man. And some of the angels refused. When He demanded that they bow down, that they kneel to the first man and woman, these angels flat-out refused. They said no."

"And so they were punished," Gerta guessed. "For God did not like to be defied. It is the nature of kings to dislike defiance."

"I guess it is. And so the angels who refused were to be banished..."

"They were to be made outlanders, unwelcome at any hearth."

"Exactimundo. And as you might imagine, some of them felt this wasn't too fair of a judgment, because after all, they had been created first. It seemed that they should be first in God's affections, and really, comparatively, they were much finer beasts."

"What did they look like?"

"They are large and radiant." There was admiration, even awe, in his tone, and Gerta wondered whether he had seen these beings. "They are made of light, not flesh or the clay of the earth."

"And their language? What does it sound like?"

"They have none. They each understand the thoughts of another of their kind and immediately."

"Ah, Isold told me of this power. Some men can do this as well."

"I guess they've learned. At any rate, these angels wanted to appeal God's decision..."

"Kings dislike a challenge to their authority." Gerta shook her head disapprovingly. "Such deeds lead often to war and bloodshed."

"Well, war is what happened, and to make a long story short, the defiant angels lost so they were banished, as per the original decree."

"And anger burned hot within them," Gerta guessed. "For they believed yet that they had been treated with injustice."

"You're good at this. It's as if you know this story already."

"It is not that uncommon a tale. The angels are different, of course, but men and kings have such battles all the time."

He muttered something that sounded to Gerta like "Isn't that special?" although she could make no sense of such a comment. She chose to ignore it, as she ignored so much of his talk.

After a moment, he continued. "So, one of them decided that the problem really was God's, that God had failed to see the weaknesses of His new creation and in so doing, failed to appreciate the marvel of angels."

"This is rational. Men and women are filled with weaknesses, and we know from the tale of Adam and Eve that this God is not enamored of those who succumb to the weakness of temptation."

"So, this angel—a fallen angel if you will—created a looking glass."

Gerta shivered, though she could not imagine why and felt suddenly aware of the weight of her bronze mirror within her bag. "I do not understand this looking glass."

"Think of your mirror, and how it shows what is far away. This glass was similar, but clear."

Gerta struggled to envision such a device and failed.

"Imagine that you could cut water," he suggested. "Imagine that you could cut a slice of water..."

"Ah, or rock crystal!"

"Right! Now imagine that you could hold it up to your eye and look through it, and see matters that you could not see without it."

"Sorcery," Gerta said flatly.

"Some called it that. This looking glass showed wickedness where good was only apparent otherwise. It showed the truth, and it showed that men were far less ideal than God imagined. It showed the dark impulses of their hearts, it showed their secret desires and it showed their envy of each other. It showed the mingling of good and evil everywhere. And so, because the glass showed the truth and the fallen angels believed that it would persuade God of his error, they seized the mirror and flew as one toward God to show it to him."

"Flew?"

"Angels have always had wings."

"You are one of these angels," Gerta guessed. He did not

answer her so she assumed she was mistaken.

"The glass was heavy, though, heavier than expected, and the journey was farther than the angels remembered from their fall. And so it was that they dropped the glass and it fell to the earth— much, in fact, as they had done. But unlike them, the glass shattered into thousands of tiny shards and scattered in the wind. In that instant, the glass was spread throughout the domains of men and even beyond, tiny dark slivers of it wreaking havoc wherever they fell."

"How so?"

"Many men had a shard of glass stick in their eye, and afterward, in all that they saw, they perceived only the evil within it. And some people had a splinter of ice lodge within their heart, turning it to ice and making them scornful of their fellows. Some foolishly thought the piece they found to be a pretty treasure. They turned it in the light, looking through it at the world, unaware of how it poisoned their view of all they saw.

"And in the wake of this, men tasted the fullness of their own evil: they killed each other over trifles, they let envy breed within their hearts, they let lust guide their actions. They forgot all they had been taught about compassion and respect for their fellows, and each cared only for himself." He paused. "And they called it truth."

Gerta considered this. "I thought it was the fall of man from the Garden of Eden that was responsible for all evil, that Eve bore the burden of banishing all of us from the Garden."

"And the glass only makes it worse. No illusions about what you're facing, not with the glass."

"Is this glass yet in the world?"

"Of course. It's what followed me; it's what drives Gundobad. The Cath Palug was wrought to serve it..."

"Like the serpent in the garden."

"No!" her companion said sharply. "Not at all like the serpent."

"It seems to me to be much the same," Gerta said, simply because the notion provoked him.

"It's not the same at all!" He seemed to take a steadying breath, though precisely what had vexed him, Gerta could not guess. "The Cath Palug does what it does. It doesn't think or weigh possibilities: it was created for a single purpose and it fulfills it. If anything, it has more in common with the apple. It's an instrument, or a vehicle, but not a force in itself."

Gerta struggled with the import of this. "Then there is a greater force, one which created the Cath Palug, just as the apple was created as a tool."

"I tell you, you are good at this. Are you sure you don't know this story already?"

Gerta shook her head. "But what purpose does the Cath Palug serve? The death of men cannot be of so much merit as that."

"Well, they're not all supposed to die. It just forgets itself and gets kind of carried away, especially when it's hungry."

Gerta frowned in recollection. "When my father still held his kingdom, the Cath Palug was more inclined to maim men than to destroy them. It killed children and small animals, but oft let injured men escape. We thought then that its power had limits, but this is clearly not so."

"It was doing what it was made to do. The Cath Palug's claws and teeth are fashioned of that dark glass and its purpose is to see that glass spread among men."

Gerta halted suddenly, remembering how the Cath Palug's claws had torn into Cai's chest. "There is a piece of glass in Cai's heart," she guessed with horror.

As much as she hoped her companion would deny this, he nodded. "And another in his eye."

"But why did this not kill him?"

"Because neither the Cath Palug nor its mistress wishes for him to die."

"Mistress?"

"The glass has been claimed by a queen, or maybe she's become a queen by mustering its power. She's gathering all of the shards and piecing together the original glass once again. Most die soon after the shard embeds itself in their flesh, but Cai is stronger than most."

"Because he is a sorcerer himself."

"And that makes him useful."

"How so?"

"She's harnessing his power for her own, and he hasn't the will or even the knowledge to fight her. The glass makes her appear most beauteous to him."

"Surely he cannot willingly serve a woman with evil intent for him?"

"Beauty is its own temptation."

Gerta quickened her steps in her concern, then stopped and pivoted so abruptly that her companion would have collided with her had he been human. Instead, he passed directly through her, leaving her shivering and slightly disoriented.

"Don't do that again, all right?" he said, apparently similarly affected.

"But how do you know so much of this glass?" Gerta demanded. "Does she hunt you, as well?" Gerta's voice hardened. "Or are you one of her minions, sent to beguile me?"

He laughed heartily. "No, she knows little of me, as yet, which is why I can help you."

Gerta's eyes narrowed. "But then, why did the hoarfrost follow you?"

He grinned. "Because it remembers me, as surely as men and angels recall God." He paused, as if willing her to guess, but Gerta did not dare to voice her thought. "Because I made it, Gerta. I made the glass in my desire to show God his error."

❧☙

Gerta could not look upon him, not with such bright pride in his eyes and in his stance, not in combination with the travesty he had confessed. He was responsible for the glass, and thus for the Cath Palug and the horror that beast had visited upon so many people. He was responsible for Cai's fate, because he had created the means by which Cai could be injured and trapped.

Sickened, Gerta pivoted and made haste to the pass. She could hate her companion for his deeds, but then, had she not made a similar transgression? Or two?

The way became more arduous then and Gerta took the opportunity to cease their conversation. The snow was deeper toward the summit of the pass, deeper than she could have possibly expected so late in the spring. There should have been no snow, even a scattering of flowers. What force seized the land and made it unfamiliar?

Gerta thought that perhaps she could guess.

The valley rose to a sharp divide, high above them. This was the pass proper from one valley to another, and Gerta knew it, though she had not come this way since her father's passage into exile, since they had been driven from their home by the Cath Palug.

The way was steep and slippery. As she put one foot after the other, focusing on this step instead of the sum of the climb ahead, she wondered whether they would have come this way if she and her father had known more of Gundobad's nature.

Would it have been better for her father to have let Gundobad die on that battlefield years before?

Gerta was shocked by the audacity of her thoughts. The sun was mercilessly bright, the sky utterly clear, the air piercing cold. Gerta imagined that her breath turned to ice as soon as she exhaled, and surely, it made a frosty cloud before her. There was frost upon the front of her cloak, ice formed of her own breath.

"Does it seem colder to you?" her companion asked.

Gerta nodded, grasped the rocks and pulled herself to the summit of the pass. "I expect no less at this height," she managed to say. She breathed deeply after her climb and the cold air stabbed inside her like a thousand icy daggers.

The view from the high point of the pass was stunning, exhilarating, and she was suddenly glad that she had made the climb. The valley claimed by Gundobad was spread before her, his abode barely discernible in the distance. The entire valley was covered in a shimmering, glittering blanket of snow, so fresh and so white that it hurt the eyes to look upon it. From here it looked to be untrammeled, pristine.

"Perfect," Gerta said softly, seduced by the sight.

"Bite your tongue! That's what she wants you to think!"

Gerta glanced about herself in confusion. "But the snow is beautiful, despite being out of season..."

"It is death. You're looking upon death not perfection, though there's one who would like you to confuse the two."

Gerta frowned. "Who?"

"The foe you go to confront, of course. Some call her the Snow Queen." Apparently contenting himself with that ominous comment, her companion moved ahead. He moved with a lithe grace that was more apparent as he became more substantial, a lean muscled strength that was appealing. He might have been nude, Gerta could not be certain, for there was a brightness about him that made it difficult to look upon the details of his form for long.

Her lips tingled and she turned her back upon him, feigning a last look at the valley behind them. She licked her lips without intending to do so and found an unfamiliar taste upon her own mouth. That reminded her of his outrageous comment and she wondered how Cai would taste.

How would he kiss? Would he claim her or would he coax her?

How long would it take her gift to abandon her? Gerta pulled her mirror from her satchel hastily, needing to affirm the presence of her gift. Her heart skipped as she turned the mirror upward, for she feared that she would see nothing within it any longer.

A woman's face was there, the sight so clear, the woman so present, that Gerta jumped. The woman smiled at the sight of her, as if in welcome, as if she could see Gerta as Cai had done.

There was something familiar about her, though Gerta could not immediately identify what. Her skin was fair, her flowing hair as white as the snow, her lips as red as blood. She was beautiful in a haughty way, alluring yet distant.

It was her eyes that made Gerta pull back: they were oddly pale, a silvery blue that put Gerta in mind of a wolf, or ice upon a frozen stream. There was something hungry about her smile, something that made Gerta wish she had not looked in the mirror in the first place.

"Begone," she commanded in a whisper, but the woman's smile only broadened.

She raised a finger, beckoned as if confident that she would be obeyed. Only then did she fade from sight.

Gerta swallowed in fear. She knew she had not dismissed or frightened the woman away. The woman had left of her own choice. And the woman had looked upon her, Gerta knew it well, just as Cai had done.

She sat down for a moment in the snow, fetching the bread from her bag to cover the fact that she was thinking. It was impossible for another to command her mirror. She knew this as surely as she knew her own name. Yet two sorcerers in one day—for the woman could be naught else—had seized control of Gerta's mirror.

Perhaps it was not truly her mirror any longer.

Perhaps this was part of how the gift was lost.

Perhaps there was more in this world than she knew. Gerta shuddered, for she did not know that any sorcerer would aid her if she overstepped herself in this quest: Isold was dead and Cai was enchanted, and she knew no others of her kind. Gerta ate the bread, not truly tasting it, then stood and made to climb again.

There was naught for it. What she had begun would only be resolved by continuing, by aiding Cai.

From that point, the path ascended only slightly, winding a course around the rocky outcroppings of the mountains. They would not see the vale on the opposite side until the following morning, perhaps midday. In better weather, this pass was rife with bandits, but that was one threat they would not face. So few used the pass in these days that the bandits had abandoned it as well.

Gerta hastened after the shadow of her companion, half-expecting that he would know what she had done.

"Having a last look?" he asked, and it took Gerta a moment to realize the ambiguity of his question.

"The vale of Burgundy has been my home these past four years," she prevaricated. "It is not so easy to turn away."

"I'd think it would be easy to walk away from Gundobad and Sigismund." His words slowed, deepened, warning Gerta that she might not like his next words. "Or maybe it's your father who's easy to leave behind, given how he's let you down."

Gerta did not answer him, for it was not his affair. "You have not yet told me your name."

"So many names, so much time." His tone was cavalier. "Maybe I should let you pick one from the wide and varied selection."

"You make a jest of a simple question."

"Because it's not really a simple question. But never mind, I'll pick one for you, one that has some resonance for you and your times."

"You make it sound as if you have known other times."

"Well, I have. That's the problem with being immortal. Actually, seeing other times isn't the problem—getting them mixed up is the issue. I'd love to have a reference book, you know, maybe something called The Evolution of Everything, so I could avoid anachronism and embarrassing mistakes. It would have to be a slender volume, so I could sling it along easily on my travels."

"Anachronism?" Gerta repeated the unfamiliar word with care.

"That's referring to things before they've been invented. Like suggesting that we take the train to your father's realm. The Venice-Simplon Orient Express will be a pretty nifty way to get through these mountains, although really, it will go under them. An engineering marvel and a damn fine way to travel. Beats all this tromping around in the snow, hands down."

"You speak madness. There is no other way to get across this pass. Even a horse must be led. And no man travels under the mountains."

"Well, that's my point. This isn't the time for the Orient Express, though it's the place, or pretty close to it. So, talking about it or even better, taking it, would be anachronistic. I'm good on the big stuff, but every so often something small trips me up. You don't have forks, for example."

"I do not know this word forks."

"They're eating implements, like a little spear. Really good for snagging a piece of meat from the stew without getting gravy on your fingers."

Gerta frowned. "My fingers have always sufficed."

"To each his own. The point is that I know better than to ask you for a fork. It'll be Renaissance Italy before anyone has one.

The big stuff is easy—salt, for example, is a given, any time in Europe after the Romans."

Gerta's belly growled. "You could cease to speak of food and much associated with it. It would make the journey pass more amiably."

"Hungry, are you?"

"Are you not?"

"There are a few advantages to not being wrought of flesh. Not many, but that's one of them. Never hungry. Never have any results of having eaten, if you know what I mean. That basic biology stuff has nothing to do with me, and that's pretty much okay by me." He heaved a breath. "Sex, now, there's some biology that could work for me. Do you realize what a problem it is to have lust but not have any outlet for it?"

"Nay." Gerta spoke crisply, speeding her steps at this awkward topic of conversation. "Tell me your name."

"Let me finish my point. It's the subtle stuff that trips me up. Like sex. What do people think about sex in these times? What's appropriate? Do you even kiss? Cunnilingus or fellatio or neither or both? It's all so complicated and so easy to screw up—pun intended—inadvertently." He sighed. "And usually, sex is a closed subject, a little socially taboo topic, so it's not as if I can just ask anyone."

"Your name," Gerta insisted, impatient with his meaningless chatter. "What is your name?"

"How about Loki? You could call me Loki."

Gerta halted and stared in his direction. "This is your name? You are named for the Norse god of mischief?"

"I've been called that, that's for sure."

Gerta shook her head in astonishment. "But that is audacious beyond belief. It is blasphemy to call a pers—someone—anyone after a god."

"Happens all the time."

"But Loki is not a god whose wrath I would invite with such a jest. He was..."

"What?"

"Unpredictable." Gerta deliberately chose a less potent description than "evil".

Her companion chuckled, the sound coming from everywhere and nowhere. "Trust me, Gerta babe, Loki won't take offense. We've got an old connection. I think it's a good name to use here and now. Kind of ties in with the whole Dark Ages motif." He nodded, seeming to assess it. "It's working for me."

"You speak nonsense again," Gerta said with some exhaustion and began to trudge onward.

"You look tired." He sounded sympathetic, which Gerta distrusted.

"This despite my not having carried a woman of one forty or one fifty."

He laughed. "Tell you what, Gerta, here's a little bonus for you. A frequent traveler upgrade, so to speak."

Gerta ignored him. She was too tired to jest and felt the cold too keenly to find him amusing. Her fingertips were chilled, her toes were cold and the snow was deeper than her knees with ice beneath it.

She made slow progress through the pass. Worse, it was starting to snow. She wondered whether she truly could walk all the way to the woodcutter's hut without rest. To sleep in this cold would be treacherous, for she might never awaken. A sharp fear lent new vigor to her steps.

"You're gonna like this one, Gerta. You see, just around that corner up there is a little hut."

"There is not."

"Oh, it's there. It's off the path a bit, kind of cleverly disguised. It's not really four star accommodation—no in-room mini-bar, for example, or room service, more's the pity—but it's there. And as an extra bonus, a limited time offer, the murderous bandits who lived there are gone, scared off by the lack of business. They did leave behind some dried meat."

Saliva gathered in Gerta's mouth. "You lie. Loki lied all the time and if you are his namesake, then you must lie, too."

"Not this time. Remember that Loki lied when it was useful to lie and he told the truth when that was useful, too."

"Loki used others for his own purposes."

He smiled with dangerous charm. "And you wonder how I got this nickname."

"Show me this hut. Prove to me that you do not lie this time."

"There's a small catch."

Gerta regarded him with narrowed eyes.

"A toll, if you will."

"I knew there would be a trick. Loki was a trickster."

"Well, you can guess my price."

"I will not lie with you."

He laughed merrily. "You've got to love smart women! I'll settle for a kiss, Gerta babe, just one smackeroo. What do you say?"

Gerta clenched her teeth for they threatened to chatter. The snow was falling thickly and the sky was darkening. She heard a distant howl that might have been of a wolf. Loki watched her, eyes a-glitter, smiling with a confidence that made her long to trick him in turn.

"One kiss," she said, holding up her finger. "If you do not lie."

His smile flashed. He darted ahead of her. She was hard-pressed to keep up to him, but then, she supposed he was motivated as she was not.

But when she stood before the hut in truth, Gerta nigh fell to her knees in gratitude. It was here, it was solid, and it was so well-hidden that she would have walked directly past it. There was even a piece of dried meat hanging within it and wood for a fire.

"You did not lie."

"Not this time."

Gerta met the anticipatory gleam in his eyes and felt a tingle within herself. Loki had earned his kiss, and she was not fool enough to deny him his due.

IV

oki was positively gleeful. He hovered close as she kindled a fire, blew in her ear as she ate some of the meat. Fingertips tickled the back of her neck, the occasional kiss landed like a butterfly upon her flesh while she felt the cold's grip upon her ease. He did not leave her be and Gerta knew why; she was delaying the embrace she owed him and he clearly knew as much.

Yet he was content to merely tease her. Sigismund would have cast her to her back already and forced her to surrender, had he had such justification.

Gerta slanted a glance in Loki's direction, noting how his eyes shone. Her lips burned in recollection of his kiss, and she realized that he had not assaulted her. Even when he stole that kiss, he had coaxed her to join him in the pursuit of pleasure.

"You do not simply seize what you believe to be your due," she said, appreciating the difference between him and Sigismund.

"Please," he said, holding a hand over his heart. "I'm not a barbarian." His gaze flicked over her and his smile turned rueful. "Not that there's anything wrong with that."

Gerta poked at the fire, coaxing the flames to burn higher. Smoke unfurled, filling the hut before it found the hole in the roof. "Do you know what occurred in Gundobad's hall?"

"Let's assume that I don't." Gentle fingertips trailed across the back of Gerta's neck, sending a pleasurable tingle over her flesh.

She shoved to her feet and paced. "When the Cath Palug came to my father's realm and proved that it could not be dislodged, we were forced to flee our home. The lands were laid waste; many men had died; the people were dispirited. My father turned to Gundobad, King of Burgundy, because he had once saved Gundobad's life in battle, and so Gundobad owed my father a boon. He agreed to accommodate us, in recognition of that debt." Gerta shuddered. "My father had only fought with Gundobad. He did not know that the man was mad."

Loki watched her closely and she was aware of the heat of his proximity. She strove to not look at his lips.

"Gundobad inherited his throne from his father and was to share authority with his three brothers. He has already murdered his brother, Chilperic, and drowned Chilperic's wife by tying a stone around her neck. It was whispered that she was witness to her husband's death and Gundobad feared her accusation."

"Murdering your family. Nice crowd you're hanging with."

"We learned this after our arrival, but had no place else to go. No one dares defy Gundobad. His other two brothers might as well be serfs for the fawning obedience they show him."

"They're afraid."

"They are wise to be afraid. My father, too, is afraid of Gundobad, for we are securely within his power."

"Yet you defied him, didn't you? I'm thinking that barred door to your chamber wasn't part of the plan."

His gaze was too bright, too perceptive. Gerta swallowed and looked at the floor. "Three days ago, Gundobad declared that my father and I were in his debt, that any boon he owed my father was well paid."

"I'll guess that he made a specific demand to pay that debt."

"Me." Gerta lifted her chin. "He decreed that I should wed his son, Sigismund."

"Daddy's boy?"

"Sigismund desires whatsoever he sees and he has no compunction about using violence to possess what he desires."

"Your father did not decline?"

"He dares not defy his host." Gerta swallowed, for what she had to confess was an error on her part. "But I could not tie myself to Sigismund. I could not surrender myself to violence and sacrifice my gift as well. And so, in my desperation, I did what I had been taught never to do—I used my mirror against its purpose. I tried to summon aid. I sent the call to which Cai responded." She met Loki's gaze steadily. "And in so doing, I summoned the ice, though I never meant to do so, and thus, I summoned you."

"No." Loki shook his head. "Newsflash, Gerta babe: nobody summons me. They can invoke and I will hear, but I'm no dog that comes every time it's called. Self-determination would be my banner. If I answer, it's because I choose to do so."

"Then why did you come to me?"

He smiled, a smile so filled with intimacy and affection that Gerta felt herself blushing. "Here's a little secret, just between you and me: I usually only come because there's a good deal to be made."

"What manner of deal?"

"One to my advantage, of course." He winked. "Or maybe I came because you needed me. You're kind of cute, in an uptight virginal barbarian way."

"Is this a lie, Loki? Is this a tale to serve your ends?"

His smile broadened. "Not all of it." His gaze fell to her lips and she felt the heat of his glance as surely as a touch. Her fingertips rose to her own mouth and his eyes brightened.

"I owe you a kiss," she whispered, barely recognizing her own voice so breathless was she.

He nodded, but made no move to come closer. "I'm waiting."

He waited. That was all the encouragement she needed to pay the debt to which she had agreed. Gerta hesitated only a heartbeat before she stretched out her hand. Her fingers passed through him the first time, chilling as they did so, but Loki shook his head.

"Remember how you use the mirror," he advised softly.

Gerta understood. She closed her eyes. There was a way of thinking, a focus that was yet unfocussed, which she had learned in order to use her mirror. She let her mind slip, let the smell of wood smoke and the taste of dried meat and the heat of the cabin fade away, let the vision of Loki form in her thoughts.

Then she reached. She smiled when she felt his chin. His jaw had a strong line. His skin felt smooth though she could discern the faint prickle of whiskers. She let her hand slide up to his ear, his throat, the thick ebony waves of his hair. She trailed her fingertips across his brow, felt his dark eyebrows beneath her fingers, traced the line of his nose.

Her fingertips came to rest upon his lips. They were firm, curved in a slight but confident smile. She let her fingers move back and forth, caressing him, learning the shape of him.

And he permitted this. Gerta dared to open her eyes, to look into his, and felt that she looked into the depths of the night sky. His eyes were an indigo so dark that they might have been black of hue, and they were filled with stars. The longer she looked, the dizzier she felt.

More bold than ever she had been, Gerta eased to her toes and replaced her questing fingertips with her lips. She tasted Loki's gasp, she let her hands fall to cup his jaw, and she leaned into his kiss. She opened herself to him, for she owed him no less, and was stunned by the wave of pleasure that claimed her.

To her astonishment, he guided her gently, angling his head, lifting one hand, cajoling her response with his tongue. She understood intuitively that she was being tutored, and she followed his lead, echoing his every gesture and feeling her ardor rise with each caress.

She was trembling when she stepped away, and she did not know how much time had passed. Her lips were swollen and softened, a knot within her had been loosed. The fire had burned down a bit, though the flame in Loki's eyes shone brighter than ever. He was more substantial, as well, and it was more difficult to look through him.

He exhaled mightily and shoved a hand through his hair as he whistled. "You're one quick study, Gerta," he teased then winked.

Gerta flushed crimson and turned to tend the fire, unable to keep herself from smiling as Loki laughed. She saw him flexing from the periphery of her vision, watched him stretch his wings out to their full dimension with a kind of joy.

"Why do you gain so much power from a caress?" she asked.

He turned to her, surprise in his expression. "Because there's a big power in lust, in desire and sex. Some cultures celebrate that; others suppress it. There's a potency in your caress, in everyone's passion. I've taken it upon myself to teach you how to harness it, how to direct it, how to wield it like the weapon it is."

"Why?"

He grinned. "You'll see."

And he would admit no more than that.

Gerta is dreaming.

Gerta stands in her father's court. She knows what will happen, for she has had this dream nightly for five years. She stirs in her sleep, fights against the dream, knows that she will lose.

The dream always triumphs, and so it does this time.

Her father, regal in his vestments, adorned with his crown and surrounded by his courtiers, looks tired. He faces a dire challenge to his suzerainty, and he is losing. The most stalwart warriors in his company have already been conquered by the Cath Palug, and on this day, he has called for all the people who answer to him to gather, to hear his edict.

Gerta stands with Isold, her mentor and friend, and feels Isold's agitation. Isold has seen something in her mirror, though she will not speak of it, no matter how Gerta pleads with her. Gerta feels caught up in a tide of events that she is powerless to halt.

Her father raises his hands for silence. "I have decided, upon consultation with my counselors, that the Cath Palug is the work of a sorcerer."

Isold straightens and Gerta knows that she has not been consulted. Perhaps she is insulted.

"And the person best equipped to defeat the curse of a sorcerer is not a warrior, as we have witnessed in the loss of our finest and most valiant men. It is another sorcerer." A murmur passes through the company and Gerta's father turns his gaze upon her. She starts, fearful of what he will decree, knowing that she is not ready for such a challenge. "Or a sorceress. Isold, I command you to undertake this task."

Chatter erupts in the chamber, though Isold stands straight and unsurprised. Was this what she envisioned? She steps forward and bows low. "With respect, my lord, I may not succeed in this task. I would not have your court be left without a seer."

"Without a kingdom, I have no need of a seer." At the company's evident dismay, Gerta's father softens his pronouncement. "And there is always my daughter, after all."

"Your daughter's education is incomplete," Isold says with a firmness Gerta is certain her father does not expect of a minion, even a gifted one. "Who will tutor her if I do not return?"

"This is not a question for you to ponder," the king says sternly. "It is your duty as one sworn to me to welcome any command I make of you."

"All know that seers answer to a different code," Isold says with resolve. She turns to Gerta, her gaze hard. "I swore to teach you all I know and that

commitment is far short of fulfillment. Do you, Gerta, release me from our sworn agreement?"

The entire company turns to Gerta, their manner expectant. Some are hopeful, some are condemning, most are fearful for the ravaging attacks of the Cath Palug has struck terror into their hearts. Gerta sees only the fierce green of Isold's eyes and knows this to be a test, knows that she is not ready to make such a choice. She shakes her head slightly in confusion, that gesture drawing her father's ire.

"Gerta! Do not defy my will in this!"

She bows her head, steps away from Isold and lifts her hands high. "I absolve you of your vow," she says in haste, as if the words must be said quickly or not at all.

The company murmurs approval, her father makes a grunt of satisfaction, but Isold's gaze is unswerving. Her steady regard feeds Gerta's certainty that she has erred.

"So be it," Isold says abruptly and turns away. She marches directly out of the hall, and Gerta watches her go in silence, knowing that she will never see her beloved mentor alive again, knowing that she held the power to save Isold in her own hands yet chose not to wield it.

Gerta awakened with a cry, her palms sweating and her heart racing. She sat up, shivering, and wrapped her arms around herself, willing the shards of her dream to leave her.

"Guilty conscience?" To her astonishment, Loki was stretched out beside her, not a handspan between them. She could feel his heat and for a treacherous moment considered the merit of being consoled.

Then she moved away from him, stumbling toward the dying embers of the fire to stir them to life. Isold. She had betrayed Isold. Had she similarly betrayed Cai with her summons?

Aware of Loki's amused glance and suspecting that he knew of her dream, Gerta went outside to relieve herself. She forced her way to a place where she could not be seen from the cabin and shivered as she lifted her skirts. The cold nipped at her bare skin, urging her to hasten. She watched the snowflakes falling and was amazed by their size: they were as big as the end of her thumb. No wonder so much snow had gathered during the night. She tipped her head back and studied the pale hue of the sky. Snowflakes swirled downward from the pewter sky in hordes that had no end.

There would be no sun on this day. She would have thought it too cold to snow, but clearly she was mistaken. Newly aware of their predicament, Gerta returned to the hut in haste. "It is cursed cold this morning, colder than last night."

"You could kindle a fire here. There is still a bit of wood."

"Nay. It is snowing with vigor. We must descend from the pass as quickly as we can, lest we are trapped here." Gerta seized her pack even as she spoke.

"Does that happen?"

Gerta shook her head. "I have never seen snow like this in the pass, even in winter. And it falls at relentless speed."

"Almost as if someone or something meant to trap you in the pass."

Gerta looked up in surprise. She thought of the woman's face in her mirror and itched to look into the bronze disc again. She sensed that her companion would not approve and stilled her impulse, even though it was scarcely his place to dictate her use of her own mirror. "Who is this Snow Queen? From whence did she come?"

"Well, that's a tough one. She's been around for a while, that's for sure, almost as long as me."

Gerta slung her pack onto her back and tightened her belt around her cloak. "Then you can tell me what you know while we walk. Once through the pass, we will head for the abode of a woodcutter. He lives on the edge of my father's realm but has always been kind to me. I am certain he will see me fed and both of us kept in warmth this night." Gerta sighed and frowned. "I had hoped to make his hut by midday but it will take longer in this storm."

"Then tomorrow will be a long day, with a fight at the end of it."

"There is naught for it."

Loki smiled, as if tempting her to consider other options, then unfurled his wings. They touched the roof of the hut, spanned its width, and were not fully extended.

"It is not so distant from here. Could you fly us in haste?"

"Altitude," he said with a shake of his head. "The air is thinner at altitude and gives less lift. It's heavy work to fly over mountains."

The gleam in his eyes left little doubt of what precise deed he would require to have sufficient strength. An answering heat raged within Gerta, but she denied it.

"Impossible, and you know it well. We walk." Gerta glanced about herself, ensuring that the cabin was as she had found it. She packed the rest of the dried meat, then opened the door. An icy wind swirled around her ankles as she fastened the latch on the door, but she leaned into the wind and strode into the storm.

She glanced back after a dozen steps and could not even discern the outline of the hut any longer. She schooled her panic, knowing it would not serve her well, and strode onward. She could feel her companion's presence, just behind her left shoulder, and curiously, though he was often an irritant, she was glad to know he was there.

"The Snow Queen, now," Loki mused, his voice so close by Gerta's ear that he might have been sitting on her shoulder. "Well, there's a lot of speculation as to where she originates, but let's go with the Norse theology, as that's most familiar to you."

"There is no goddess of winter in that pantheon."

"Not a goddess but a patroness. There was a giantess named Skadi, a real beauty, a huntress who favored winter. In fact, she was said to be in command of winter, for she preferred it and ensured its grasp upon the land."

"But perpetual winter would mean death to the people."

"Nobody said she was a fun date. Death was her provenance, as well. She was a keeper of dark secrets—a sorceress, if you will—and a keeper of men's souls. Now, her father was killed by the gods and so she came to them in a fury, seeking reparation in the death of a god. Loki—" he coughed lightly "—charmed her into making a deal that was less onerous to the gods."

"So you are named fairly as one who seeks to turn matters to your own advantage."

He ignored that, though Gerta had not expected otherwise. "Skadi was persuaded to marry a god instead of see one killed, but she was given the chance to choose which one. I seem to remember things getting pretty wild and a lot of mead being drunk in the pursuit of Skadi's smile, but at any rate, she did finally smile and further she agreed to pick a partner by his feet."

"His feet?"

"You see, she thought she was clever. She was attracted to Balder, most handsome of the gods, and was certain she could identify him by his feet and thus get herself a handsome god of a husband."

"But Loki killed Balder. Did that occur before or after?"

"Uh, before, so Balder wasn't there. Skadi didn't realize that, so she picked and it turned out that she chose Njord."

"God of the sea."

"And he was one happy camper, let me tell you, because he needed a wife and Skadi was one hot piece of business. Skadi was less impressed and blamed Loki for her situation. We got them a bit drunk and kept them happy and things seemed to begin on the right foot, so to speak."

Gerta noted that Loki seemed to find this amusing, though she could not see the jest. He seemed also to be confused as to whether he had actually been present at these festivities—instead of the actual god—but she supposed that was the god Loki's vengeance for the frivolous adoption of his name.

"Ultimately, Njord took his wife back to his home, which was on the coast. While she was there and while he coaxed her smile, winter retreated from the land—it's that heat we make in bed, that power I was telling you about. This seemed pretty much peachy, but Skadi couldn't stand the sound of the gulls. The constant breaking of waves drove her crazy and she insisted that she couldn't sleep. So, the happy couple went back to her father's home, which was in the mountains and completely snowbound."

"And winter touched Njord's land again."

"Right. But in Skadi's father's place, Njord couldn't sleep because of the howling wolves and the whistle of the wind through the pine trees. He needed water to be happy, being a god of the sea and all, and was as restless as his wife was happy."

"I will guess that they made an arrangement."

"They did: nine months in her home, three in his—that tells you something about how badly Njord had it for her. And the Norse got nine months of winter and three of summer as a result of that deal, the divine rhythm being echoed in the world we know and love. The marriage didn't work out in the end, though—irreconcilable differences, you know— but the cycle of the year stuck even after Njord went back to the sea full-time."

"And Skadi?"

"Well, I guess she needed a hobby because that's when she started collecting souls. They're a hot commodity in the divine realm, you know. Collect the complete set, and all that."

"I did not know."

"And really, appropriating souls gives her a longevity she wouldn't have otherwise." He mused, seeking a comparison. "Like rainwater filling a barrel over and over again."

Gerta understood, though there was little she could say. She began to doubt herself as the snow rose higher and higher. How could she defeat an opponent who had devoured souls and assumed their power for eons?

Gerta stumbled out of the pass much much later that day. The snow had risen as high as her waist and it had been an ordeal to continue to push through it. She could not feel her toes, or her fingertips, and the end of her nose and her earlobes were so cold that she feared they would shatter if she touched them. But she seized the familiar outcropping of rock that marked this end of the pass and pulled herself past it.

She stood in her father's kingdom, her breath leaving clouds in the bitter cold, and shook with relief. The snow was still falling, but it had been blown from this side of the pass. The mountainside was slick with ice, ice that had been polished to a sheen by the wind, and Gerta was too tired to fight against it.

Truly, there was no need to do so. She sat down on the ice and began to slide on her buttocks, letting the downward slope of the mountain labor in her favor. She crossed her legs, pulling the back of her robe over her knees. With her pack in her lap and her head bent low, she slid ever faster down the mountainside.

The wind snapped at her hair and loosed her braid, tearing her hood back with icy fingers. Pellets of snow stung her face and drove themselves down the neck of her robe. They stung the back of her hands, but Gerta did not care.

She could see the woodcutter's hut before her, a shadow among pine trees, a welcome haven after her efforts of this day. She knew that the fire would be raging, that there would be a pot of soup or stew hanging over the flames, and that Egan would welcome her with a bellow of joy.

Indeed, she could think of little else in her anticipation.

But there was no thread of smoke rising from Egan's hut, which was a marvel in this weather. Gerta dug in her heels and slowly eased herself to a stop. The ice had formed in swirls around the trunks of the pine trees and with her last bit of speed, she was flung into one of those swirls. She came to a halt before the woodcutter's door with such a graceful flourish that the storm might have deposited her there apurpose.

Gerta thought about the woman's face in her mirror, then pushed such whimsy from her thoughts. It was coincidence, no more.

She spied the silhouette of Egan himself, a great bear of a man dressed in furs, on the far side of the hut and her heart soared. He had not turned to greet her, but truly, her arrival had made little noise.

"Egan!" she cried, struggling to her feet.

He did not answer, did not so much as move.

He must not have heard her.

Gerta hastened toward him. "Egan! I would beg your hospitality this night, if you would be so kind to an old friend."

Still he said naught. Still he did not turn. A shadow of dread touched Gerta's heart. She seized his arm and he did not jump.

"Egan!" She shook him, but he was still and immobile. His face was yet averted, so Gerta stepped around him, though she gasped when she looked upon him fully.

There was ice in his moustache and beard, ice even across his cheeks and nose. His eyes were open, staring, his lashes frozen into tiny icicles. He did not blink. He did not breathe.

"He is frozen!" Gerta said, taking a step back.

"Like a popsicle," Loki agreed. "Guess we'll just make ourselves at home."

Gerta stared at Egan, knowing something was amiss. She had seen men who had died in winter's embrace, for men lost in storms and recovered later were oft brought to her, in case they could be healed. They were always dead beyond doubt, their flesh a curious cold hue. But Egan did not look dead. He looked alive, if encased in ice.

He was enchanted. She knew this with sudden clarity and guessed what she must do.

"We must take him with us, into the hut," she said with authority. "We must thaw him."

"Oh, that's a really bad idea."

"It is the only deed that can be done! He is bewitched, it is clear!"

"Are you sure you want to go there?"

"I can do naught else! Egan has been an ally to my father. I cannot abandon him like this."

Her companion sighed with forbearance. "One of these days, Gerta babe, you're going to learn to take my advice."

"I am never deaf to sound counsel, but I must think of others beyond myself."

"Well, don't blame me for the results." Loki sat on the woodcutter's stump, clearly unwilling to lend any aid.

"You are heartless," she informed him. "To not assist another just because there is no immediate advantage to you is reprehensible." Loki examined his fingers with apparent fascination.

Gerta exhaled in frustration, then bent to her task. She pushed and shoved at Egan, but his feet were frozen to the ground. It would have been easier to move a tree.

After some effort, she discovered the sledge that he used to bring wood back to his hut and his axe. She positioned the sledge behind him, then hacked at the ice that bound his boots to the ground. It was heavy labor and she was already exhausted.

Loki whistled tunelessly, apparently fascinated with the sky and falling snow. Gerta cursed him soundly and he blew her an impertinent kiss. Her hair fell into her eyes and the cold nipped at her, but Gerta persevered.

Finally Egan fell, toppling like a great tree to the sledge. She had to scramble to make certain that he did not roll off it. She caught her breath for only a moment before hauling him toward the hut.

"You could be of some assistance."

"Do you really want me to waste my power on something so pointless?" Loki straightened. "Now if you were interested in bolstering my power, I could afford to expend an increment here and now."

Gerta hauled on the sledge again. "Nay!"

"The thing is that chastity offers a simple kind of power, but it's a power that comes from denial, from negating the fullness of what you can be," Loki mused. "Potency, sexual or otherwise, comes from the positive side of the coin, from not just the awareness of what is possible but of doing it. And you know, if you believe as much, then nothing is impossible."

"Eternal life is impossible."

"Babe, you're in the presence of Exhibit Number One."

"You dream."

"It's not an exclusive club, you know. You could be immortal, too."

"I cannot!"

"Not as long as you believe you can't be. That's how it works. Whether you believe you can do something or you can't, you'll be right. Neat trick, isn't it?"

Gerta refrained from comment. She reached the door of the hut, panting from her efforts, then hauled the entire sledge inside. Egan stared unblinkingly at the roof and Gerta shivered at the sight of him.

She set to kindling a fire and soon had a blaze on the hearth. She held her own hands out toward the flames and halfway feared that they would melt rather than revert to their former warmth.

When she looked again, Egan was beginning to drip upon the floor. Gerta knelt by his side, wiping away the ice from his face as it melted. His flesh was cold, but she fancied she could feel his pulse in his neck. She pulled the sledge closer to the fire. Within moments, his cheeks looked more ruddy, though it could have been a reflection from the flames.

Gerta's belly growled and turned to seek something to eat in his simple stores. There was some smoked pork and a few root vegetables so shriveled that Gerta was not completely certain what they were—or what they had been. She found an onion and was encouraged that they might eat well this night. She took Egan's cauldron outside and packed clean snow into it, then lugged it back into the cabin, intending to hang it over the fire.

She had only just crossed the threshold when Loki yelled a warning.

V

ook out!"

Gerta spun at Loki's cry and found Egan standing before her. She had an instant to marvel that he was revived, before she noticed his unnaturally wide stare.

Then she glimpsed the flash of a descending blow.

Gerta cried out and leapt backward. The axe blade missed her by the barest increment.

"But Egan, what..." she managed to stammer before he came after her, swinging again. She dropped the cauldron and held up her hands, the blade slashing across her palms so that she cried out in pain.

"Egan!" she screamed, but he brandished his axe again. The blade flashed and Gerta ran.

She darted behind one tree and another, horrified by how Egan followed her. He swung his axe over and over again, whenever she was within striking range. He wielded the heavy tool as if it weighed naught at all, so accustomed was he to it.

But there was something amiss. Egan moved at a strangely slow speed, as if against his will. He did not falter but neither did he move more quickly. His features were expressionless, his stare blank. Gerta did not understand what had befallen him but she instinctively knew one truth: Egan would only halt when he killed her.

Unless she killed him first.

Horrified at the prospect, Gerta knew that she had to do something soon lest she be slaughtered. She leapt behind one pine and Egan swung his axe so hard that it was nearly buried in the trunk. The tree shuddered beneath the force of his blow.

That gave Gerta an idea.

"You will never catch me, Egan," she said with a confidence she did not feel. "You move too slowly, it is clear."

There was no anger in his expression, though he followed her.

She taunted him, drawing his blows and ducking out of range in the last moment, until she led him to the largest tree.

Gerta held her ground as he raised the axe blade. She stood stalwart as the axe began to descend. She did not move one step as the blade sliced through the air, directly toward her neck.

And just before the blade kissed her skin, she jerked backward. The axe blade whistled past her and buried itself in the trunk of the tree. Egan tugged at it but the force of his blow had been too considerable. He was so determined to retrieve his axe that he seemed to have forgotten Gerta.

Gerta raced back to the cauldron she had dropped. To her relief, when she turned, Egan still fought to free the axe. She crept up behind the woodcutter, hating what she had to do, then swung the iron pot at the back of his head.

He tumbled like a felled tree and Gerta hit him again in her terror. He twitched and Gerta hit him again and again. It was only when he fell still, when the blood flowed from his wound, that she dared to cease.

Gerta circled Egan's fallen body, panting at the travesty of what she had done, her heart still racing. Her tears welled that she should have to injure a man who had been so good to her. Confusion and exhaustion made it impossible to halt her tears once they had arisen.

"What did I do?" she whispered, as her first tear loosed itself.

A hand shoved her suddenly from behind and she fell, sprawling across the inert woodcutter. Gerta shouted in dismay and struggled, but still her tears fell upon Egan's face.

There was a strange sizzle emitted from the point where the tear touched his face.

Gerta frowned. "What have I done?"

"Another!" Loki insisted, for it was he who had shoved her. "Shed another tear!"

"I do not understand..." Gerta made to rise, not liking whatever force ruled these events.

She did not make it to her knees.

"Listen to me for once, Gerta!" Loki raged, infuriated as she had never seen him. "Weep! You must weep. It is all that can save him!"

When Gerta stared at Loki without comprehension, he swore, then slapped her face so hard that she gasped. Gerta's tears sprang forth again, a trio of them falling upon Egan's face. Again, there was that odd sizzle, as if something melted beneath them.

"More!" Loki made a growl of frustration. "People think saliva is the universal solvent but, really, it's human tears. You're compassionate, Gerta, use it!" He took a ragged breath. "Think about ol' Egan here and what's happened to him. Think about his fate without a soul. Think of how he must be suffering—and weep for him!"

Gerta surrendered to her mingled grief and confusion. The tears fell across Egan's face, until finally a shudder slipped through his body. The hue of his skin changed then, turning grey as Gerta knew dead men should be.

Her last tears made no sound when they fell upon his flesh. Loki bent past her. He pulled Egan's eyelid back, and there, nestled in the socket, was a long sliver of black glass.

"Ice," Gerta whispered, remembering his tale all too well.

"Ice," he agreed. Gerta made to take it, for she was curious, but Loki snatched it away. "I'll take charge of this," he said and she could not see where he secreted it. He then closed Egan's eyes with care.

"He looks peaceful now."

"He is at peace now." Loki looked around them with narrowed eyes. "You can sleep now, Gerta. You'll be safe here tonight."

"Even from you?"

He spared her that wicked grin. "I only take what's offered. You should know that by now." He winked. "But if you're offering..."

Gerta looked at Egan, her thoughts churning. "Is this what has happened to Cai?" she asked and saw the answer in Loki's abrupt solemnity.

Before he could answer, feminine laughter sounded across the snow-covered field. The sound rang out from the pack Gerta had dropped. It was the woman in Gerta's mirror, her laughter loud and cruel and yet ringing like a thousand silver bells. Gerta stared at her pack in horror, recognizing that distinctive laugh.

The woman in the mirror was Isold.

"You looked!" Loki said with disgust, clearly not understanding the full reason for Gerta's dismay. "Did I tell you that the mirror could be used against you? Did you listen? No, of course not, it's too easy to heed my counsel and make our lives simple. No, you had to show yourself to her, so that she would know we were coming." He bent, eyes gleaming, and she felt him seize her shoulder. "One thing, Gerta, one small detail that will shape everything. Maybe you could stir yourself to remember."

"What?"

"Did you tell her about me?"

"We did not speak."

"Were you thinking of me? Were you aware of me in any way? Was there a shadow of my presence in your thoughts? Because if you did—" he sighed and shook his head "—then the gig is up, girl."

Gerta did not know. She shook her head, unable to give him the response he clearly desired with any conviction. He released her shoulder and turned away from her, his disappointment in her clear.

"What will she do to Cai?"

Loki barely glanced back. "He has ice in his heart and his eye. You work it out."

Gerta looked at Egan, a humble woodcutter possessed of no magical powers who had nearly killed her. She saw now that the winters had been harsh for him, that he had lost weight and that his face was more deeply lined than she recalled. She touched him, whispered a blessing, then stood on unsteady legs.

There was a lump in her throat at what she had to do to right her own error in summoning Cai but a resolve in her heart beyond anything she had ever known. Loki paced, impatient and displeased, and perhaps not in best mood to hear any offer from her.

Gerta took a deep breath, for she knew what she had to do. "I will surrender my chastity to you this night," she said, watching Loki turn to face her in his astonishment. "If you will fly us to the Cath Palug's cave in the morning."

There was a glint in his dark eyes. "Out of uncontrollable

passion for me?"

Gerta shook her head, unable to lie.

"You're doing this for Cai. A guy could be insulted by that, you know."

"I would do this to right the error I have made. It is often necessary to surrender something precious to oneself to make reparation for the damage one has done."

He sobered. "To earn redemption."

Gerta shrugged, not truly caring about such details. Their gazes locked and held for a long moment and she feared in his silence that he meant to deny her. He was so changeable, so incomprehensible, that she was suddenly aware that she could not predict his choices.

Then, Loki strode toward her with a confident swagger and cast his arm across her shoulders, guiding her back toward the hut. "We're on the same page, Gerta, don't worry about it. And lucky girl, I'm going to make this worth your while. See, I've had a bit of practice despoiling maidens." He winked. "You're going to like this."

But Gerta was not so certain. Her chastity would be surrendered, surrendered much sooner than she might have hoped and surrendered to a being she would never truly understand.

She did not need her mirror to fear that portent.

Gerta awakened to find herself alone in Egan's hut. Embers glowed on the hearth, and she lay on the hard straw pallet for a moment, savoring the warmth both outside and inside of her. She had the sense of forgetting a dream upon awakening, for she could not precisely recall meeting Loki abed: each whisper of recollection that she pursued, thinking it would lead to a fuller memory, slipped from her grasp and disappeared.

She did feel curiously replete. There was a thrum within her, a new potency that she had not known in herself before. Yet all the same, it was a part of her, and hers to command.

She was more glad to be alive than ever she had been.

She rolled over and saw that Loki had brought Egan into his own hut. The old woodcutter lay upon his own pallet, his features composed as if he slept. It was better thus, for no animals would despoil his corpse before he could be buried properly.

Gerta rose to seek Loki, a new spring in her step. She opened the door of the hut and halted in amazement. He stood not a dozen paces away, stretching his great black wings as he had the previous morning.

On this day, however, he was so radiant that she was nigh blinded. He shone, as if lit from within by some dark fire, a light wrought of shadow but impossible to look upon fully all the same. He turned, perhaps at the sound of the door, and smiled. Gerta had to avert her gaze from his brilliance.

"Loki, I do not remember what occurred last night. Is this some kind of sorcery?"

He laughed, a triumphant sound that filled her ears. "It's a gift, Gerta, a little prezzie from me to you. I think you'll be happier not knowing exactly what you've done." She dared to glance at his face and he blew her a cocksure kiss. "You can thank me later, babe."

He savored her discomfiture for only a moment before he stretched again, his massive wings casting a shadow across the white, white snow. It seemed to Gerta that he was twice the size he had been before. Once again, she had the sense that she had summoned forces far beyond her understanding and control, though this time she said as much.

"Loki, I am afraid."

"Sensible reaction, I'd say."

"Loki, do not jest. I fear that going to the cave of the Cath Palug is an error, that we will only make matters worse for Cai."

"You think there's worse than what happened to Egan?"

There was truth in that. Gerta bit her lip. She studied her toe and spoke her thoughts with care. "If Skadi consumes souls and takes their power for her own, how can I ever hope to defeat her? I have not even finished my apprenticeship."

"And...?"

She looked up. "What do you mean?"

"And there's something you're not telling me. Cough it up."

Gerta took a deep breath, glad in a way to surrender this secret. "I saw the Snow Queen in my mirror. I looked to ensure that your stolen kiss had not claimed my gift and she was there. I could not name why she looked familiar, for she has changed much..."

"But you know her?" Loki did not seem to be surprised.

"She is Isold." Gerta glanced up but Loki did not react to this. "You must understand, Isold was my mentor. She knows far more than I do, for I never completed my study beneath her tutelage. And I did not stop my father from dispatching her to face the Cath Palug, even though I could have done so. She must hate me for what has happened to her."

Loki turned and came toward her. Gerta did not look up and still she had to squeeze her eyes closed for the glory of him burned her eyes. He touched her chin and she noticed immediately how much more substantial he was: he might have been wrought of flesh, so firm was the press of his hand against her face, might have been flesh if not for the slight sizzle that followed his moving caress.

Wrought of light, Gerta remembered, and felt awe.

"You forget your assets in this battle, Gerta," he said gently. "You have the greatest power of all, and you don't even count it."

"What is it?"

"You have a purity and innocence of heart. I made you forget last night so that you would still have that in your arsenal." And he bent, against all expectation, and pressed a kiss to her brow. The imprint of his lips seared her flesh and continued to burn after he had stepped away.

"Climb on my back, Gerta," he invited as he crouched before her. "We're late, we're late, for a very important date." He cast her a grin, pleased by yet another jest that she did not understand. Gerta smiled in return, encouraged despite herself.

Then he took flight and she gasped aloud.

Her father's realm was destroyed. Gerta's heart broke as she looked over Loki's shoulder and saw the damage to the land below.

"No place like home, huh?" he said and she shook her head.

"Nay, it was not like this. There were vineyards here, and

orchards, and gardens outside every hut. The meadows were filled with blossoms and the streams were filled with jumping silver fish. There was abundance in my father's realm before the Cath Palug."

She shivered, Loki's rare silence persuading her that he did not believe her. "It has been five years since winter came to the land and still it has not left. Five years of winter. Look! Even the pine trees turn to brown, for only the larger ones are rooted deeply enough to survive."

"There are no buds on the tree branches."

"The fruit trees are dead. No spring can awaken them now."

"Nothing like the kiss of death," Loki said.

Sadness seized Gerta and she feared their quest was a futile one. Even if the Snow Queen was defeated, even if winter left this realm, would the trees ever break into leaf again?

"Please fasten your seatbelts and return all chair backs and trays to the upright position," Loki said then, much to Gerta's confusion. He spared her a grin. "We're here."

She peered over Loki's shoulder in anticipation. The opening to the cave of the Cath Palug was surrounded by trees, curious trees that she did not remember.

Loki flew low and Gerta realized that it was a forest of men. They stood frozen, ice dripping from their helmets and their weapons. Horror was captured in their expressions and Gerta understood that they had been in the act of going to Cai's aid when they had been trapped.

"Cai's companions," Loki said grimly.

"Frozen like popsicles," Gerta agreed, not understanding Loki's earlier words but recalling them. He laughed under his breath, as if surprised.

He landed gracefully before the opening to the cave and Gerta imagined that she could smell the blood of hundreds of warriors from within its shadows. She shuddered, squared her shoulders and glanced to Loki. He nodded, and they stepped into the cold darkness of the cave as one.

To Gerta's surprise, Loki shone like a black opal in the darkness, releasing a faint luminescence that lit their steps. There were bones scattered across the frozen ground, remnants of armor and weapons and men. Gerta's bile rose but she forced herself onward.

To Cai.

They found the Cath Palug not a dozen steps inside the portal, snoring. Gerta was reluctant to leave it alive behind them, but Loki beckoned, then continued into the yawning darkness beyond.

An abyss opened behind the cave, Gerta saw with astonishment. They followed a path ever downward, a path that offered no choices of direction, then stepped into an enormous cavern. A mountain had been hollowed for this chamber, it was clear. It was so large that Gerta could not see its end in any other direction.

The floor shone, like fine polished marble, and the roof was beyond Gerta's abilities to discern. Stalactites hung from that distant roof, Loki's light making their tips glisten in a familiar way.

"Ice," Gerta said softly.

"Got it in one," Loki agreed, his voice barely a breath. "That explains a lot." He knelt and touched the floor with one hand, reverence in his gesture. Gerta followed his move and saw that the floor shone like obsidian. It was cracked a thousand times in a thousand directions, shattered into millions of tiny shards.

And then she realized what it was. Loki ran a hand across its surface and she wondered whether he had expected to ever see his dark looking glass assembled into one piece again.

He lifted his head, then pointed across the ice. Far in the distance, Gerta could just discern a throne. It was massive, twisted in shape and high of back.

"It must be on the other side of this cavern!"

"It's in the middle," Loki said with conviction.

Before he could suggest their course, Gerta gasped aloud. She spied a man upon the ice beside the throne, a man who ran his hands ceaselessly over the surface of the mirror as if he could do naught else.

And she knew without doubt who he was. He would be tall in proximity, and fair, and possess eyes of clearest green. So great was Gerta's relief to find Cai alive that she ran to him.

There was a listlessness about Cai that Gerta could not reconcile with his earlier confidence. Her footsteps faltered when she noticed this. He traced cracks in the surface of the ice with a fingertip, then apparently forgot what he was doing and began again. Over and over again, he did this, driven by a compulsion Gerta could not name.

She framed his face in her hands and forced him to look at her. His gaze was vacant, his mouth slack. Gerta thought of the proud sorcerer who had confronted her in her mirror, thought of his surety, and found her horror rising at what he had become.

What a travesty that a man of such potency could be reduced to this! There was a mark upon his temple, a mark of silver filigree that resembled the imprint of a woman's lips. Gerta traced it with her fingertips and knew that the Snow Queen held him in thrall with a mere kiss.

Gerta instinctively touched her lips to the wound and Cai shuddered at her caress. She understood then the purpose of Loki's instruction, understood with sudden frightening clarity. She kissed Cai before she could consider the wisdom of her course.

He did not resist her, nor did he respond to her touch. Gerta used every gesture Loki had taught her, poured all of her passion and hope and desire into her kiss. She understood that she could not have done this deed without Loki's tutelage, and still she feared she did not know enough. She felt desperation, then, just before she gave him up for lost, Cai's lips moved slightly beneath her own.

Gerta gasped in joy. She deepened her caress with new fervor, feeling Cai's response increase with every heartbeat. She felt him thaw, felt the ice recede and knew a joy beyond any other. She kissed him, she offered him all she had to grant.

So great was her relief that Gerta wept, wept a river of tears that flowed over Cai's upturned face.

"Well done," Isold said crisply.

Her voice was at such close proximity that Gerta jumped in alarm. She broke her kiss and glanced over her shoulder, aware all the while of Cai's wonderment. She felt his gaze upon her, felt his fingertips touch her chin, but she dared not look to him yet.

She was still dizzy herself, and their woes had only begun.

Isold smiled, though there was no warmth in her expression. She appeared much older, her brows and hair seemingly touched by frost, but the steadiness of her gaze had not changed. "But then, you always were a dutiful pupil." She arched a brow. "If a faithless one."

Gerta was stung to silence by the reminder of her betrayal of her mentor. A waft of cold air assaulted Gerta as Isold swiftly leaned past her. With long fingertips, Isold pulled back Cai's eyelid, taking no care to be gentle. He winced as she claimed the shard of black ice from his eyelid. He moved slowly, like a man awakening from a deep sleep, too slowly to halt Isold's efficient gestures.

"Perfect!" she said when she claimed the shard of black ice from his eyelid. She reached beneath his jerkin, following the same course as the Cath Palug's claws, and extracted a second shard from his chest.

Cai took a shuddering breath and coughed. He shivered, seemingly to his very marrow, then looked around himself as if unaware of where he was. The filigree mark on his temple had turned an angry red. He quickened, even as Gerta watched and the shrewdness she had witnessed previously returned to his gaze.

"Chaste little Gerta," Isold murmured. "Who could have imagined that a virgin could have stirred a man beneath my power?"

"You bade me remain a maiden," Gerta said cautiously, sensing that there was something of import in this. "The better to preserve my gift as a seer."

Isold laughed. "The mirror is what it is, Gerta, and it shows what it will show. Such vessels answer to a higher authority than a little seer like you."

"You lied to me, then."

"Indeed I did. A sorceress of my potency could see much farther in your mirror. I saw myself, reigning upon Skadi's right hand before ever I came here." Isold nodded. "It was my destiny, as evidenced by my own name. 'Rule of ice', that is the meaning of the name Isold, and truly, I do rule the ice as Skadi's trustee." Her smile turned cruel. "I collect souls for her, which sates her, and one day I shall wrest the last vestige of power from her lax grasp."

Gerta had never suspected that Isold had used her!

Isold smiled. "I saw you, coming boldly to challenge me, burdened by guilt but still possessed of a chance of success. And so I taught you, Gerta, that you must be chaste, that no man must lay a hand upon you, the better that you might have no opportunity to awaken the sorcerer whose soul Skadi desired more than most." She shrugged and granted Cai a skeptical glance. "But who can guess what will stir a mortal man?"

"I do not understand. I sent a summons for aid three days past and Cai came to assist me." Gerta felt Cai claim her hand. His fingers were still chilled but his grip was resolute.

Isold laughed again. "You believe that you sent the summons? Gerta, child, your power is not sufficient to command the mirror. I heard your attempt and turned it to my own purpose." Her eyes gleamed with pride. "I summoned Cai, though I made it appear that you did so. He would never have heeded me otherwise."

"There be truth," Cai muttered.

"It matters little," Isold said. "Now, you will surrender your mirror to me, and perhaps I will be merciful." Her hungry smile granted Gerta no confidence in that possibility.

Gerta clutched her pack. "But my mirror is as a part of me..."

"Have you not realized the truth? How did I find myself such a witless pupil?" Isold sneered. "Have you not guessed from what the mirror draws its power?" She gestured broadly and Gerta's gaze was drawn unwillingly to the seemingly endless expanse of dark ice surrounding them.

Isold leaned close to whisper. "Your mirror shows truth, does it not?"

Did Gerta even wish to have such a vessel in her possession? Cai gave her a nudge and a glance, and Gerta agreed with his impulse. She surrendered the mirror to Isold, gladdened to be rid of its burden.

The sorceress clutched it in her hands and closed her eyes. She gritted her teeth as she crushed the bronze mirror in her hands; she arched her neck and exerted such a force of will that Gerta could not look fully upon her. The mirror melted within her grasp, melted to no more than a whiff of dark smoke.

And a long shard of black ice.

Isold smiled in triumph. "This is the last of it," she confided. "Now the glass will be complete, as once it was."

She cast the three shards into the air and they moved seemingly of their own volition to find their places in the puzzle of the ice. Gerta feared the result when they slipped into their places, though she knew not what to expect. She clutched Cai's hand and he clutched hers and neither of them took a breath.

Naught happened.

Isold frowned and looked about herself in confusion.

"Missing something?" Loki asked, and sauntered across the ice toward them.

Loki was much smaller and more shadowy than Gerta expected. He might have been a kitchen serf, bent under the burden of his labor and faded from exhaustion. She could not even discern his wings.

The flight must have been a greater strain for him than anticipated and Gerta felt a new fear. He was cocky, though, confident as always, his swagger in marked contrast to his appearance. His smile had a fearsome brightness and his eyes shone with what might have been anticipation.

Loki the trickster. Gerta had little time to consider this, for he moved his hand and something flashed within his grasp.

"You're missing one last piece," he informed Isold with a measure of insolence. "Wanna jump for it?"

"Who is your humble companion, Gerta?" Isold demanded.

"I could not undertake such a journey alone," Gerta said hesitantly. Loki gave her a look and she fabricated a tale, following his silent bidding for once. "He is no more than a minion, pledged to my father. You know that my father surrendered his best men to the Cath Palug years ago."

Loki's eyes widened slightly and Gerta did not doubt that he would have much to say about that description. It sated Isold though, and persuaded her that he posed no threat.

She extended her hand regally, clearly believing that he was no more than a feeble man. "Give me the shard."

"I don't think so." Loki bounced it on his palm. "I kind of like it. It's shiny, you know?"

"I know not who you are, but your defiance is unacceptable," Isold began to fume. "Give me the shard!"

"We could arm wrestle," Loki taunted, tossing the shard of black ice from one hand to the other. Isold snatched at it when it was airborne, but without success. "Thumb wrestle. Draw straws. Or—" he granted Isold an arch glance "—you could seduce me into giving it to you."

Isold stilled and smiled a cunning smile. "That can be arranged."

"Goody goody." Loki stood his ground and again Gerta had the sense that he barely restrained himself.

Isold leaned forward and kissed his brow, lavishing her attention upon him. Loki whistled, turning the shard in his hand, utterly oblivious to her.

"What is this?" Isold murmured, then kissed him again.

"That's it?" Loki asked when she lifted her lips from him. "That's the best you can do?"

Isold was clearly astonished that he had not readily succumbed. "Once more," she demanded and he nodded with insouciance.

"Why not. Maybe the third time's the charm, hmm?"

Isold drew herself taller and caught Loki's face in her hands, bending toward him with purpose. She kissed his brow, clearly funneling all of her power into the embrace.

It was to no avail. She stepped back and regarded him warily. "You are no minion."

"My turn," Loki said. He flicked the shard of ice off his thumb and it flew through the air, gleaming as it sought its place in the shattered ice. In the same instant, Loki seized Isold and kissed her full on the lips. She managed to make a strangled cry and no more before she began to loose substance. She struggled but Loki did not release her.

Indeed, Gerta thought that he deepened his kiss. His grip was clearly relentless, his kiss consuming. Isold became more and more shadowy, yet he released her when she was no more than a wraith.

"Take that message to my old pal Skadi," he bade her. He snapped his fingers and the wisp of what had been Isold disappeared.

Cai gasped and Gerta felt the last shard of ice snap into place. There could be no mistaking it. The lake of ice lit suddenly, illuminated with that shadowy opalescence along all of its cracks, then shimmered and fused into one glass again.

And Loki began to laugh.

❧

Gerta watched in dismay as Loki grew larger and darker. He was more substantial than ever he had been, blacker and bigger and more fearsome. He was exultant. His laughter shook the walls of the cavern and resonated within her very marrow. He looked down upon them in his dark majesty and the radiance of his eyes fairly blinded Gerta.

She feared then that she had erred in truth, that she had been used for a wicked purpose. Had Loki used her as Isold had done?

Beside her, Cai straightened and she admired his fearlessness. "What will you do?"

"No more and no less than what I came to do." Loki smiled and the sight sent fear dancing down Gerta's spine. "No more and no less than Gerta helped me to do."

Gerta and Cai exchanged a glance of trepidation.

"I will destroy it, of course." Loki shook his head as he looked across the expanse of dark ice. "Though it's a damn shame. This is a fine piece of work."

Gerta looked at him in shock. "But, but why? You said you had made it."

He lifted a finger as if to chide her for doubting him. "And I did. But it was wrong to make it, wrong to try to show God his error." He swallowed. "It was pride I showed, not truth."

"And you mean to make reparation," Gerta guessed, recalling his earlier comments.

"There is only one way to right a wrong, only one way to earn redemption. You've got to fix what you screw up." Loki heaved a sigh. "Destruction is the shadow of creation. Some cultures celebrate this, though most choose to forget it. The bottom line is that I, as the creator of the ice, am the only one who can ensure its destruction."

"But how?" Cai asked. "It has been shattered before and survived in pieces, which was worse."

"Tears!" Gerta guessed.

Loki grinned at her. "Tears."

"You do not weep," Cai observed.

"We seldom weep, but mortals have potent tears. If I take pieces of ice to places of suffering, places where tears of compassion are shed, then it will be melted, one chunk at a time."

"But it is so vast," Cai protested. "It will take eternity."

"Isn't it a good thing that I'm immortal?" Loki commented. "I've nothing but time on my hands." He cried out a command, a word in a language Gerta did not know and never wished to hear again, and raised his hands skyward.

The ice followed his gesture, rising and buckling. Fissures opened upon its surface, and instead of shards, it was broken into pieces about the size of a man. Gerta clung to Cai as the ice beneath their very feet uprooted itself. Loki seized one piece, then ran across the broken ice and bounded into flight.

The remaining chunks of ice, to Gerta's amazement, shuddered, lifted, then pursued him. The cavern was filled with spiraling chunks of dark ice, seemingly caught in a whirlwind. They all moved upward and away, following Loki.

When the storm of their passing had subsided, Gerta realized that she and Cai must have been swept along, for they stood together in the cave of the Cath Palug.

The Cath Palug was dead.

"I suppose it survived its purpose," Cai said when he bent to examine it.

"Or it could not survive without the ice."

Cai shook his head. "In this cavern was a dark power, to be sure. This is no sorcery I would know." He touched the great beast and it rolled bonelessly to its back.

Its paws had been cut off.

Gerta retched at the sight, though Cai, more accustomed to battle, merely frowned. "Look. Two of them are embedded in my shield," he said, pulling his shield from beneath the beast's corpse.

"And the other pair are there." Gerta pointed to the jumble of bones from other fallen warriors, where the two paws had fallen. She saw now that the ground was stained with the Cath Palug's dark blood. Cai studied the corpse of the fiendish cat, then grinned.

He pulled his sword from its chest with satisfaction. It had been embedded to the hilt in the beast and its blade was stained with that dark blood.

His eyes narrowed. "The Cath Palug dragged me into its lair," he said, as if his recollection was faint.

"You must have defeated it here," Gerta said. Their gazes met and for a moment, they both knew that that had not been the case. They stared at each other in mutual awareness of the marvel they had witnessed, of the surety that they would soon forget it, then a cloud passed over their recollection.

"It was ferocious and thirsty for your blood," Gerta said, impressed by the valor and strength of this man. Her father would surrender her hand to him, she was certain, and truly he deserved no less for his noble deed. "Yet you did not falter."

Cai looked at her and smiled, the warmth in his eyes making Gerta flush. "How could I, when such a fair maiden was at stake?"

Gerta's face heated and she averted her gaze, awkward in the presence of a man so virile, so attentive. They were alone and she was aware of the scent of his flesh, the heat of his presence, the sound of his breathing.

Cai chuckled, a hearty sound that warmed her heart. He slid his fingertips down the length of her arm, conjuring a faint recollection within Gerta. She caught her breath at his boldness, admired his tenderness. She watched his hand, shivered when he reached the end of her sleeve and his warm fingers trailed across the bare flesh of the back of her hand. He interlaced their fingers, capturing her hand within his, then lifted her hand to press a kiss into her palm.

His gesture was so simple, yet so potent. Gerta must have dreamed of this moment, of his first caress. She looked at Cai, looked at him fully, seeing her destiny in the bright sparkle of his eyes. Her heart pounded with an awareness of him, his height, his breadth, his gentle manner and his wisdom, and she knew that she would learn much in this man's company.

She knew she would gain far more than she had lost.

"Be my bride," he murmured.

"Prize, bride, it's all pretty much the same in a barbarian culture," Gerta said, then clapped a hand over her mouth. From whence had such words come?

Cai laughed, undeterred by her uncommon speech. "Praise be for that," he murmured, then bent to touch his lips to hers.

They stared at each other in marvel when he lifted his head, then heard the singing of birds. Filled with the marvel of spring's return, Gerta took Cai's hand within her own and led him into the garden of her father's realm.

Coven of Mercy

Vampire romances haven't been my thing. I read a lot of Anne Rice twenty years ago or so and some Chelsea Quinn Yarbro—maybe I just drank my fill with that round of reading, so was never tempted to return to that particular well.

As a result, when I was invited to participate in the **Mammoth Book of Vampire Romance II** several years ago, I very nearly declined. I couldn't imagine that I had a vampire story to tell. I decided to wait until the morning to get back to the editor, and that night—as so often is the case—I had the most interesting idea. It was a concept for a vampire romance that did really appeal to me, probably because it colored outside of the lines of the subgenre's expectations.

This short story is the result of that idea. Be warned—it's not a typical vampire romance.

It's interesting to re-read it now, because Micah still catches at my heart. I'm intrigued to know the rest of his story—and I know that he has friends. As short stories often do, this one gives just a glimpse into a world, and I'm tempted to revisit it to learn more.

hate the month of March. It's an indecisive month, hovering on the cusp between winter and spring. Indecision drives me wild.

I like clear-cut strategies, battles that are victories or failures. Nothing in between.

March hovers, indecisive whether it should herald warm and sunny spring, or more winter—cold and overcast, the skies thick with falling snow. It ends up in that mucky zone, somewhere in between. Freezing rain and relentless grey, dampness and dull days, are followed by teasing intervals of sunshine. It's unreliable, untrustworthy, despicable.

Give me black or white. Give me winter or spring. Give me February or April. You can keep March.

My mother died in March; maybe that's part of it. Diagnosed early in the month, gone by the end of it, hers was a chaotic and whirlwind departure, a roller coaster ride of triumphs and setbacks. That journey to death—the one no one wanted to take, the one that changed everything forever—is echoed for me every year in the weather.

March makes me restless and impatient, sharp and irritable.

That year was no different.

My hospital was a research hospital. That gave me the option of working in the labs, researching instead of practicing. There are no mucky grey zones in the labs—a new drug is effective or it isn't—and that polarity always worked for me.

I had a bit of a reputation on the wards, where I would be called in as a specialist on the tough cases. "Icicle" Taylor cut to the chase, took risks, won more than she lost. Each case, for me, was an array of statistics, a flotilla of blood test results, and I chose the armaments with which I would engage based upon experience and the sum of results to date. I never wanted to know the patient—that was just extraneous detail. I never wanted to familiarize myself with the territory in dispute.

I just wanted to win.

But that March, one patient wasn't having any of that. Mrs. Curtis was in her forties and had a wry smile. She refused to let me slide in and out of her life without making a connection. She continued to insist that I call her by her first name, for example, even though I never did. She always wanted a conversation when I slipped in to check her charts or progress. She introduced me to her family and friends. There are many points of contact in an aggressive routine of chemotherapy and radiation, and Mrs. Curtis put every one to work in her effort to charm me.

In a way, she waged her own campaign against my clinical detachment while I fought the disease that had invaded her body.

She had one advantage she'd never realized and it was the one that made the difference—she looked like my mother. She was taller and more buxom, but that glint in her eye, that ability to see right through my carefully composed lines to what I really meant, was my mother back from the grave. It caught at my heart, ripped a hole in my composure, and exposed a small vulnerability.

So, I was even more determined than usual to ensure that Mrs. Curtis was a triumph. My mother, you see, had lost her battle right before my eyes. Mrs. Curtis was my chance to prove that I wasn't some helpless twelve-year-old forced to stand aside and watch while her life disintegrated before her eyes.

Mrs. Curtis was a territory I intended to win back from the enemy, one cell at a time.

And that's why I was back at the hospital close to midnight that night, on the way home from a date that I hadn't wanted to keep. It had been a double date, set up by a friend despairing of my "perverse affection" for solitude, and it had been a disaster. They all were. He'd been nice enough, but not nearly as fascinating as the mutating opponent I met in the lab every single day. And he didn't understand what it was to be passionate about anything—other than football and sex. I'd tapped my fingers on the table and smiled thinly throughout the meal.

We were probably all relieved when the check came.

I'd immediately gone back to the hospital to look over the most recent bout of test results, just to make sure I hadn't missed anything. I knew I hadn't, I never do, but it gave me the excuse to look in on Mrs. Curtis again.

She was probably awake. We shared a kind of insomnia, a restlessness in the middle of the night that only conversation cured. She had a private room, so I knew I wouldn't be troubling anyone else.

I needed to talk to her about doing another biopsy anyway. The last had been painful, deeper than anticipated. I'd feared that the subsequent radiation would finish her before the cancer did. But Mrs. Curtis had rallied, as she always did.

So, unfortunately, had my determined foe—the cancer.

The ward was quiet. I've always preferred the hospital at night. During the day, it can be fraught with emotional energy, people demanding answers and desperate to do something to help. I'd never done well with that kind of anxiety.

I was always better with test results, percentages, calculations, cold hard math. Winter, if you will—relentless but consistent, instead of the capricious and fleeting charm of spring.

In the quiet darkness, the hospital was more pure in its function. Monitors beeped and intravenous tubes dripped. The machines ran the show, which worked for me. Patients slept. Visitors had left. Guerneys were moved as the dead journeyed quietly down to the morgue. The nurses focused on checking of patients and keeping records.

I savored the dimness of the lights and the emptiness of the lobby as I crossed the threshold that night. I was looking forward to seeing Mrs. Curtis, too, even with the discussion ahead of us. The elevator came immediately, and in the comparative silence, I heard the whirr of its mechanism as I stood alone in it.

I nodded to the night nurse, Miriam, one of the most watchful and competent of the nursing team. I hesitated outside Mrs. Curtis's room, my steps frozen at the sound of voices.

She had a guest.

How could that be?

I looked at my watch. It was almost midnight. Outrage rose within me that anyone would disturb a patient as she healed, but then Mrs. Curtis laughed.

It was a different laugh than the one I usually heard in her presence. Low. Breathy. Sexy.

"I can't dance now!" she protested in a tone of voice that indicated she'd like to be persuaded otherwise.

"Of course you can," a man insisted. His voice was low and rich, a murmur that made me shiver.

"The IV..."

"We'll ignore it."

"But there's no music," Mrs. Curtis argued, her tone light. Flirtatious.

Did Mrs. Curtis have a lover? She'd never mentioned it, but then, I made a point of not asking after personal details. I knew nothing about her life, and until this moment, that had suited me just fine. I peeked around the edge of the door, curious.

There was a man on the far side of Mrs. Curtis's bed, standing with his back to the window. He had dark hair and dark eyes, and seemed to be younger than Mrs. Curtis. He was handsome, handsome enough to make me yearn for something I hadn't had in a long time. He was wearing a black leather jacket, black jeans, and a black t-shirt. A silver earring gleamed from his left earlobe. No pretty boy—he was older, knowing, a little bit world-weary.

Sexy.

Familiar.

Although I knew I'd never seen him before.

Mrs. Curtis had braced herself on one elbow, her hair a tangle of silver and russet on the back of her neck. Her skin was pale and she was thinner than I'd realized. The back of her hospital gown was open, and I was shocked at how clearly the individual vertebrae were delineated. The IV in her right hand looked enormous in comparison to her delicate hands.

"Isn't there?" he asked, his smile broadening. He had a sensual mouth, a full and mobile one, and his smile looked positively decadent. I couldn't identify his accent, but it was European. Exotic.

And then I heard the waltz. It seemed as if an orchestra had struck up in the ward, although that made no sense. The music lilted through the room, barely audible to me in the doorway, but achingly beautiful.

Mrs. Curtis was laughing at the man, who watched her as if she was the most beautiful woman in the world. A lump rose in my throat at his kindness.

Or maybe the state of his infatuation.

"How did you do that?" she demanded.

"Does it matter? Or should we simply dance?" He offered his

hand to her, palm up, and I was struck by how tiny her right hand looked when she placed it in his. How wrong that IV needle looked in the back of her hand, with its three strips of tape.

I had never seen Mrs. Curtis healthy.

I had never before heard her laugh.

"Okay," she agreed, conspiratorial. "Let's dance."

He gathered her in his arms, bodily lifting her from the bed. My mouth went dry at the tenderness in his expression. She was all bones and pale skin, a rag doll, a wisp of the woman she must have been.

She slid her hands up to his shoulders, rapturous in his embrace. He smiled down at her, loving, possessive, gentle.

She laid her head on his shoulder and sighed. I saw her eyes close. I saw the glimmer of a tear on her cheek. She looked so fragile and faded, like a rose left in a vase too long. I thought he was going to kiss her and I knew I should look away.

But his gaze suddenly locked on mine.

That one glance stopped my heart cold. I was caught.

But there was no surprise in his expression: he'd known all along I was there. That realization shook me, rooted me, made it impossible for me to move.

He knew me as well as I knew him.

Impossible.

He had smoldering dark eyes, eyes filled with a thousand shadows, eyes that seemed to see straight through to my heart. His hair was long, tied back, his features could have been sculpted out of marble. But his dark eyes, his eyes saw so much.

More than I allowed anyone to see. I wanted to avert my gaze, to hide. I saw the glimmer of a smile, as if he were amused by me.

Then he bent his head and sank his teeth into Mrs. Curtis's neck. Mrs. Curtis gasped and arched her neck, as if in pleasure, then laid her cheek upon his shoulder in surrender.

I knew that my eyes had to be deceiving me. There were no vampires in real life.

But the blood was flowing, easing from the corner of the stranger's mouth to slide down Mrs. Curtis's fair skin. The rivulet was red against her pale flesh, and he drank steadily. The music soared and swirled as I gaped at them, then I saw her fingers go slack on his shoulder.

That made me move.

"Stop it!" I almost flew across the room, intending to pull him bodily away.

He stole one last massive gulp, then straightened. By the time I crossed the room, he'd laid Mrs. Curtis back in her bed with that remarkable tenderness. He was a good foot taller than me, broad and imposing, but I shoved past him in my haste.

He stepped gracefully aside, as if he'd meant to move all along. I bent over Mrs. Curtis, checking her monitors and her IV, placing my fingers under her chin.

Her pulse was weak, irregular, but still there.

The music, the lilting music that seemed to have drifted from another world, faded to nothing. I doubted I had even heard it in the first place.

"It's too late," the stranger said quietly. At close proximity, I was even more aware of his potent voice. It was more than low— it was languid. Melted chocolate on fruit.

Dark chocolate.

Tropical fruit.

I could feel the heat of him beside me, feel his scrutiny, almost hear his pulse. He was flesh and blood, like me, not an illusion.

Not a fable.

Before I could decide that my eyes had deceived me, I saw the proof: there were two perfectly round punctures in Mrs. Curtis's throat.

He *was* a vampire.

I sputtered, far from my usual coherence. "How could you do this? Who are you?"

His smile broadened, but there was a tinge of sadness in his eyes. I had the sense that he knew more than I did, but I was too angry to care. "My name is Micah," he said softly.

Mrs. Curtis's pulse faltered beneath my fingers and I forgot his alluring gaze. I reached past him and slapped the alarm button for Miriam. "We need an infusion, Miriam, stat," I said, not waiting for her query.

She knew where I was and would call up the blood type.

The stranger, meanwhile, had stepped around the end of the bed. He leaned over Mrs. Curtis and, before I could stop him, touched her throat gently with his fingertips. The gesture was reverent, that of a lover saying farewell.

When he lifted his hand, those two round holes were gone.

As if they'd never been there.

I blinked and stared, but the flesh was perfect.

I had seen them, though. I had seen what he had done.

Mrs. Curtis sighed and her head fell to one side. The pulse monitor began to sound an alarm.

Everything happened quickly then: Miriam arrived with the blood and we worked together, two other nurses following instructions. Mrs. Curtis's vitals rapidly went from bad to worse. Her pulse rate slowed and became erratic. Her breathing became more labored, rattling in her throat, her skin became paler. Nothing we did made a difference. Miriam was the perfect partner, both of us knowing exactly what had to be done when.

But it was too late.

My hands were on her scarred chest when Mrs. Curtis's heart stopped right beneath my palms. I would have kept trying, but Miriam touched my shoulder.

"There's no point, Dr. Taylor," she said quietly, and even knowing she was right, it was hard to lift my hands away.

This battle had been more important to me, although they all were critical. I blinked back unexpected tears as Miriam pulled the sheet over Mrs. Curtis's face. The two other nurses left quietly and I took a shaking breath. I turned away from the sight of Mrs. Curtis's still figure.

I'd lost.

The night was inky black beyond the windows, a perfect echo of my mood.

No. I hadn't lost. I'd been cheated.

By Micah.

I spun, finding Miriam halfway to the door. "That man, Miriam, did you see him? Where did he go?"

Miriam gave me a quizzical look. "What man, Dr. Taylor?"

"Mrs. Curtis's visitor; you couldn't have missed him. You must have passed him on your way in here with the blood."

She frowned. "I didn't see anyone but staff tonight."

"Maybe he works here." I shrugged. "He was with Mrs. Curtis when I arrived, talking to her. He was tall and dark, about thirty-five, leather jacket and long dark hair..." I faltered to silence as I realized Miriam had no idea who I was talking about.

"I think I'd remember a man like that," Miriam said with a smile. "Are you sure, Dr. Taylor?"

I glanced back at Mrs. Curtis again. I knew what I had seen. Why hadn't Miriam seen him? I remembered the way he had made the marks of his feasting disappear, and bit my tongue.

No one would believe that I'd seen a vampire.

And I wasn't going to ask Miriam about bats in the ward.

Miriam crossed the floor, her shoe soles squeaking on the linoleum. She touched my elbow briefly and I started in surprise. No one ever touched me, especially not at work. "Time to go, Dr. Taylor." She gestured to the door and I knew she was right. Lingering wouldn't change anything.

"I'll call her family," Miriam said kindly when we were in the hall.

"Does she have a partner?"

"A sister. I have the number. I'll tell her how hard you tried." Miriam studied me, then smiled. "Go home, Dr. Taylor, go home and get some sleep."

I was confused by her compassion. "I'm fine. I'll go down to the lab..."

She exhaled sharply and looked stern. "I understand that you did rounds at seven this morning, and now it's almost midnight."

There was frost hanging from every word of my response. "I always work long hours." And they were no one's business but mine.

"But you don't always see people who aren't there, Dr. Taylor, do you?"

I could have argued that the stranger *had* been there, that I knew what I had seen, but I saw that Miriam wouldn't be persuaded. I nodded an acknowledgment, thanked her and returned to the elevator.

But I didn't go home.

I went to the cafeteria and nursed a coffee from the vending machine, reviewing everything I had done, seeking the error in my judgment. I always do this kind of examination, always try to improve my strategy.

I'd done nothing wrong.

I just hadn't allowed for vampires in my statistical analysis.

Vampires. Maybe there was something to Miriam's concern. Maybe I had been pushing myself too hard. I was tired, there was no disputing that.

But how can anyone sleep when the battle is so relentless? Cancer never sleeps and it takes advantage of every weakness. It would win, maybe even while I was sleeping, and I couldn't let that happen. There already weren't enough hours in the day.

It was getting light when I ditched the cold coffee, then left the hospital. If nothing else, I'd shower and change my clothes at home before returning for morning rounds. I tried to swallow the lump in my throat to keep from looking back to Mrs. Curtis's room. I ignored the cars of my co-workers pulling into their parking spaces.

I was halfway across the lot when I saw the stranger leaning against the front fender of my car.

Waiting.

For me.

He had that amused smile again, which was more than enough to set me off.

❧

I was across the parking lot in record time, fury and exhaustion making me more volatile than usual. "You killed her!"

The stranger didn't move away from my anger. He leaned one hip against my car, his arms folded across his chest. He was dark and large and could have been carved from stone.

No, he could have been sculpted from stone. He was beautiful, his dark eyes thickly lashed, his mouth sensuously curved. I felt an awareness of him and our proximity, an awareness I resented.

He was a predator, a murderer, a vampire. He might as well have been on the enemy side.

Micah. It was a name that suited him. Just a little bit different.

Unexpected. Old and strong.

I glared at him. "You did, didn't you?"

He inclined his head slightly. "Yes." He moved slowly, elegantly, every gesture thoughtful. He closed his eyes briefly, his features touched with a sadness I didn't understand.

"How could you do that?"

"I have to feed."

"Isn't there someone else you could kill? A criminal or a wild animal? Someone who deserves to die?"

"Everyone will die, deserving or not."

"But she was going to live. I was winning..."

"Maybe she's at peace now."

"No. She's dead now."

He was amused again. "Not in heaven?"

I was as impatient with this idea as ever. My father and I had argued this up, down and sideways and I knew my position well. "There is no heaven and there is no hell. There is life and there is death and everything else is just romance."

"*Just* romance?"

"There's no point in self-delusion. Get away from my car."

"You need to understand..."

"I understand everything, thanks. You *fed*, and she died because of it. That's evil."

He didn't move. He frowned and averted his gaze, and I thought that maybe I had touched his conscience. But to my surprise, he spoke with regret and changed the subject. "Once I had a child," he began softly, but his own history didn't interest me.

"I don't care. No matter what you've lost, you have no right to decide whether another person lives or dies."

He met my gaze steadily and parted his lips, letting me see the sharp points of his fangs. "I have every right."

"No. No. Vampires don't exist," I said. I jammed my key into the lock of the door on the driver's side. He still didn't move.

"Then who killed the woman?" he asked mildly. "You?"

"No! I was the one who would have saved her. You stole that victory away."

"Victory?"

I heard my own fears in that single word. "Sure, it was back, but it hadn't won yet. I had a treatment plan prepared. We would have gone after it, hard." I held his gaze, knowing my own was filled with accusation and anger. "I would have *won*. I would have saved her. But you stole her first." I took a deep breath and glared at him. He watched me steadily, those full lips curving in that damned amusement. "You cheated me and you cheated Mrs. Curtis."

"Are you sure?"

"Yes!"

But I wasn't and he knew it. You can never be sure. Remission might be permanent or might not be. I'd been sure that Mrs. Curtis's previous round of treatment would finish the cancer, but the blood tests don't lie.

He was watching me. "Don't you want to know the rest of the story?"

There was something seductive about his voice, something that I feared I would find compelling. There was something more seductive about the notion that he knew more than I did, and that he would share. Why did I recognize him? How could it be possible?

How could I not remember?

I felt charmed by him and didn't trust the jumbled feelings I felt in his presence. I was aroused. I was furious. I wanted to know how he kissed. I wanted him to disappear forever. "No," I said with a heat that was rare for me.

His eyes twinkled, their darkness lit as the night sky had been lit with stars. "What if I don't want to go?"

I shoved him and he moved from the fender of my car. There was nothing virtual about him. He felt muscled, as if he worked out, solid and real, and I tingled in an unwelcome way.

"You can't stop the coven of mercy, Rosemary," Micah whispered, his words making me catch my breath.

"How do you know my name?" He'd known which car was mine, too.

"I know a lot of things." He arched a dark brow. "I've watched you for a long time. Not everyone prefers solitude."

His words startled me, in more ways than one, but he didn't

have a shard of doubt. He was too smug, too sure.

Maybe a little bit too much like me.

I needed to get some sleep.

"There is no coven of mercy and there was no mercy in what you did. Get away from my car."

"Is her death what's really bothering you?" he asked, his words low. "Or is it that you lost a chance to win? Is this about the person or the score?"

I slapped him then, hard, right across the face. His head jerked to one side and the red mark of my hand showed on his cheek.

I was afraid then, afraid for a moment that I'd pushed him too hard.

What he did next astonished me.

He looked at me steadily for a long moment in which my heart thundered in terror, then he pivoted with the grace of a giant cat. He strode silently across the parking lot, toward the surrounding scrub of trees.

The hospital was new, built slightly outside of town, surrounded by undeveloped land. There were scrubby trees and a little creek, a tangle of undergrowth and a nature trail. There was still snow there, caught in the bit of brush, and the tree branches were dark and bare.

The sky was turning pink in the east by then, and my hands clenched as I watched his dark figure move away. His boots crunched on the snow, as real as I was. I was so angry that I was tempted to go after him, argue some more, shake him.

Kiss him.

A car door slammed near me and I jumped, surprised to find Dr. Bradley stepping out of his Subaru so close at hand. He ran the labs and was my boss. "Are you all right, Dr. Taylor?"

"Good morning, Dr. Bradley." I forced a smile.

He didn't smile, just came to my side, his expression concerned. "Have been here all night? Again?" He was paternal, a good twenty years older than me.

I made a gesture of futility, not knowing how much I wanted to share and too tired to work it out. "I was just going home for a shower."

"And arguing with yourself about it."

"What?"

"You were shadow-boxing when I pulled in."

"No, there was a guy here..." I recognized immediately that Dr. Bradley hadn't seen the stranger.

Just like Miriam.

I stopped talking before I condemned myself.

Dr. Bradley cleared his throat. "I know you've been working really hard lately, Dr. Taylor, but indulge me, will you?"

I was wary. "What do you mean?"

"You look exhausted and have for a while. I'm wondering about your iron and iron stores. You're probably not eating well any more often than you're sleeping well. And I'm probably being cautious, but your expertise is valuable to the team."

He smiled, softening the impact of his words, but I got the drift. No one was glad to have me around, but they liked my abilities. Someone like Dr. Bradley would never understand why a lack of human connection didn't bother me.

Even if, this time, it did. A bit.

"Meaning?" I asked in my most professional tone.

"That prevention is the best medicine. Indulge me and get a routine suite of bloodwork done. We both know that it'll be easier to improve your iron counts sooner rather than later."

"There's nothing wrong with me. I just didn't sleep last night."

"When did you last have a physical?"

I shrugged. I wasn't the only one who never got around to it.

He smiled, the way he always did when he wanted something extra from his staff. For once, it worked like a charm on me. "Just humor me." He winked and turned away, giving me a last wave. "I'll leave the requisitions on your desk this morning. Promise?"

"Sure, Dr. Bradley." It wasn't as if I was afraid of needles and test results. And I had felt as if I was running on empty lately. I knew I just needed more sleep, but it wouldn't hurt to have my hemoglobin checked.

I got in my car, went home and had a shower.

Then I drank the better part of a pot of good coffee and came back to work. Cancer doesn't need to rest, after all. The battle rages, even when we leave the field. Maybe it moves faster when we aren't looking.

Coven of mercy. What had the stranger meant?

His name was Micah.

Micah.

Two days after Mrs. Curtis's death, her last batch of test results came back from the lab. There was also a reminder from Dr. Bradley that I hadn't given my blood samples yet. I crumpled the message and tossed it out. I'd just been too busy for details.

I wasn't going to look at Mrs. Curtis's results, as I was still unable to accept what I'd seen. But on some level, I needed to prove to myself that I'd been right, that Micah had been wrong, just in case I ever saw him again and could tell him so. I needed data to argue my point of view.

I knew this was ridiculous—that I needed to muster my resources to argue with a vampire—but couldn't put it out of my thoughts. I argued with myself until close to midnight.

Then I gave it up. I got a coffee from the vending machine, sat down at my desk and clicked through on the file. I stared at the numbers for so long that my coffee got cold.

I checked them four times. I assumed initially that they had to be wrong, but they were completely consistent. The cancer had efficiently progressed while we'd thought we were killing every last cell.

Against all expectation, it had turned even more virulent and metastasized. It had used the highways and byways of her lymphatic system to colonize every corner of her territory. Despite the treatment regimen. Mrs. Curtis had been so much more ill than she had appeared to be. The counts were staggering and impressive.

Cancer had already won. I had maybe slowed its progress, but I hadn't come close to stopping it.

I remembered how Mrs. Curtis had cheerfully suffered through her more recent bout of treatment, enduring more no matter how violent her reactions were. I had been so sure that short term pain would lead to long term gain. I had never underestimated the disease so much.

I felt a bit sick that she'd gone through that for nothing.

Just like my mother.

Yes, my mother's treatment had been just as futile. I'd found copies of the correspondence with her doctors in the house after my father's death, when Rick and I were cleaning things out, still refusing to speak to each other. I had reviewed them with the eyes of a trained oncologist, seeing then the inevitability of her counts. She was diagnosed too late for the treatment protocols available then to turn the tide.

I had known at twelve that she would die, even without that training, and I had been right. Later, I saw that there was mercy in the speed of the disease's progression. Three weeks of knowing, two weeks of suffering, then the battle had been won.

It wasn't always that kind.

I stared at Mrs. Curtis's charts.

Coven of mercy. I recalled Micah's words and had to consider them. If Mrs. Curtis hadn't died two days before, would these two days of treatment have been merciful? No, of course not. Chemotherapy and radiation are seldom easy, and we would have had to hit her harder this time. I had to face the truth.

With counts like this, she would have been gone in a week or two anyway, barring a miracle.

I felt a presence at my side and knew who it was. It was the warmth, the watchfulness, the scent of leather that gave Micah away.

"You knew," I said, without looking.

"I knew," he agreed.

I spun in my chair to face him, surprised at his size and intensity. He was all male—brooding thoughtful male—and he filled the bit of spare space in my crowded small office. "How?"

He frowned and folded his arms across his chest, scanning the floor as he sought the words. I liked that he didn't dismiss my question, that he didn't rush into explanations.

I felt a strange sense of union with him and was struck by the fact that it was easier to talk to him than any other person I'd known.

"We can smell it."

"Cancer?"

"Death." His gaze collided with mine, his eyes filled with enigmatic shadows. "You have to understand that it's our biological need to feed on blood. Some of us choose to use that need for compassionate ends. Some of us choose to feed strategically."

"Why?"

His smile was fleeting and his eyes gleamed as he watched me. "Some of us have an inexplicable fondness for humanity." He shrugged. "Or maybe we just remember the pain of being mortal."

"You're immortal, then?"

He nodded.

"But every day, you have to kill somebody?"

He shook his head. "The hunger comes with some regularity, but not daily. Exertion affects the appetite, as does quality and quantity consumed."

It made sense to me, in biological terms. I could understand him as a different species better than as a fable. I looked at my computer screen again, fighting the sense that I could fall into his eyes and lose myself forever.

I looked up. "We. You said we. How many of you are there?"

"The coven has twelve members right now..."

"Shouldn't there be thirteen?" I joked but he didn't smile.

"Yes," he agreed, then continued with his original point. "We are committed to mercy, to using our power to improve the lives of individual humans."

"To killing."

"Sometimes it is kinder to die. Sometimes suffering achieves nothing but pain."

That was a sentiment too close to my own recent thoughts. My tone was more sarcastic than he deserved. "So, you're all stalking cancer wards and palliative care units?"

He didn't respond to my tone, which only made me feel rude.

"We all have our tendencies and our passions. Beatrice is sensitive to victims of abuse, perhaps because of her own history. She knows some scars cannot be healed. Adrian hears the anguish of broken children, and Lucinda shares her kiss with the old and infirm. Ignatius can be found in war zones, Petronella in areas struck by famine, Augustine near outbreaks of plague."

"And you?"

That sad knowing smile curved his lips. "I have my own quest." His words were soft and he seemed to have turned inward, away from me. I felt the loss of his attention and the weight of his grief and had to say something.

To my surprise, I didn't want him to leave. "Tell me about your child," I invited. His gaze locked with mine, a familiar sorrow lighting its shadows, then he swallowed. "You said you had a child. Tell me."

Micah shook his head and stood, facing the window and the night. I was struck that he seemed overcome with emotion. I had thought that he would be a monster, a cold and calculating predator, but his anguish was raw.

And I was astonished by my own wave of compassion for him. I stood, but couldn't bring myself to go to him, to touch him.

"Boy or girl?" I asked quietly, not expecting him to answer. He sighed—a shudder that rolled right through him—and glanced over his shoulder at me.

That gaze, so filled with torment, caught at my heart. I couldn't look away.

"Elsebietta," he murmured, reverence and love resonant in every syllable. He swallowed. "Her mother died in labor and they said she would be a sad child." He fell silent for a moment, and his voice was thick when he continued. "But she was as radiant as sunlight." He raised a hand, closing it on nothing. "She was my joy. The center of my world."

I had to ask. "Did you kill her?"

The quick shake of his head was no lie. "It was before, before the coven." He swallowed. "I had to watch her die, and then there was no point in living anymore."

"But you're alive now."

"The coven came to me and I found their proposition appealing."

"Why?"

"Elsebietta had consumption. There was no real treatment and no cure. She wasted to nothing before my eyes." He inhaled sharply, then eyed me. I couldn't avert my gaze. I knew that consumption was an historic diagnosis that contemporary researchers believed meant tuberculosis. Another thief of a disease. "My daughter needed my help and I had nothing to give her."

I swallowed then, knowing that sense of helplessness all too well. We had been to the same place, Micah and I.

"Only her hair held its color." He smiled, lost in recollection. "It was so beautiful, like spun gold."

I knew then that his wife and daughter had been blond, like me. My hair has always been wavy and unruly, so I have kept it tightly controlled, captured beneath dozens of pins and clips. I saw the yearning in Micah's eyes, though, and I wanted to console him, this haunted man who mourned his only child.

It was such a small thing to give. Even if I was clumsy with such gestures.

I unpinned my hair and shook it out. It fell just past my shoulders and seemed to writhe with pleasure to be free for once. I shoved the pins in the pocket of my lab coat and looked up to find his dark gaze fixed upon me.

Filled with admiration.

In an instant Micah was beside me, although I never saw him move. He lifted a hand and gently captured one tendril between finger and thumb. That secretive smile touched his lips again.

"So soft," he whispered, then bent his head and kissed that lock of my hair. When he glanced up, those dark eyes were near mine, that mouth so close that I could almost feel it on my own lips. I caught my breath, felt my eyes widen, and saw that sparkle light his eyes. There was a moment in which we stared at each other, a moment in which time stood still, a moment in which there was nowhere else I wanted to be.

Then he kissed me.

I could have stepped back. I could have ensured that he never touched me. But one kiss, one kiss was nothing. A taste. A tease. A temptation.

And it had been so long since I'd kissed anyone.

I let him kiss me, and he seemed to understand that I wouldn't give much, not without being persuaded to do so. The first touch of his lips was as light as the brush of a butterfly's wings. Ethereal. Almost illusory. I made some small involuntary sound—one of disappointment—and he bent close again, his kiss soft upon my mouth.

Persuasive.

Tender.

I thought of Micah helpless to save his child. I thought of the wife he had lost. I recalled my own mourning of my mother. I remembered how our small family had dissolved and scattered in her absence and guessed that he had experienced a similar loss. The same sense of having no direction. Of being lost. Adrift.

Alone.

The isolation must have been worse for Micah. I had had my father, barricaded as he had been in his own grief. And my brother, Rick, now on the other side of the world and estranged. We had had the comfort of each other's physical presence, at least.

But Micah…Micah had been all alone.

I kissed him back. There was solace in the common ground of sorrow, purpose in consoling another. Our kiss was sweet and gentle, but then it changed. Then it became more sensual, more rooted in desire than in consolation, more demanding.

More exciting.

I opened my mouth and gripped his shoulders, leaning against him as he caught me close. He knew when to entreat and when to wait, how to drive me crazy as if we'd been lovers for years. I wanted more. I wanted it immediately, and I knew he tasted that in my kiss.

It was unlike any kiss I'd ever had, making all others look like pale shadows of this perfection. It was the kiss I had always wanted and I realized, as he let his tongue tempt mine, that I had been looking for just this kiss.

Then I felt the brush of Micah's sharp tooth against my lower lip. There could be no stronger reminder of the predator he was.

And I heard music.

I broke the kiss and backed away from him in fear.

He let me go, watching as intently as I'd come to expect. "Now you look alive," he murmured with satisfaction.

I pivoted to check my reflection and was shocked at my own appearance. My hair was loose and wild as it had never been, my eyes sparkling, my lips swollen. I looked like a woman who had been thoroughly kissed, and as different from my usual prim self as could be.

I would have blamed Micah for that, but when I turned back, he was gone.

As surely as if he had never been. My hands were shaking as I scooped up the scattered pins from my hair, and I pulled my hair up so tightly that it made me wince.

I could still taste that kiss, though.

I knew I would relive it in my dreams.

We aren't supposed to become involved.

We learned that in med school. Oncologists should be professional and detached, in order to make the best logical decision for treatment. We are the rudders, the realists, the rational ones. It's the only way to balance the emotions we encounter, the ones that cancer rouses.

It's the only way to fight the battle over the long term. I may have been called Icicle Taylor, but I haven't been the only one with my moat filled and my portcullis dropped. I have waded through buckets of emotional reactions every day since graduation, but always kept my eyes fixed on the prize.

Maybe it's not an accident that I chose to stay in research, to be a specialist called in for tough cases, but never the primary contact.

But two years before this particular March, a little boy named Jason had reached in and grabbed my heart.

He had been all of five years old when he came to the ward with leukemia, the adored elder child of a devoted couple. They were a picture-perfect husband and wife, trim and attractive, affluent and kind, professionals. They were affectionate with each other and with their adorable son and daughter. They were the kind of people who get what they want, and what they wanted was their son healthy again.

They would do whatever it took.

Jason was solemn, with a tangle of dark hair and eyes that seemed too big for his face. He had beautiful dark lashes and a surprising ability to understand what was really going on. His leukemia was aggressive and I was testing a new drug. Their oncologist, pushed by Jason's parents to do more, called me in.

I was not used to being noticed in these situations. I'd explain the drug or the protocol, the risks and advantages, the unknowns, then step back and let the patient's oncologist handle the rest. I witnessed but didn't really participate.

Jason was the first to challenge that. We were at the end of our meeting, the oncologist summing up the strategy for Jason's parents, when this boy reached out and grabbed my hand. I jumped. I had thought they had all forgotten my presence.

"Will it hurt, Dr. Taylor?" he demanded, his eyes wide.

I was so surprised that I couldn't lie to him.

"Yes," I said. "But if you can do this, you will get better."

His mother caught her breath sharply. His father watched in horror. The oncologist closed his eyes. The tension in the room was palpable.

But Jason studied me, his gaze searching mine. I stared back at him steadily. I knew we would win and I let him see my conviction. His lips set and he nodded then, as committed to the course as I was.

And he was a trouper. Never complained. I went to his second marrow transplant as an observer, unable to stay away. The first hadn't been easy and the second was likely to be worse. Jason had seized my finger in pre-op, insisting that I hold his hand.

The whole team was shocked when Icicle Taylor agreed.

I was more shocked when Jason ran to give me a hug on the day of his final discharge. No one had spontaneously hugged me since my mother's death. I didn't think to hug him back. I was surprised and touched, and although I had rationalized it since, I still relived that moment of triumph.

It was a battle we had won.

But a week after Mrs. Curtis died, Jason came back.

Capricious, deceitful March.

I'd been working even more hours, cross-checking everything, determined not to let anyone down the way I'd almost let Mrs. Curtis down. Dr. Bradley was a genial nag about my apparent inability to give the lab some blood. I'd never logged so many hours and I was exhausted, but I felt on the cusp of a breakthrough.

Until I saw Jason's parents in the ward. My heart stopped cold with the knowledge of why they were there. I have never wanted to be wrong as badly as I did then. Headaches, lassitude, infections that wouldn't go away, night sweats. His parents knew the truth as well as we did.

Jason had always reminded me of somebody I couldn't quite remember. I was so shocked at the sight of him this time that I realized who he resembled.

He looked like Micah. He had the intensity of focus and thoughtfulness that characterized Micah. That solemnity, that intensity, that watchfulness. Never mind the dark eyes and dark hair, the beautiful features.

It made no sense. I had met Jason *before* Micah.

No. That wasn't true. I remembered suddenly that I *had* seen Micah before. He'd been at my mother's funeral, a stranger on the perimeter of the gathering of mourners, watching.

Watching me.

My father had told me to pay attention and had been impatient with my insistence about the stranger. He had said that there was no one there.

I had never told anyone about the dreams I'd had later, dreams of that same man who didn't exist. I had shoved the recollection of those dreams aside, like so much else that made no sense that year.

Once recalled, I couldn't forget them. Micah had been watching me.

Why me?

I had a dreadful feeling about Jason's prognosis. We ordered the tests and tried to make cheerful noises, but the oncologist on the case and I avoided each other's gazes.

I was there the night the tests came back from the lab, a little ping from my computer indicating that the file I was watching had been updated. I didn't get coffee, just sat and read.

The results were terrible.

Inescapable.

I shut the door of my office and wept. Optimism isn't nearly a good enough weapon. I know the statistics and the survival rates as well as my own name. I looked again at Jason's blood work, even though I knew.

I was caught. We couldn't deny him treatment. I couldn't be fatalistic. I couldn't send Jason home to be happy for as many months—or weeks—as he had left. But I didn't want to put that darling boy with his trusting eyes through a treatment ordeal that wouldn't matter at the end.

I didn't want him to suffer more than he would anyway.

I wanted mercy for him.

I knew that Jason's parents would spare no expense and no trouble in their quest to see him cured. They had proven to be great allies in his past treatment regimen.

But this time they would fight, and they would lose.

And so I cried. I sat alone in my office and I wept for the futility of it all. I wept for Jason and his parents and the fact that he would never grow up to be the heartbreaker I wanted him to be. I wept for Mrs. Curtis, believing at the end that she was dancing with a handsome man. I wept for my mother, and my father who had never been able to talk about his own pain, and my brother who had run as far away from the past as was physically possible. I wept for Micah and his lost wife and his beautiful daughter.

It was late when I had shed all my tears—two decades worth of them—and the night was still and dark. I wiped my face and blew my nose and decided I needed some sleep. I was straightening my desk when I grimaced at another e-mail from Dr. Bradley. The message from the day before was still unopened as I'd assumed it to be a nag about iron supplements. This one was marked urgent.

Some people don't like to be ignored.

I had done the blood work, for goodness' sake.

I rolled my eyes and flicked open the file, guessing that he'd been right in his diagnosis. Low iron is a common problem among women, and I knew I wasn't that special in biological terms. I certainly didn't practice good self-care.

But it was a referral to the head oncologist on our team.

I clicked through to my own blood tests and sat back, stunned. My hemoglobin was down, but my white blood counts high. Worst of all, Dr. Bradley had requested a cancer antigen test, because of my family history, and its high result told me all I needed to know.

My old adversary had moved the field of battle into my own cells.

Cancer is sneaky. It takes advantage of your mistakes. I've learned that, but I had left one flank undefended. My mother, after all, had died of ovarian cancer. Her death was what got me into this line of work. I wanted the power to do something other than stand by and watch for the inevitable. I've made a lot of saves in my time and spearheaded a lot of research. I've done good work.

Maybe that's why it came after me. Maybe I was too worthy an opponent. Maybe that's why it took advantage of my genetic weakness.

It had certainly taken advantage of my slip-up. How long had it been since I'd had a physical examination? A suite of blood work done? A Pap smear? I just never had the time. Or maybe, I'd thought I was invincible, since I was fighting for the good guys.

It didn't really matter. I knew too much about treatment, about pain and suffering, and I knew the statistics. I knew that the oncologist would review my family history and immediately order an ultrasound of my lower abdomen, and I knew what he would find. I understood suddenly why I couldn't shed that round belly I'd developed, and it wasn't the food in the cafeteria.

I had a tumor and, with these counts, I would bet that it had already metastasized. It made too much sense. I knew that by the time there are symptoms of ovarian cancer, it's all over.

Even more damning, I had known my mother would die, with unshakeable certainty, when she was diagnosed. I had the same conviction that this cancer would take me, too.

Maybe I had always known that. Maybe that was why I hated March so much. Maybe it was a kind of foresight.

I didn't cry for myself. I'd cried all my tears for Jason and for Mrs. Curtis. I was too angry that the fight would go on without me, that the battle would rage without my contribution. It wasn't fair. I was surprised by how much I wanted a different answer than the one I routinely gave.

I looked out the window at the night, seething.

Micah was leaning against the fender of my car again, and he looked as if his gaze was fixed upon my window. I understood then why I was the only one who could see him. Just as Mrs. Curtis had seen him.

He was waiting for me.

And I knew why.

❧

"You knew," I said when I was still twenty feet away from him.

Micah inclined his head in agreement, that same graceful gesture, but there was no amused curve to his lips this time. He was as watchful as ever, though.

Still.

I couldn't simply stand, not with this chaotic need to do something swirling inside me. I was excited, agitated, uncertain. Could I battle my old enemy in a different way?

"I need to walk." I headed for the scrap of wilderness around the parking lot.

Micah followed. I walked quickly, striding through the brush, ignoring the patches of snow underfoot and the brambles snatching at my clothes. It felt good to push my body, a denial of the disease that lurked inside my cells.

When I finally halted and spun, there was nothing but Micah, his glittering eyes and the stars overhead. I was aware of the warm strength of him, aware of the lump in my throat.

I saw no need for pretence. "Tell me about the coven."

"We offer relief to those who suffer, especially those who suffer needlessly. It's a choice on our part."

"When treatment is futile."

"When there is no chance of healing."

"Like Elsebietta."

He nodded once and looked away, still tormented by that loss. "It was hell."

I knew exactly what he meant and so I did what I never do—I

reached out and touched him. I offered solace.

He eyed my hand, then reached down and captured it in his. My heart skipped at the heat in his eyes and I sounded breathless. "So, you joined the coven."

"I saw the chance to diminish suffering." He grimaced and bent his head, staring at the glint of the creek. "I follow the edicts of the coven of mercy, but I've been looking for something different than the others. Something more."

"Like what?"

He looked at me so quickly that I couldn't look away, his eyes gleaming. "I don't want to be alone," he whispered.

I swallowed, guessing his implication. "You said the coven is short one member."

He nodded once. "I asked for the right to fill that place. I have been waiting for a dance partner for a long time."

"How long?" I knew the answer, but I had to hear it.

"Twenty years, this very month."

"I thought I saw you at the funeral," I guessed. "But no one else did."

"No, you could only glimpse me then. It was too soon." He smiled. "But you dreamed me. I managed that."

He was right. "Why me?"

"Because I saw the same passion in you that burns in me."

I caught my breath and looked away, dizzy at the implication. I heard the music begin, sounding as if it carried from a distant orchestra, and panicked. "But Mrs. Curtis died."

"Because I didn't stop."

I eyed him, seeing that he looked paler than he had, seeing a gauntness to his cheeks. "You're hungry."

He nodded, licked his lips and looked away. "I've been waiting for you, Rosemary."

"For a long time?"

He smiled. "Always."

"And I would be able to do what you do, to give mercy?"

"Yes."

"But I would be your partner?"

"Maybe. Maybe not. We can only try when we have similar powers and objectives." His smile was fleeting, barely curving his lips. "I'm inviting you on an adventure."

It was an invitation that I was destined to accept. Another chance, an opportunity to make a difference, an adventure…and Micah.

There was only one element in my past, only one detail that I wanted to resolve. "Will you show mercy to Jason?"

He shook his head and my heart sank. "I think he should be yours."

In a way, my decision had been made when I saw my own test results. I offered my other hand to him, palm up. My words were thick, my voice not sounding like my own. "I've never learned to waltz."

"I'll teach you," he pledged. He pulled me into his arms and that music became louder. It was evocative of another time and place, romantic and sweet and ethereal. As seductive as he was.

"How do you do that?" I asked.

"It's easy," he whispered and I believed him. I felt his hand on my back, his chest against mine, then he pulled me close. His breath fanned against my ear, my neck, and I gasped at the tiny prick of his teeth.

Then my blood was leaving me, its heat flowing from the wound on my neck. I felt him drink, felt him take the life force into his body. With every beat of my heart, Micah felt stronger and larger, firmer and warmer. And with every beat, I felt less substantial, weaker.

I was becoming a ghost. The cares of the world fell away from me and I saw the course of my life with perfect clarity. I saw that every step had been on the same journey, bringing me to this place at this moment with this man. I relived that forgotten glimpse of Micah at my mother's funeral, reviewed those dreams, and tasted the force of destiny in my life.

I saw the pattern in my dating, my dissatisfaction with all those dark-eyed, dark-haired men, none of whom could hold a candle to Micah. I saw my own impatience with any relationship that was not a perfect communion and knew what I had been seeking.

This.

Him.

I saw how the past shapes the future, but gained a sense of how the future could shape the past. My life had brought me inexorably to this destination, to this junction, to this destiny.

Who could tell where the adventure would lead from here?

I wanted to know.

And just when it seemed that I would cease to exist forever, just when it seemed that I was no more substantial than the wind, Micah lifted his head. He bit his own hand, then fitted my mouth to the wound. The blood was salty, not truly to my taste, but he coaxed me to drink of it.

Once I had started, I couldn't stop. Micah's blood flooded through me like a draught of starlight. It set me tingling with a physiological change that I knew I would have to analyze later. For the moment, though, there was only the sense that I was changing, becoming something closer to ice and moonlight than before.

I was trading the sun for the moon, in more ways than one. I felt stronger and more vital, purposeful and focused. When Micah made me stop drinking, I believed I truly was invincible.

Finally.

I smiled at him, seeing him fully for the first time. He was larger and darker than I'd imagined, the secrets in his eyes more profound. His skin was finer, his presence stronger, his hair more luxurious. My desire for him had multiplied tenfold.

My gaze was sharper, my ability to perceive detail almost dizzying. All of my senses were heightened and my body was stronger. I flexed my hand, awed by the change. There was so much to learn.

And all of eternity to do it.

Then I lifted my arms, astounded to find myself rising above the earth by will alone. I looked down upon the collapsed body of Dr. Rosemary Taylor, that mortal shell I needed no longer. She laid on the bank of the creek as if she were sleeping, no more a part of me than the shoes I'd kicked into my closet.

Micah offered his hand and we moved like the wind through the air, the speed leaving me dizzy and disconnected from space and time. I knew where we would go and trusted him to take me there.

Jason awakened to find me by his bedside. He smiled, this thoughtful gem of a boy, trust filling his eyes. I heard the music again, that ghostly waltz, and my throat tightened at its import.

"Would you like to dance, Jason?"

He looked between me and Micah, with uncertainty. "Will it hurt, Dr. Taylor?"

"Never again," I vowed and he searched my gaze as he had once before.

And then he smiled.

"Okay." Jason opened his arms to me.

I smiled and leaned closer, gathering the precious burden of him into my arms as Micah watched. I smelled the death in Jason and my heart swelled that I could give him this gift.

This mercy.

"Listen to the music," I murmured.

"Pretty," he said and closed his eyes, his dark lashes thick upon his cheek. He'd never awaken again and I was fiercely glad of that. I bent my head to his sweet neck, tore the flesh and drank until he was gone.

Until he was at peace forever.

Micah brushed my fingertips across the two puncture marks, showing me how to remove the proof of our presence. His hand was warm over mine, protective, and as I stared at Jason, finally so tranquil, I was fiercely glad of the choice I'd made. I had become something new and was determined to use my power as Micah did.

For mercy.

So, I smiled when Micah took my hand in his and I squeezed his fingers in mine. He smiled at me, his eyes glowing with promise, then led me on our adventure.

I went willingly. There was so much to learn, and all the time to do it. I had been waiting for this opportunity and I knew that I—we—would make the most of it.

Forever.

The Ballad of Rosamunde

Rosamunde was a character introduced as a foundling in my Claire Delacroix medieval romance, **The Scoundrel**. From that point, she became entangled in the lives of the families at Ravensmuir and Kinfairlie, and by the time of my Jewels of Kinfairlie series, Rosamunde had taken over the family business of trading in religious relics from her foster father, Gawain. She was always one to defy expectations, serving as both a warning and an inspiration to her nieces at Kinfairlie. In **The Rose Red Bride**, Rosamunde was lost in the caverns beneath Ravensmuir when that keep collapsed. I'd always thought Rosamunde would star in her own book, but since she was an older heroine, a pirate queen, and not exactly virginal, my view wasn't shared by my publisher. By the end of the Jewels of Kinfairlie trilogy, Rosamunde's fate was still unknown. I'd always figured she'd find her way out of the realm of the Fae somehow and always believed that she deserved a happy ending, too. I just didn't see a way for me to tell that story to you.

Several years later, I was invited to participate in another anthology, this one being the **Mammoth Book of Irish Romance**. It was evident (at least to me) that the realm of the Fae must be connected, at least beneath Ireland and Scotland, so this was my chance to tell Rosamunde's story and give her that second chance at love. It also seemed only natural that Rosamunde, of all the characters who have strolled into my office over the years, would be the one to star in a ballad, particularly one sung in taverns.

Rosamunde's story was edited due to space constraints in that anthology. It appears in its entirety in the new trade paperback edition of **The Snow White Bride** and in a digital-only edition by itself. The story of the family at Kinfairlie continues in my medieval romance series The True Love Brides, which begins with **The Renegade's Heart**.

Galway, Ireland—April 1422

he hour was late and the tavern was crowded. Padraig sat near the hearth, watching the firelight play over the faces of the men gathered there. The ale launched a warm hum within him, the closest he was ever like to be to the heat of the Mediterranean sun again.

He should have gone south, as Rosamunde had bidden him to do. He should have sold her ship and its contents, as she had instructed him. Galway was as far as he had managed to sail from Kinfairlie—and he had only come this far because his crew had compelled him to leave the site of disaster.

Where Rosamunde had been lost forever.

Instead he had returned here, to the site of his upbringing, to his mother's grave and the tavern run by his sister and her husband. It had an allure for him, with the bustling port and the cobbled streets, the high gates and the memories, but he would trade it in a heartbeat for a voyage over the seas with Rosamunde.

Perhaps Galway would have to do.

Padraig enjoyed music, always had, and song was the only solace he found in the absence of Rosamunde's company. He found his foot tapping and his cares lifting as a local man sang of adventure.

"A song!" cried Declan, the keeper, when one rollicking tune came to an end. "Who else has a song?"

"Padraig!" shouted his sister. She was a pretty woman, albeit one who tolerated no nonsense. Padraig suspected there were those more afraid of her than her husband. Much like their mother in that. "Sing the sad one you began the other night," she entreated.

"There are others of better voice," Padraig protested.

The company roared a protest in unison, and so he acquiesced. Padraig sipped his ale, then pushed to his feet to sing the ballad of his own composition.

> *'Rosamunde was a pirate queen*
> *With hair red gold and eyes of green.*

A trade in relics did she pursue,
Plus perfume and silks of every hue.
Her ship's hoard was a rich treasury,
Of prizes gathered on every sea.
But the fairest gem in all the hold
Was Rosamunde, beauteous and bold.
Her blade was quick, her foresight sharp,
She conquered hearts in every port."

"Ah!" sighed the older man across the table from Padraig. "There be a woman worth the loss of one's heart."

The company nodded approval and leaned closer for the next verse. Even his sister stopped serving, leaning against the largest keg in the tavern, smiling as she watched Padraig.

"Trade in relics, both false and true
Her family trade she did pursue.
No man cheated her and told of it,
For Rosamunde allowed no debt.
She vanquished foes on every sea
But lost her heart to a man esteemed.
Surrender was not her nature true
But bow to his desires, she did do.
She left the sea to become his bride,
But in her lover's home, Rosamunde died.
The man she loved was not her worth..."

Padraig faltered. His compatriots in the tavern waited expectantly, but he could not think of a suitable rhyme. He remembered the sight of Ravensmuir's cliffs and caverns collapsing to rubble, the dust rising, his men holding him captive so that he couldn't dive into the disaster in search of Rosamunde. He put down his tankard with dissatisfaction, singing the last line again softly. It made no difference. He had composed a hundred rhymes, if not a thousand, but this particular tale caught in his throat like none other.

"Her absence was to all a dearth," his sister suggested.

Her husband snorted. "You've no music in your veins,

woman, that much is for certain."

"The son she bore him died at birth," the old man across the table suggested.

Padraig shook his head and frowned. "There was no child."

"There could be," the old man insisted. "'Tis only a tale, after all." The others laughed.

But this was not only a tale. It was the truth. Rosamunde had existed, she had been a pirate queen, she had sailed far and wide in the buying and selling of religious relics, she had been both beauteous and bold.

And she had been lost forever, thanks to the faithlessness of the man to whom she had surrendered everything.

Padraig mourned that truth every day and night of his life.

He cursed Tynan Lammergeier, the man who had cost him the company of Rosamunde, and he hated that they two might be together forever in some afterlife. It was wrong that a man who had not been able to accept Rosamunde for her true nature should win her company for all eternity.

Because Padraig had loved her truly.

His mother had warned him that he was his father's son, that he would be smitten once and his heart lost forever. It had shocked him all the same to find her counsel true.

But he had held his tongue. He had spoken of friendship in his parting with Rosamunde, not the fullness of his heart.

Now he would never have the chance to remedy his error. It had been almost six months since Rosamunde had gone into the caverns beneath Ravensmuir, Tynan's ancestral keep on the coast of Scotland, six months since those caves had collapsed and Rosamunde had been lost forever, and still Padraig's wound was raw.

He doubted it would ever heal.

He knew he'd never meet the like of her again.

Padraig sat down and drank deeply of his ale. "Let another sing," he said. "I am too besotted to compose the verse."

"Another tale!" shouted the keeper. "Come, Liam, sing that one of the Faerie host." The company stamped their feet and applauded, as Liam was clearly a local favorite, and Padraig saw a lanky man rise to his feet on the far side of the room.

He, however, had lost his taste for tales. He abandoned the rest of his ale, left a coin on the board, and headed for the door.

"We will miss your custom this evening," his sister said softly as he passed her. Her dark eyes shone brightly in the shadowed tavern, and he knew that she saw more of his heart than any other. She never asked for details, though, simply offered him a place to stay.

"A man should be valued for more than the volume of ale he can drink," Padraig replied, blaming himself for what he had become. His sister flushed as if he had chided her and turned away. Padraig raised a hand toward her, not having wanted to share his anguish, but she bustled away to serve another patron.

He could do nothing right.

Not without Rosamunde.

Was her loss to be the shadow over all his days and nights?

Far beneath the hills to the north of Galway, Finvarra, High King of the *Daoine Sidhe*, templed his fingers together and considered the chess board. It was a beautiful chess board, with pieces of alabaster and obsidian, the board itself wrought of agate and ebony with fine enamel work around the perimeter. When he touched a piece, it came to life, moving across the board at his unspoken will. His entire fey court gathered around the game, watching with bright eyes.

Finvarra was tall and slim, finely wrought even for the fey, who were uncommonly handsome. His eyes were as dark as a midnight sky, his long hair the deep blue black of the sea in darkness, his skin as fair as moonlight, his tread as light as wind in the grass. He was possessed of both kindness and resolve and ruled the fey well.

His hall at Knockma was under the hill and as lavish a court as could be found. The ladies wore glistening gowns of finest silk, their gossamer wings painted with a thousand colors. The courtiers were armed in silver finery, their manners both fierce and gallant, their eyes glinting with humor. The horses of Finvarra's court were spirited and fleet of foot, gleaming and beauteous in their rich trappings hung with silver bells. He had steeds of every color, red stallions and white mares, black stallions and mahogany mares with ivory socks. Each and every one was caparisoned in finery to show its hue and strength to advantage. The mead was sweet and golden in Finvarra's hall, and the cups at the board filled themselves with more when no one was looking.

But all the fairy court was silent, clustered around their king's favored chessboard. They watched, knowing that more than victory at a game hung in the balance.

As usual.

Finvarra did not care for low stakes.

Finvarra played to win.

The spriggan, Darg, sat opposite the king and fidgeted. Recently of Scotland, the small thieving fairy had traveled to Ireland in the hold of the ship of Padraig Deane, a blue-eyed and handsome pirate possessed of a broken heart. Caught trespassing in Finvarra's *sid*, a crime punishable by death, the spriggan played for its life.

Finvarra, in truth, tired of the game. The spoils were not so remarkable and the spriggan was a mediocre opponent. The splendor of the board, indeed, he felt was wasted upon the rough little creature. Certainly, his skill was.

Then Finvarra heard the distant lilt of human song.

"Rosamunde was a pirate queen
With hair red gold and eyes of green..."

As was common with Finvarra, the mention of a beauteous mortal woman piqued his interest. He turned his head to listen, just as the spriggan interrupted with a hiss.

"A laughing trickster Rosamunde did be, but she did not have the best of me."

"You knew this mortal?"

Darg raised a fist. *"Stole from me! That she dared, but I did steal her from her laird. She would be dead but for me; now she owes me her fealty."* The spriggan cackled, then moved a pawn with care. It was a poor choice. *"Not dead but enchanted she doth be, while I choose what my vengeance shall be."*

Intrigued, Finvarra snapped his fingers and his wife, Una,

brought his silver mirror to his hand. She knew him well. She caressed his hand as she passed the mirror to him, but Finvarra ignored her gesture of affection.

He didn't imagine her sniff of displeasure, but Una's pleasure was not his current concern. Not when there was a beauteous woman to be possessed. He murmured to the mirror and its surface swirled before his eyes, the image of this Rosamunde appearing so suddenly that Finvarra caught his breath.

Then his blood quickened.

Una, always able to read his response, spun on her heel. She strode from the hall, her ladies scurrying after her like so many sparrows. Finvarra was oblivious to his wife's mood.

This Rosamunde was not just beautiful, but there was a set to her chin that hinted at a spirited nature.

Finvarra had to know more. He touched the queen, his favored piece, sliding his finger up her carved back. She strolled across the board in perfect understanding of his intent, halted on the desired spot and tucked her hands into her sleeves meekly.

If only all queens might be so biddable.

"Check," he murmured with a smile.

"No! I shall not die, not by your whim!" The spriggan erupted from its place in fury, jumping across the board and kicking pieces left and right. *"I demand we play the game again!"*

Finvarra shook his head.

The spriggan scattered the pieces onto the earthen floor, then lunged at Finvarra. There was no contest between them, the spriggan being only as tall as the king's golden chalice. Finvarra struck the ill-tempered creature with the back of his hand, sending it sprawling across the floor.

The elegantly attired fey stepped away from the spriggan, whispering at its poor manners. It hissed at all of them, then made to run. Two elfin knights seized it, holding tightly while it bit and struggled.

"I have no interest in your life," Finvarra said with soft authority. The spriggan froze, staring at him in confusion. It was a crafty creature and Finvarra deliberately stated his terms so that there could be no deception. "I would trade your life for a specific treasure in your possession."

Darg's eyes narrowed into hostile slits. *"No gem do I see fit to spare..."*

"The woman," Finvarra decreed, interrupting what would likely be an impolite diatribe. "I trade your life for that of your captive, Rosamunde."

The spriggan regarded him warily. *"I fear you make a jest of me and would be freed 'fore I agree."*

Finvarra rose and clapped his hands. "There is no jest. When Rosamunde graces my court, you shall be free to leave." He reached forward and snatched at the spriggan, holding it so surely in his grip that it paled. He lowered his face to its sharp features, glaring into its eyes. Darg squirmed. "Deceive me, though, and I will have your life as well as the woman."

Darg's eyes gleamed and Finvarra knew the creature would willingly deceive him. He beckoned to his armorer, who produced a fine red thread at his master's bidding. Finvarra knotted that thread securely around the spriggan's waist. It appeared to be made of silk but was strong beyond measure and it held the spriggan to Finvarra's command. The small fairy struggled and fought against the bond, grimacing where it touched the skin.

"It burns, it does, the knot too tight," Darg snarled. *"You cheat when I would do what's right!"*

"Only I can unbind this thread, and I will only do so when you have fulfilled our bargain."

Darg continued to pluck at the thread, its displeasure clear. It cast a glance over the company, then its lips tightened. It straightened and addressed him with surprising hauteur. *"As you command, so shall it be. You shall see that Darg lives honestly."*

Finvarra smothered a laugh. He didn't doubt that the creature would try to break both cord and vow, but he knew such efforts were doomed to failure. "Tomorrow sunset," he decreed. "I would have her by my side for the Beltane ride two nights hence."

The spriggan grimaced at the time constraint, but before it could argue, Finvarra made a dismissive gesture. "It is enough time. Should it not be..." He raised a brow and the thread bound around the spriggan's waist tightened an increment. Darg screamed, swore agreement, then scampered across the court, muttering. Three elven knights followed it at a discreet distance, ensuring that it left the hall upon its mission.

Finvarra eyed the path Una had taken, heard the distant sound of her sobs, and decided to remain in his hall a bit longer. He clapped and called for music, for he was feeling as celebratory as Una was not.

After all, soon he would have a new prize to savor.

Rosamunde dreamed.

If she had been asked, she would have said that her expectation was to dream of Tynan through all eternity. But her dream took her farther into the past, to an abbey on the coast of Ireland.

She had been summoned there by the bishop, eager to increase the revenue of his remote diocese with the acquisition of a holy relic. Pilgrims brought coin, and the faithful had already made their journey to Compostela. Many did not have the inclination—or the funds—to travel to the Holy Land itself. This bishop saw opportunity, as did many of his ilk.

He had not been pleased to have a woman answer his summons, however. Although she knew nothing of him, Rosamunde was well accustomed to his perspective. He had addressed her man first, assuming him to be the leader, but Eugene had been quick to step back and gesture to Rosamunde.

The bishop's lips had tightened, and Rosamunde had been certain of his intent to cheat her.

They had met in a cell that had been used by a solitary monk centuries past, the cone-shaped dwelling of fitted stones perched on the coast. The remote setting had been convenient both for Rosamunde's ship and had provided the discretion necessary for such a purchase.

It was also dangerous, a treacherous facet of her trade.

It had been a windy night, with storm clouds rolling from the western horizon. The flame had danced wildly above the bishop's lantern, even inside the cell. That man had been swathed in a great dark cloak, its hood drawn to disguise his features, and accompanied by a pair of men.

They stood silently behind their lord, one at his left and one at his right. They wore no livery and their expressions were impassive. Rosamunde did not doubt that they were instructed to forget whatsoever they saw on this night. Whichever relic the bishop chose would be 'discovered' in the crypt of the church shortly.

One man had eyes of brilliant blue and a steady gaze. He watched Rosamunde openly, which surprised her. She strove to ignore him.

"I expected Gawain Lammergeier!" the bishop complained.

Rosamunde smiled. "My father surrendered the family trade to me some years past. He sails forth no longer."

"Have you not a brother?"

"My brother chose the family holding as his legacy."

The bishop snorted in disapproval of the situation. It was clear that he did not want to trade with her, but at the same time, he wanted a relic. His pale hands moved with agitation beneath the hems of his sleeves.

"Perhaps you would like to see what I have brought," she said, knowing he would be tempted. She had brought the best of her current inventory, after all.

First there had been an embroidered blue cloth, purported to have been worn by the Virgin. It had the muck of authenticity about it, but its appearance did not inspire devotion. The bishop made some cursory remark in praise of it.

There had been a broken crown of thorns, one possessing the best provenance of any Rosamunde had seen in recent years. It was likely still a fake. Rosamunde had seen too many crowns of thorns to have faith in any of them. The bishop stroked it, admired it, considered it seriously.

"How many crowns of thorns can there be, my lord?" asked the man with the blue eyes. "There is said to be one in Paris and another in Palestine."

"Is this the genuine one?" the bishop demanded.

Rosamunde shrugged. "Who can say?"

The bishop drummed his fingers. "There must be no question of authenticity, and I cannot imagine how the crown of thorns might have made its way this far."

Finally, there was a coil of dark hair. Clearly old, it was still lustrous and long, braided neatly. There was a faint scent of perfume to it, although Rosamunde suspected that this had been enhanced over the years. Best of all, it was encased in a jeweled reliquary of masterful craftsmanship, adorned with images of Jesus treating Lazarus. That reliquary was within a wooden box of no apparent distinction.

Although the bishop grimaced at the sight of the wooden box, his eyes lit when the reliquary was revealed. "What is that?"

"It is said to be the hair of Mary, the daughter of Lazarus." Rosamunde opened the reliquary and the bishop took a deep, delighted breath. "She who anointed Jesus with perfume when he came to her father's house and washed his feet with her hair."

The bishop pretended to be torn, but Rosamunde knew which he would choose. And choose the hair, he did. They negotiated the price, then he gestured to the man behind him.

The other man, the one with the compelling blue gaze, watched Rosamunde steadily throughout the whole transaction. She sensed that he also knew the bishop intended to cheat her. She locked her hands behind her back, giving Eugene a silent and hidden signal.

The exchange was made, the coin counted and deposited in Rosamunde's purse, the relic and its reliquary surrendered to the bishop's man. Compliments and formalities were exchanged. They parted, Rosamunde's intuition warning her all the while. Eugene was at her back as they left the cell, both of them scanning the land to the left and right as they returned to the dingy.

Rosamunde was glad to see her ship, still moored where she had left it. The light at the stern had been lit, the one with the red filter, so she knew that the ship had not been assaulted in her absence. There was no sound of pursuit.

Perhaps her intuition had been wrong.

She emitted a high whistle, a signal to Thomas waiting in the dingy out of sight. She and Eugene broke into a run, anxious to be away.

Rosamunde was not prepared to find Thomas dead, bleeding in the bottom of the boat.

She was not prepared to have two other men assault her in the darkness, to be leapt upon and beaten. It happened quickly, upon turf she did not know. The purse was ripped from her belt, Eugene was stabbed, the other two relics fell to the ground.

Her blade was snatched, she was struck across the face and fell to her knees. A man seized her from behind. The other attacker lunged toward her, his blade flashing, and Rosamunde feared she was done.

She certainly was not expecting the blue-eyed man to leap out of the shadows behind her attacker.

"Oi!" he shouted and the attacker spun in surprise.

The blue-eyed man sliced him from gullet to groin and kicked his carcass into the sea. The one holding Rosamunde released her and ran. The bishop's man pursued him, stabbed him until he moved no more, then returned to Rosamunde.

She met the determination in his gaze as he handed her the fully laden purse that had been stolen from her.

"I sicken of his thievery," he said softly, his voice as steady as his gaze. Rosamunde checked Eugene and was glad to find that he yet breathed. The blue-eyed man helped her move him to the dingy, Eugene wincing as he was rolled into the boat. Thomas, unfortunately, was beyond aid. Rosamunde would see him buried at sea, which would have been his choice.

She looked up at the man who had saved her. "I thank you for your aid."

"You are most welcome." He glanced inland, then back at her and smiled, a quick conspiratorial smile. "I fear I have lost my employ this night. Have you need of another man on your ship?"

Rosamunde found herself liking this man a great deal. "I always have need of men with stout hearts and quick blades." The bishop's henchmen did not move, a sign of this man's effectiveness. "Have you a name?"

"Padraig Deane."

Rosamunde shook his hand, liking the heat of his skin, the firmness of his grip. It was not in her nature to remain on land, and she always yearned to be back at sea. But this man made her think about lingering.

"Welcome, Padraig. There is no better compliment than knowing a man can be trusted with one's own life." She saw him smile, glimpsed his flush, then they gathered the relics and the fallen men. She watched the moonlight play on his muscles as he rowed them all back to the ship. He was determined, stalwart, unafraid to do what he believed to be right.

And Rosamunde wondered how she had failed to see the full merit of Padraig in all the years he had served her.

What lifted the scales from her eyes now?

Padraig wandered the streets of Galway, paying no attention to his course until he reached the gate in the Norman wall. He glanced back toward the harbor, then ahead to the hills cloaked in starlight and shadow. He chose to pass through the gate and walk out of town, knowing that the way was not without risk. He was but half-Irish, half of town and half of country, though there were those who would have little interest in the details.

He did not care about his fate as much as he once had.

And he had no taste for human company on this night. He should love it here, the place where he had been raised, but instead he felt at home only upon the sea.

Rosamunde had been the same way.

He walked as the moon rose ever higher in the sky. He walked as the church bells sounded far behind him. He walked as the stars glinted overhead.

He heard the rustle of small animals in the underbrush and the tinkle of running water. He felt the ale loosen its hold upon his body and grief well in his heart.

He paused in the middle of the road, hours after his departure, and cast a glance back toward the sleeping town. His feet ached and he knew he should turn back.

Padraig just made to do so when he heard a woman singing, singing more beautifully than ever he had heard anyone singing. It could have been an angel he heard, and he was drawn to the sound.

He could not hear the words, and hastened closer.

"Una was the Faerie queen
Fairest woman ever seen
Wed centuries to her king

Love meant more to her than his ring."

The ground rose ahead of Padraig in a mound, a low hill covered with grass. A circle of large stones surrounded the crest of the hill, like a crown upon it, and a hawthorn tree grew outside the circle of stones.

The hair prickled on the back of his neck for he had learned at his mother's knee to be cautious in the presence of the fey. If nothing else, this was the kind of place they favored.

He could barely discern the silhouette of a woman atop the hill. She was sitting on a stone in the midst of the circle, combing her long hair, and he knew she was the one who sang. Two women sat at her feet, one with a lyre the like of which Padraig had never seen, the other humming along with her lady. They were all lovely, ethereal in the moonlight.

Her voice had a lovely lilt and Padraig wished to hear more of her song. He walked closer, trying to move silently as he didn't want to startle the women.

To his astonishment, as soon as he stepped within the circle of stones, the lady with the comb turned to confront him. She smiled, her hand falling to her lap as she sang directly to him.

With proximity, he could see more than her silhouette. Her hair was golden, as bright as sunlight, her eyes as blue as a southern sea. Padraig walked closer, awed by her loveliness.

> *"But Finvarra had an appetite,*
> *For mortal women, both dark and light.*
> *He vowed he'd have the pirate queen,*
> *Held captive by the spriggan's greed.*
> *One glimpse of the fair Rosamunde*
> *Had left him filled with lust and love.*
> *And so his wife did come to dread*
> *Her spouse taking Rosamunde to his bed."*

Padraig blinked. Surely she could not be singing of his Rosamunde?

The woman stood up, revealing that she was tall and slender. She wore a dress that was fitted to her curves and swept to her ankles, one as blue as her eyes and rich with golden embroidery. There were gems encrusting the hem and cuffs of the gown, and it seemed to Padraig that her slippers were made of silk the color of moonlight.

Or perhaps she was wrought of moonlight. She seemed insubstantial as she walked toward him, both of this world and not. Was he dreaming? The hem of her skirt seemed to dance with a will of its own, and lights glinted around the perimeter of the stone circle. He remembered will-o'-the-wisp, the fabled lights of the fey, and knew he had strayed into their enchanted realm.

Only when the woman was directly before him did he see the numerous small courtiers holding the hem. They could not have stood as high as his knee, not a one of them, and were dressed in green livery. Their faces were sharp, their eyes narrow, and their hair caught with twigs.

Padraig remembered her own words and knew whom he encountered.

The Faerie queen, Una.

"Greetings, Padraig, sailor of the many seas," she said, her voice as melodious in speech as in song.

"Greetings, beauteous queen." Padraig bowed deeply, knowing well the price of insulting one of the fey.

"Perhaps you have guessed that I have summoned you here. I heard your song and knew that our goals could be as one."

"Heard my song?" Padraig glanced over his shoulder, unable to glimpse the lights of the town. "But that was miles away. You could not possibly have heard..."

Una laid a fingertip across his lips to silence him. Her touch was as cold as ice, as smooth as silken velvet.

She smiled. "She is not dead, your Rosamunde." Her lips tightened and she averted her gaze. "And now my husband, casting his glance over all of Faerie, with aid of his treacherous mirror, has glimpsed the slumbering Rosamunde. He means to make her his own on Beltane."

"I mean no offense, my lady, but Rosamunde is dead," Padraig spoke with care. He knew of the fey inclination to trick mortals. "I saw the fallen rock, I tried to retrieve her from the destroyed caverns. She cannot have survived."

Una smiled. "The spriggan Darg took her captive when she might have died."

"Darg!" Padraig exclaimed. He recalled the deceitful spriggan well, and its determination to have vengeance upon Rosamunde.

Una watched him carefully. "You know this creature."

"Indeed, I do, my lady, although I believed the spriggan to be yet at Ravensmuir."

Una's smile faded. "No. It came here in your ship."

Padraig frowned. There had been items disappear on their last voyage, including the ale that he knew the spriggan liked so well. It was possible that Una spoke the truth.

"It trespassed in our *sid*. It has wagered with my husband and lost, so it will bring Rosamunde to him tomorrow. You must steal her from him."

"My lady! A man who steals from the Faerie king will not live to tell the tale of it!"

Una smiled. "With my aid, you will not be detected." She pressed a golden ring into his hand. "Wear this and you shall pass unseen in any company."

The ring was cold, as cold as the tomb. Even having it in his hand filled Padraig with dread. He was not afraid to risk his life for Rosamunde, not even of inciting the wrath of the fey king, but there was one more thing he needed to know.

"With respect, my lady, I would be certain of the desire of Rosamunde. It seems to me that it would be most fine to live at the Faerie court. She might not wish to leave."

Una laughed but not because of his compliment. "You must have heard the old riddle, the one with truth at its heart."

"Which is that, my lady?"

Her eyes glinted with humor. "What gift is it that a woman wishes most from a man?"

Padraig shrugged, not knowing the answer. Riches? Comfort? Love? There were so many possible answers that he could not choose. He suspected the answer depended upon the woman.

Una leaned closer. "To have her own way." Her eyes shone with brilliant light as her courtiers giggled around her hem. "I suspect you are a worthy lover, Padraig Deane, and in tribute to your love, I give you a gift."

"You have already been too kind..."

Before Padraig could finish, the Faerie queen framed his face in her hands. She leaned closer, her cold breath caressing his skin, then she kissed him full on the lips. He tasted death and loss, a chill that shook him to his marrow.

And Padraig swooned.

Rosamunde dreamed of another day in her past.

The sky was pink, a sure sign of trouble in the morning, and the dark clouds racing overhead made no better forecast. All the same, Rosamunde's heart leapt at the familiar cliffs that rose before her, the cliffs surmounted by the keep she knew as well as the lines of her own hand.

Ravensmuir.

Governed by Tynan, stern but fair, the man who had taken her to his bed, the man who had vowed subsequently to never wed her. The man who had chosen this pile of stones over Rosamunde.

Twice.

In her dream, she was certain she would relive that last encounter, that final fatal rejection, that she would see him again.

But she did not. She dreamed again of Padraig, of their final parting.

Rosamunde stood on the deck of her ship, staring up as the land rose closer, her heart pounding with trepidation that Tynan would see her approach, that he would meet her in the caverns below the keep. She was in the moment of approach, felt her own hope and anticipation, yet at the same time, knew what had happened subsequently in those caverns. She knew again the twinge of dread she had felt that morning and knew it had been a warning. Although Tynan had apologized to her, he had once again chosen his holding over her.

And he had died.

Had she not died, as well?

Padraig came to stand beside her on the deck, but this time when Rosamunde turned to her most trusted friend, she saw him with clear eyes. He was tall and hale, was Padraig, experience tempering his expression and his choices. His dark hair was touched with silver at the temples, she noted, and there were lines from laughter etched around his eyes. His tan made his eyes look more vividly blue, and she was struck by his vitality.

By his masculinity.

With the clarity of hindsight, she saw what she had missed day after day in his company. Padraig was of an age with her, and they had shared a thousand adventures. He was unafraid of her truth, much less of her temper. He was quick to laughter, he was clever, he dared to challenge her when he believed her to be wrong. He was deeply loyal and she had always been able to rely upon him.

Her heart began to pound at the magnitude of her error, at her own blind folly.

"I will go into the caverns alone," she said, feeling the words she had once uttered as they crossed her tongue in this dream. Her quest had been the retrieval of a silver ring, once given to her by Tynan, demanded by the spriggan Darg as the price of its assistance, but returned by her to Tynan after his rejection. It had not been hers to take, but on this day, she had returned to steal it to ensure the future of her niece.

"I will accompany you," Padraig said, determination in his tone. They shared this resolve to protect those they loved, Rosamunde realized, this ability to stride into the shadows so others would not be compelled to do so.

She and Padraig had walked the periphery of society together, daring all as they challenged convention.

At each other's backs.

While Tynan had upheld convention. He had found Rosamunde useful, he had accepted her favors abed, but he had never respected her or intended to honor her. It was no surprise in hindsight to realize that Tynan could never have loved her in truth.

"No, not this time," she argued in her dream, just as she had argued on that fateful morning.

She saw Padraig for what he was. She saw the ardor in his eyes. She saw his fear for her. She saw his valor and his loyalty, and she guessed the secret of his heart.

And Rosamunde regretted that she had surrendered her love

to the wrong man.

She had suspected as much on that day. The ghost of the realization had teased at her thoughts, urged her to choose otherwise, made her words tumble forth with uncharacteristic haste. "Take the ship," she told him, in this dream as she had then. "See me ashore, then take the ship and sail south to Sicily."

It had been their jest, all those years, that they would one day sell everything and live out their lives in Sicily. They had both preferred the sun's sultry heat there to the chill of the north.

"But what of the contents?" Padraig's displeasure was clear.

"Sell them, sell them wherever you can fetch a fair price for them and keep the proceeds for your own."

"But..."

"I owe you no less for all your years of faithful service." It was a facile lie and they both had known it, even then.

"But the ship?"

"Sell it as well, or keep it for your own. I do not care, Padraig." Rosamunde uttered that heartfelt sigh, acknowledging the shadow of dread that touched her heart. "I have had wealth and I have had love. Love is better."

It was a lie. She had never had Tynan's love. She had had the illusion of his love, and had been seduced by that. She had had no more than the physical expression of his love, and that was a paltry offering.

On the other hand, Rosamunde saw in her dream that Padraig's love had been before her, awaiting her invitation, for years.

"You will fare well enough," she said in her dream, and the declaration of her gift of foresight struck her as ironic. "I have seen it and we know that whatsoever I see will be true."

"What do you see for yourself?" Padraig asked softly, his survey of her so searching that Rosamunde could scarce hold his gaze. He frowned and looked away. "I always said that you saw farther than most, but could not see what was before your own eyes."

There was a truth in his claim that she had missed on that red-stained morning. She declared her destiny to be at Ravensmuir, seeing in her dream how the notion displeased Padraig.

How could she have missed such an offering?

How could she have overlooked the affection of one who knew her better than she knew herself? She had been a fool and lost her life because of it. If only she had another chance, she would seize the opportunity Padraig offered.

"Farewell, Padraig," she heard herself say. "May the wind always fill your sails when you have need of it."

And Padraig embraced her, catching her close. She could feel the muscled strength of him, the resolve of him, the power he oft held in check. In her dream, she closed her eyes and savored what she had lost through her own folly.

His voice was husky when he spoke. "We have fought back to back a hundred times, Rosamunde, and always I will consider you to be my friend." His blue eyes filled with heat as he regarded her. "You have been my only friend, but a friend of such merit that I had need of no other."

"No soul ever had a friend more loyal than I found in you," she said, her heart aching at her own folly.

"I did," Padraig said, his words fierce. His gaze bored into hers, then he turned away, staring at the cliffs of Ravensmuir. "I did," he added softly.

And in her dream, Rosamunde did what she should have done on that day. She reached out. She touched Padraig's shoulder. She saw his surprise when he turned toward her. Then she caught him close, hearing the thunder of her pulse in her own ears, and kissed him.

It was a sweet, hot kiss, a kiss that sent a torrent of longing through her. It was a kiss tinged with regret, filled with love, a kiss of yearning and potency. It left her dizzy. It left her hot.

It left Rosamunde wide awake and blinking at a ceiling she could not place.

Was she not dead?

It appeared not. She was simply alone. She touched her lips, caught her breath, and dared to wish for that second chance.

Padraig awakened abruptly, his heart racing and his breath coming in quick spurts. He was hot and he was tight, the taste of

Rosamunde upon his lips.

He had also slept, apparently, in the field.

The sun was rising in the east, gilding the hills and setting the dewdrops ablaze. He stared around himself. He was alone. He was cold and his clothing was damp with dew. The stone circle was a dozen steps away, silent in its secrets. The women were gone, if indeed they had ever existed, and there was no music echoing in his ears. No lyre, no small faeries, no footsteps in the grass.

Padraig heard a man shout at a cow as he drove her along the road to town.

He ran his fingers through his hair and his tongue across his lips. He tasted the kiss of Rosamunde again, closing his eyes at the rush of pleasure he'd felt beneath her touch.

Rosamunde had never kissed him.

Except in his dream.

He had indulged too much the night before. It was the ale, confounding him, feeding his desire and leading him astray.

Padraig shoved to his feet, grimacing at the distance he had to walk back to town. His feet were still sore and his head ached. He made to brush himself down, removing the twigs strewn across his clothes, and realized there was something in his hand.

It was a stone. The stone was round with a hole in the middle of it. It was the color of gold. Was this the golden ring he believed the Faerie queen had given him?

Padraig smiled at his own foolish dream. He had been in his cups. Still, a stone of such a shape was unusual. It might be lucky. He was possessed of all of the superstitions of a seafaring man and a few more besides, courtesy of his mother's upbringing in these hills and her respect for the fey. If nothing else, it would be an error to cast the gift aside where the donor might witness his rudeness.

Padraig pushed the stone into his pocket and strode through the damp grass. And as he walked back to his accommodations in Galway, he savored the memory of Rosamunde's kiss.

Even in a dream, it had been a sweet prize and was enough to put a spring in his step.

"But Rosamunde, she had not died
In truth she breathed still.
She was a captive of the fey
And lost beneath the hill.
Such marvels she did see while there
Such beauty, wondrous still
Still Rosamunde did not wish to be
Captive beneath the hill."

The spriggan Darg was not a creature Rosamunde was glad to see.

Solitude was better than the company of this thing.

That the small fairy had a red cord knotted around its waist was curious and surely did not improve the creature's mood. It hissed and spat, pinching her to wake her up then nipping at her heels to hurry her along.

"Make haste, make haste, the king is not inclined to wait."

"Where are we going? I thought Faerie was like limbo."

Darg chattered unintelligibly, as was its tendency when it was annoyed. The creature led her more deeply into the caverns beneath Ravensmuir and Rosamunde was glad to leave her past behind.

It wasn't truly the caverns beneath Ravensmuir, though. Those caves and their pathways were well-known to Rosamunde, having been her secret passage to the keep for decades. As a child, she had played in them, learning their labyrinth, delighting in their secret corners. But they were dank and made of grey stone, dark and filled with the distant tinkle of running water.

She did not know the passageways that Darg followed. Rosamunde had never spied that entry lit with golden light until the collapse of the cavern and the death of Tynan. She suspected that Darg had opened a portal for her, but knew not where it truly was.

This cavern could not be fairly called a cave or even a labyrinth. Indeed, Rosamunde did not feel as if she was underground at all. There was brilliant golden sunlight, the light that had spilled from that unexpected portal. The sky arched high, clear and blue, over verdant fields. The air was filled with music and fine singing, and every soul she saw was beautiful.

It took Rosamunde a while to realize that she only saw nobility. There were aristocrats riding and hunting, borne by finely draped steeds so majestic in stature that the beasts rivaled the famed destriers of Ravensmuir. The women were dressed in silk and samite, their garb of every hue, their long hair flowing over their shoulders or braided into plaits. They wore coronets of flowers, and gems were plentiful on their clothing, even wound into their hair. Many played instruments as they rode. Golden flutes and silver lyres abounded in this strange country. The women's laughter sounded like music as well.

The men were just as well wrought, tall and slim, muscular. There was a glint of mischief in every eye. Their armor shone as if it was made of silver, their banners were beautifully embroidered and their steeds galloped with proudly arched necks. Silver bells hung from every bridle.

The land itself was bountiful, the trees lush with fruit and flowers blooming on every side. Rosamunde thought she saw fruit of gold and silver, and flowers wrought of precious jewels, but Darg did not delay their passage so she could look more closely. Birds sang from every tree, their song blending so beautifully with the ladies' tunes that Rosamunde felt they made music together.

Just passing through the beauty of this realm, even at Darg's killing pace, lightened Rosamunde's heart. It healed her wounds and made her believe that she might live on, even without love. It made her think of the future with an optimism that she had believed lost.

It made her wonder where Padraig was.

It made her wonder how she might get from here to there.

"Where are we?" she shouted to Darg, who hastened ahead of her, muttering all the while.

"A foolish mortal you must be, to not know the land of Faerie."

Faerie. Rosamunde was a pragmatic woman, one who had never believed in matters unseen or places to which she could not navigate. Was she dreaming?

A butterfly lit on her shoulder, its wings fairly dripping with color, its beauty far beyond that of any earthly insect.

Rosamunde realized with a start that it was a tiny winged woman. The fairy laughed at her surprise, a sound like tinkling bells, then darted away, disappearing into the blue of the sky with a glimmer.

"And why do we not linger in this magical realm?" Rosamunde asked Darg.

"*Late we are, late we must not be! Finvarra waits impatiently.*" The spriggan tugged again at the red cord knotted around its waist. It spat in the grass with displeasure, then snatched at Rosamunde. "*Hasten, hasten, by the moon's rise, we must be safely at his side.*"

"Who is Finvarra? And why do we go to him?"

"*Questions, questions, instead of haste! Your queries do the daylight waste! We have far to go without rest: Finvarra will accept no less.*"

They crossed a bridge, the river running beneath looked to be made of mead. Rosamunde caught a whiff of its honeyed sweetness and saw a cluster of bees hovering at the shore. A beautifully dressed suitor offered a golden chalice of the liquid to his lady, who flushed, fluttered both wings and lashes, then accepted his tribute.

"But why do we go to this Finvarra? Who is he and what hold has he over you?"

Darg spun abruptly, facing Rosamunde with fury in its eyes. "*A match I lost, the price my life. His demand was you as his new wife. High King of Faerie is his task, a man whose patience does not last.*" Darg wrestled with the red cord, then released it with disgust. "*This bond he knots, it burns me true; 'til you are his, this pain my due.*"

"You traded me to the Faerie King?" Rosamunde demanded, bracing her hands upon her hips. "What if I have no desire to be his toy? Or that of any other man, for that matter? I will not go complacent to his court, no matter what you have promised."

"*I pledged my word, I swore my life; Finvarra will have you as his wife!*"

"I think not." Rosamunde turned her back on her vile captor, having no inclination to make such a submission easier. She surveyed the beautiful countryside and spied a man tending a pair of horses that were drinking mead on the bank. He was handsome, and his gaze was bright upon her.

His hair was as dark as midnight, and if she narrowed her eyes, he could have been mistaken for Padraig.

Save that Padraig had neither wings nor pointed ears.

Perhaps he could aid her in finding Padraig.

When the Faerie knight smiled, Rosamunde found herself smiling in return. "I will take my heart's ease here instead," she said to Darg and turned her back upon the creature.

"No!" Darg screamed, as once the spriggan had screamed before in Rosamunde's presence. She glanced back warily, then ran when she saw the spriggan had become a large and menacing black cloud. When enraged it could change shape with frightening speed—the last such eruption had led to Tynan's death by shattering the caverns.

"*I saved your life, it's mine to give,*" the spriggan shouted. "*I trade it now so I shall live!*"

Rosamunde ran as quickly as she could, feeling the other faeries watching her with bemusement. She could not outrun Darg's fury, however. Her heart sank as the dark cloud enveloped her, surrounding her with fog as black as night.

Then she was snatched from the ground, as helpless as a butterfly caught in a tempest, and carried away. She thought she heard someone cry out, but Darg did not slow down.

Finvarra's wife. King or not, Rosamunde had no interest in his attentions. The very fact that he would trade a faerie's life for a woman, with no consideration of any desire beyond his own, was no good endorsement. She struggled and fought, knowing it was futile, and she wished again for a loyal friend to fight at her back.

Padraig. How could she have been so blind?

Padraig fondled the strange stone in his pocket as he returned to the tavern that night. It was falling dark, the sun blazing orange just before it slipped beneath the horizon.

He could not dispel his dream of kissing Rosamunde, and in truth, he did not want to do so. The dream had lifted the shadow from his heart, made him feel that there might be some purpose to his life even without his partner by his side.

"You are fair pleased with yourself tonight," his sister said as she set ale before him. She smiled and propped her hands on her hips to regard him. "A conquest was it then?"

Padraig laughed for the first time in a long time. "Naught but a dream, but 'twas a fine one."

"I wager it must have been," she said, her smile teasing. "You dreamed then of a lady?"

"None other than the Faerie queen," Padraig agreed amiably. "And she gave to me a token."

His sister sobered. "Did she then?" Her wariness reminded Padraig strongly of their mother.

"A ring with the power to make a man invisible to others." Padraig chuckled at the whimsy of it all, then reached into his pocket to show her the stone. He thought she would be amused by the evidence of his drunken dream, but when he pulled the gift from his pocket, it had become a golden ring again.

Padraig stared at it on his palm and blinked in wonder. "But a moment ago, it was a stone," he whispered.

His sister caught her breath and took a step back. "A Faerie gem." She crossed herself quickly. "Mind your step, Padraig. A man does not easily elude the favor of the Faerie queen."

Padraig barely heard her warning. He knew all the tales of the fey, courtesy of his mother. He simply could not believe that the ring had changed twice.

But then, if it was fey, the charm upon it would hold for the night and not the day. He stood and, leaving his ale, looked out the door of the tavern. Sure enough, the sun had set completely and twilight, that time so potent for the fey, had fallen.

He gazed at the circle of gold. What if his dream had been true? What if this ring truly did have the power Una had stated? What if he could reclaim Rosamunde from the realm of the fey?

What if his dream of that kiss had answered his question— what was Rosamunde's honest desire? Did she wish for him as well as freedom?

But before he dared enter the Faerie mound, before he dared to abduct a woman destined for the High King of Faerie's bed, Padraig would be sure of the ring's powers.

He left a coin for the ale, having no taste for it any longer. He strode out into the streets of Galway, slipped down an alleyway, then donned the ring.

To his astonishment, when he stepped back into the crowded

thoroughfare, a man walked right into him, frowning at the obstacle he could feel but not see.

Padraig spent an hour testing the ring's abilities, but it was clear that no human eye could discern his presence.

Next he would check it among the fey. He borrowed a horse and rode like a madman to the stone circle where he had heard Una sing the night before.

"Thus Rosamunde's lover true
Did meet the Faerie queen.
Thus he gained the magical ring
That let him pass unseen.
And so it was that he did choose
To witness his lady's plight.
He held his breath and donned the ring
At the Faerie sid that night."

"He saw his lady Rosamunde
All garbed in white and gold.
Her hair was braided thick with jewels,
A star was on her brow.
Her girdle was of finest silk,
Her shoes of purple leather.
So radiant was her countenance
He'd never seen her measure."

Rosamunde was displeased.

To be sure, the court was fine enough, and the hospitality was generous. She had been assigned some two dozen ladies in waiting who cared more for the careful plaiting of her hair than she ever could have done. She liked the splendid fabrics, the jewels and the evident wealth.

She did not like that she had been unable to escape Darg, much less the creature's hoot of triumph when Finvarra had removed the red cord. The spriggan had disappeared so quickly that it might not have ever been.

She did not miss the vile creature.

Finvarra was a handsome man, confident in his appeal. His eyes were strange, or at least they did not seem to match his countenance. He looked to have seen no more than thirty summers, his body young and strong, his face unlined and handsome. But his eyes, his eyes were filled with the shadows of experience. There was the memory of sadness there, of joy, of triumph and defeat. Had it been her choice to meet him, had she met him when both were unencumbered, Rosamunde might have been intrigued by the Faerie King.

As it was, she saw that his fascination with her was no more than lust. She would be a conquest, a mistress, a frippery to be tossed aside when he became bored with her charms.

Rosamunde had never been so little and had no desire to be as much now.

Indeed, his interest reminded her of Tynan's supposed love, and she would spurn it as she had failed to spurn it previously. If nothing else, Rosamunde would learn from her error.

Then there was the matter of Finvarra's wife, Una, who had retreated to the far side of the hall. Una, no small beauty in herself, had gathered her ladies about her and they clustered there, whispering and pointing.

Finvarra ignored his wife so deliberately that Rosamunde guessed she was but a pawn in some ongoing match between king and wife.

It was far less than what she wanted of her life.

She had tried to escape, without success. These maidens purportedly assigned to ensure her pleasure were also charged with keeping her captive. Their hearing was sharp, their sight sharper, their vigil complete.

Rosamunde folded her arms across her chest, smiled thinly and refused to participate in the festivities. If Finvarra's interest waned, perhaps she would be cast out of the realm sooner.

It seemed an unlikely prospect, given the gleam in his eye when he glanced her way, but Rosamunde had precious few options.

She disliked this role of a woman pampered. She disliked having no choice over her direction, having no ability to shape her own fate. It was utterly at odds with the way she had led her life, and Rosamunde fairly itched to return to what she knew.

First, somehow, she had to escape this court.

The music was intoxicating, so loud and sweet and melodious. The fey danced with a vigor that was astounding, seeming never to tire. The bounty of food on display was enticing, all manner of sweets and confections offered for the pleasure of the company. The mead smelled wonderful indeed, but Rosamunde feared the loss of her wits should she drink it. She simply stood and watched, and the hours drew long.

It was hours later when the faeries began a vivacious dance. It was clear that Rosamunde's maidens were captivated by the music, their eyes dancing and their toes tapping. Rosamunde encouraged them, one after the other to take the floor, until finally she felt unobserved.

It would not last, but she would savor the interval.

No sooner was she alone than a man's hands closed over her shoulders. He stood close behind her, whoever he was, his breath in her hair and his chest at her back. Rosamunde jumped, then felt her eyes widen at a familiar murmur.

"At your back, as always," Padraig said, the feel of his breath on her neck making her tingle. "Say nothing, but listen."

Rosamunde felt her heart skip and feared her maidens would hear its tumult. She tried to quiet her response, but she felt the strength of Padraig's fingers on her shoulders, the warmth of him against her back. She glanced down but could not see his hands.

"An enchantment," he murmured and she heard the familiar humor touch his tone. "I know not how long 'twill last."

Rosamunde's mouth went dry. She didn't doubt that Padraig would be at risk, if they realized there was an intruder in their midst. She scanned the hall, endeavoring to be casual in the survey, and realized that none could see Padraig. None even guessed his presence.

Then Rosamunde felt Una's gaze land upon her and saw the woman smile slightly.

Could Una see him?

Or was she simply gladdened that Rosamunde did not enjoy the celebrations?

"I do not know how much you know," Padraig said in quick

whisper. "You are in the *sid* of the High King of the Faeries, Finvarra, and he means to make you his mistress."

Rosamunde nodded ever so slightly.

"Choose, Rosamunde, choose whether you would remain in this place or whether you would have me aid your escape." Padraig's voice dropped low and his grip tightened slightly. "I am not without my own expectation, you should be warned. I should have confessed my love for you years ago. I would love you. I would be with you. I would endeavor to make you happy."

Indeed, the man could not fail at that task. Rosamunde closed her eyes, overcome with joy at his words.

"My right hand if you would stay here," he murmured. "My left, if you would be mine."

Without hesitation, Rosamunde raised her hand, as if to straighten her hair, and brushed her fingertips across Padraig's left hand. She felt him catch his breath.

Una's smile broadened, turning smug, then she plucked a sweet from a proffered tray. The Faerie queen's eyes gleamed and Rosamunde feared her deception.

"Eat nothing," Padraig warned. "Drink nothing. If you consume so much as one morsel, you will be captive here forever."

Rosamunde touched his fingertips to indicate her understanding. She was fiercely glad that she had not taken a bite since her arrival.

"Tomorrow night, the fey will ride out in procession for Beltane. You must go with the company. You must ride as close to the perimeter of the group as you can. I will come for you."

And Rosamunde would somehow learn the terms of release before then. She did not doubt that Padraig would face a challenge in gaining her freedom.

Rosamunde felt the burn of his lips against her nape. She closed her eyes, wanting to turn into his embrace, her chest tight with the gift of his presence.

Then Padraig was gone, like a shadow swallowed by the night.

And there was only the glitter of Una's knowing gaze locked upon her.

What treachery had the Faerie queen planned?

"And so the pair did plot their scheme;
So did they plan to keep their dream.
But the ring's charm did not hide all:
Una saw the mortal in her hall.
The Faerie queen had no good intent;
Loyalty to her spouse had been spent.
None could have joy while she did not;
And so Una schemed her own plot.
Padraig might capture his love lost,
But Una ensured too high a cost."

It was Beltane, and Padraig was enough of his mother's son to know that anything was possible on this night of nights.

On this night and on Samhain, the fey were at their most potent.

He made his preparations, fully aware of that.

He bought the horse that he had borrowed and the ostler was pleased to be rid of the beast, given that it had gone missing the night before. Padraig had the steed for a better price than he might have otherwise. He prepared it with care, ensuring that there was no iron in its harness, less the fey realize it was not one of theirs.

It was a fine stallion, a high-stepping black horse with a proud gait. Its mane was long and dark, its eyes lit with a fire that made him wonder whether it knew more of the fey than he. It was said that the Faeries bred the best horses, and there was majesty in this one's lineage.

It had not even shied at the *sid*, but waited calmly for him at the hawthorn tree.

He declared his intent to sail with the morning tide and had his ship provisioned for the journey. His sister extended her hospitality again, but Padraig knew they were too different for him to remain in her home. Her husband was not so unhappy to see a reputed pirate leave. Padraig cleared space in the hold of the ship to create a stable for the horse, for he had no inclination to simply leave it behind.

He tried to sleep, that he might be at his best when night fell. When the darkness slipped over the land, when the Beltane fires were lit in the hills, Padraig walked his horse to the old Norman gate. His heart in his mouth, he mounted and rode out into the night, slipping the ring onto his finger when he left the road.

"His steed was proud, as black as night
He donned the ring, was lost to sight.
The steed ran on, proud and bold,
His hooves thundered on the road.
The lover knew he faced his test;
Without his lady, he'd know no rest.
Lit by the fires on ev'ry hill,
The heat of his ardor knew no chill.
Padraig rode for his lady heart,
Would the fey queen keep them apart?"

Padraig reached the stone circle, but found only silence within it. The wind was still, the ground dark. He feared he had come too late, that the host had already ridden out—or that perhaps they had guessed his intent and chosen to forgo tradition to keep the prize of Rosamunde.

There was much he would forgo to keep her by his side.

Then the wind rustled in the branches of the hawthorn that grew to one side of the stone circle. His stallion snorted and tossed his head, then Padraig heard the clarion call of a distant trumpet.

The single note was clear, as clear as a mountain stream, as lovely as a summer morning. The sound melted his heart, dissolved his inhibitions, filled his veins with starlight and resolve.

The earth in the middle of the mound cracked; it gaped wide. A portal opened in the ground, one wide enough for four horses to ride abreast. Padraig glimpsed the hall beneath that he had visited the night before and his grip tightened on the reins.

Golden light spilled from the hidden court into the night's darkness and the Faerie host rode forth. Music accompanied them, the tinkle of ten thousand silver bells mounted on a thousand harnesses. Their steeds pranced with pride, confident of their splendor and beauty. The Beltane fires on the adjacent hills burned higher as if in tribute, their flames stretching to the stars.

And the fey laughed.

Padraig stared in awe at their magnificent display.

"Then lo, he saw the Faerie host,
Their company more beautiful than most.
He saw the silver and the gold;
He saw the Faerie knights so bold;
He saw the maidens garbed so fine;
He heard the music, saw the wine.

The will-o'-the-wisp danced on the hill
Fey light glimmering and never still
The stars seemed to have come to earth
As the Faerie host rode in mirth.
And so it was he glimpsed his lady,
On the left of the King of Faerie."

There were horses in the company without riders, or perhaps their riders were too small to be seen. Padraig would have eased his steed to join the company, but the beast seemed to know his expectation—it marched alongside, as if it had done as much a dozen times before.

The Faerie host flowed over the hills, eased down to the valley and ascended the next hill. Small Faeries darted toward the occasional cottage, claiming whatever gifts had been left for them. They shared the milk and ale with their fellows, lapped the porridge and cast gold coins in their wake. Each Beltane fire they passed snapped and crackled in acknowledgment of their passage, and Finvarra laughed at the sight. His wife, riding on his right, smiled but there was no joy in her eyes.

Neither was there joy in the steady gaze of Rosamunde.

Padraig eased his horse closer to the royalty, stroking its neck to encourage it to pass between the other beasts. The stallion needed little encouragement, and Padraig considered the possibility that horses felt a natural attraction to the Faerie King.

Just as the Beltane flames acknowledged his presence.

Padraig did not know how long they rode, nor how far. He thought solely of getting closer to Rosamunde without attracting attention, and he made consistent progress in that goal. They crossed a vale and ascended another hill. When they reached the top, the shining dark water of Lough Carrib was visible, gleaming at the foot of the hills. There were more stars on this night than he had ever seen and the moon rose high in pearly splendor.

When they began to descend the hill, Padraig's horse eased so close that he could touch the hem of Rosamunde's dress.

It was time.

"He spurred his horse, he galloped near
He seized the lady he loved so dear.
He stole her from the Faerie host
Claimed she Finvarra desired most.
The fey did scream, the horse did run,
Finvarra shouted 'twould not be done.
'Hold fast, hold fast,' Rosamunde cried
'For she would steal you from my side.'
And so he held with all his might
Even as Una unleashed her spite."

The company jostled for position as they began the descent. The fey were celebratory, and less disciplined than when they had first left the hill. Their laughter was louder and their songs more merry.

Padraig lunged through the company with purpose. He dug his heels into the stallion's side, and the horse leapt with power. Padraig snatched Rosamunde from her steed, his arm locked around her waist, and placed her on the saddle before him.

Then he fled.

As the stallion raced down the hill, the golden ring upon Padraig's finger cracked in half. It fell from his hand and was trampled beneath the horses' hooves, leaving him revealed to the fey.

"Impostor!" they cried. "Thief!"

"Fetch my mistress!" bellowed Finvarra.

Padraig gave the horse his heels. The steed raced down the hill ahead of the Faerie host, running so quickly that the ground was a blur beneath their feet.

"Faster," Rosamunde urged, glancing back. "Faster!"

Padraig heard Una's song rise sweetly in the distance, but did not trust her ode.

"Padraig!" Rosamunde said, locking her arms around his neck. "She means to make you spurn me. Be not deceived."

Padraig guessed the test he would face a heartbeat before it began.

"They will turn me to an ancient crone
A woman wrought of sinew and bone.
A cold, rotted body from the grave
Hold fast, my love, you must be brave.""

In his embrace, Rosamunde turned to a hag, appearing to have endured a thousand years of hardship. Her skin was wrinkled like ancient leather, her eyes yellow and her teeth missing.

She cackled at him, this apparition, and looked fit to devour him. Padraig could see the bones of her skull beneath the loose flesh of her face, he could smell the fetid stench of decay, and he felt the clutch of her skeletal fingers on his neck. Everything within him was repulsed and his urge was to cast her aside with all speed.

Padraig told himself it was but a spell and held fast.

"Next I'll be a writhing snake
With a toxic bite your life to take.
I will be as slipp'ry as an adder
My release lies solely in your power.""

Rosamunde changed then to an enormous snake, green and

slippery in Padraig's grasp. The snake bared its fangs and malice lit its eyes as it reared back to strike. He had not doubt its bite was poisonous, but he did not release it.

There were, after all, no snakes in Ireland. Padraig knew that this, too, was but a fey trick.

He heard Una's song, realized it was growing in volume, and knew there would be worse to come. Three tests there would be, he guessed as much, and they would become more fierce. He held fast to the writhing green snake and hoped he could keep hold of Rosamunde. The horse ran, outdistancing the shouting host at its heels.

The snake twisted in his grip, as elusive as a fish, but Padraig held tightly. He reminded himself of Rosamunde's valor, how she had challenged more than one aristocrat in the wrong, like the cheating bishop he had once served, and that gave him the strength to persevere in his challenge to the fey.

The water of the lake drew ever more near, and he wondered what the horse would do. He thought to direct it around the body of water, then Rosamunde changed shape again.

"'And last I will become a flame,
As hot and fierce as ever came.
A Beltane fire, orange and hot
My love, my love, release me not.'"

In the blink of an eye, Rosamunde became a fire in his embrace. The brilliant light of the flames nearly blinded Padraig and surprise almost loosened his grip.

He cried out and tightened his grasp upon her. The fire burned his skin, the flames licking at his flesh. He closed his eyes to the sight of his own body burning, to the smell of his destruction. He held fast to the column of flame, even as he feared he could not have the strength to endure against the fey.

Padraig thought of the way Rosamunde's hair looked in the sunlight.

He recalled her bold stance on the ship as they sailed to adventure. He thought of the light in her eyes when first they had met. He thought of her determination, even when the spriggan Darg had stolen her charts and trapped the ship in a calm.

He recalled her pride in her nieces and her joy in seeing them well wed. He thought of her passion and her pride and he fortified himself with the truth of why he loved this woman with all his heart. Padraig squeezed his eyes shut as the pain built to a crescendo.

He could not lose his love.

He recited the Paternoster, on impulse, recalling his mother's counsel. Tears stung his cheeks as he said the familiar prayer. *Our Father...*

The horse halted abruptly, reared, then it ducked its head. Padraig was thrown over its neck and gasped aloud when he landed in the lake with a splash.

He sank low, still holding fast to Rosamunde, and the cold dark water of the lake embraced him. He felt the flame in his embrace turn to a woman again.

A naked woman.

A naked woman he loved more than life itself.

And Padraig knew he had triumphed. They broke the surface together, Rosamunde's smile enough to light Padraig's nights forevermore.

When they might have spoken each to the other, a man cleared his throat at close proximity.

Finvarra stood on the shore, holding the bridle of the stamping black stallion. "And so the contest goes to you," the High King of the Faerie said. He stroked the horse's nose with affection and the beast nuzzled him. Finvarra smiled and his eyes glinted. "I shall take this horse into my care, seeing as it was once stolen from us and is rightfully returned."

Padraig understood why the horse had not been startled by the fey, why it had been so at ease joining the host. Recognition was possibly why it had been allowed to join the company in the first place.

He understood then why it had thrown him and saved Rosamunde. Padraig fancied that the horse had intended to reward him for bringing it back to Finvarra.

"You are a man of more cunning than most." Finvarra smiled.

"I should have liked to have played chess with you."

"With respect, my lord, I have little to my name and nothing I would choose to lose." Padraig kept his arm around Rosamunde, noting how the king's gaze flicked between the two of them.

"Should his devotion falter," Finvarra said to Rosamunde. "You are always welcome at my court."

"I thank you, my lord, and thank you also for your hospitality," Rosamunde said with a bow.

"You and your fellows will always find welcome at our home," Padraig added with a bow of his own.

Finvarra smiled, his gaze trailing to his wife, who remained upon her steed and at a distance. "It is no crime to covet a beauteous gem," he said softly, "but a rare triumph to possess one. I salute you, Padraig Deane. May your love never be tarnished."

With that Finvarra turned and led the prancing horse back to the company. Padraig felt the chill of the night air on his wet skin as he stood with Rosamunde fast at his side, but he could not tear his gaze away from the departing company. He doubted he would ever see them again. They rode forth, passing over the hills like a vision, leaving only the echo of their silvery laughter behind.

And Rosamunde.

"Thank you," she said, smiling up at him.

"You are welcome. I am glad to see you hale again." Padraig stared down at her, knowing his desire but afraid to speak of it too soon.

Rosamunde, as was typical of her, showed no such restraint. She twined her arms around his neck, sliding her fingers into his hair. "I am sorry, Padraig, that I erred so badly. I love you, I think I have always loved you, but I wish I had seen the truth of it sooner."

Padraig bent to touch his lips to hers, his heart swelling that his dream should be his own. "I know that I have always loved you," he murmured against her mouth.

Rosamunde laughed. "Then I shall have to spend the rest of our lives atoning for my error."

"I do not think it will be so onerous."

"Nor do I!"

Padraig laughed at the prospect, then he sobered. Rosamunde's eyes were richest green, filled with a conviction that stole his breath away. "Marry me, Rosamunde. Marry me and seal our bond for all to see. I have little to offer you but myself."

"Your ship."

"Your ship, and the contents are yours as well. I have only myself."

"It is more than enough. I will wed you, Padraig, and I will honor your love every day and night of my life.

It was everything he had ever wanted, and yet more.

Rosamunde's kiss sent a welcome heat through Padraig, a heat that her presence would never fail to kindle. Padraig knew that whatever he had suffered had been worthwhile, for he had gained his heart's desire.

When he lifted his head, her eyes were sparkling and her cheeks were flushed. She glanced about herself and shivered. "Tell me, though, that we can sail to warmer climes."

"I thought Sicily," Padraig said, smiling as pleasure lit her expression. "With the morning tide. All is prepared."

Rosamunde laughed. "A man of confidence, and one in pursuit of my own heart."

"I thought I possessed that prize already," he teased, loving the sound of her answering laughter.

"You do, you do." Then Rosamunde raised a hand to his cheek, as solemn as he had ever seen her. Her voice dropped to a fervent whisper. "Oh, Padraig, never doubt that I am yours." A tear glistened in her eye, a tear that he knew was rare for this bold woman. "I may have been late to see the truth, but I shall never forget it now."

"I shall never let you forget it," he retorted, then winked. Rosamunde smiled and he swung her into his arms, then strode from the lake. He had an idea of how they might warm themselves before the walk back to town.

One glance at his lady told him that their thoughts were as one. Yet again, they would challenge convention. Yet again they would follow their hearts. But from this day forth, they would do so together.

It was as close to heaven as Padraig Deane ever expected to

be.

"Padraig gained his lady's heart,
She vowed they'd never be apart.
Rosamunde was a pirate queen
With hair red gold and eyes of green.
Her lover true did hold her fast,
Showed all the fey his love would last.
They ne'er forgot those of Faerie,
And lived out their days most happily."

266

An excerpt from
The Rogue
Book #1 of the Rogues of Ravensmuir

Dear Reader:
Seductive and mysterious, Merlyn was the laird of Ravensmuir—never had
a man so stirred my body and soul. I gave myself to him—willingly,
trustingly, passionately—and we soon wed. Then a horrible revelation
emerged, shattering my innocence and my marriage…

Five years later, Merlyn returned to my doorstep, desperate for my help.
The scoundrel swore he was haunted by memories of me, that a treasure
locked in Ravensmuir could clear his name. Yet I could not surrender to
his will again. Now he is said to be murdered and Ravensmuir has fallen
into my hands.

But even as I cross the threshold of this cursed keep, I hear his whisper in
the darkness, feel his caress in the night, and I know that Merlyn has told
me but part of his tale. Should I do as is right and expose his lair? Or
dare I trust my alluring but deceptive spouse—the rogue who destroyed my
heart?

— Ysabella

"A beguiling medieval romance from Delacroix…readers will devour this rich
and compulsively readable tale."—Publishers Weekly

Turn the page to read an excerpt from
The Rogue
by Claire Delacroix

he raven came first.

It landed upon the window sill in the kitchen of the silversmith's wife and croaked so loudly at me that I nearly dropped my ladle into the hot wort.

"Wretched bird! Shoo!" I waved my hand at it, but it merely tilted its head to regard me with bright eyes. "Fie! Away with you!"

I knew as well as any the repute of these birds, but had less desire than most souls to be in the company of a creature so associated with superstition.

I had sufficient trouble without being found in the company of drinkers of blood and harbingers of death. The silversmith's wife would be rid of us for once and for all, if anyone in this village whispered that I kept a raven as a familiar. Such tales were all nonsense, of course, but I dared not risk an inopportune rumor.

"Shoo!" I flicked a cloth at the bird, which seemed untroubled and unimpressed by my antics. The creature bobbed its head and seemed to cackle at me, no doubt enjoying my discomfiture.

"Begone!" I picked up an onion, the bird watching me with knowing eyes all the time, then flung it across the kitchen with all my might.

I missed the raven by a good three hand-spans, though the onion splattered against the wall most impressively. The bird screamed and took flight, uninjured and apparently insulted, which suited me well enough.

I sighed and rubbed my brow as I eyed the mess. I not only had to clean the onion but would have to explain to my patroness why I had seen fit to destroy her foodstuffs—without admitting to the presence of the raven, lest her superstitions be fed. How sweet it would be to have no need of Fiona, with her sharp face and sharper tongue!

I had learned long ago, though, that there was nothing to be gained in bemoaning one's circumstance. I stirred the wort again and fought the urge to grumble.

My ale is fine, I dare say, the very finest. But with no kitchen, no pot, no spouse, the law decrees that I cannot be granted a license to brew. My ale has long provided what little coin my family had, so I am compelled to brew. What choice have I but to ally with this wife or another?

Fiona it was, for she would have me as her partner, if by her spouse's command. It would take a more foolish woman than I to not perceive that though I did most of the work, Fiona kept most of the coin—and one less aware of nuance than I not to note that coin and spousal approval were not sufficient in Fiona's view to suffer a witch in one's kitchen.

We were convenient to the silversmith and his wife, and it was for this, not a matter of principle or Christian duty, that they tolerated us. I have learned not be surprised that charity is so circumscribed, nor that principles can be so readily forgotten.

Once this massive pot was strained and flavored with my particular combination of herbs, I hoped for brisk sales over the holiday season. The ale would spoil in several days and, as I worked, I worried anew that I had made too much.

I could not risk the loss of any of my investment in ingredients. Competition was fierce in Kinfairlie for ale-making, there being so few other sources of profit. I had a good repute, but the harvest had been mean and all the other brewsters would be making similarly large batches.

I frowned and stirred the wort while it came to the boil. Making ale is a tedious trade and one requiring much heavy labor. I am not afraid to work, indeed I welcome labor. A heavy day ensures a solid night's sleep, at least, and a reprieve from the multitude of worries that plague me.

This day was the first day of the so-called Twelve Days of Christmas, though I should undoubtedly have to explain to young Tynan again and again why there were fourteen days in total so designated. The prospect made me smile.

The wort began to sputter and splash. It was a feat to move the cauldron from the fire myself, but I would have to do it again. I cursed Fiona, who contrived to be absent whenever her assistance might have been helpful. The pot was large enough and hot enough that even once it was away from the heat, it continued to chortle.

It was when I had wrestled it from the fire and halted to wipe my brow that I heard the hoof beats. I turned, eyes narrowed, and listened.

Three fleet steeds, their hooves shod with iron. Dread prickled down my spine. Not plough-horses, for they pranced too lightly. Palfreys lightly burdened, perhaps. And a fourth steed. Larger. Faster. I listened, wanting to be certain, my heart thumping with its own certitude.

The fourth beast was a destrier. There could be no doubt.

I closed my eyes, swallowed, and prayed that the beast's rider was not who I feared it might be. There was no reason it should be him. After all, Kinfairlie's meager tithes have been hotly contested since the liege lord and manor were lost. We were accustomed to various nobles assaulting the town in search of tribute.

Especially before a holy day.

The hoof beats came closer. When the raven cried, even at a distance, I knew.

The silversmith's house faces the main square of Kinfairlie, where markets are held and criminals are hung, and it was here that the new arrivals came to a halt. I stiffened, but did not go to the door. The steeds' hooves clattered to silence, the destrier neighed and no doubt tossed his head.

"I seek Ysabella of Kinfairlie!" roared a man, his voice achingly familiar.

Merlyn. My heart lunged for my throat.

For years, I had imagined how we might meet again, how I would scorn him with blistering wit, yet now I merely whispered his name beneath my breath like a besotted damsel. In truth, I did not know whether to be frightened or relieved, to be joyous or disappointed. He had come in pursuit of me, after all this time, a boon to my pride if not a good omen for my future.

"Ysabella!" he shouted anew, and I wondered if he was drunk.

I glanced over myself and smiled wryly at the embellishment of fermented malt upon my skirts. No doubt the hair had escaped my braid, my face would be hot and nigh as red as my hair. It was a far cry from the reunions I had so oft envisioned, when I was garbed in richness and hauteur, my words as sharp as lances.

My appearance would do very well to show my spouse his importance—or lack of it—to me.

I crossed the kitchen and opened the heavy wooden door.

Even though I braced myself, my heart stopped. Merlyn was just as imposing as before, his two young squires fighting to control their palfreys. He was garbed in the black and silver he favored, the hues of his house, the hues that made him look more dangerous and dashing than even he was. I looked hastily at his companion. Stalwart Fitz was still with Merlyn, his face only slightly more lined than before.

"Good morning to you, Merlyn," I said, feigning an indifference I hardly felt. "What brings you to Kinfairlie?"

He urged the steed closer, then dismounted, casting the reins aside. His smile was confident, roguish, and enough to set my very flesh to flame. His gaze swept over me, leaving a tingle in its wake and I gripped the door lest I cast myself at him like a harlot. His breath made a cloud against the sky that darkened too early in this season.

"Well met, *chère*," he murmured, with the intimacy one reserves for lovers.

I flushed scarlet, heating from nipples to hairline. Worse, I could not summon a sound to my lips.

Merlyn knew it, curse him, and grinned with wicked satisfaction as he closed the distance between us.

I could not draw a breath. I knew the dark truth of Merlyn, and yet, and yet despite all of that, despite my moral certainty that he would burn in hell, I still yearned to touch him again. He infuriated me, yet I had not felt so alive in all the years we had been apart as I did in this one moment, holding his gaze in winter's cool air.

I had assured myself that my attraction to Merlyn had been born of my ignorance, but he approached with all his wretched surety and the loss of my ignorance did not keep his allure at bay. Far from it. If anything, I desired him more ardently than ever.

To think that I had long fancied myself a clever woman.

"I seek you, *chère*," he said, his words husky.

I caught the scent of his flesh and lust unfurled within my gut, memories flooding my thoughts of nights—and days—spent entangled in each other. I squared my shoulders, determined to resist him and failing utterly.

"What else?"

He claimed my hand and bestowed a kiss upon my knuckles, his eyes filled with an answering heat that weakened my knees.

I snatched my hand away, hating that I so quickly fell beneath his spell once more. "And it has taken you five years to remember the way to Kinfairlie village? God in heaven, Merlyn, even the slowest child can walk to Ravensmuir in a day."

I inclined my head curtly, excusing myself, and retreated into the kitchen. I knew full well that he would follow, though I bristled when he did so. I stirred the wort vigorously, showing a belated care that my investment did not burn.

"You might at least leave the door ajar," I snapped. "But then, when have you had a care for my reputation?"

"Always, despite your conviction otherwise." Merlyn's words were more harsh than I expected. I pivoted and his gaze locked with mine as he flicked the portal closed with his fingertips. He did not apologize, he did not so much as blink.

I raised a finger. "You..."

He interrupted me with resolve. "I am your legal spouse, and there is no law writ that says a man cannot be alone with his wife."

I turned back to the brew and stirred it with an enthusiasm undeserved. "And you have developed a sudden interest in law?" I asked archly. "How strange. I was certain that your sole commitment to the law was to break it."

Merlyn laughed. I felt him pause behind me and heard him doff his gloves. He cast them on the board beside me and I caught my breath when I glimpsed them from the corner of my eye. Had he chosen scarlet ones apurpose this day? Did he mean to prompt memory in me?

I knew him well enough to understand that nothing, but nothing, was accident with Merlyn Lammergeier.

Even knowing he approached, I still jumped when his warm fingertip landed on my bare nape. His gentleness always caught me unawares. I inhaled sharply, hoping my indication of disapproval would halt him.

It did not, but then, I had expected as much. I stared at the wort as Merlyn's finger traced a beguiling path around the neckline of my ancient dress. I felt the barest whisper of his breath before he kissed me beneath the ear.

I jumped truly then, swatted him and moved to the other side of the cauldron. I looked daggers at him, but he was unrepentant.

"The fire still burns," he murmured, his eyes gleaming. No doubt he reveled in having some power over me.

"Trust me. It is doused beyond reviving." I scrubbed the hot mark of his kiss with one hand as he laughed.

Merlyn blew me a kiss across the cauldron. "I have missed you, *chère.*"

The Rogue
Book #1 of the Rogues of Ravensmuir

Available Now!

Deborah Cooke sold her first book in 1992, a medieval romance called *Romance of the Rose* published under her pseudonym Claire Delacroix. Since then, she has published over seventy novels in a wide variety of sub-genres, including historical romance, contemporary romance, paranormal romance, fantasy romance, time travel romance, women's fiction, paranormal young adult and fantasy with romantic elements. She has published under the names Claire Delacroix, Claire Cross and Deborah Cooke. *The Beauty*, part of her successful Bride Quest series of historical romances, was her first title to land on the New York Times List of Bestselling Books. Her books routinely appear on other bestseller lists and have won numerous awards. In 2009, she was the writer-in-residence at the Toronto Public Library, the first time the library has hosted a residency focused on the romance genre. In 2012, she was honored to receive the Romance Writers of America's Mentor of the Year Award.

Currently, she writes contemporary romance and paranormal romance as Deborah Cooke. She also continues to write medieval romance as Claire Delacroix. Deborah lives in Canada with her husband and family, as well as far too many unfinished knitting projects.

Visit Deborah's websites:
www.deborahcooke.com
www.delacroix.net